Waterlines

Waterlines

Jenny Markert

water, water everywhere
clean and
flowing free
forever

Waterlines
by Jenny Markert

Editor and designer: Wendy J. Johnson, Elder Eye Press
Interior and cover photography: Jenny Markert
Author photograph: K.E.A. Photography

A publication of Elder Eye Press (www.ElderEye.com) – a design and concierge
publishing house dedicated to designing with the best design practices for legibility
and clarity, to benefit all eyes, of all ages.

Elder Eye Press
PO Box 142
Crystal Bay, MN 55323, USA
www.ElderEye.com

First Edition, 2022

Markert, Jenny
Waterlines / by Jenny Markert
ISBN: 9798837477188 (alk. paper)
Library of Congress Control Number: 2022911930

This is a work of fiction. Aside from some real geographic locations and businesses,
all other locations, names, characters, events, and incidents are the products of the
author's imagination. Any resemblance to actual persons, living or dead, or actual
events is purely coincidental.

Manufactured in the United States of America by the KDP Independent Publishing
Platform.

For the storytellers
and those who champion the Earth
and all the marvelous creatures who live here.

"I will arise and go now, for always night and day
I hear lake water lapping with low sounds by the shore;
while I stand on the roadway, or on the pavements grey,
I hear it in the deep heart's core."

– William Butler Yeats

CHAPTER 1

Floating

Lake dwells
      dreamlike
        floating
          mirroring mire
            swirling paisleys
      sparkling light.
        Wind basks in the trees round the lake
                while distilled air hovers
             awaiting witness
        one to see and hear,
      rise and fall,
to spiral, breath by breath, here and now, in time.
         Earth cues the ephemeral elixir
           tap, tap, tap vibrates
             the maestro
        Dawn's orchestra, leaning,
       led by light
      melody by melody
     into day.
        Sun pulses pink peals along the horizon as
wind unfurls extensive exhales. Rhythms roll into the land. Treetops
begin to sway. Fall grasses bend and flutter.

A light steady breeze develops over the lake—mustering air, water,
and even thought molecules into mingling as our heart-beating witness
wanders in.

A woman, standing at the edge of a dock, stares into the molten silvery
plain. She's stood at these shores many times, having grown up on the
lake. She hugs her shoulders to stay warm. This lake has been her friend—
nonjudgmental, consoling, inviting. But today, she must detach. The lake
vibrates cold and distant, subdued, like a mirror that reflects no emotions,
no personality. She won't know it anymore. This very moment it changes. Her
heart drops a little, realizing. It can't be frozen in time. Even in her memories,
it's too dynamic and evolving.

Peace and quiet are hard to find here except maybe at dawn. Most summer docks have been hoisted out of the water, and emptiness haunts the atmosphere. She has become used to being alone but rarely feels any peace in it. Years of yoga and meditation have taught her how to sit still, but she has no idea how to be content. She shakes the old familiar realization out of her head. She gazes across the surface, distinguishing shades of steel undulating in the forlorn ripples, robotic, hypnotic, resonating an end like the season on the brink of change. Her ears feel a change in pressure; a slight ringing comes and goes. Holding back tears that feel like they might never stop, she presses her eyelids down with her fingertips and thinks about the water. Energy shadows of it play against the back of her eyelids, in her inner eye.

As if Earth is a sorceress and her lakes are her kettles, brewing all kinds of who knows what, water's psychedelic auras roil random images into her mind's eye and conjure up memories.

A little girl with wet hair, running along the shore,
                         feet shuffling through the lapping water,
           giggling, arms out like a bird, she's soaring.

Then, her hand holding the main line, a sail gleaming in the sun,
           whitecaps sloshing over the splashboard.

Then he is there,
his face blurred underwater, his eyes searching, open wide and waiting.

                         She shivers a little then clenches her eyes. Her ears pique. Water's soft waves lap, one over another, along the rim of the lake, like feathers strumming harp strings, rhythmically purring echoes.

Rising from the rippling depths, coming from afar, closer and closer inside her mind, a thought surfaces; letters,

like musical notes,
reverberate,
                    circling
to a point.
Words spiral along,
all in a   willowy   windy   whisper

           . . . here . . . stories . . . linger . . . hear . . .

She doesn't know where the thought comes from, but it feels familiar. Like a voice she recognizes or a melody she knew. Then more thoughts come tumbling in.

She sees why water allures. Water is a paradox, a mystery, presenting and harboring subtle and titanic qualities

holding and releasing, hiding and revealing, carving and eroding
rush and trickle,

    fog and freeze,

        drown and transform . . . ever

the same, always new.

                    Water has spirit. Epics reside in her dimensions.

In the ripples and currents,

    relinquished to the infinite layers,

        and vaporizing along the edges,

            truths and tales trellis.

Lakes have wombs, gestating history and memory and culture and life. They harbor the present and whisper as midwives of the future. Water reflects everything yet is transparent. It awaits, inviting insight. Water is Calypso's capsule and cape. Music. Earth's eye, Earth's blood. Earth's life. Life's world is weaved with water.

She inhales, uplifted and inspired. Her focus comes back to the scene of the present, and she gazes determinedly, attempting to memorize the water. Her eye catches something floating along out in the water. It looks somewhat like a green and orange plaid shirt, weirdly bright in the overcast. She wants to go, but she's compelled to identify what is

    waywardly

        floating,

                drifting   shoreward.

Is it a half-soaked pizza box? A deflating water toy? A missing life preserver? A lost spinnaker . . . ?

She has brought her camera, she suddenly remembers. She grabs the bulky telephoto lens and holds it up, slowly searching with the lens for the floating object. Back and forth across the water, she scans. Finally, she spots the target. She zooms in and studies it a bit before the realization hits, and she gasps and jerks the camera, almost dropping it. She hesitates but has to look again.

Holding the camera up, she sees it is real indeed. A giant bloated turtle. It floats belly up, splayed, far beyond dead. Her gut drops. She wonders how it died. How big it must have been in the prime of its life—maybe the size of a serving tray? Probably bigger. How old it must have been! Ballooned and distended, it has expanded to the size of a wheel on a truck; its legs bulge out from its mosaic underbelly. She cannot see its head; it has been cut off or is so sharply tweaked backward it has disappeared from sight. She doesn't want to know.

Did it die swiftly or of old age? Why does it float recklessly through the big wide-open lake? Do turtles die this way naturally? She wonders. Only one other time had she seen a turtle as big as this one might have been when it was alive. Could it be that *same* turtle? So many years ago! Her eyes fill with tears, thinking of the horror of drowning, of the forsaken turtle, once graceful and full-on, no joke dazzling, pulsing with life, and now . . . its surrendered state, limp and ominous.

The old man's stories come to mind, about the frontier people mutilating the indigenous people, left for dead along the roadsides,

dragging them through the streets behind their wagons and

putting explosives in their ears and nostrils.

Sickening nausea pulses through her. No matter what, she will never come to terms with that human behavior. It comes back to her mind again and again. She has tried to think of the extent of the damage just those actions alone have caused on the Earth, but she has yet to get to the end of it. What is it in humanity that would ever allow for such cruelty? It can't be boiled down simply to ignorance. Something malignant lies in knots there. She doesn't know what it would take to untangle that dark mess. But she does know she doesn't want anyone to find this amazing creature washed up on shore and abuse it for sick amusement. She will call him and tell him what she's seen. He, more than anyone, will appreciate the undertaking.

She wipes away tears and takes a deep breath. What made something so magnificent so strange?

What kind of omen is this?

She looks to the somber sky. Light penetrates the thin cracks in the drab cloud cover, giving her a headache. Wind gusts through her thin windbreaker shell.

This turtle smothered her moment, if there were to have been a moment, standing there on the dock, gazing into the gray infinity.

Yet maybe there was no *moment* to equate to this moment. She comes to the lake to say goodbye and mark a turning point. But nothing great happens. In fact, the opposite. A dead turtle shows up. What was she hoping would happen? She'd have a startling realization? She'd untie, or even arrive at, the last knot of the evil and diabolical doom, and humanity would turn itself around?

She admits to herself she was hoping for something amazing and inspiring and now feels like an idiot for hoping. Humans are so predictably and obliviously shallowly optimistic. It disappoints her to be so typical.

She continues ruminating, looking around. For a split second out of the corner of her eye, she glimpses a motion of a figure jerking backward, quickly out of sight. The modus operandi of a phantom. She looks sharp and squints as eeriness creeps along her shoulder.

Was someone just at the top of the hill looking down at her?

No one is there. A shiver escapes her.

What the hell? Enough of *that*. Now I'm seeing things?

She grabs her camera bag and hustles off the dock. She takes the steps two at a time to the top of the hill, releasing the so-called moment with every elevation, thinking about the next task. She has to let this all go, *all the shit* stewing around here. This place is washed up—like the decimated turtle. *There's your symbolic moment.* She gets to the top of the hill and starts jogging away, not bothering with a final glance back. She'll miss swimming here with her daughters, but that's about it. This lingering loneliness gots to go, once and for all

    and

                something   begins   to shift.

Despite her carefully harnessed and mastered self-control, her insides begin melting down, like old metal being repurposed. She imagines swaths of taffy-like metal dropping off her shoulders, hips, and thighs, tumbling to the ground, popping and splattering with sparks of stardust. Relaxation, or a shedding, a releasing, overcomes her whole being. Everything effervesces with clarity. Her legs tingle as they bound with zesty energy, and a different self begins to rise. A feeling of being righted, like a sailboat recovering from turtling, takes hold in her body, with a delicate, almost undetectable, euphoria in tow. Clarity. The rarity of clarity.

She sees what to do, what's been needing to be done.

Tell the story.

Why had she not known?

        It's been there all along. She doesn't know what will happen, but finally something will.

    and the dust,

            stirred up by her heels along the road,

                                        like

                                 spirit

                floated into the air behind her.

CHAPTER 2

Riparian Rifts

Drifting back many years ago, to the summer I turned twenty, maybe this story's not all that unique, but like anyone's story, it's worth telling and hearing, nonetheless. In the late 1980s, the consensus was life was pretty good for most people—in the U.S., that is. Scientists were building a neutrino detector, and minds were being blown trying to grasp the implications. We had Reaganomics. I had no real idea then what Reagan was doing in other parts of the world, like Central America, but he appeared good for people where I lived. My vision barely extended beyond my immediate here and now, and I didn't care because my life was going along nicely. I know I sound privileged, and of course, I was, to a degree, but I wasn't aware of my privilege then. I did not "come from money." I worked hard, and everyone I knew worked hard. I was well-raised in my midwestern practicality and sensibility. But I did not know the environmental, racial, sexual, and economic inequities that plagued our world then and still today. I admit I didn't really care to know. Part of this can be forgiven due to youth, I hope. But I was too caught up in my own life, and this blasé attitude I had was common around me. It had everything to do with what happened. And what happened had everything to do with how I began to wake up to the jagged ways of humanity. Still, human consciousness is evolving, which offers a drop of hope.

So, yes, mostly in the '80s, I was a blissfully unaware kid. It was my last summer at the lake, though. I lost that blissful blur, but I didn't know it at the time. I was so much in a blur, I didn't see the blur. Is that the general state of adolescence? The proverbial teenage brain? For me, the turn to adulthood happened over the course of that late '80s summer. I didn't know the cabins would be demolished for personal cathedrals. But there were hints. I knew my family didn't have a strategy to pay the rising property taxes or the "keep up with the Joneses" maintenance costs, or the fees for upgrading the dirt roads, septic systems, power grids, and whatever else the city commissioners omnipotently decided was good for the lake area.

What I hoped for the lake to be was not what the waves of the future were bringing. Quartz Lake permeated my body. God knows I swallowed enough of it. I knew her glinty scales like my own skin. But I hadn't lived enough to know what we were up against. I knew a little Minnesota land war history. I knew lakes were people magnets. But I thought Quartz Lake would somehow be different. I thought I was so old at twenty.

My dad was a kid when he first came to Quartz Lake in the 1930s. His father came with his father when he was a teenager, just at the turn of the century. When the first resort, Quartz Shores, opened amid the Great Depression, my dad's family managed to rent a cabin for the summer holiday. The lake offered city dwellers an escape from the growing polio outbreaks. My dad's family did at least a full day's labor at the resort as a way to offset some of the expense. My dad learned to paint on the resort cabins and painted at least one nearly every summer they stayed at Quartz Shores. I hold dear a fading black and white photograph of my dad and his brother when they were toddlers. In their old-fashioned bib bathing suits, standing in the sand, Dad hugs a beach ball, and his brother clutches a fishing net. Mischief and adventurous ideas seem to spin in their eyes, revealed by the grins and the twinkling. Beyond a Quartz Shores cabin, no other structure is seen in the frame. The shore looks enchanting, charmingly lake-home-free.

As the favorite summer destination for my dad's family, Quartz Shores weaves through our history. My dad and his seven siblings eventually had little cabins on the lake. Being good Catholics, all of them had many children, and for a glorious blink of time, we stitched the hem on the lake's north shore.

I was one of four kids. When I was little, we had free reign just as my dad and his dad before him. The lake was infinite in my mind. My dad recalled running to the water's edge as a boy for the momentous occasion of seeing a boat putter by. They were fascinated by the motor. He said they'd watch it as long as they could. They loved the sound of the propellor spinning the water around and the hum it made. They loved the motor-generated waves that rolled out and away behind it. They crashed to the shore like boat engine exclamation points.

The boat operator was usually the mailman, a celebrated sighting and a statement on progress indeed. My elders could recall Ojibwa teepees, birchbark canoes, and the mission across the bay.

We loved the lake and didn't tap it for a green lawn. We didn't alter the shoreline and wanted no part of filling the marshes to build corporate retreat centers. We didn't care about real estate gains. We myopically cared about our own bliss and making our own memories. And those memories weave with the tales and histories of the Ojibwa and Dakota people, in the stories we told and retold, the ones that floated up and out of the mist and down and out with the raindrops. We listened to the water. It was our song too. And we were foolishly bold in our claiming of it. But still, we held some history here. Because we loved the lake, we thought we would always have it. The Ojibwa and the Dakota thought the same. In those days of my youth, I had not yet put it together that for me to have what I had, the people who were here before me no longer had what they once had. I got that momentous

    punch to the gut

    way later. Way after it was far

too late.

          So much arrives in our consciousness too late. Told too slant.

    Is it the human condition to be unable to fully comprehend? The full impact of one's actions is not knowable in the moment the actions occur. How startling to try to grasp the fullness of some things that happen. They weigh more on the scale of time somehow. You know the ones I mean. Year after year contributing maybe even more weight to the scale, a weight not fully comprehensible by one generation, or even two, three . . .

          straining, straining

        the mechanisms of the scales

   and what will be the penultimate action? (Is there such a thing?)

      The one that breaks the scale—in some time? Or at least the

    human scale of time.

      Or is time a swing, a long now, swaying slowly swaying, but also

          ticking and ticking, ticking in infinite meters;

          and when—or how—does the pendulum ever morph?

          (Can it?)

    The polarity of the planet shifts randomly

    But maybe it's not so random

    Maybe polarity and time intertwine

      somehow.

    I waited tables that summer at the Harbor View Inn. It had been a gambling joint, a dance hall, a gangster hangout, and long back, an outpost.

    But in my day, it was a moving-toward-upscale restaurant on the water's edge that also provided water skiing, boating tours, boat repairs, and gas. It docked twenty-five to thirty boats in a naturally formed inlet on the north end of the lake, and patrons came in flip flops and baseball caps for brunch, lunch, dinner, and late-night cocktails and dancing. The parking lot was always packed, as were the moorings. It was the spot among eight or so other beachy hangouts all around the lake's periphery.

    I had just finished my junior year of college, and waiting tables gave me great spending money for school. I convinced my best friend and roommate, Margaret Hensley, to spend the summer, and she waitressed at the Harbor View too. We learned every server's motto as our manager Gina drilled into us: *never go anywhere empty-handed.*

It wasn't hard to convince Margaret to join me. She was a farm girl and never had a "summer at the lake" before, and we were inseparable as some college roommates sometimes are.

On the Friday of Memorial Day weekend, we intended to hit the road early to avoid rush hour, but it was four o'clock when we approached the on-ramp. We experienced a grueling, four-hour obstacle course through construction and bumper-to-bumper traffic.

Still, when Margaret first saw the Quartz, we were driving by the spot where the road runs parallel to the big bay, and she insisted we pull over. She threw her arms out wide and yelled, "My God—It's so big!" I loved this about Margaret. She expressed a childlike enthusiasm for anything new. It was no rural Minnesota farm lake, and it was no Lake Superior, which we saw every day while trotting across the University campus in Duluth. But she saw a different bigness. Quartz Lake pales in size next to Lake Superior, and it's not as majestic, but it's inviting and warm in a way Lake Superior, with its icy temperatures, shipwrecks, and whipping winds, can never be.

I was so glad to get to spend the summer with Margaret. We inaugurated the event with a few disco moves in the tangerine sunset. The car radio emitted Prince's 1999 for our dancing pleasure. We high-fived a few times—we were finally free for *three whole months.*

"No wonder so many people come here," Margaret said as I began to attempt to get the stuffed car back into the zooming, divided highway. "But God—four hours of hell to get here! How do people stand it?"

I hit the gas hard to avoid being rear-ended, falling in with the rushing stream of frantic travelers. Soon we again turned off the highway and weaved down a hill where the dirt road turned sharp to avoid the main lodge of one of the big but soon-to-be mega-huge resorts in the area.

"Look, Margaret, every year . . . more rental cabins." I point to the newest row, uniform in color and shape.

"Well, everybody gets to go to the lake, not just you!" She was right, but a person gets to feeling possessive. I wanted it to be a secret, but word was so out it was gushing.

Minnesotans and tourists agree Quartz Lake is one of the best jewels of the state's acclaimed ten thousand lakes. Named for the glittery quartz rocks that rim most of the shoreline, its popularity reaches the coasts. Many seasonal residents fly in on their floatplanes and private jets. People spend as much, and sometimes more, for Quartz property as they do for oceanfront. Right smack in the middle of the northern Midwest. The seemingly endless expanse of Canada just a few hours away enhanced the region's rugged reputation.

The Quartz possesses a subtle current
feeding into the Mississippi River,
with several small lakes and rivers mingling and flowing with it. Her waters dazzle an array of blues, greens, and grays, and her hard, sandy bottom draws the sport fans. In winter, she freezes up thick with rolling banks of snowy powder; her misty white vastness breathtakingly contrasts her warm and sunny summer blues. Winter once contained silence and recuperation, but now snowmobiles grind it away. Neighborhoods of fish houses, ice-paved streets, and fishing contests punch holes in the whiteness.

I explained to Margaret about winter now compared to winter "long ago" as we pulled into the cabin driveway. My family was still in the cities for a graduation party, so we got to settle in without parental oversight. We ditched the car for a last look at the lake as daylight fled the scene.

We stood on the dock overlooking the big bay. It was chilly and still felt like spring, and many residents didn't have docks out yet.

"Where's the highway where we stopped?"

"Over there, see that bald spot—no trees?" I pointed to the east. "This is the biggest bay, but the lake has three bays total. It's longer than it is wide."

"Is that your sailboat?"

"Yep. And the first windy day, we're going sailing!"

The Quartz is perfect
for sailing and for cruising. A boat full of partiers can mosey down one side and up the other, seeing a variety of homes and landscapes, and sometimes wildlife, all in an afternoon.

"Where's the mission you were telling me about? And that rock island?" It was getting harder to see because the sun had dropped far below the tree fringe. Little cabin lights began twinkling with the twilight all around the lake. This huge translucent powder blue bowl of water had dazzlingly transformed into midnight blue with the coming night, and the lake felt bigger somehow.

I pointed out both spots, which were parts of the big bay. Quartz has bluffs, sand beaches, cliffs, channels, and wetlands. Two narrow streams
connect two smaller lakes and the natural harbor. In the middle of our bay,
an underwater sandbar
stores a hodge-podge of giant rocks and boulders. At one time, the rocks formed a motley mesa of sorts and rose above the water's surface. A natural cairn. Early locals called the spot Rock Island. How and why the rocks stacked in the middle of the lake the way they did was unusual. I know this whole region of lakes was formed by receding and melting glaciers. Sometimes when I was a kid, riding around the lakes area in the car, or even by boat, I'd look out

at all of the scenery and try to imagine the whole place covered in glacial ice, and I'd try to grasp at how big it all had once been. The whole colossal, slower-than-sloth-paced movement of ice and water around the planet used to drive my mind crazy attempting to comprehend it all. To try to understand growth and rebirth on such a magnificent time cycle was to tap into another way of seeing and understanding so unrooted in the increasing speed of the passing days of now.

Today Rock Island is gone. Who can really say how much of the lake's transformation is due to natural progression or human overuse? Boulders gradually tumbled off the stack into the drop-off, but some still linger there hidden under the water, forming a dazzling, freshwater reef. As I filled Margaret up with all the lake's traits, she began to love it then, too.

"In August, we take the boat to the regatta unless we get asked to sail. Some of my cousins race."

"No, Ellie. I would be a nightmare on a sailboat. I know nothing!"

"You may change your mind!" I nodded vigorously at her as she rolled her eyes. "Never say never. We're gonna sail the old *Copper Clipper* many times before summer's over!

"Anyway, the big bay—see where it opens up right across from us?" I pointed straight ahead. "Busiest part of the lake, where the yacht club is. If we don't end up in the races, we have to go for the party. It's so fun. Cute sailor guys everywhere."

She sat down at the edge of the dock, slipping off her flip-flops to dangle her feet in the water. "So, where's Harbor View?"

I sat next to her, but we couldn't keep our feet in long because the water was chilly. We were tip-toeing our feet in, kicking them, and swirling them around. "By boat, you go around this big bluff. The restaurant's in a harbor back there. Raven's Point is another cool spot over there." I pointed directly across to the south. "It's a sandbar. People park their boats there to swim and party. Across from that," I moved my finger a little bit to the west, "is Battle Cove, where the last Native American battle supposedly happened. We'll go there by boat tomorrow, and I'll show you."

"Let's go check out the cabin," Margaret shivered, getting up.

It took several trips to unload, and it was pitch dark by the time we were done because the moon had yet to rise, but I gave Margaret a tour. Our cabin was actually two, a front and a back, mostly identical because they were once part of Quartz Shores Resort. My parents let us occupy the back cabin. My two older siblings had graduated and had jobs in the city, and my younger sister was enrolled in summer school at the University of Minnesota in St. Paul, so for the first time since we owned the cabin, the place was mostly empty. In no time at all, the back cabin would be a mess with towels, dirty clothes, clothes that had been tried on but not worn, make-up, shoes, jewelry, bathing suits, curling irons, and blow dryers.

As we went through the few rooms of the cabin, I gave Margaret a quick history of the place. What happened with Quartz Shores Resort was not unusual as far as resorts go in Northern Minnesota. When the Logan family couldn't keep it up and running, they sold the eight cabins. We had known the Logans for years, so my parents did whatever they could to be able to buy our favorite two. The remaining six went to a businessman from a Minneapolis suburb. And back then, lake property did not have the extraordinary price tag it does now, though sometimes I wish it had. If it had been as expensive then as it is now to own a cabin up north, maybe the landscape would be healthier, less populated. Who knows. If it had been too expensive, I never would have gotten lucky enough to be there at all. Most waterfront land is privatized in this country now. For people who don't have money, the best they can hope for is an overpriced and packed resort, a fee at a state or national park entrance that allows them access, or places that are still secret enough, somehow, to be unfettered by ownership. The latest question in the world of waterfronts is, who is responsible for them when they flood or dry up? The landowner, the local, state, or federal government, the causers of climate change? Who are they, and who decides? Earth has ultimate authority, but her solutions may or may not include a human future. I suspect Earth is observing our behavior to decide.

Like any good waterfront abode, the cabins had screened porches facing the lake. The front cabins had two small bedrooms, one tiny bathroom, a small kitchen, and a big living room with a Franklin stove. The back cabins had only one bedroom. At first, a bathhouse enhanced the resort with four toilets and four showers, and a laundry area. Eventually, each cabin had small shower stalls added, and the bathhouse went away.

The cabins were old and creaky. Three overhead lights, one in the bathroom, the bedroom, and the living room, were basic, and you had to pull a string to turn them on. The floors were wide-planked hardwood, and the ceilings were thin plank cherry hardwood. Each door and window had thick wood framing. There was always a pleasant wood smell in the cabin. The only modern installment in the small kitchen was our microwave and toaster oven. Margaret said, "I thought we were the last people on Earth with no dishwasher!" My parents never managed to get one installed and never wanted to. They told us we kids were the dishwashers. We spent practically every sunset washing dishes, drying dishes, and putting them away. We got really good at rotating jobs to make it fair, but of course, we still had high drama, sometimes over drying the dishes.

Every bed, lamp, table, chair, dresser, and footstool were old and worn. Three beds were on the porch in the back cabin, a double on one side of the doorway, where my older sister slept, and two single beds on the other, where my younger sister and I slept. My brother got the bedroom. All beds had matching bedspreads, wool blankets, and hand-embroidered monogrammed "QSR" white cotton sheets. The front yard was the Quartz, so we heard her musings nonstop. We drifted to sleep on crashing waves, or stillness, and sometimes wee hours of the morning storytelling. Our lot was considered small with seventy-five feet of lakefront. When my parents purchased their waterfront in the mid-1970s, it cost twenty-five thousand dollars. Fifty years later, it would be "worth" millions, even as the ethereal wildness diminished.

Margaret chose one of the single beds, using the other to pile clothes as she emptied her suitcase. I took the double. We unpacked our groceries, which were beer and junk food. As we got into bed, we began the summer tradition of talking through half the night. We each had a large bag of Doritos, and I sipped my usual favorite, RC Cola; Margaret had Bubble-Up. We were munching away in the dark. I was happy my parents weren't around, so I wouldn't have to hide the "No food in bed!" evidence from my mom. It was her habit to knock way too early in the morning to make sure we were all "in line."

"Tell me about the neighbors. That log cabin on this side is so cute. Who lives there?"

"Oh, Mrs. Wylund.

She lives by herself now.

Her husband died a few years ago.

Her kids come every once and a while with their kids, but most of the time, her place is quiet. We play kickball and capture the flag in her yard. She loves kids. She gets a little lonely sometimes, so she comes over for dinner."

"At least her kids come to visit."

"Yeah, exactly. You'll meet her. She'll probably come over tomorrow with something homemade to eat. Her strawberry rhubarb pies are amazing. And if she invites you to see her cabin, go see it. It's even older and cooler on the inside."

"What about the other neighbors?"

The Crandahls, our neighbors to the west, had the remaining one hundred and twenty-five feet of the original two hundred from the resort.

They tore down all but one of the six cabins.

The one left standing they used as a guest cabin,

but over the years

we watched them expand the porch, remodel and enlarge the kitchen,

build-in a Jacuzzi and walk-in shower,
add another full bath and a second floor
with two bedrooms and another full bath. Their
guest cabin was close, about fifty feet from our front cabin, so we were glad
they designated it a guest house. They rarely had overnight guests who weren't
gone within the first couple of daylight hours. Few could tell that their guest
cabin and our cabins were once part of the same resort.

Their main cabin was gigantic; it had about three thousand square feet
at first;
but many summers, we watched and were auditorily violated by
more construction and bemoaned the vibrations and screaming of the big
machines.
And the paradoxical scent of sawdust.
We watched from our porch the demolition of the original five.
Then we watched
the grinding
away
of a grove
of tall
pine
trees.

It didn't take long to raise the new place, and at first, it was one level. It
had four bedrooms on the far side. Eventually, Mr. Crandahl bought the lot on
the other side for an additional seventy-five feet of lakeshore.

Their sunken living room boasted an enormous fireplace constructed
with massive boulders from the lake. It was a great room before great
rooms were great. The huge kitchen had stainless-steel appliances, quartz
countertops, an island, and barstools. The home also contained a library, den,
formal dining room, three bathrooms, a mudroom, a laundry room, and a
beautiful screened porch that opened onto a multi-level terrace surrounded
by a thick green lawn and marvelous flower gardens. They had a live-in maid,
a gardener, and a nanny. Eventually, the entire house had a second level, with
more bedrooms, a giant sunroom, an entertainment room, a fitness room,
and an office. They built servant quarters over the four-car garage. They
eventually had a cook too.

How could I sum them up? She'd figure them out on her own, so I tried
for neutral.

"Oh, that's the Crandahl family. We used to get along with them better
when we first bought our cabin ten years ago. They have four kids; three of
them are our same ages. The oldest is Blake, who's Julie's age, two years older
than me. Then Angelique, who's my age. Then Donovan, Nancy's age. Then

they have a much younger son, Brandon, twelve years or so younger than the oldest, Blake."

"What's the girl like? Angelique?"

"Yeah. Well, like I said, in the early days when we were first neighbors, we had a lot of fun swimming together. The dad's a big fisherman. He always called us over to see the humongo fish he caught. We used to ride our bikes around their driveway. Donovan had a unicycle, and he'd let us take turns learning how to ride it.

"Angelique had this amazing Barbie collection. She had this big suitcase full of them, with tons of clothes and little plastic shoes. She had the condo, the salon, the dune buggy, the convertible, and a bunch of other Barbie crap."

"No wonder you liked her," Margaret sounded impressed. "I had two Barbies. That's it. I could never keep track of their clothes or shoes."

"Yeah. Well, by the third summer, more of my cousins had cabins, so we were hanging out more with them. They all went off to horse camp for like a month, so they weren't around much."

"What's the mom like?" She took a noisy sip of her pop. It was pitch dark inside the cabin, but now we could see the glow of the moon starting to lighten up the shadows.

"Ya know . . . I don't know much about her. I don't think she likes us. She comes from a lot of money, and I'm sure she thinks we're hillbillies. I remember the one and only time we stayed overnight there; she wasn't all that nice to us. But, then again, it wasn't exactly by invitation. Nancy had to have her appendix out in the middle of the night. She's sweating and crying, and my poor mom had to take her to the hospital. My brother and my dad were off on a camping thing, and we didn't have a telephone in those days to call anybody. Me and Julie were pretty young, and my mom didn't want to leave us alone. She figured she'd have to stay overnight at the hospital, so she dragged us over there about eleven o'clock and knocked on their side door."

"Wow. What was Nancy doing?"

"I think laying down in the back seat of the car. Can you imagine? My mom must've been a wreck. She didn't really hit it off with Mrs. Crandahl, so she must have been pretty desperate to go over there."

"So, what happened?"

"Well, we knocked quite a few times, and finally, Mrs. Crandahl answered in her matching robe and nightgown. I remember her slippers. They had little triangular heels and pink feathers on the front."

"I'm sure those were comfortable."

"Ya think?"

"Maybe you just thought they were high heels."

"No, I remember her click-clackin' away across the hardwood floors. It was one of the few times I'd ever seen her up close."

"Was everybody sleeping?"

"I doubt she was—Camilla's her name. She looked all made up if I remember right. But she always looks like she's ready for a party. Donovan was at camp, so she put us in his room, and he had two twin beds. We were scared. We didn't know what was wrong with Nancy at that point, but also, the place was too clean and un-homey. She didn't smile at us once."

"Maybe you woke her up," Margaret speculated.

"Maybe. Who knows. We were afraid to touch anything. And they had all these stuffed animals on their walls."

"*What?* Like what?" I heard the bedsprings squeak as Margaret moved around in her bed. She rolled up her Doritos bag and set it on the wiggly nightstand between her two beds.

"Big tropical fish and sharks, a moose head, an elk head." How easily I could picture each one, "Oh, and a beaver, and a bobcat mounted on stainless-steel pedestals by the front door. Mr. Crandahl is into hunting and fishing."

"Sad!"

"Yeah. I know. See why we got the creeps?" I sat up in bed so I could look out and see the lake, shimmering like an insane shale jewel in the moonlight. I went on. "In the morning, the dad was all jolly, and he made crepes. I'd never had crepes. We played jacks in the laundry room with Angelique until our mom came to rescue us. Mrs. Crandahl never appeared. She was probably playing golf. The whole family loves tennis and golf."

"Hence the tennis courts."

"Yeah. You'll see them out there a lot."

"Do they let you guys play?"

"They used to. We used to play with Angelique and Donovan."

Margaret yawned big, but I continued, "Frank had some guys up last summer, and they drove over their yard in a jeep and tore up their nice grass. They bitched about that, but they have tons of parties and pretty rowdy ones. Though no one has ever tried to drive over our yard. We have too many trees."

"I wonder if I'll meet them." I could hear Margaret getting all tucked into her blankets settling in. I yawned.

"You will. We'll see them on the dock. If you want, I'll walk over there with you sometime and introduce you to Angelique." Margaret was the type who liked to know her neighbors.

I couldn't explain how different our families were. It had become hard to relate to each other. Eventually, maybe inevitably—it became impossible.

CHAPTER 3

Rushing Rivers

The double-barreled exhaust pipe of a four-ton pickup chugs diesel fumes into the air vent of the car behind it. A smoldering cigarette butt flicks out the truck window and flies backward to bounce off the next car's windshield, tumbling recklessly into the dehydrated ditch. The ground swelters.

     Risk of fire,

             according to Smokey the Bear, is extremely high.

Just one high risk among countless others.

          And yet

the automobile

    represents success, freedom, power, control, and status.

View any advertisement to learn how to adore cars, trucks, RVs, boats, motorcycles, snowmobiles, any vehicle to get you from here to there quickly and efficiently. But who tallies the actual efficiency of these carbon dioxide machines? Efficient for whom? Yes, motorized vehicles take us places we want to go; they help fulfill the human need to explore and conquer, but what lies in their shadows? We know we know a better way.

    Perched on a curving highway light post, a regal bird blinks,

                    observing

                      and scanning.

    Car after car, truck after truck, the asphalt river roars with vehicles all doing the highway hop, a pulsing dance with bursts of speed,

    lunging stops, and lurching starts.

    A cacophony of chugging, accelerating, and squeaking brakes

    humming dissonance into the open sky. The light post bird inhales toxic heat.

    The freeway: hardly free—a maze of ramps, merge lanes, tunnels, and bridges connecting roads and infrastructure. In the cars, the humans stare, nearly comatose with sluggish arteries, caffeinated schedules, and road overload—billboards, construction zones, detours, and potholes. They grip their steering wheels, entranced by waves

    of red brake lights

    leading them onward.

A cradle of humming engines   coaxes   a   doze.
Speeding up   slowing down.
One driver droops a millisecond too long. Screeching brakes reel into smashing metal, burnt rubber, and shattered glass brings blaring sirens, tow trucks, more stagnation, gawkers, and gouged rubble . . . roadkill . . . road rage.
The hungry bird blinks some more; its gaze glazes.
The blacktop streams gush
                        with ego and aggression.
Hummers overpower the smelly old rust buckets, complete with extra-large gas tanks, surround sound, GPS, air purifiers, and power everything. Living rooms on wheels roll by. Houses on wheels roll by, pulling eighteen-wheeled trucks, pulling other eighteen-wheeled trucks. Screens light up the dark interiors.
An overhead camera accompanies the bird's perch,
            its rotating eye watches.
Where are the people in their mobile metal cages going?
Racing to get ahead,
            they find they are already behind,
                        no matter the time.
Hostility begets stress, stress begets hostility
aligning in the cells. And the forest fires burning, burning against the dying light.
And . . . Yet
                Exodus—to the great wild North!
    The sprawling Midwest's escape destination.

Up to the lake for hunting and fishing, partying, or retreating.
The human condition is stressful,
                    every PhD agrees.
Prevailing protocol is escape.
We all need to get away from it all.
    It's Friday when the even madder, the maddest of the mad, mad, rush begins. Freeway never stops, no matter how choked and stumbling it may go. One freeway, one scenario, one state, one country,
    one day,
            every day
                    in time.
When and where it stops, nobody knows.
Uniformity, destruction, and construction spread, all in the attempt for a little peace and quiet. A jockeyed journey for the nostalgia of the vastly

vanishing wildness. Not only wildness but history and culture and memory and traditions and ancient wisdom of the Earth are evaporating.

The drive, the craving for what the people once had, or more precisely, what they think they're entitled to, is the very thing that killed it.

Some came for land. Some came for fur. Some came for lumber. Some for fish and deer. Some came to connect more deeply with the land. Some came to escape oppression and to experience religious freedom. To become more a part of it. To discover their true selves by learning how to fit and thrive in the unpredictability and complexity of the landscape and her moods. Some are driven by curiosity to learn more about the world in the most hands-on way. Exploration and discovery are innate in every living being. The show must go on. Unless imbalance, violence, poverty, fear, coercion, or depression pummel the life spirit to a pulp.

There was a time,

elders say

when traveling through the northern wilderness was harrowing.

Some rode the rails.

Some carved canoes out of trees and paddled their way.

Horses, buggies, wagons, sleds.

A rare few still remember the introduction of the great automobile. A rare few live in remote enough places; there are so few left.

But soon, no one will know what life was like before cars. Hopefully, some will know what life is like after them.

How long does it take to cross the Boundary Waters by canoe?

To traverse the Iron Range on snowshoes?

How much would a person's mind be blown by walking across the Dakota plains with no technology in hand? What insights would be gleaned by such an endeavor? Would nature, your nature, allow you to survive?

Asphalt trumps dirt for speed;

And we gotta get out of this place, quick.

If it's the last thing we ever do.

In the "old days" no overhead lights showed the way.

No surveillance equipment recorded you as you passed.

The pace was slow

but compelling.

Families packed their Model Ts. They cranked engines fueled by a handful of pennies. Picnicking on blankets on the side of the road and waving to the occasional passerby, travelers did not prioritize schedules and competition.

Going North was a luxurious escapade, a grand adventure, a chance at renewal or even rebirth. Not knowing what might happen unearthed the experience differently.

The journey informed the destination.

Until the journey transformed the destination.

Transportation has turned ubiquitous and boring, and we no longer feel the Earth under us. Fossil fuel dragon breath is killing us. We fly through the air with the greatest of ease, soaring the skies on wings made of steel rocketed by jet fuel and propulsion technology. And what's next? We sit so high off the ground in our computer-chipped SUVs with power steering and anti-lock brakes. We do not grasp our movement, our own wake, under our own feet. We do not personally expend the energy to get ourselves places. We do not see the relationship between energy expended and distance attained. Energy expended is disconnected from the multi-faceted and high costs of that expended energy. It has become a non sequitur in human consciousness. The energy required to see the world and tell all my friends about it is not calculated in terms of environmental health and sacrifices—only dollar signs and selfies and posts and likes. Dollars spent do not cycle back to nature, to the world. They go into the pockets of the oil barons, the media moguls. They go into the coffers of the tourism and travel industries. More glossy trifold brochures.

We continually take from the Earth
we consistently fail to give back.

We want our disposable cups and straws and spoons. We want our meals fast, easy, and fresh. We want our gas cheap and our accommodations luxurious. We want roadside amusements and convenience in the swipe of a finger.

Can anyone count the drive-thrus?

What was the first road sign?

How many cars existed on the planet when the road was first paved?

How many now? A quick online search says one billion. One billion cars today, and the quantity is expected to double within fifteen years. Two billion cars. How many rubber tires is that? How much fracked oil?

What will be the limit? Just create more electric cars . . . and then more . . .

How will we come to understand our limits? And who is "we"?

Who will decide?

What does an Ojibwa elder think about a large billboard for a chlorinated water park? Did Van Gogh think his paintings would one day become 3D, or want them to be?

Does anyone remember when stoplights didn't exist?

How much time has ticked away waiting for the red light to change?

Travelers still traipse their way north, but the asphalt pavers have pulverized the journey.

Cell phones and iPads have derailed conversation, storytelling, and dreaming.

Presence. What it means to be present.

Have they inspired solutions? Really? Where do solutions come from, if they come?

Generations of tree societies collapse under the swift and mighty whim of the motorized chainsaw, the foolish flame,

Nets and nets of roadways have been cast across the wilderness. Surviving animal citizenry must recalibrate where to go next.

The majestic bird, wings folded, clutching the metal light post, pitied or unnoticed, continues to scan for edible scrap, finding a noxious shred of roadkill smeared dangerously close to the rushing combusting engines. It adapts to big risks

or dies.

Longer ago than our dark-skinned and great grandparents, the world did not roar and rumble with traffic.

The original people and the voyagers footed the shaggy unknowns of this glacially sculpted land. Animals were wild. Cautiously and mostly with humility, they journeyed forth. In this time, they seemed to better understand the true price of travel and mobility because they paid it with their bodies.

Nature dwellers came to know it and learn.

They knew wind whispered messages yet unframed by letters and words.

We cannot imagine that.

They could not have imagined this.

What can we not imagine

for

the

future?

Can

humans tackle

the frothy, frazzling frontiers of our horizon?

It's not so distant now, the irreversible
destruction of human greed and deliberate ignorance. We still try to dictate
the weather.

Maybe we can, as a way

to manifest our human need to conquer?
Can we conquer our Earthly mistakes?
Can we conquer the mistakes of our human history?
Our treatment of one another, human and non-human citizens of this planet?
And of Earth
and all Her life?
Will we?
Or are we too tired?
Will we continue to waste time with our foolish optimism?
Our fashionable narcissism?
What is the price of redemption?
Can we pay it?

Who is here to hear and answer?
Who? Who?

CHAPTER 4

Bubbling

Sunday was the first day we worked at the Harbor View. The after-church crowd was big on brunch, and I knew the place was going to get stuffy. I was worried about not knowing what the hell I was doing, but I quickly forgot about being clueless when I noticed a gorgeous guy on the dock. As I watched him during that first hour while we set up for the onslaught, I realized I *had* to meet him. His blond curly hair gleamed white in the sun. It was hard to imagine it wasn't chemically altered, but when I did finally get near him, I could tell the sun had bleached it out, though it was still only June. His face and body were even more beautiful up close. His eyes glimmered a deep golden-greenish brown like a tropical rain forest lake, and his smile—it will charm me for eternity. Dimples like parentheses. Skin so smooth and tan it looked spreadable like peanut butter. I learned all this by volunteering to take lunches out to the dock. It was part of our employee perks to get a free meal with each four-hour shift.

Four guys worked the docks; one was a gas guy, and another was a tour guy. The other two were younger, and though all four landed boats, when necessary, the younger two worked solely as boat valets. Each was cute, but the blond was *beyond* cute. Being around him made me squirmy. Waves of nervous attraction interrupted my breathing. He was the tour guy, but when he wasn't on the tour, he was pulling water skiers and docking, gassing, and repairing boats.

I pushed open the glass door to the patio with my hip and made my trek across the patio and down three layers of steps, balancing four grilled hamburgers, with chips and a pickle, on four plates stacked up my arm, with my apron full of pop cans. The other waitresses, none of whom volunteered, kept an eye on me, waiting for a wipeout. From that day on, I delivered those lunches all summer and never once tripped. I did, however, once tip a plate slightly, causing the pickle spear to roll off. My foot then happened to punt it just before it hit the ground, and it sputtered across the terrace, bouncing to a halt with a splash in the diet Coke of a customer on the lower deck. I released a quick, hysterical giggle, but when inquiries were made, I never owned up.

When I went out there that first day, the dock guys weren't busy. But most days after that, they were too busy, and I had to set their plates next to the register where they rang up the gas. They had to eat intermittently, taking bites as they hustled back and forth. How they enjoyed eating amid gas fumes, I don't know. That first day, the gorgeous one stood in the shallow water behind a small fishing boat, working on the engine. He had tools and parts on the dock, and he squinted in concentration. I watched him as I approached. He didn't look up to notice me, but the dock rattled with my quick steps.

"Neal, chows on, man, get over here," one guy hollered. He looked up at last, and as I happened to be staring at him, I noticed he looked right at me. I watched as he hoisted himself like a gymnast onto the dock and came over to where I stood with the plates. I felt my knees go a little weak. I re-focused on distributing the plates.

The gas guy looked at me, "You're the delivery girl, huh?"

"Yup. Nice to get out of the air conditioning."

"What's your name? I haven't seen you here before," the gas guy said. He was also very cute, with thick brown hair and bright blue eyes, dark tan, tall, muscular.

"Yeah, first year. But I've spent a lot of summers around here. I've been to this restaurant a million times," I answered, trying to look at him with the sun behind his back. I held up my hand for shade. "My name's Ellie. What's yours?"

"Steve." He held out his hand to shake. "Your nametag says 'Jenna.'"

"Yea, good one, huh?" His hand was warm and strong. "It's supposed to say 'Ellie,' of course, but someone screwed up." We finished shaking hands.

"Wow. Big time, I'd say." He took a huge bite of his burger and then mumbled, "Are you gettin' a new one?"

"Nametag? I don't know. I don't care. It's kind of fun being Jenna," I concluded, starting to walk away. Then I stopped and swiveled back. "What are the rest of y'all's names?"

"I'm Neal," said the heart-stopper, looking at me intently. "This is J.R., and that's Robbie." He pointed to the two younger boys. Then he smiled at me. I had to blink hard a couple times because I couldn't believe he was talking to me. "Thanks for the food."

"No problem!" I held up my hand. "Don't get sunburn!" Then I had to hold my hand over my heart, completely out of breath even before I trucked up the steps, two at a time, back inside.

Margaret suddenly appeared at my elbow. "Oh, my God. Those guys are so cute! I can't believe you didn't fall down the steps with all that food!"

"Oh, my God. That blond guy? Neal? He's even *more gorgeous* up close," I giggled, squeezing her arm.

"Fine, you take him. Neal? I'll take the dark-haired guy. What's *his* name?"

"Steve. Yeah. He *is* cute. Tall. Friendly too. Margaret, we are going to have so much fun!" We both squealed. Yes, like teenage girls that we just barely weren't. Then we had to split because the rush hit.

Margaret and I worked most shifts together, which made it more like hosting a raucous party than schlepping food for tips. Margaret was awesome. Good-natured, easy-going, and full of fun, she captured the attention of any group of people she walked into. And she had no competition. Margaret was the ultimate catch. On top of her brains and huge personality, she was pretty much a drop-dead stunner. Farmgirl stock. I hate to say it, but I mean, really . . . big bright eyes, deep and expressive. Cheekbones to die for. She had legs like a racehorse, smooth and muscular. Her thick, long, golden blond hair could have commanded any shampoo commercial; it was naturally wavy and shiny. She had perfect teeth and a radiating smile. She bore her good looks with zero effort. If she had any ego, I never saw it. But I could somehow stand next to her and not disappear. She made me better looking. Maybe it was my contrasting dark eyes, dark hair, and dark skin, or maybe it was my nice feet, I don't know. Maybe it was her aura of authenticity.

As the shift wound down, Cindy, one of the other waitresses, told us about a party. Donny, the cook, was having a small get-together, and apparently, he was picky about who got invited. After we'd been there a while, I realized that Donny's roommate, Patrick, was a bit of a drug dealer. We were cool I guess, because we worked with Donny. And we were good enough partiers. We often stayed out till dawn, but we were learning the crucial survival skill of pacing ourselves. We had heard too many men refer to drunk women as "freebies," and Margaret and I witnessed too often the dark side: blacking out. We knew "date" rape was far more common than anyone would admit. So many of our friends had been raped. I never really could fully relax at a big party. It was just too risky. Hard drugs were definitely around then, and maybe they were different from today's drugs, but they were just as damaging. I saw a few college friends toil through the hell of cocaine addiction in those free-for-all eighties. Little did we know meth and opiates were on the way. Luckily, I never understood the appeal of snorting anything, and I never had a dime to spare for a drug habit. College had dibs on my money. But Margaret and I could dance and yammer with the best of them, especially if the circumstances were right.

They weren't exactly right that night because I was driving, but the party was a rager. Summer was just kicking off, and everyone was pumped up. Margaret doubled over in fits of laughter while talking to Donny, who was not normally at all funny, at least not while standing behind the grill, sweat on his cheeks, stabbing slabs of animal flesh. I lingered in the kitchen, sucking down a foamy beer poured from the tap when the kitchen door cranked open. Blake Crandahl and two of his buddies blasted in. I almost sniffed beer through my nose. But I managed to control myself with the thought that he might then look at me, and we would have to acknowledge each other. Or worse—he would look at me, recognize me, but not say a word. Which is exactly what happened.

First, he shook hands with Donny, then skimmed over me, putting his eyes on Margaret. He moved over to where Patrick stood by the refrigerator. His buddies got cold pours from Donny while Blake negotiated with Patrick. All three of them took hits off a roving joint, then another joint emerged, and the rage continued.

Some of us moved into the living room, where water skiing competition highlights played silently on the television. The Doors' *L.A. Woman* blared pretty loud for people trying not to look like party animals. Were we trying to not look like party animals? I'm not sure.

But I am sure the neighbors would have complained, except there were no neighbors. Though the house was only a few blocks from downtown Pineville, a sleepy little town, it was tucked into a slot of woods and perfectly private. At peak party, a line of people waited to get in the front door, and four kegs were simultaneously flowing in that hazy, smoke-filled house. I doubted everyone was invited by Donny or Patrick.

I laughed and chatted away with Cindy and another guy, Charlie, a bartender at the View, when I noticed Margaret talking to Blake in the dining room. He appeared to be totally digging her as I tried not to care. I watched them walk through the kitchen into the garage to the keg.

I stopped my slow drinking about midnight, knowing I'd have to drive down Main Street, where cops lurked everywhere. The party was still going strong well past two in the morning, but I was ready to shove off, especially because there was no sign of Neal, the cute guy from the dock. I didn't know whether to take it as an indication he was nerdy or that I was a burnout, but either way, I had a twinge of disappointment. Maybe I had set my hopes on an improbability.

Margaret disappeared at some point, and so had Blake and his two friends. I didn't know what to do, but I figured she was with Blake, and he could easily drive her home. It wasn't like her to pull a disappearing act, and I was just about to give up on her reappearance as I snuck out the front door. Avoiding the puke on the sidewalk, I heard a vaguely familiar-sounding car pull up. Eric Clapton's guitar blared as Margaret got out, planting a foot on the dirt. I squinted through the open car door at Blake behind the wheel. He grabbed her arm and pulled her toward him, and they kissed lightly as I approached.

"Hey! How's it going?" What else could I do? I had to say something. Margaret could definitely hold her own, and I knew where to find Blake if he tried anything nasty. I thought he was a guy with class, but I wasn't sure he was or even if that actually mattered. I worried just a little. This was just around the time when we were hearing about guys putting the "date rape" drug in girls' drinks. I just didn't know.

"Oh, God, Ellie! Shit. Thank God you haven't left! I gotta go, Blake," she withdrew her arm and shut the car door.

"Ellie Marlow, is that you?" Blake leaned over slightly to look at me. His sudden friendliness shocked me. "Your friend's Ellie Marlow? D'ya know we're neighbors?" He slurred just a touch. Then glancing at me, he blurted, "How the hell are ya, Elle? I never see you guys anymore. Didn't know you're around this summer."

"Yeah, we're around, Blake."

"You guys are neighbors? Up here? Oh, my God!" Margaret gushed.

"Yeah, small world, huh?" He replied lamely.

"Well, we gotta get goin', Blake. See ya!" I muttered, walking away. He responded by pouring on the gas and screeching away, leaving a stinky exhaust cloud.

"My God, Margaret! Do you know who that was?" We walked arm in arm to my little car. "That guy's icky! Stay away from 'im."

"Are you kidding? He's gorgeous! And brilliant. He's an athlete . . . and single, and . . . he *loves* me!" She twirled around in the middle of the road. Annoyingly. "You didn't tell me your neighbor was so *cute*! And . . ." she held up her finger, "he has excellent taste in music. Are his brothers cute too?"

"*What?* No! I've never thought *any* of them were cute." I laughed because I thought she had to be kidding.

"Well, we went for a drive. His friends were there, too," She explained as we got in the car. "God! I think I could pass out right now just picturing him."

"You *are* kidding, right?" I frowned, looking at her.

"No, I *mean* it."

"Margaret," I lectured, turning the key. I started driving. "I've known that guy almost my whole life. He's a pig . . . a gross, arrogant" I struggled for the right word but could only manage "dickhead!"

"*How* can you say that? How many times have you *actually* talked to him? You only know what you *think* you know. You really hardly know him."

"Okay, you're right. I've barely ever spoken to him, even when we were little. That might be the longest conversation we've ever had right there. He's never bothered to acknowledge me. The point is, he thinks he's hot shit."

"Okay. Tell me about him then. Why's he an asshole?" She put on her seatbelt. We turned down Main Street, and I began searching the nooks and crannies for cops. I drove slowly and carefully. I was pretty sure I wasn't drunk, but I told myself that's what they all say. I was definitely sobered by the thought of Margaret and Blake Crandahl.

"Well, for one thing, he *does* have a girlfriend. He's been dating her every summer since junior high. Candice. She lives in a gigantic house across the lake. You can see the sun glare off their windows, like a friggin' beacon. I'll show you tomorrow. And that's her *summer* house—where the mission used to be. I have no idea where she lives during the winter, another mansion in moneyland. And, he was at that party buying drugs, ya know." My rant over, I took a deep inhale.

"He broke up with Candice. He told me *all* about her. She's in Europe this summer. He said she flipped out when he broke up with her but then apparently decided to go to France with some other guy, so they're completely through. And so, what about the drugs? We smoke plenty of pot ourselves."

"Okay, Margaret. I'm just warning you. I don't trust the guy. I don't like him. You're *way* too awesome for him."

I didn't want to admit Blake was cute. I occasionally had, secretly, a little bit thought so. He had a movie star quality. This, the two of them had in common. That dazzling all-American girl and boy thing. But Blake had never once glanced my way. I didn't want to like him. I'm not sure if it was deliberate, but his lack of interest in my existence hurt. I didn't want to let him off the hook for seeming oblivious. I felt some level of falsehood in him or insincerity. Maybe it's just that he was "too good" for me. Or he thought he was. Or I thought he was. But maybe it really was just oblivion. I still don't quite know and probably never will.

CHAPTER 5

The Parhelion Effect

Her dream is a nightmare, really. And annoyingly, it randomly reoccurs. She falls through space, as if in a tube, like a gray industrial tunnel that may or may not be slimy and bumpy with rust and mold and other substances or creatures unknown.

Dropping

with no cushion to soften the landing

leading to panic

it's always the same.

Eleanor wakes up startled, in sharp inhalation, preparing for the crash that never happens.

On this morning, though, the dream takes a new turn.

She wakes up

not in heart-racing anxiety,

but all floaty

and light.

Eleanor opens her eyes, stares at her ceiling. Wow. What was *that?* She glances at her nightstand and turns off the alarm just as it's about to go berserk. She rolls over and pulls the covers around her, settling into a luxurious moment of early morning silence and warmth. A big believer in dreams, she figures this new development must be a good sign. *Today, of all days!* She replays it in her mind, oddly happy at the way this version turned out.

As usual, she is falling, tumbling

through a tunnel morphing into any number of scenarios

this one is as if through the color gray, a void, spinning

through the inside of what she can only say

feels like a cardboard paper towel roll.

Feeling out of control, dreading what's coming . . . then her body being righted, like she's strapped to a parachute, and it's just popped open.

She's floating out the bottom of the gray tunnel,

slowly and with control, into bright sunlight.

It's a beautiful day. She can see the trees, outrageously green, like giant broccolis coming up below her. Then she's flying, as if being held and carried by a silent bird, along the willowy wind over the stretched-out forest. She's soaring,

kicking ass through the sky,

and feeling like a feather in an updraft. That's when she wakes up.

She's moving upward instead of downward toward the usual doom. Interesting development. Curious happiness settles in. Unusual. Lately, she can't even watch the news or listen to the radio. There's always doom all around. Racism, corruption, climate crisis, species extinctions, pandemics. She's been lethargic and resigned in what she considers might be an early midlife crisis. She turns over to get up, glimpsing at the clock. It's six thirty-six a.m. and the beginning of an unprecedented day.

Eleanor plans to give notice—yeah, quit, actually quit, where she works as a copywriter for a big-ass marketing firm in downtown Minneapolis. That's the first hurrah. She's prepared for the fact that her turbo-boss, Roxanne Radcliff, might not accept it. She knows no one in their right mind these days quits their job. She knows this may indicate she may be starting to become a little unhinged.

She's also going to mail a letter on the way to work. This letter will most definitely alter her life if she has any luck. That's the second hurrah. Eleanor has planned and visualized, and scraped every penny for this.

It's amazing how getting a plan and sticking to it unpredictably brings people and events into a person's life. She ponders this as she hurries through a hot shower, towel drying her wild hair and grabbing clothes from the closet.

She remembers stuff, all while she's getting ready for work, taming and twisting her hair back into a clip, slicking it with gel, applying make-up, and slipping into her sharply-creased, white-collared shirt, fitting it snugly beneath the generic gray suit.

She remembers she was coming up the driveway to her one-bedroom condo, just north of downtown, in her two-door Accord; she hit the garage button and waited for the door to swing open, her engine idling. She looked at her clean dashboard. A thought came in. *So, this is my neat and tidy little life. This is it.* As the door opened wide, she drove in, parked, and turned off the car. Sitting in the garage stall, she dropped her head back against the headrest, closed her eyes, and took uneven breaths, lost in thought. The car tweaked a little as the engine cooled.

Since college, she watched her friends and siblings trot off to exotic places and excellent careers and make families. Eleanor was busy pulling up a sort of invisible screen around all sides of herself. She didn't see how life would manifest so perfectly for her. Somewhere along the line, and she was pretty sure when, things started to go haywire with her destiny.

She didn't think about it too often, but how had this gone on for so long? She didn't want to wake up and realize when she was forty, or even worse, fifty, where had the time gone? But this is exactly what was happening.

Yes, she holds favorite aunt status with nieces and nephews and friends' kids. Yes, she travels. She loves trips to New York to see her friend Jessie, and she lived a few years in Oregon and Northern California. But most of her excitement has been solitary.

Yes. That moment sitting in her parked car was significant. A come-to-Jesus meeting with self.

A total of two almost-significant boyfriends in almost twenty years is hardly something. Achievements? She catches her eyes in the mirror and squints. No comment. Here she is, getting ready for work: alone, celibate. Perfectly sustaining a vague and hollow life.

But in the acknowledgment of that brutal truth in the garage that day, something besides the car tweaked.

The next pivotal moment occurred not long after when she first did yoga. For years she relied on running and swimming laps at the community pool. But after noticing on several occasions the totally put-together woman in the condo next door trot off with a yoga mat, she decided to try it. As she stood in mountain pose atop the spongy yoga mat in the middle of the cold gym at the rec center, something in her heart began to unfurl like a microscopic fern sprout.

As she visualized herself standing tall and strong like a mountain, she felt a presence. She realized over a lot of practice that the presence was her big self, but also a former self, a self she knew long ago in younger years.

A happy self, confident and willing. Wide-eyed and wondering. Not hurt or hesitant, dull or afraid.

Years . . .

how they came and went.

So much pain crackled below her surface. It seemed insurmountable to process it or move beyond it. But in those early, super mind-tripping classes, she stumbled across a lost aspect of herself asleep inside. She realized yoga could be the vehicle to journey toward her own redemption. She immersed herself and became a teacher. Yoga was beyond real. Yoga was a way to travel to new destinations and escape and conquer demons with relatively low energy expenditure costs. Talk about seeing the world. The internal landscape was vast and varied, as exploration-worthy as the seas and space.

Five years came and went since that first class. For four years, she studied and practiced intensely. She completed her teaching training and took night courses in business, all while she worked her grindstone job and hoarded cash—enough for six months of living expenses. None of this infringed upon her personal life.

Eleanor put her computer bag together with all her take-home work. No wonder she succeeded in collecting money all these years in corporate life. As long as a worker drone makes the office the center of her life, she will continue to have an office from which to collect paychecks.

No longer! Screw the copywriting job. Nearly giddy, she slides her nylon-covered feet into her business heels, giving them a little Dorothy Gale tap. *My days of stiff socks and shoes are numbered.*

She grabs her bags and keys, her mind racing with possible scenarios that may occur when her boss hears the news. She forgets the envelope sitting next to her alarm clock. Amid the aggravating starts and stops on the freeway, she remembers it. Glancing at the car clock, she bites on her finger, pulling the cuticle until it bleeds. She can't go back to get the stupid letter. If she does, she'll miss Roxanne, who, at nine a.m. sharp, will be in a stockholder meeting. Oh well. It's just going to have to wait.

Eleanor has thought it all out. The *I-quit* conversation has to take place *before* the stockholder meeting. It needs a forced ending. Roxanne'll have to go. She hates being even close to late to meetings; in fact, she's normally the first one in the room. And Roxanne fires up about stockholder meetings—all the talk of profit margins and employee bonuses. She's VP of marketing because she busts balls and frequently sends, and expects to receive, emails at all hours of the day and night. And she keeps a bottle of Bailey's in her bottom drawer to top off her endless cup of coffee and streaming cigarette smoke. Eleanor smiles, thinking how extremely corporatized Roxanne is. She's a caricature. She's too unbelievable to be true, which makes her all the more annoying.

The envelope will still be sitting there when she gets home, but not for long. She'll get it, turn right around and head for a mailbox. If it doesn't get mailed today, she thinks to herself, it might somehow never get mailed. Weird things happen. Life has given her enough examples of unfulfilled dreams. But then, the updraft dream floats into her head . . . *that dream* and that *ending*. She holds on to that sensation as she enters the darkness of the underground parking garage.

Eleanor pulls into her designated spot and ascends the elevator to the fifth floor. She stops briefly at her desk to drop her bags. She looks around, and though she hears tapping on keyboards, she sees no one. She feels her pocket for her resignation letter, then she stands up straight, pulls her skirt down a little, and strides toward Roxanne's office, pausing just outside the door to brace herself.

The door is closed, as usual.

She knocks. No answer.

Unusual.

She hears mumbling. So, she knocks again, waits, then opens slowly and peaks in. Roxanne is on the phone and gestures adamantly for Eleanor to hurry up, come in, and shut the door, which she does. Suddenly Roxanne erupts, giving Eleanor a start.

". . . I don't care what *you* have to do! This needs to happen TODAY. I will not be responsible for those babies!" She pauses, dragging on her cigarette, gesturing again to Eleanor to sit down.

". . . Yes. Oh, believe *me*, I will. And if I don't hear from you by nine-thirty, I will hunt you down. I *will* be physically standing at your desk by ten o'clock. Do you understand?" She listens a moment, shakes her head, and rolls her eyes, then slams down the phone. She looks up at Eleanor, who has yet to sit down. She is staring intently.

"Yeah! Hah!" She jerks her cigarette. "This story is gonna be the topper! You'll need to sit down for this one." She gestures again to the chair. "Can you believe it? I am the new *legal guardian* of my sister's *two* brand new babies!" She laughs shrilly, barely subduing hysteria.

"What?" Eleanor stares some more.

"Would you *sit down!*" She snuffs out the cigarette, pulling out a fresh one from the pack next to the phone. "Have you got a minute?"

Smoking is against the law in the building, but Roxanne defies reprimand. She keeps her window perpetually open, but it hardly covers the reek that lingers around her office. Eleanor still hasn't sat.

The conversation is already way out of whack.

"*Sit!* You won't believe this story. You just *won't!* I am deep in *shit*, I tell you."

"You know you shouldn't smoke in here, Roxanne."

"Shut up, would you? God, how *long* you've been saying that! Can you see I'm a little stressed?"

"Why? You don't want to be the guardian?" Eleanor feels her heart drop. She's never known Roxanne not to rise to a challenge, no matter how ridiculous or impossible. Roxanne doesn't bow out of anything.

"Are you *completely* out of your mind? I am fifty-six years old! In four years, I will retire from this God-forsaken *dung heap*. I am *not* going to spend my hard-fought freedom wiping baby butts and driving a minivan. I tell you." She scrunches her face in anger and frustration.

"Whose are they? Why would someone make you a legal guardian then, especially if your opinion is—"

"Oh, *God*, Eleanor. How do I know? I just *walked in* this morning, and I have a message from some *caseworker* about my *sister's twins!* They were just born! I didn't even *know* she was *pregnant!*"

"You've told me some real doozies before, Roxanne. But really . . . what are you talking about?" She watches Roxanne turn and dig into her file drawer behind her. The back of Roxanne's head seems small. Her hair is uncharacteristically unkempt, looking a little like a bird's nest.

"God*damn* it!" She mumbles, rifling through the files, cigarette pinched between two stiff fingers, weaving a line of smoke. She is unable to find what she's looking for. "Oh, forget it. I'll tell you the whole story. It's not like I can make the stockholder meeting anyway. I'm in a crisis here! . . . unless . . . you go and take notes for me. Ha, ha."

"Hey . . . I will . . ." Eleanor's voice goes up. She's not sure how to bring up her resignation now.

"No. Sit. You might as well be the first person to hear this unbelievable story. And it really is *unbelievable*. Even for me. Adopting babies? Is that what I'm supposed to do with my life, just as I'm on the brink of retirement? I'd rather go to prison! And really—there's not much difference."

"Prison or parenthood, really?" Eleanor's voice drifts. She sits down.

A vision of the envelope, sitting on her bedside table, which contains the forms to begin adoption proceedings, flashes through her mind. The image delivers a rush of heat through her chest and shoulders as her face reddens. *How weird is this?*

"Okay. What happened is this," She pauses, ignoring Eleanor's question while dragging on her cigarette. "My sister Heather is dead. She died yesterday at like *dinnertime*." She rolls her eyes. "I'm out with Richard and Natalie having dinner, and my sister's in some hospital, dying. In *childbirth*. She bled to death. That *stupid* girl never went to a doctor?!"

"Oh, my God. Roxanne." Eleanor looks at Roxanne's face, which is so spun with rage it would be comical if it wasn't disturbing. "I'm so sorry! Oh, my God . . ." Eleanor sighs, and her voice trails off. She leans forward to maybe touch Roxanne's hand, but one hand is busy smoking, and the other is twirling a strand of her short curly hair. She looks again at Roxanne's face. The rage tenses her jaw.

"Yeah. Well," She talks calmly for a moment, "Now I've supposedly got her two children. She wrote some eight-page letter, according to this *dimwit* social worker," she gestures at the phone. "This delusional woman read me parts of the letter. It seems my sister had some sort of *premonition* she was going to die in childbirth. She has no idea who the stupid father is, some fucking asshole. It was a drunken, one-night stand at a *casino*. All I know is, his name is apparently 'Brandy.' Go figure."

"Shit. Wow . . . I can't believe . . ." Eleanor mumbles. She wants to stand up and yell *I'll take them! I'm dying to be a mom! Give them to me!* But she waits for Roxanne to proceed. Roxanne's leg jiggles under her desk. Eleanor asks, "Do they have names? Did she name them before she died?"

"Names? Sure, they have names. Ah, let's see, what did she say? Not that it really matters. Ah! Hope and Joy. Can you *believe* it? My sister the hippie." She forces a false laugh. Then she erupts, "You know, she *bled* to death! Who *dies* in childbirth these days? I thought we were beyond that! My God, this isn't a third-world country! She waited too long to go in! By the time she finally waddled her sorry ass to the emergency room, the doctors had no idea what they were dealing with. Placenta Previa, apparently? And no, I don't know what that is."

Eleanor looks perplexed. Roxanne stares at her for a second, then storms, "What the *hell* do I know? I'm just telling *you* what the social worker told *me*. She left me a message at *six a.m.* this morning!"

"Is it legal to leave that kind of information on a voicemail?" Eleanor asks, truly wondering what kind of woman would relay all that tragic information into a voice message.

"Oh, she *didn't!*" She says, irritated. "I called her back, and she picked up the phone on the first ring. This is probably the best case she's ever worked on in her pitiful little life. A woman dies in childbirth. Two babies left homeless. Right up these people's alley. Social workers *love* this shit. And, oh! Believe me!" She points her cigaretted-hand up to the sky. "I'm not *keeping* them. I have no-o-o intention of playing mommy! But I'll tell you, I *was* speechless for a minute there. Can you *imagine*—me, speechless."

She doesn't ask it as a question, so Eleanor doesn't really know how to respond.

Roxanne continues, "Then I *freaked out*. I screamed. I told that stupid *social worker* I was turning them straight over to her. *She* can raise them! I'm out of my mind." She inhales, then takes a long breath out, smoke billowing like a toxic cloud.

She gestures her cigarette out toward Eleanor, "Maybe I'm in shock. I don't know. You get it, though, right?"

"Ah, I—"

"I can't *raise* them."

Eleanor is about to protest, but Roxanne continues. "Heather, goddamn her. I could just kill her for doing this to me!" Ash falls off the tip of her cigarette.

"She's already dead," Eleanor mumbles quietly. "Now two little tiny babies, two little girls, will never know their mother. . . ."

"Stop blathering, Eleanor. That is NOT helping. And stop saying 'oh my God' every other second! I've got enough to deal with without *you* falling apart!"

"Well . . . okay. What else did the letter say?"

"Oh, more Heather blah blah blah *bullshit*," she tweaks her head back and forth with each blah, "something about fate and destiny. I didn't listen, to tell ya the truth. I was too pissed off to listen to that *idiot* on the phone. She's sorry we fell *out of touch*. She wishes we could have *become close* again." She uses her fingers like quote marks. "Like we ever were! The last time I spoke to her was at our mother's funeral. Four years ago. We went to the bar, did a couple shots together, then she went her way, and I went mine. We couldn't stand each other. We're so different in age, too. She was a partier—a hippie—a free-wheeling, stupid *liberal*. Always broke. I'm a conservative corporate VP. What could we *possibly* have in common?"

Hmm . . . maybe alcohol, for one thing, Eleanor thinks. She squeezes her eyelids together tight. With her eyes shut, she tosses out, "I thought she was married. Didn't you have me buying her a wedding present a few years ago?" She pinches her tear ducts with her thumb and forefinger just to feel a bodily sensation. The whole day so far hasn't felt exactly real.

"She *did* get married. How *fucked up* is that? He died in a plane crash not long after. I didn't go to his funeral. It was in Washington."

"Why is that so fucked up?"

"She was a *flight attendant!?*" Roxanne's eyes are wide and incredulous. "She got laid off a while ago, though. She left plenty of messages asking for money. I never called her back. Maybe I should have. Maybe she wouldn't've been out at the casinos trying to win herself a fortune or a man. Typical Heather!"

"Well, maybe there's another family member, an aunt, or cousin or something, who would take them?" Eleanor asks hopefully, raising eyebrows.

"Wake up and smell the baby puke, Eleanor. I *have* no relatives. Parents are dead. My mother's twin sister, dead. My father's one and only brother is an old drunk wandering around Wisconsin, last I heard. He never had children. There's no one. My sister says in her letter, she has no one but me. She tries to butter me up, saying she knows I'd be a great mom. And she thinks *deep down*, I've always *wanted to be* a mom. Can you *believe* her?" Another Roxanne exhale fills the small office with a haze of blue smoke. Eleanor feels a headache coming on.

"So, I heard you say something about nine-thirty when I walked in. What happens at nine-thirty?" Eleanor asks, wanting to cough but suppressing it.

"Well, that good-for-nothing social worker was good for one thing. She's going to set up foster care while this whole mess is sorted out. I have to file some paperwork with the state, something about giving up custody.

"I called Edmund. He'll kick some ass and get this taken care of quick. I mean, Holy shit! We've got the huge millennium campaign about to hit the shelves! I can't be wound up in all this! This kind of shit can drag on for months. But that's why I pay that goddamn lawyer the big bucks. He better get his shit in gear, or I will *fire* his ass!" She stamps out another cigarette.

"What about your sister?"

"Oh, *yeah!* And that's another thing. She leaves me her whole estate to deal with! Not like there is anything! I have to arrange some sort of *funeral.* Hah! I don't even know if the woman had any friends. No goddamn money, that's for sure. I feel like I'm in a Charles Dickens novel, all this poverty—and orphans.

"Who's gonna show up to see *her body* put into the ground? I'll probably just have a blessing or something, get her cremated. The last thing I need is my mother visiting me in my sleep!" She glances at Eleanor, who seems to be staring at her in disbelief. "What? I just read your box copy for Scrooge! What the hell! Thanks to you, I've got ghosts in my head."

"God, Roxanne. . . . I don't know. I think you need to just slow down a minute. You have to call the paper and put in an obituary. Maybe some of her friends will read about her death in the paper. I mean, you don't just disappear one day without someone missing you. You should try to figure out who the father is."

"Fuck, Eleanor. *You* figure it out! *You* call the funeral parlor! *You* call the paper! *Here!* Use my phone!" She tosses her cell phone at her, and it bumps to a stop at the edge of the desk. "Then call a private investigator!"

"Sorry. Sorry. I'm not trying to make you feel bad. I'm . . . I'm just in shock, too, I guess. It's so fucked up when someone dies so—so *suddenly*—like that." Eleanor pushes the cell phone away. She feels like she is going to get sick. "It's so strange." She pauses and looks down at her hands, which are wringing. "I'm sorry this all fell on you. It's so not fair. I'm sorry. I really am."

"That's why I've got child protection services," Roxanne says conclusively. She squints at her computer's screen clock. "That bitch social worker has thirty minutes to call me back and tell me she's got someone taking charge. *They* can figure out who the father is. I don't care. But he's probably *not* the type to play daddy, for Chrissake!"

Eleanor does a few neck tilts. Then she blurts out, "Okay. I'm just going to say this, and . . . I know you're going to get mad . . . but I'm gonna throw it out there anyway." She inhales. "I really think you need to think about this."

She says slowly, "This is a big deal." Roxanne looks at her, irritated.

"I mean, giving up custody of your two blood nieces? They're your *family.* Your sister wants you to raise them. She *picked* you. Can you really do that to her?"

"*What!* Eleanor. How can you *even* say that? You should be asking how could *she* do that to ME! How dare *she!* I haven't talked to her for *four years!* This is *incredible!*"

"Well, maybe you should think about it, like for a night or two. This is a big decision, Roxanne. You've been their guardian for less than a day. Maybe you could love being a mom."

"Elea*nor*. Listen to me. It's NOT going to happen. I don't care *what* happens. It's NOT going to *happen*. If they have a shitty life, it's HER fault. NOT MINE!" Her words come tumbling out, "I mean! Am *I* the one running around having one-night stands with strange men at casinos? She doesn't even know the guy's *name!* What kind of a *life* did she think she could give them? An *unemployed* flight attendant? She didn't even *know* she was having *twins!* She never went to the doctor because her medical benefits *ran out?* Who lets their medical benefits run out? And be pregnant! What kind of mother would do that? Believe me, Eleanor, they didn't have much of a chance anyway. And *goddamn* her for dumping *her* responsibilities on *me!* She's done this to me her *whole* life."

She grabs the almost empty cigarette pack and shakes out a new one, placing it gently on her lips and lighting it without even looking. Eleanor sighs. She watches her inhale, waiting for more. Her hand flies around. "I'm *not* going to feel guilty about this, Eleanor. And don't you try to make me! It's not *my deal!* I did not *have* children because I don't *like* children. I don't want to be a mom. I've *never* wanted to be. If I did, I would already *be* one!" She breathes in heavy for a minute.

"Maybe I should adopt them." The words roll out before Eleanor thinks to stop them.

"*What?*" Roxanne lowers her head and stares at her.

"Well, here's the weird thing, Roxanne," Eleanor suddenly leans forward in her chair, grabbing her elbows on her lap. "You're going to think this is crazy, but today on my way to work, I was going to mail an application to adopt a kid. Oddly enough, I forgot the envelope at home. But—I, *I do* want to be a mom."

"Eleanor. You are *so* whacked out of your head! What are you *talking* about? You want to be a *parent?* You're not even *married!* You want to be a *single* parent? Do you know how *expensive* children are? And we're talking TWO children. TWO!"

"I know. I know. I *know* I'm not married!" How many times did she have to acknowledge it? "I really doubt I'll ever *get* married." She hears herself, weirdly, sounding adamant, like Roxanne. "But I make enough money. I want to do something! I want to make a difference. I want to be significant to someone." Then she stops talking, realizing she might insult Roxanne. She knows Roxanne is married, but she also thinks the marriage may be completely hollow, at least that's how it seems, based on Roxanne's comments about her husband, Richard.

She feels a fight rising inside to make this happen. Thoughts flood in. *These girls need a good home. God knows what will happen with child protective services . . . foster home after foster home . . . maybe being split up. How weird, this coincidence . . . the dream!* She continues, "I mean, look, Roxanne. You know me.

Wouldn't I be a good mom? If they go to child protection, who knows what'll happen? They might get split up. We could do some sort of private adoption, couldn't we?"

"Okay. Well. Here's something for you to chew on, *Miss* Mother of the Year. If you adopt them, you have to quit." She says flatly, assuming this will put the kibosh on it. "I cannot have you working here, bringing in stories about those babies. I would have to insist we cut all ties, Eleanor." Silence. Pause for effect. "I mean . . . if you're serious about this. Are you? You didn't *really* fill out adoption papers. Did you?"

"I shit you not, Roxanne, I did. And as I was driving to work, realizing I forgot to mail the application, I wasn't even mad at myself for some weird reason. I wondered if there was some reason I forgot. How crazy I walk into your office this morning, and here are two baby girls needing to be adopted? Maybe it's fate like your sister said."

"I don't think it's the fate she envisioned, Eleanor."

"Well. Okay. Maybe not. But what do you wanna do? Hand them off to some massive institution to be chucked around like baggage? Not knowing who or what will be their fate? Or sign over the guardianship to me. I'll walk away. I'll quit. I'll—"

"Stop. Don't fuck with me, Eleanor. You're willing to quit *your job* over this? So much for your good salary, then, right? How will you be a mom to two children if you're unemployed?"

"I'm not messing with you, Roxanne. I am dead . . . totally serious about this." She leans back in her chair, crossing her legs. "Let's talk severance."

"This is ridiculous, Eleanor." She shakes her head. "Don't waste time."

"Come on! Roxanne. Seriously." Eleanor raises her brows again. Willing her energy of influence over Roxanne. "Why won't you take me seriously?"

"What? What do you want?"

"Let's just talk it through," she adds, "see if we could come to an agreement."

Roxanne leans back in her chair. Her favorite thing is to negotiate and win deals. "I *could* make it easy for you to walk away. But you'd have to promise never to call me to talk about this *ever again*. I will have that written into the legal papers!" She waves her hand around some more but stops suddenly. "But wait *one big fucking minute!* What am I talking about? I can't let you go right now. I need your help on this millennium thing! You can't *leave*, we're going into the busiest season, and I have no one else to work on this crap! Forget it!"

"Okay, okay . . . wait! Don't shut the door on this yet! Give me a chance." She talks faster. "I can do the work from home. The packaging's done! All we have left is the event itself. I can do my part from home. And they're babies; they sleep a lot, right?"

"How the *hell* would I know! Eleanor, you are—"

"Come on, Rox, give me a chance! I really want a shot at this! I really can work from home. I'll come in for meetings. I'll find someone to babysit. I'll hire a daycare person. I have teenage nieces!"

Eleanor doesn't like the whiney sound in her voice, and she doesn't want Roxanne to think she's desperate or pathetic, but she also doesn't want Roxanne to close her mind. Once she gets going in one direction, it's hard to bring her back around. "Wouldn't you like to know who they went to?" In midstream, she wonders if this might be a strike against her. "Your sister would be so grateful if you gave them to me."

"You're gonna get your *ass* kicked, Eleanor." She laughs a little. "If you do this, you can't back out! I mean it! You really have to quit." She pauses thoughtfully. "We could hire you as a freelancer through Christmas. Give me time to find a new writer." She points her finger at Eleanor, "But you, *listen!* I will make your life *a living hell* if you fuck with me!"

"I . . . I'm *not!* I won't." Eleanor sighs. "I'll sign all the legal documents you want." Eleanor tips her hand toward the phone, "Get your lawyer on the phone. Then call Tom. Get me a good severance, and I'll walk away and never look back."

"Shit. Eleanor. Maybe *you* should think about this for a few days?" Roxanne leans her head forward and raises her eyebrows. "When they get addicted to drugs when they're teenagers, you can't call me to bail you out. I *won't* help. I won't know you. I won't give a damn *who* you are."

"Well, same goes for you. You can't call me and ask to throw a birthday party or host a bridal shower for them one day in the future. And you can't take them to Disneyland."

She laughs. "You are *delusional.*"

"Come on. Let's talk severance. What will you say to everyone—about my leaving?"

"I would just say you quit. No one but Tom has to know."

"Okay. I want at least nine months' salary." Eleanor begins calculating. "And I need an exit bonus. Twenty percent?" Her boldness startles her. "Something along those lines?"

"I'll do my best." She can see a hint of pride in Roxanne, that she has learned the art of negotiating. Or maybe she's just happy there's someone concrete to foist the babies onto. The phone rings. Eleanor stands up to leave. Roxanne picks up the receiver and holds it to her chest, saying, "I'll talk to this woman and see what's up. Get me a coffee? *Please?*" She smiles and blinks exaggeratedly.

Eleanor nods. She opens Roxanne's door and shuts it quickly to contain as much smoke as possible. She stands outside the office a moment, taking a deep breath, flapping her hands to swish away lingering smoke. She has to appear normal. There's no way to explain the exuberance. She feels dizzy, sick with cigarettes and joy. She suppresses a gigantic, beaming grin, holding it down to a slight smile. As she walks away, she does a little skip step; she just can't help it. Dorothy Gale, indeed.

There's a full kitchen on the ground floor of the building where she can grab Roxanne's coffee. The elevator dings, and the door opens. *Empty! Yes! Where is everybody?* The whole floor is weirdly quiet. She hasn't even sat at her desk yet. She wonders what Melissa's doing. Melissa sits across from her. She's a young mother, and her cube is plastered with baby pictures of her son and daughter. Melissa has been a motivator in Eleanor's decision to adopt. She and Melissa are the same age with polar opposite lives.

The elevator doors open into the large cafeteria. She orders a scrambled egg and hash browns. She slides her tray down the metal bars to the cashier and pays. She pours a large coffee and grabs an extra cup, slipping four creams in her suit pocket. She sits in an obscure area, though only six people are there anyway.

She looks down at her food, blinks, holding her eyelids down tight. She feels the breath moving in and out of her lungs like waves rolling up and down a shoreline. She thinks, *My God. I'm gonna be a mom! This could be it!*

Two secretaries emerge from the elevators, talking. Eleanor watches them order eggs and waffles. They pay, then head right in her direction. Eleanor wishes she had grabbed a magazine or something so she could look busy. Instead, she's just sitting here, probably projecting some glazed look of wonder or fear. She knows them somewhat. They've commiserated over the years about the tyranny of Roxanne and her maniacal demands. Her unpredictable temper is known to all.

"Hi, Eleanor. How are you?" They approach with trays in hand. "Mind if we sit here? We're keeping our eyes on the elevator. We're avoiding Tom. He always has a pile of crap for us after stockholder meetings. We're hoping he finds Amy." They laugh.

"Sure. I'm trying to get up the energy to deal with Roxanne."

"Oh, yeah. I bet she's peachy after one of those meetings, huh?"

I roll my eyes.

". . . We were just talking about my aunt. She has a summer cabin up north and is thinking about selling."

"Don't mind me." Eleanor holds up a hand, then looks down at her food.

". . . Anyway, he starts going ballistic on me. He's like, 'Look, Tammy, I'm sick of you making all these big decisions without talking to me first.' I'm like, 'Scott, I didn't tell her we'd buy it. I just told her we'd come look at it.' But I know my aunt wants us to buy it. She wants to sell it to someone she knows. She doesn't want it to be torn down. She's strange that way."

"You wouldn't tear it down?" Angie stabs at her waffle.

"I don't know. It only has two bedrooms. A tiny garage. If Scott and I have kids, we'd want a bigger place."

"But it's just a cabin. It's not like you'd be living there full-time."

"Well, according to Scott, we're not looking. But she's only asking *ninety* thousand for it. It's a steal."

"What'd he say about that?"

"He starts going off about how we can't afford the down payment."

"Where is it?"

"It's on Quartz Lake. Well, it's not actually *on* the lake. It has shared lake access with a bunch of other cabins. It used to be a logging camp, I guess."

At the mention of Quartz Lake, Eleanor's ears perk up. She hears a microwave beeping somewhere close. She blurts, "Did you say Quartz Lake?"

"Yeah. You know it?"

"Gosh, yeah. I love that lake." Eleanor shakes her head. "Sorry to eavesdrop."

"Ah. No big deal. We're just talking real estate. My aunt's gettin' too old to get up to her cabin much anymore. But she wants to sell the place to someone she knows."

"Is it on the market?"

"Not yet. She's asking around."

"Wow. I wonder if she'd let me look at it?"

"Are you in the market for a lake cabin?"

"Well, actually, yes," Eleanor doesn't explain she isn't looking to buy a cabin but to relocate, to get out of this massively expanding city. "My family used to have a cabin on Quartz Lake a long time ago. I love it up there."

"Really?" Tammy takes a sip of her diet Coke. "Well, God, yes. I'll give you her number. You gotta call her. She doesn't want it torn down. Apparently, that's what people are doing now, buying old cabins and ripping them down, building big mansions in their place."

"Yeah. That's what I hear. I haven't been up there in a long time. I wonder how much it's changed," Eleanor scoops the last bite of her hash browns into her mouth.

"Well, stop down at my desk. I'll give you her number. If you're serious."

"Okay. I can't believe you were talking about Quartz Lake. How weird is that?"

"Yeah. Kind of freaky."

"But . . ." Eleanor swallows hard. "It's not the only freaky thing that's happened to me today!"

"Really?" They both look at her intently.

"Oh, no, nothing," Eleanor waves her hand. "Every day with Roxanne is freaky, let me tell you." They all laugh.

Eleanor gets up and pushes her chair back, grabbing the coffee in one hand, pulling off the second cup underneath. "I'll definitely be down in a little bit, Tammy. I really want to talk to your aunt. Unless, of course, you think you are going to look into it for yourself."

"No, really, my husband nixed that idea. I'd just be happy knowing I helped make a connection for my aunt." Eleanor fills the empty coffee cup and tops off her own before she leaves.

Up the elevator and down the hall, she knocks lightly on Roxanne's door, then goes in quick. Roxanne is writing intently. She looks up, "Well, it's about time. Gimme that!" She reaches for the coffee, takes off the lid, and takes a sip. She holds up her hand when Eleanor tries to give her the creams. "I talked to my lawyer. It may take a few days, God, hopefully not more than a week, to write up the papers. But he says we can make it happen.

"The idiot social worker doesn't think it's a good idea, but clearly that's why she's an idiot. Edmund says it can be done, and I'm banking on him. He thinks it's a great idea." She takes another sip and sits back in her chair a little more. "As I've been sitting here, I started thinking about what a good idea this is."

"Edmund is with us on this?"

"Yes. He is. And I won't have to feel bad about fucking up their lives after the hand they've *already* been dealt. You might actually be a good mom, Eleanor. I don't know." She stops suddenly. "Have you changed your mind?" She looks hard at Eleanor.

"No!" Eleanor says quickly, "Not at all. No."

"I haven't talked to Tom yet. He's in the damn meeting. But I'm thinking you should get the hell out of here before someone comes by. Take the day, go home. Write up a resignation letter. Get your affairs in order. You're about to turn your life upside down, you know."

"Yeah. I'm sure I have no idea."

"Take *two* days. Think about this hard, Eleanor. Don't fuck up my life, and don't fuck up yours." She stops to take another sip. "Call me here Wednesday morning. Early. If it's a go, I'll FedEx you the papers. Hopefully, I'll have them by then. I'm not fuckin' around. If you change your mind, I need a backup."

"Roxanne, I'm not going to change my mind," Eleanor smiles broadly.

"I don't know if they're fucked up, you know. They could be *really* fucked up. The social worker says they're fine and normal. But what does she know? For all I know, she drank throughout the entire pregnancy. Then you're going to have fucked-up kids with fetal alcohol syndrome. Two of them!" She pauses. "I can't believe Heather's dead. I can't believe all this has happened to me today." Her brashness never ceases.

"Oh. You're telling me," Eleanor shakes her head, "So weird."

"Well, get out of here, then," she sort of shoos her, "without a scene."

Eleanor looks up, "Sure." She catches softness in Roxanne's face, a little limpness around the eyes she never noticed before. They smile at each other for a second.

Roxanne stands up and thrusts her hand out, "Leave the yogurt blurbs on your desk for me, okay?"

"Yep. The whole file is there, pretty much ready, so you just have to negotiate the final details," Eleanor says, shaking hands. Just saying the word "negotiate" to Roxanne brings her the warm fuzzies.

Roxanne walks around behind her and opens the office door wide, looking into the hall. Smoke escapes en mass. She turns to Eleanor. "You're really good, you know. Make sure you really want to do this. Give up your job. It's a huge decision. And don't think you're walking away scot-free. I *am* calling on you about the millennium edits." A grin forms on her face. She peeks her head out, loudly whispering, "The coast is clear."

Eleanor heads out and down the hall to get her stuff. Besides the yogurt material, she has a deadline on a different account to wrap up. She'll call Roxanne. Roxanne ties up loose ends. It's her specialty. She quietly approaches her cube, but Melissa isn't there. She grabs her purse. She can empty her cube on Saturday when no one's around. *Oh, my God, car seats. Two of them. Shit. Infants? What the hell am I doing? What if they do have major problems?*

As she steps into the elevator, again seeing no one, she feels for the resignation letter again. Still there. She smiles widely, then bites down on her lips a little, trying not to laugh. She stops by Tammy's desk for the aunt's number. Then the elevator opens to the giant windows on the ground floor. Sunlight pours into her like a warm drink. Eleanor steps out into the hallway. Recalling that dreamy, feather-in-an-updraft feeling, her feet hardly touch the ground.

CHAPTER 6

Reed Rhythms

My fear of Blake and Margaret quickly becoming an item became a reality. But luckily, a distraction came along to help me stop dwelling on it. First, I continued to discourage Margaret from having anything to do with Blake, but he was wheeling and dealing a whole set of fancy tricks for her. Even I was startled by his seeming sincerity for being crazy about her. He came by the cabin, just quick stops, either picking Margaret up, or dropping her off, or dropping off fresh flowers (*from where?*), a pair of expensive sunglasses (Margaret dropped hers in the lake within days of arriving, and they had come from the gas station), tennis outfits, a new tennis racket, movie tickets, need I go on?

They really got along,

especially when Margaret kicked ass on the tennis court. She was a volleyball player, a track runner, and a regular old jock; tennis for her was a no-brainer. They went out to dinner by boat, played miniature golf, and basically spent every free moment obsessing over each other.

I hated that his good looks and charm were growing on me. Up close, he was pretty cute. They looked alike, somehow, with that golden girl-slash-dreamboat kind of vibe. She had Daisy Buchanan appeal, but luckily, Margaret also was smart, practical, hard-working, and real. But Blake? He did have a sort of sexy Gatsby mystery quality. He still didn't talk to me much, but in front of Margaret, he dripped with syrupy sweet interest, though I wondered just how stupid he thought I was to not see it was an act. No matter what she said about him or how she gushed, I couldn't shake my skepticism. She said it was because I was bummed she wasn't around to do stuff with. And that was true, but I would have been happier had she found Steve, the tall, dark and handsome guy at the restaurant. That might have upped my chances of bumping into Neal too.

It was painful that I never saw Neal outside the brief moments I dropped off lunches. I never had an opportunity to start a conversation with him or any of them. They were into their guy things—engines, boats, cute girls in bikinis riding by. And I never saw him outside the restaurant or heard his name. It bummed me out to think maybe he was a dork somehow, that he didn't know where the parties were or how to get invited to them, or that he wouldn't just go to a party in hopes of running into me there like I did. Still, I didn't care. The charge of air I felt when I was near him overwhelmed me. He couldn't have been *that* dorky. I couldn't believe someone so cute, so athletic, so mechanical, could be so outside the social scene. I began to theorize about why I never saw him and decided he was shy, but how could I have known,

until the day I finally did run into him.

I was alone, my usual state since Margaret became enthralled with the neighborhood playboy, and it was a beautiful summer afternoon. I didn't have to work. I paddled the canoe into the channels where my siblings, cousins, and I had spent many exuberant hours exploring and chasing turtles and butterflies. Along one edge of the shoreline, the channels were narrow passages of water like a short weaving creek. They seemed to have a subtle current, maybe even some deep springs. The ribbon-like waterway held a zen-like quality because no matter how windy the lake may get, the channels were always still, dark, and deep. They were easy to get to in the canoe by following closely along the shore all the way around to the other side of the bluff from where our cabin was. Even if the lake gave you big sassy waves, you could endure it in your canoe, knowing you would be held safe once inside the barrier walls of the channels. We knew well and loved this mostly secret place. It had a smell all its own, a mixture of cattails, waterlilies, clean water, and musky cedar. Nowhere else could you find more white, yellow, and soft pink waterlilies on the lake. They never failed to mesmerize me while I paddled my way through their midst. If fairies lived anywhere, this was the place. And the best thing was we rarely encountered other people in there. Most boats were too big, and most tourists back then didn't have a clue about the lake's most enchanting feature.

Quartz was a little wavy that day, but of course,

the channels were smooth.

I had a stack of books to read, but I had one, in particular, I wanted to read in exactly that setting. I was an English major with dreams of becoming a writer or some type of editor, but I was not disciplined about reading all the texts I'd been assigned that last semester. I had taken a class on the American Renaissance writers, and we had dipped into some of the essays of Fuller, Emerson, and Thoreau. Thoreau had me captivated, even though others in the class complained about his pontifications. I'd never been exposed to such inspiring and insightful writing about nature, and growing up as I did, in the realm of this flamboyant lake, I was a budding nature lover. What better subject to contemplate, kicked back in a canoe, surrounded by birds and trees rushing in the wind, than Walden Pond? Thoreau's perspective was heavy and contemplative and required solitude, at least for me, so I geared up with an anchor, my unabridged *Walden*, lunch, and enough beers.

Paddling quietly to myself, bombarded by nature, I came to the bridge/ tunnel, which was really just an old, gray industrial metal tube humans plopped down to connect one channel into the next. As the tip of the canoe came through the soft shade of the tunnel into the blazing sunlight, I almost knocked into a kayak coming from the other direction. The kayak moved to let me out, and when I emerged, I almost tipped over when I saw the kayaker was Neal.

"Oh, my God. Hi," I blurted out, completely astounded. Here he was right before my very eyes. And I had been thinking about him right then too.

"What?" He said, smiling at me.

"I said 'Hi.'" I could feel my face getting hot.

"Fancy running into you here," he beamed.

"Yeah. How weird is that?" I paddled around him, not knowing if I should keep going or stop or what. I watched him as he began to turn his kayak around to follow in my direction.

"Where ya going?" He asked, setting his paddle in his lap.

"Oh, I come in here sometimes when the lake is wavy. I was just gonna hang out and read my book."

"Oh, you wanna be by yourself?" He asked innocently.

"Well, that's what I planned, but I'm open."

"You wanna go sit on the bridge?" He tips his head toward it. "I was just about to park my kayak."

Oh, my God! "Sure."

"I have some good chow. I can serve *you*, for once," he said. Then he maneuvered his kayak and pulled up parallel to the narrow lip of the embankment. I watched him smoothly hop out. He stood on the little wisp of sand and pushed the rear of the kayak out, holding the nose. I steered the tip of the canoe next to him. He pitched his kayak up on the sand, then steadied the canoe for me as I clambered out. There I stood on the same slip of shoreline right next to him. I felt unsteady as if I were still standing on a canoe in the water. I felt faint. I actually wobbled, and he actually steadied me by holding my arms. It was electrifying. We both laughed. I'm glad he didn't do the stupid brotherly thing and pretend to almost push me in the mucky water.

I didn't have a line other than the anchor, and there was really nothing to tie it to, so he pulled my canoe up onto the grassy edge. We climbed the short hill toward the bridge. The sides were round and a little slippery with rust and crusty paint. I had to concentrate not to slip and humiliate myself. But the stars behind the brilliant blue sky shined in alignment on us that day. Who knows why I remember the details so vividly? I have a few theories, but nothing concrete.

"Oh, what're you readin'?" He asked when he saw my book.

"*Walden.* Do you know it?" I flipped it over so he could see the front.

"You're kidding," he said. I watched as he opened his backpack and produced the same title. It was such a crazy and cool coincidence I momentarily stopped breathing. We took a quick deep observation of each other's faces; a steady smile came over his face. The shimmering of his eyes focused directly and unwaveringly on me. I didn't blink, but I too began to smile, and a wish on a star, like a blown kiss on a star, took flight.

After what seemed like a long moment, I started talking because it was so quiet. "I was supposed to read it for my lit class last semester, but I sort of blew it off. Not because I didn't want to. I just somehow never did. So now I'm going to read it for real. I loved discussing it in class. Everyone else hated it, so that made me like it more." I heard myself rambling, vowing to shut up.

"Oh, you're a rebel, huh?"

"No, I just think most of us are comatose most of the time. I'm mostly comatose, too—but I don't want to be," I yammered, hoping I didn't sound like a phony. I didn't want to project some fake image of myself like I was some intellectual or some pseudo-intellectual bimbo.

"Yeah, me too. I'm pretty out there."

"What do you mean?" I asked. We were getting out our food now. He had French bread, avocados, slices of cucumber, nectarines, chips, and iced tea in a plastic jug. A gourmet kayaker. The skin on the backs of his hands was so dark it looked unconnected to the light skin on his palms. It was the same with his arms and forearms.

"Well, you know. Take school. Aren't you surrounded by people who want big, fat, high-paying jobs, or at least your classic politician, lawyer, business type? I just don't see myself doing that."

"Well, what do you want to be? How many years till you graduate?"

"I just graduated—from the U. I'm teaching for a year while I apply to get into vet school. Hopefully, I'll get in."

"Really? So cool. What're you teaching? You have a job?" I sounded like such a dweeb. I couldn't believe I was sitting there, in the middle of nowhere, with this beautiful human spectacle. No wonder I never saw him at parties. I had to force myself to look away from his face; it was mesmerizing.

"Well, I got my B.S. in Biology and Chemistry, with a Secondary Education minor. And I somehow got a job teaching ninth grade Science in Horton."

"High school teacher! You barely look old enough for that job!" I couldn't believe it. I could only imagine how the ninth-grade girls were gonna swoon. We started sharing food. And then we yakked for about two hours on that rusty old tunnel bridge. The day only grew more luscious and breezy. The glinty light, and maybe it was the unknowable neutrinos too, electrified all the colors around us, and the birds harmonized with the wind. The lily pads flapped excitedly while the waterlilies bobbed their heads. I wonder if the turtles and the butterflies watched us sometimes like we watched them. And I wondered if they had thoughts to think, and what they might think of us, there, if they did.

We stared at the clouds as they billowed and floated like spirits across the sky, and we talked about dreams and hopes, TV shows, movies, school, friends, everything. We were observers and participants in nature, worshipping the sun, tripping the frequencies with Bob Marley-level positive vibrations. Thoreau would have been stoked, especially because we opened neither copy of *Walden* that day.

It was one of those rare early summer days when you can feel the potential of more summer still to come. The water was still chilly and crystal clear; the air was still a tinge crisp at the edge of a long wind. The wildflowers were on the brink of bursting their blooms. The birds conveyed a special note of exuberance in their hymns. Everything turned skyward, crowning this day, Queen.

Neal had dreams, big and inspiring. He wanted to buy a chunk of land and have his own farm with a riding stable with a sanctuary for old and injured horses. He wanted to mix it with a camp for disadvantaged kids. And I wanted to be a part of his vision. Did I have dreams of my own before he gave me his? Sure, I did. Doesn't everyone? But they are murky and hard to remember. Suddenly all I could think about was the next time I could see him, talk to him, and stare into those dreamy eyes. I'd make him my career. Women gaining footing in the workforce? My time and my education had groomed me to want to make things better for women, to honor the women who pioneered before me, and for my someday daughter. I had cared about becoming independent and finding my own path, but sometimes love decimates any singular dream for glory, attainment, or independence. Sometimes women, and men too, just want to become partners, collaborators, co-creators.

We didn't have a long stage of teaser conversation or witty repartee in our courtship. I guess we had done enough of that over the burger plates on the dock at work every day. We just jumped right to dreams and aspirations. I felt like I had known him for a long time. Like the dial of time had just spun forward from behind to catch up.

"Where do you live up here?" I asked.

"My grandparents live on Lake Erma. My sister and I have spent our summers with them as long as I can remember."

"It's so weird I've never seen you."

"Is your cabin on Quartz?"

"Uh-huh. Did you ever go to the roller-skating rink?"

"Oh, hell yeah. On rainy days. Afternoons from one to four."

"Same with us!"

How had I never seen him before? We had to have been at the roller rink at the same time. I don't care how young I had been; I would have noticed him. He was unforgettable. "Did you sail in the Regattas?"

"No, we never had a real sailboat, just a little Butterfly. Erma is so long and narrow, you know, so it takes just the right wind."

"Is that why you kayak?"

"Partly. I love how it glides through the water. I know I probably sound like a freak, or whatever, but big speed boats aren't my thing."

"Yeah. I know. Isn't it strange how people get in their boats, race across the lake full blast, then turn around and race back? I don't get that."

"Me either." We laughed. Every time he looked down, I kept noticing how perfectly his hair waved, curling around his face. His eyebrows were perfectly shaped and thick and a little darker than his hair.

"You kind of seem obsessed with boats out there on the dock all day," I noted. "How do you know how to fix engines anyway?"

"My grandpa," he said. "He's taught me everything. First, how to figure out what the hell's wrong with'm, then what to do to fix'm. It makes me insane."

"You seem pretty entranced whenever I come out with the burgers."

"I'm pretending, so I don't get caught staring at you," he grinned. I felt lightheaded.

"Uh-huh," I smiled hugely.

"No, I mean it. Your friend's totally cute, too," he grinned some more, shading his eyes with his hands.

"Yeah. Her name's Margaret. I'm sad to report she's decided to go out with my next-door neighbor. Your run-of-the-mill jerk."

"Too bad."

"You're telling me."

"Well, I have to get paddlin'. I gotta help get dinner on the table," he stood up. "Wanna go for a jet ski ride tomorrow?"

"Yes," I answered, trying to stop smiling. "You're into jet skis? With all that gas and noise?"

"Hey, I'm not against all machines. I really like the ones that work."

"I work nine to four."

"I'll pick you up at your dock after work, but we have to be off the lake an hour before sunset, being on a jet ski." He lifted my canoe and pushed it into the water, and held it steady for me so I could get in and not tip myself into the mucky water.

"Oh, I didn't know that. I've never been on a jet ski." He gave the canoe a little push, and I floated out and away.

"You'll love it. They're like motorcycles on water." He launched his kayak. He stepped into his seat and sat down, then he added, "I'll make sure not to zoom down one end of the lake and then zoom back."

"Hah. You don't know where I live, do you?"

"Tell me tomorrow. On the dock. Then I can stare at you while you talk to me," he smiled, eyebrows raised. How readily he gave himself away.

I watched him glide away down the channel; the long reeds swayed beside his kayak. I caught the last sight of him as he rounded the corner, and he turned and waved. I wanted to blow him a kiss, but I restrained myself. I sighed and stared at the sky. It was enough that he knew I waited to see him go before I went back through the tunnel again.

I was perma-giddy that once-in-a-lifetime summer. It's embarrassing to remember it now, except I like to remember the innocent eagerness of my then self. We living entities change so much with age and experience. I see this in the lake; it too is ever-changing and evolving, rotating toward something else entirely from what it originated as. No matter how we spin and tumble along on our journey, most every living thing begins in radiant charm. Somewhere deep in the core, there is still the golden beginning. It's all contained within. The beginning contains the end, and the end contains the beginning. And the ends and beginnings reverberate with other ends and beginnings. The cycles of life are bigger and longer and more interwoven, unwieldy, and circuitous than we can comprehend.

At twenty, I was naïve to cycles and forces and powers beyond a person's control, like a child is unaware of the impact of an ocean-sized wave. How it can pull you down and drag you across the rocky bottom, gasping for air, hoping to be alive when the ordeal is over. How one wave can make you terrified of the whole ocean.

I didn't know, then, what ordeals were. But even had I known, I would fall for him still.

CHAPTER 7

Cambial Currents

In the quaint, blink-of-an-eye town of Pineville, one of the few remaining original buildings on Main Street displays a totem pole to mark its storefront. At the peak stands a bald eagle, wings half spread, with feathers splayed like fingers. Its stern face and beady eyes convey enviable confidence and a little Old Testament God aura. Below it are some less regally represented creatures, a gopher, a rabbit, and a fish.

Was it sculpted to represent the concept of the food chain—nature's innate order? Is it an honorary symbol of someone well-loved and respected? Is it a fake totem made out of wood-like plastic meant to imitate or mock a real one? Who knows or cares enough to find out? Who is the artist, and what was the artist's inspiration?

Why does it take heritage archeologists to tell us what to value? Artistry of every form is overlooked and undervalued, yet, without it, life loses context, its fabric loses texture and warmth.

An artist carving a totem hidden in a tree trunk seems impossible without some element of spirit. Relationship, ritual, and ceremony are integral to a totem's existence. It heralds of realms invisible in the visible, a symbol of higher thought mostly overlooked in the midst of a small town barely noted on a map—a landmark, a beacon, a sign of the times.

And in these times, it is old, awash in gray, and nearly colorless; its preservation, the people seem to think, will take care of itself. Yet maybe the point of a totem is to decay with time. Do we value it by preserving it or by letting it be? Maybe it stands to convey the influence of time on art. Maybe it stands to teach us; a flagrant image to contemplate, to learn whatever it is we need to learn. Maybe it's meant to tell a story and be a story.

One remnant of a story about the totem one might hear at the local bars was that it had been commissioned by a resort owner to decorate his lodge and highlight local culture, even though totems weren't actually common in Midwestern Native tribes like they were in the Pacific Northwest. The resort owner was not happy with the totem because he had wanted, in addition to the eagle on the very top, a rabbit, a wolf, and a grizzly bear. The Ojibwa artist who sculpted the totem didn't see how a grizzly, or a wolf for that matter, could be below the eagle, so he didn't follow the design he was commissioned to create. The resort owner refused to pay for the totem, and it was sold for a meager amount to the opportunistic owner of the trading post. Who knows if the artist got any money at all? Who knows what the artist acquired in the making of this art—no accurate price or bearing can be calculated.

But where the totem pole came from, who carved it, who commissioned it, who purchased it, and who placed it atop the storefront are all very vague. Many stories have been told, but none are verifiable with documentation,
               like a deed of sale or a commission contract.

Who stands to gain by such paper trails? Not enough "whos" are concerned about the legality of anything if it can be obtained otherwise.
                           Treaties . . . anyone?

          Reparations?

In the early 1900s, the totem building functioned as a trading post for trappers, loggers, settlers, old-timers, tourists, Native people, railroad workers, prospectors, people on the run, businessmen, and bankers. It became a saloon, then a pizza shop, a liquor store, and recently and finally, a trinket shop, stuffed full of gifts, gag items, and clever knick-knack paddy-whacks, most of which are culturally appropriated: toy tomahawks, drums, dream catchers, mini-tipis and totems. There, for all to see, try on, and purchase, are plastic-beaded leather moccasins made in China and the Dominican Republic. Does anything tie back to its original source anymore?
          Totus Tuus?

The tourists, among others, don't care. Most of Main Street caters to the new breed of tourists, offering big-windowed stores filled with highly over-priced collectibles confidently displayed. They just need something to buy. And quaint little nooks with benches for selfie-taking.

For many years, this town only had a main street, but over time, it filled in
               with a grid of streets anchored by a few churches,
a bank,
     a baseball field,
          a community center,
              a hardware store,
                    a funeral home, and a
convenience store.

Within a matter of a couple of decades, the quaint little village burgeoned with spec houses,
          rows of condominiums,
              strip malls, fast food, drug treatment centers,
                   more gas stations, more churches, more banks,

and real estate agencies.

A casino sprang up

to replace the bingo parlor

on the outskirts of town, encompassed by the Indian

reservation.

Tourists still visit the town hall, treading down the long hallway to wait in line for the bathroom. The walls are a tapestry of old black and white photographs.

Ancient model Ts,

sturdy women in full-length skirts, aprons, and hair buns,

barefoot children with fishing rods,

Ojibwa and Dakota tribesmen and women in their

natural clothing, Main Street as a narrow, rutted road.

At one time, a train station shuffled in the people, but the depot was replaced by the town hall, where its old picture now resided. The totem is captured in these photographs, too, but it's been spiffed up with layers of paint over the years.

Joseph Gerhardt, the man who converted the trading post into a saloon, supposedly still haunts the place. He built a large house on the south side of Piney Lake, the small lake on the outskirts of Pineville. He walked to work, tending bar and serving deli sandwiches to locals and travelers. He was a German known for homemade sauerkraut, barrel pickles, and sausages. He was also known for his backroom gambling. When Gerhardt purchased the outpost, it didn't have the totem. Supposedly, he claimed it in a wager won.

Gerhardt had a strong, beautiful wife, Helena, who gave him a large family of eight children. As earnings were good, he and Helena purchased more land on the south shore of Piney Lake,

and had eight small cabins built with local lumber purchased cheap, one for each child to enjoy someday.

While the kids were young,

the Gerhardts rented out the cabins.

They became the first resort owners in the area. Renters were easy to find; people who came to the totem pole would inquire about lodging, and Joe had the answer. Joe and Helena called it Piney Shores. Then they purchased more land, this time on the north shore of Quartz Lake. They hired a crew and built more cabins to rent. They called this resort Quartz Shores. Soon visitors came yearly and reserved the same week or two every summer, and both Piney and Quartz Shores soon became sought after summer vacation spots for many Midwesterners who had begun to discover the lake country.

Joseph and Helena grew too old to handle all their booming businesses and eventually sold the Totem Pole Saloon. Their older children took ownership and management of the two resorts, but when the Totem

Pole Saloon changed hands, it's said, old Gerhardt never quite let go of it emotionally. He would visit the bar often and stay long. Beautiful Helena became "an old battle-ax," and he drifted along with his alcohol. She wanted to spend her golden years traveling. Tragedy struck when a drunk driver killed their eldest son, who had been running Piney Shores. The irony did not escape Helena, and she left old Joe to fend for himself. She moved to San Francisco with the two youngest children, and they never came back.

Old Joe fell once again to caretaking Piney Shores
     after his son was gone,
             but the resort slowly crumbled from neglect.

Eventually, Piney Shores, like the Totem Pole, was sold to a new owner. Joe lost touch with his kids, most of whom had left the state, and the two daughters, who ran Quartz Shores Resort, were said to have disowned him—too many drunken sob sessions over his dead son and missing wife. Not long after things had gotten to that point, Joe Gerhardt drank himself to death and was found all alone, in his old saloon, in the second-floor storage area, collapsed in a box of plastic straws.

Gerhardt's two daughters sold Piney Shores but continued to run Quartz Shores together with their husbands and growing families. The subsequent owner of Piney Shores remade the place, upgrading, modernizing, and expanding it. He added more amenities, and the clientele gradually shifted from working-class families to the upwardly mobile. This development proved successful, and the resort thrived for another fifty or so years.

A childless couple from Denmark took ownership next. When they retired, they put the resort on the market and moved to a warmer climate. This time, the new owner did an even more drastic upgrade,
     tearing down the cabins,
          and putting in a large hotel-like structure.

It brought in more paying people and cost less to maintain. It was less unique but more profitable. The new owner didn't live on the premises, and when the resort hotel somehow didn't do as well as before, he decided to get out.

The next owner envisioned bigger plans. He was into
     development
          and favored the tear-down and rebuild strategy. He reconfigured the four hundred and fifty feet of shoreline that was Piney Shores into nine double-unit executive townhomes, renamed it "Timberland Heights," and
     sold each unit as a single-family home,
          making big cash
             and many enemies in the process.

The heavy boat traffic,

all the downed trees,
      and the way the city-ish makeover imparted itself on the landscape,
            with bright lights fuzzing up the dark sky and the
dark water
      all night long
         disturbing the locals.
Elevated auto traffic irritated the town, too.
      They sued the developer for violating building codes,
         but he paid his fines and
            continued re-sculpting the roadway and shoreline.
Large trucks brought in
    piles of giant granite boulders,
        and metal scoops dug out
         the weedy shallows and fish breeding grounds so heaping
piles of sand
           could be spread out for the Timberland Heights
private beach. More and new townhome residents moved in and loved the
new shoreline. Older and non-human residents got squeezed out. Indigenous
diversity shrank as property values surged.

The beach made a fat, bald spot on the shoreline, and big boulders
formed an impassable retaining wall along both sides. Residents loved the way
the water
           lapped against the rocks
             and echoed across the lake. Old-
timers complained about the engineered sound-manipulations of nature.
Town meetings were held, more fines were paid, but no alterations came.
How does one undo something already done? Repairing and restoring is a
nuanced and nebulous process. Who will do it for how much?

And all the while, Joseph and Helena Gerhardt's two daughters spent
their lives raising their children and maintaining their resort until they too
sold for profits and tropical breezes. Who could blame them? Progress will be
had. The resort was broken up and sold off. Long-time visitors found different
places to stay, some purchased cabins. Some were lured to the big resorts
offering many amenities, pampering, and bigger, year-round lodging and
entertainment. This is the way of the world. It's all good, say the players.

This one growth pattern, among many other potential manifestations,
dominated and continues to reign in Minnesota lake country. Such growth
has depended on the fur trade, timber industry, the railroad, rock and
mineral mines, gambling, real estate, outdoor recreation, and tourism. The
latest boom is the high-tech West Coasters jetting in to work remotely for
their mega-corporations. Such success has not depended upon the rights and
dignity of the region's inherent inhabitants. Such unshuttered progress allows

every kind of exploiter access. Cue in the zebra mussel, the Eurasian milfoil, the emerald ash borer, the Japanese beetle, the capitalist, the real estate magnate. Even if we'd all rather not have it be true, we all no longer have a choice.

Across regions and times, populations ebb and flow, and cycles start and finish. Quaint one-road towns transform into
boarded-up buildings or thriving small towns. Ponds morph into meadows, and maybe meadows roll through the centuries into forests. People grow and change, or fritter and waste, and pass on what they sow. Hard-working Natives and settlers, lake sedge, Canadian rye, wild rice fields, loons, and falcons who have loved and cherished these ice-age sculpted realms,
are drying up and blowing away
as fast-moving, toy-lovin' tourists and techies and their systems and ways flow in.

Nature is "improved" to make room for more people, real estate, economic growth—for unharnessed, unquestioned *progress*. How strangely undisturbed progress is by the common but fleeting human tendency to regulate.

While all they are really meant to do is be holy and sanctify beauty, land and water   stretch and bend   to accommodate progress . . . but stretching and bending unrelentingly
becomes straining and breaking   irreparably.

Scars form.

What is done
cannot be undone. The only way is forward. Progress must progress.
Yet
how does land breathe, covered with asphalt and cement? How do our feet feel the earth?

How does water flow, though dammed?

How do lake bottoms breathe under layers of strange mussel mucus? Where can birds clutch their talons? Where do the seeds of the grasses take root?

They float like questions on the shallow, temperamental breeze,
but they have no place to take root in the dry and shrinking wilderness. The delicate diamonds of dreams, the seeds of the future, are hard to discern amid echoing chainsaws
and zooming four-lane highways.

Where can the babies, the pups, the fledglings be wild?

. . . and the totem pole, with its withering gray eagle, rotting and crumbling.

How long will it last?

And who

       will

              see

when it is gone?

CHAPTER 8

Traveling Zen

Our first official date, when he picked me up to go jet skiing, is a vivid and much-replayed memory. It comes to me most on big-wind days, when the sun flings millions of little diamond shards of light across the far, watery horizon, and the waves crash heavy and loud, frothy, and backlit to transparent seafoam green. On these windy days, the lake reveals an ominous side, deep and powerful, a churning cauldron. It was like this when I got home from work that afternoon.

Margaret and I worked the same shift, as we often did, so we came home together, excited for the night to come. Blake was having a party at his house, and Margaret invited me to bring Neal over if I wanted after we were done frolicking on the lake.

"Margaret. I've only been in their house a few times, always as an alien. I highly doubt I'm dragging Neal into that."

"Ellie. He's having a keg. It's gonna be fun. He's got a band coming."

"Wuuooo. What's the big occasion?"

"I don't know; his roommate from college is coming up and staying a few days, I guess."

"Well, I hope I don't come over there and find you draped over the keg, or worse."

"Haha. Very funny. I really want you to come. Give me an excuse to leave so I don't crowd Blake and his roommate. Blake is begging me to stay there all night, but I want him to be able to hang out with his buddies, girlfriend-free, ya know."

"Well, it depends on how great this goes with Neal. I might just want him all to myself." We were changing to go swimming. It was always so fun to swim after work. On wavy days, the lake was warm like bathwater. Margaret liked to swim as much as I did, which seemed strange for someone who grew up surrounded by cornfields. She was a superb swimmer too. We usually swam to Quartz Lake Lodge, a big resort about a half-mile down the shore to the east, then we'd turn and swim back. Because it was so wavy, though, we opted for inflated inner tubes and floating around on the topsy-turvy waves. The sun had airbrushed pink and lavender into the clouds of the late afternoon sky, and the wind held steady.

When Neal arrived, he wasn't stressed about the waves or finding the place. I was shocked he made it. I had given him only a rough description of where the cabin was and how to get to it via boat, and he didn't even know my last name, so I wondered if the date would actually happen. But there he was, pulling right up on the sand, ignoring the dock. From the back cabin, I saw him land, and my heart leaped. I went down to meet him. Margaret went for the couch with her book.

"Hey!" He greeted me as I approached. "Are you ready for this big wind?" He used his eyes and tipped his head to point out at the lake. I shivered a little bit with unchecked adrenaline.

"I'm surprised you made it!" I lifted my voice above the roar. "Can we do this on such a wavy day?" He handed me a life jacket.

"Yeah, sure. It's fun. We'll cross to the west side to get out of the wind," he gestured. "We're gonna get drenched a little bit on the way over there, but the water's warm."

"Okay. Let's go for it." I wasn't really too worried. When we were little, my dad would take us out in our beloved old boat with the open bow. Me, my siblings, and a bunch of cousins would kneel on the floor of the boat in the front and wait for the big waves to crash over the top of the bow and drench us. My dad would drive so slowly, straight into the waves. He could somehow get the boat to rock down just as a wave rolled up. The ensuing tryst of boat and water was, for a split second, unnervingly unpredictable, until, like a plucky waterfall, the wave showered us with glee. It was a blast and a rush. I zipped up the life jacket. I was hoping the jet ski might offer something similarly thrilling. But I knew full well what the even bigger thrill was.

Neal turned the jet ski around. He looked back at me and said loudly over the roar, "Ready? When I get on, you have to grab the back end and push us out a ways. Then hop on quick, and I'll start the engine. Okay?" I nodded, and he got up and over the big, long, cushioned seat and started prepping the engine. It started with a loud hum, and I started pushing. It was hard to push it through the waves. It was like a reckless horse, but I managed to shove it forward and hop up as he put it in gear. Taking off, I had to wrap my arms tight around him, which was heavenly, even as we smashed up and down in the shore break. I just tucked my head into his shoulder and held on. The motion of the jet ski was so wildly up and down it was hard to get a sense that we were actually moving forward.

Out on the open water, the waves were massive, giant dips and arches. I worried we might get pushed over sideways. But as we cut through the chop, we fell into the rhythm. Neal hit the curves just right to avoid most of the spray. He wasn't going fast, hardly fast enough to gain distance, but the motion was hypnotic. He turned his head toward me and hollered, "You doing okay?"

"Awesome!" I shouted back, nearly in a daze. "I'm lovin' this!"

"Sorry, we have to go slow," Neal continued, turning his head again.

"Are you kidding? It's the perfect speed."

"Yeah. Exactly. Too fast, and one of us'll fall off. Prob'ly you," he laughed. We were quiet for the rest of the ride across, unless we crashed through a particularly monstrous wave, or it crashed over us, curling around the front of the jet ski and over the windshield. Then we both got soaked and laughed with the rush of it. It was hot, so the water felt good, even in the wide-open bay with the wind. When we finally glided into the calm, shielded water, the contrasting tranquility was amazing. Funny how bodies of water can have many different moods occurring all at the same time in different locations. Sometimes I think about how much a mood can be lifted simply by a cloud getting out of the way of the sun. And how unsighted people understand this so much better than sighted people usually do. We are really so much more intertwined with our landscapes than we think we are. When we zoomed into the flat calm of the lake and slowed down that day, I remember it was as if I could feel my own pulse, and the water sloshing around in my very own body started to settle down within me too. I'm sure some of it was nerves and adrenaline getting rinsed out too.

Neal slowed the jet ski to a stop, and we pulled all our wet clothes off down to our bathing suits. Neal tucked everything into a compartment, and we jumped off the back a few times, swimming around the jet ski as it drifted for a bit, but when it headed straight back out for the wild waves, Neal tied a line to the front end with a small anchor and tossed it into the lake. He dug out goggles and flippers for both of us.

"It's great to swim along underwater here and watch for fish and turtles," he said as he produced all the equipment, handing me my share.

"Do you know this shoreline at all?" Neal asked, tightening his mask. I was ecstatic he didn't ask if I was a good swimmer or if I was game.

"A little. I know it comes out flat and sandy—for about one hundred and fifty feet, then it drops off, right?"

"Yeah. I dropped the anchor near the edge of the drop-off, not too close. You can swim for like a mile along this nice ridge." He pointed with his hand down the long shoreline.

"We sometimes let the sailboat luff here and swim around to cool off because it's nice and sandy. But I've never gone down to investigate. Let's go."

As we got our bearings underwater, I looked at him, and he made me laugh. He looked like a weird sea creature. His skin was dark tan, his eyes radiated bluer in the blue hue of the water—mesmerizing. His hair flowed all around his face, a wild halo of white curls swishing with the water. I almost giggled out loud. I had to come to the surface for a breath. He popped up as well.

"Are you ready?" He smirked as he looked at me closely again. "What are you laughing about?"

"Nothing." I suppressed more giggles. "How long can you hold your breath?" I asked, a little cautiously. I didn't know how long I could stay under. I was sure I couldn't keep up with him.

"I have no idea. I've never timed myself. Luckily, it's not too far to the top to catch another breath. Come on." And he surface dived, his flippers breaking out of the water with a splash. Then he disappeared into the depth. I took a big gulp of air and followed him. My eyes were glued to him. He was a sight to see as a swimmer. Smooth, strong, and steady, he moved through the streaming green-blue under haze like a bird fish. I tore my eyes away to catch a look at the bottom. It was true; we were right on the edge. The bottom was about six to eight feet down, then it literally rounded off and dropped steeply. The water turned from blue to green, to dark gray, to black, and bottomless, depending on your angle and where you looked depth-wise.

The shallow sandy side was such a contrast, dazzling orange-brown with ripples like staggering, slow-mo streaks of lightning, streaming, unbroken for as far as the eye could see. Underwater weaves of magnificence. Not a weed in sight. One of my favorite things is to go underwater and look up at the surface. The light and color combo are entrancing. Nothing in the world can parallel the feeling of floating and swimming underwater and being able to see all around you. There may be other, more thrilling experiences, maybe, but nothing that compares.

We came up for a breath.

"Wanna keep going? I haven't seen any fish or anything, have you?"

"No, but I'm lovin' the color of the sand and the light ripples. It's like watching lightning in slow motion."

"So amazing. I love being underwater," he breathed deep. "Let's go a little further. Sometimes I see turtles over here."

"Big ones?" I perked up on that note. "I'm not sure I want to see a big turtle coming at me."

"Come on. We probably won't see him."

"*Him?*—a specific turtle? A friend of yours?" I laughed.

He didn't answer but gave me a sly, half-grin. Down he went again. I hesitated but followed. We were swimming side by side, and I was about to look over at him to see if he was ready to give up the search, when I saw up ahead in the deep, dark gray, a faint shadowy motion. I watched as it came clearer into view, and sure enough, it was a turtle, as big as a couch pillow. Or maybe my perceptions were distorted through the water's magnification. It was swimming along the ridge of the deep water, about four feet deeper down than we were. It swam to about twenty feet in front of us, and it still kept coming. Trying not to panic, I began to kick myself backward, preparing to turn and bolt, but Neal touched my shoulder. His hand was warm and gentle. I looked at him, and his eyes got bigger. He tilted his head at the turtle, saying *stop . . . look*. I suppressed my panic and froze as the turtle approached.

Its spectral quality was astonishing. I thought I could be hallucinating. Its appendages were supple and sinuous, while its shell was smooth and firm.

It swam

      buoyantly

          like a balloon, weightless, though it probably weighed . . . twenty pounds? As it got closer, I saw how its hook claws and lily-pad paws pushed the water backward for propulsion. Its scaly hide was snakelike and hypnotic. Sunlight electrified the ancient nature of its skin. It glowed neon in a mosaic of tans, greens, blacks, orange, and yellow.

I looked directly into its beady eyes when I finally caught them, from about maybe eight feet away, and it seemed to look right back at me. We got a real good look at each other, and I felt a grandfatherly presence. Not even remotely sharklike, it had, instead, the aura of Yoda. The turtle seemed to be able to tell everything about me through a wizened orb filter. It seemed cautious but accepting of me. It seemed to know I was impressed. I assumed it was male because its tail seemed long. My brother told me males have longer tails than females. I didn't know, but I felt like I was staring at an elder. It was unexplainable.

I had no idea what it may have thought of me. I didn't have the time to wonder. I was too mesmerized by it to think beyond the moment. All I could do was perceive. Then tears welled up in my eyes, and my goggles steamed up.

I realized I had just seen the most beautiful creature I'd ever seen in the real world, not a zoo. It was a wild vision I never expected to see but have remembered ever since. All my life, I had been terrified of creatures slithering around underwater. I was sure they were coming for me. For the first time, I was not afraid. This water dweller was not coming to get me. It did not seem to change his course along the drop-off at all. It observed me but seemed to remain unmoved by me. We watched it go by underneath us, and as it came nearly parallel to us, it swiftly turned and instantly disappeared into the deep as if it had never been there. I stared after it, and I could feel the wake of its powerful back legs as a subtle blast of water hit my face.

It all must have happened fast because I was still holding my breath. But I needed air quick. Suddenly we were at the surface, breathing hard and looking at each other. He, of course, was grinning.

"What'd I tell ya!"

"My God," I paused to breathe hard. "That was amazing."

"I see that guy a lot over here. He likes to prowl the edge. I watched him catch a decent perch one time. That was really cool."

"I've *never* seen a turtle that big. I can't believe it. I didn't know such big turtles lived in this lake anymore."

"Were you scared?"

"Hell, yes!"

"Well, he didn't hurt ya, did he?"

"Well, he could have taken a pretty big chomp out of me if he wanted to. His jaw was huge."

"But don't they seem intelligent? Wise old turtle. The way he moved and didn't alter his course as he came toward us. It's like he wanted us to watch him, don't you think?"

"For sure. He waited to dive down right as he came up to us."

"He was definitely showing off for you," Neal pulled his mask off behind his head and looked for the jet ski. "He didn't do that for me. He's become familiar with me." He wiped his eyes.

"You ready to keep going? I just wanted to see if I could see him. I wanted you to see him."

"That was *really* cool. Yes. Thank you." My heart was so full I was speechless. I had my goggles off, and I wiped my eyes. My cheeks were wet, not with lake water but tears. I could not believe how much this guy blew me away. Within the first hour of our first date, I had a life-changing experience. A childhood fear I probably never would have shed otherwise got cracked open. I'm not saying I'm not afraid to swim in deep dark water, but I can sometimes make myself do it now, and—I'm a lot less afraid of big turtles.

We crawled back on board and began cruising down the shore toward the state forest beach at the complete opposite side of the lake from where our cabin was. We beached the jet ski and meandered down the shore. I looked for interesting rocks, and Neal plunked an old piece of driftwood into the lake and launched rocks at it. He unpacked a picnic, another item stashed in one of the compartments of the jet ski.

"This is like the ideal date, man. You do this with all your chicks?" I asked as we settled on a nice stretch of wide sandy shore, a light wind at our backs. The beach was deserted except for us.

"Actually, I don't go on dates like this," he said, cracking a bottle of wine. "I don't date many girls, you know, especially up here. Most of the time, my sister and I hang out with my grandparents. I honestly didn't think I'd get you to come out on the jet ski in those waves. But I took a chance on coming over anyway. Most girls wouldn't go out in that stuff with some guy they hardly know."

"Really." I doubted this. I mean, the guy was nearly irresistible.

"It was pretty crazy, you gotta admit. But the way back won't be as rough, going with the waves," Neal said.

"Yeah, plus, the lake usually flattens out as the sun sets. But even more crazy than those waves was that turtle. I still can't believe I saw that."

"I know. Turtles are so amazing, don't you think?" He broke off some French bread and handed it to me after slathering it with butter he had in a little plastic bowl.

"Yes. Even more now. We used to catch turtles in the channels, you know, where I bumped into you?" I asked.

"Yeah, I bet those channels are full of turtles. Have you ever swum around in there?"

"Are you kidding? *Way* too many weeds and mushy mud holes for me!" I held up my hand. "For the record: I will *never* do that; let me just say that right here and right now."

"Just checking. I don't think I would either, actually, so don't worry."

"We used to take the turtles back to our cabin and race them. If you stand about twenty feet back from the shore and hold the turtles right at the sand, their legs get wiggling even before you set them down. Then when you do, they bolt so fast, you can barely catch 'em before they escape for good."

"I bet. I don't know if I'd want to catch them," Neal said.

"Well, I wouldn't catch a big dude like that one. We really took care not to hurt the turtles we'd catch. We'd feed them minnows and fill the rowboat with water to let the turtles swim around. The turtles would bite the minnows' heads and then devour them whole. It was freaky. We'd only get to keep them overnight. My mom would make us take them back where we caught them. The best part was releasing them, and watching'm disappear. They literally go straight down from the boat."

"They were probably glad as hell to be back in the neighborhood."

I laughed. "Did you ever read *The Grapes of Wrath?*"

"Yeah. That chapter on the turtle?" We both grinned at each other. "I love how he describes in such minute detail all the perils the turtle has crossing the highway," He paused. "That one we saw has to be really old to be that big, don't you think?"

"I'd say. I've always wondered what they do when winter comes. Do they swim around under the ice like fish?"

"You know what they do? They burrow deep down in the mud and go into, like, hibernation, like a bear. They tuck themselves into their shells and become like a rock."

"You mean at the bottom?"

"Yeah, I think. Or maybe along the shoreline?"

"How much do you think that turtle weighs? It was so sleek, so aerodynamic. It looked like a Frisbee, or a UFO, or something."

"Totally. Did you see its claws? Bet he weighs at least fifty pounds." He tipped his wine glass back.

"Did you see the chip on its shell, by his tail?"

"Yeah, that's how I know I keep seeing the same one. I recognize that chip. Must be a battle wound."

"Maybe he got hit by a boat."

"I doubt he ever gets anywhere near a noisy boat engine. Don't you?"

"Yeah. My dad told me he used to see snappers that big out at Rock Island when he was little. Like a whole family of them, five or six, at least. He said they were so big, you could see them, roughly, with your naked eye from the shoreline, like a green dot. You know where our cabin is now? My dad's family used to stay right in that same area when he was a kid."

"Wow. How cool. Did he ever go out there for a better look?"

"Yeah. Funny story. One time he went out there with his brother to see if they could catch one. They had a couple of big nets. They got within about fifteen feet of a couple of 'em. And they didn't dive into the water like he thought they would. They sort of stood up on their front legs and hissed."

"Yikes. That's wild. Never heard 'em hiss. Maybe they considered the rocks their territory."

"Yeah, my dad said they were so scary that they backed away. They didn't even turn the canoe around. They just paddled backward. They were afraid the turtles might charge at them."

"I wouldn't wanna feel that jaw biting down on any of my body parts, that's for sure." He looked at me with a grin. I barely resisted the urge to tickle him; it nearly overwhelmed me.

"My dad said one summer when he was about sixteen, they came back, and they never saw the big turtles again. The rocks had disappeared from the surface, too."

"Strange. Wonder what happened to them."

"Yeah. I dunno. Maybe as the rocks drifted apart into the deep water, the turtles had to find a new spot. But why did all the rocks disappear so suddenly between one summer and the next?"

"Maybe the DNR had the brilliant idea to take the whole thing down, and the turtles migrated to another part of the lake. But we know they still exist, or at least one does."

"Yeah." I finished my wine. "That was so cool."

"So, your family's been coming here for a long time, huh?"

"Yeah, my dad's dad came here as a kid. And here we are, almost a hundred years later."

"My dad came here as a kid, too. But not every summer. Just, like, when he was a teenager. As an adult, he and my mom came back and found a cabin they liked. And here we are."

"Do you hike that trail a lot?" I wondered, gesturing with my head to behind us where a path started weaving up through the steady line of shrub and pine. "We used to come over here sometimes with my dad for nature walks."

"Yeah. Same here." He beamed. Another parallel universe scenario. "Actually, the land I want to buy for my horse camp is right back up in there."

"Is it on the water?" I asked.

"Well, it backs up to this parcel here, which is state forest, you know. Someday I'm sure it'll be for sale for huge bucks."

"No way, it's state forest land."

"I hope you're right, but I have my doubts," he said.

"You gotta take me there and show me the land. I'd love to see it. I'll write marketing materials for you—as long as you teach me about horses."

"Do you know how to ride?"

"I'm one of those people who signs up for group rides with a guide."

"Well, no wonder we never met. You were out here sailing in regattas, and I was in the woods swatting flies and trotting around on a horse."

"Maybe you can take me riding sometime. I've always wanted to know how to ride better."

"Definitely. My grandparents had two horses, but they got too old to care for them. They had this guy do it, then he ended up buying them. He lets me ride them, though, whenever I want."

"Next time you need a partner, count me in." I just couldn't get enough of him, and I probably sounded desperate, but I couldn't stop myself. "My neighbor's having a party tonight with a keg and a band. Wanna go? I told Margaret I would get her out of there later."

"Sure. I'll have to come by car, though, after I drop you off. I have to check on the old folks. Want to get going?" He stood up and offered me a hand.

"Sure. But just so you know, I'm a little tipsy. If I accidentally let go and slip into the lake, you'll try to rescue me, right?" I grabbed his hands as he hoisted me up.

"Only if you're tipsy enough to kiss me," he for once wasn't smiling. He pulled me next to him.

"You're not supposed to ask, ya know; you just sort of slip one in there."

"Oh. Alright then?" All at once, he leaned over, and his mouth fell gently onto mine. A warm, yummy kiss. The kind of kiss that stays embedded in the heart and soul for centuries. I could go on and on about that kiss. I wanted to keep kissing him, fall down like they do in the movies, rollover on the blanket, and let the world fade away . . . but he stepped back after a good long moment and pulled my hands around his waist, and we found ourselves hugging. His arms grew with warmth, and I felt embraced by his whole body and his presence which was vibrant and encompassing. I smelled his skin, which made me drunker. Best hug ever.

He told me I was the coolest girl he'd ever met, next to his sister. He said he never thought he'd ever meet someone like me. I could only choke out, between break-the-seams smiling and giggles that rippled through my whole body, that I felt the same exact way. I don't know how I got back to my dock. The rest of the date is and was a blur. The memory ends at the kiss and the hug, except I remember watching him crash through the waves on his jet ski as he receded into the water away from me. I have a lot of memories of watching people in boats driving off into the waves, disappearing into the horizon of the lake. I guess these scenes capture a certain melancholy often intertwined with memories. A sense of letting go, a feeling of longing for something that is moving away from you. Something in the moment itself and something bigger.

I walked in a daze to the cabin to wait for him to come back, assessing all the new information I had just discovered about him.

He lived with his grandparents, who were in their eighties. His grandmother was nearly blind, and his grandfather was recovering from a stroke, but he adored them. His parents died in a car accident his junior year of college, and while a lot of people would freak and drop out of school, Neal went the other way. He grew up fast. He had to be responsible and mature. He said his vision for his future became clear that year following their deaths. He said they visited him in his dreams and gave him motivation. He talked about them with such love and respect. I never knew anyone to talk about death so openly, with so much acceptance and understanding. He had no anger. It was strange to me. I wondered about his maturity, and I only wanted to know him more.

His only sibling, his sister Jessica, spent the school year in New York City, studying art history at NYU. But she had begun to battle depression. She was three years younger, and he missed her, sometimes more than his parents, he said. She was still touchable, and he hated that she lived so far away most of the year. He couldn't wait for us to meet. I couldn't wait to meet her either, because she was more of him to discover. Everything about him, every aspect of his life, was more for me to love. The more I learned about him, the more he grew in my esteem. No discernable flaws. Maybe he smiled just a little too much; maybe he tended to look on the bright side and not see others' flaws in an annoyingly too perfect, too golden, sort of way, especially considering the cloud of losing your parents that tried to rain him out. I also believe I was good for him. He needed more family, and I had one. He loved my family stories, and he loved that I wanted to hear his. He could tell me stories about his family before his parents died, and he wasn't ashamed if he teared up and cried. I was amazed to get to know a person like him. I felt so lucky that the places and times of our lives finally brought us together.

As the summer days wore on, I sometimes went on the Harbor View boat tours just to hear his voice and watch him unabashedly. He stood at the front of the boat with his microphone and smiled and winked at all the old ladies. He teased kids with jokes and funny faces. He didn't have a speck of self-consciousness, and my presence, which would have made me dopey if the roles were reversed, pumped him up. He referenced me when telling ghost stories and legends about Battle Cove or Raven's Point, ". . . and my friend Ellie over there, who's lived on this lake her whole life, can back me up on that." Or "Just ask Ellie, my friend in the back seat there, to tell you how big the waves can get out here on the open bay." I just shook my head, gave a little wave, and smiled at him and the crowd as they sized me up. In those moments, I just wanted to melt into him. I was lovesick, and I am sure I was annoying, but I could

    not

       help

          myself. Luckily, Margaret, who spent the most time around me, was in a similar state over Blake, so we could both gush and sigh and understand each other.

Neal liked to kayak to work in the wee small hours of the morning, and his first tour started at eight a.m. Besides him, I knew not one person who woke up that early and was happy about it. His kayaking was a drag because I liked to have his wee small hours of the morning. We never ran out of things to talk about, and we liked to hang out on the porch and listen to the wild world outside; I tucked into his arm, feeling a warmth and safety unknown before. When Margaret traipsed in, our solitude flew away. The door would squeak loudly when Margaret turned the handle, and he'd sneak out with a quick parting kiss while Margaret hit the bathroom and I felt a hole in my bed.

Summer progressed divinely. It may have been the most golden summer of my life. It certainly contained infinite amounts of happiness. That summer still provides me with happiness sometimes. Margaret and I went to many parties, we had a lot of fun expanding our social skills and lives, but mostly it was me falling giddily off the proverbial cliff and Margaret conveniently doing the same. Neal was around, getting to know my brother, sisters, and parents as they came and went on long weekends. I was so enamored; how could they help but love him too? So many bonfires, stories around the campfire, midnight walks and dips, swimming contests, boat rides, bike rides, swimming and diving escapades, nature explorations by foot and by hoof, and margarita parties. So many Harbor View anecdotes. Cousins all down the shore came to know and love him too; we all felt he had been a part of us forever.

CHAPTER 9

Ripples

Two old-timers, who look a little like a pair of barred owls, sit at the local bookstore in their quaint, northern town, rounded over their steaming hot coffee mugs. Horton, like so many fading small towns across the Midwest now, has more boarded-up storefronts than thriving ones. The rare bustling business is usually a sandwich chain or a filling station. Everyone and everything are moving out along the new four-lane highway where the passersby pass. Horton exists purely because of lake country, but unlike nearby Pineville, which somehow holds onto its quaintness and tourists, Horton is sub-par. Downtown Horton, which includes about eight or nine square blocks, offers a handful of dingy bars, a couple dusty hardware stores, a shoe repair and used clothing shops, a bank, a rundown supermarket, one department store, and many abandoned businesses. One business, Harvest Moon Books & Brew, selling new and used books, somehow survives in the backwater. Locals come for the espresso, though the books don't hurt.

The longtime owner, who is half Ojibwa and born and raised in the area, doesn't much care about attracting customers. He hasn't done much to the space to make it modern. Years ago, it was a beer hall, long and narrow, with a long wooden bar running along one side. The bookstore kept the bar, using it as a counter for sales and for patrons to sit and sip hot drinks and ponder their new book purchases. The one well-lit area, with overhead lighting, contains the bookshelves lined up in the back half of the space, perpendicular to the front window, with new and used books separated into distinct sections. The bookstore still has the original flooring, large black and white square tiles, which the owner covers here and there with a variety of red, patterned rugs to cover the floor's flaws. The furniture shows off the owner's nonchalance for taste. The only commonality is that each piece contains some shade or design of red. Couches, red spray-painted, wooden parlor chairs, love seats, and wing-back chairs are placed wherever they fit, some tucked between the bookshelves, set up with shaky old reading lamps and small, square tables. White holiday lights strewn along the cement walls and wooden ceiling beams give the place a warm, campfire feel, sealing the deal on overall coziness, despite the hard, cold tile. Caribou Coffee chains may attain the campy atmosphere, but never the kitsch.

The two old men, friends since their high school basketball days, sit in their usual spot at the bar where they people-watch inside and out. They've been coming for years every wintery Saturday when it's too unpleasant for their old bones to be out ice fishing. Behind the bar, the owner, a big, tall, dark-skinned man with long white hair always tied at the base of his neck, busies himself grinding coffee, and tapping buttons on the cash register. He joins their conversation here and there. They're abuzz because
the vacant storefront across the street
is finally showing signs of life.

"Look'it that fancy new glass they're puttin' in. What'dya s'pose that's all about?" They all look.

"It looks frosted, in a sort of web. Do ya s'pose it's a pornographic video store?"

"Richie, you're a one-track mind!" The owner scoffs and wipes the counter.

"Well, explain that glass to me. Why would anyone take that clear glass out in favor of the cloudy stuff unless they're up to something?"

"Who knows. Maybe it's a doctor's office or a shrink. God knows this town has enough lunatics. That'll be a thrivin' business. Ha!"

"I tell ya, gentlemen. Yesterday I saw what they did to the inside. It's wide-open in there, with *cork* floors, fancy in-floor heating, and floor-to-ceiling mirrors on two of the four walls. Explain that to me," says the owner. He pours himself a mug of coffee.

"Boy, oh boy, Red. Now I'm curious. Did you see the owner around?"

"Nope."

"Probably some new fan-dangled exercise joint. Ya seen the new one out on Burdock Road, next to the Quick Mart? Whasit called again, Barney?"

"Sweat Your Ass Off? Or somethin' ridiculous like that!" Barney chuckles. "I've yet to see anyone go in or out a there."

"Young people today. Boy, I tell ya, in my day, there was no such thing as a fitness center if that's what ya wanna call it. We got our exercise doin' hard work!"

"Yeap. I know it. Kids are all over-indulged these days. My granddaughter—obsessed with her looks! She's only thirteen, and she wears more make-up on any given day than my wife has in her whole life. We can't get over it. And her clothes! I don't know what my daughter's doing, raisin' her to think she's a movie star. I don't like thinkin' about how much they spend on frivolity."

"So self-obsessed, these kids. It kills me. I can't have a decent conversation with any of 'em. All they do is play with their cell phones. Materialism run amok!"

"And all the news can tell y'bout is another murder or suicide, and fear-mongering about nuclear weapons, global warming, and the damn pandemics. It's like we're already in another world war, but not."

"All right, you two. Quit your bitchin'. You're a couple'a old coots, and you say the same damn things week after week! Have you old slugs put your icehouses out finally? I been watchin' people drive by pulling their icehouses. The damn river is frozen already; it's been so cold for so long."

"Mine's out. But I can't go out unless I'm with someone, according to Betty. She's afraid I'm gonna croak out there. I'll be preserved in the ice because she won't be coming out to find me."

"Oh, you'd be a pleasant discovery for some snowmobiler."

The windows, all steamy from the inside, hint at the stiff below zero temperatures lingering the past several days. Die-hard winter enthusiasts are outside, but the wimps find their way to the hot drinks.

"Mine's out too, but I gotta tell ya, I keep thinkin' about spending the damn winter down south. I'd rather be drinking ice tea under a palm tree."

"You? A snowbird? No way. You'd go crazy in all that shrubbery and Chemlawn."

"Naw, it'll never happen. The wife's so busy with the grandkids, she'll never part. Hey, look. There's a lady goin' in there with a big box. See'er?"

Everybody looks again, and through the steam, they watch the woman disappear through the thickly wood-framed, old-fashioned glass door, carrying a huge cardboard box. The old men are silent, hearing the impassioned conversation of the two community college teachers sitting behind them at a table. One is reading something aloud to the other.

". . . total irony! Our desire for unfettered freedom is pistol-whipped by the militarization of the borders! And the protruding falsehood of freedom taints the entire globe. Somewhere out there is the dream of peace, but the citizens are armed just in case." The other man nods his head in agreement.

Next to them are two high school students. Textbooks and papers spread all over their table, coffee mugs leaving brown rings on their worksheets. Their backpacks slump at their feet, stuffed with heavy books, notebooks, vape stuff, their cell phones, and crinkled-up candy wrappers. They furiously punch away on their calculators, not talking or working together. Each is listening to different music through tiny earpieces.

A young couple sits, side by side, chatting and laughing, heads close together to avoid being overheard. They have a computer propped up between them with a travel website up. The woman taps notes into her Palm Pilot, while the man steers his finger around on the mouse pad. Both have their cell phones on the table beside them.

Outside, the woman who had been carrying the box is crossing the street. She heads toward the coffee shop, while framed by two little girls, one on each side of her, holding her hands. The door opens with its usual jingle, and they come in with a cold blast. All three are bundled up with thick woolen hats, scarves, and mittens. The woman's long brown hair streams out in waves from the bottom of her hat. As they grab a table to sit, they take off their hats and coats, and the little ones, who are twins, unveil their blonde, curly, still baby-fine hair, wildly full of static, disheveled, and undeniably adorable. Their round faces, brown eyes, and dimpled smiles brim with excitement at the thought of donuts and hot chocolate. The woman settles them, both about three years old, in their own chairs and pulls out coloring books and crayons from her backpack. She pulls a chair over and sits down after piling coats and gear on the next table.

"Now, let's see, Joy, I know you like frogs. Do you think there's a picture of a frog in here you would like to color?" She nods, sticking her lower lip out slightly. They open the book and begin flipping through the pages.

"Here, Mama. Stop. I want to color this one!" It's not a frog, but a fairy, surrounded by big flowers. Perfect.

"How about you, little Miss Hope? Let's look for one for you." They flip through her coloring book, this time more slowly, passing many pictures after pausing a few seconds to consider the details. They finally settle on one of a kitten, looking cross-eyed with a dragonfly on its nose. Both get intently into their coloring as the woman pulls out paperwork and sets it down in between the two coloring books.

"No, Mama. You can't put that here. We don't have enough room."

"It's okay. I'm just setting it here while I go up and order. Then I'll grab it and another table, so we have enough room, okay?"

"Okay. Can I have some hot chocolate?"

"You are too familiar with coffee shops, little miss!" She grins at her, attempting a quick smoothing of Joy's hair.

"Me, too, Mama!" They both swing their legs back and forth under the table. "And we want white donuts, too, Mam. We'll be good. You go; we'll wait here," Hope nods vigorously and smiles in total agreement.

The woman moves to the bar, where Barney, Richie, and Red are talking, though they've been watching the whole thing. She leans on the counter and waits for Red to come over.

"Hi. I'd like to order a soy mocha, medium, please. And can you make hot chocolate for the little ones? Like kids' size?"

"For here, then, right?"

"Right."

"You got it, soy mocha and two kids' hotties. Anything else?"

"How about a blueberry muffin. Yeah. That sounds good. And, two powdered sugar donuts."

"Surely." Red moves toward the pastry shelf and grabs the tongs to pick up a giant blueberry muffin and place it on a small plate. "Do you want plates for the donuts, too?"

"Yeah. Thanks. That'd be perfect."

"So, you're movin' in next door, huh? We've been watching the goings-on. What're ya doin' over there exactly?" He sets the plates down with the goodies. He reaches down for a knife and hands it to her.

"It's a yoga studio," she smiles hesitantly, glancing down the bar at the two old codgers who are barely trying not to stare. "I hope it'll be opening in about two weeks. I have to have my sign painted, but the painters are telling me it's too cold to paint outside. I won't be able to get the sign up until mid-spring."

"Kind of an unusual spot for a yoga studio, I'd say," Richie mutters. "Hope you can make a go of it."

"Don't know many people 'round here that do yoga," Barney adds.

"Well, how would you know, Barney? Your idea of exercise is driving to the coffee shop," Red says, handing the woman two kiddie drinks. "I think you have the one and only studio in the area that I know of, ma'am. That's gotta be a good thing."

"Well, I've been teaching yoga classes at lots of the big resorts around here. They're always crowded, and most of them are locals. I teach a couple different yoga classes at the community center in Pineville, and guess what? Every class gets bigger and bigger. I think people are starting to like it. You should try it. Come on over and join a class. I'm offering a senior class Monday, Wednesday, and Friday mornings at eleven, so if you know anyone who wants to feel great and beat the cold and winter blues—send 'em over okay?"

"What's yer name?" Red asks as she walks away to deliver the hot cups. She reminds the girls to be careful, the drinks are hot, and not to spill, then she comes back over to the counter, makes another trip with the donuts, and then comes back one more time for her mocha.

"Eleanor Marlow. And you?" Eleanor holds out her hand. Red reaches across the counter, and they shake.

"Red. Red Tatéweh. I'm the owner," Red says. He turns to pour the soy into her mug. "You like whip cream?"

"No thanks," Eleanor says. "We should form an alliance then, Mr. Tatéweh. I'm sure we'll be seeing a lot more of each other since we'll be neighbors. And I'm a coffee junkie."

"You can call me Red. But I have to tell ya, I'm not too informed about yoga, some new trendy exercise, huh?"

"Well, actually, it's hundreds of years old. Started in the Far East. But it's caught on in the U.S. for a while now," Eleanor says, keeping her pitch short. She takes the mug and takes a careful sip, glancing over at the girls to see them scribbling away.

"What're ya callin' yer place then?"

"Ah. *Currents*," Eleanor answers, trying to sound self-assured. She'd been wrestling with the name.

"Oh, like a water theme. Or river, I guess, since we're next to it, huh?" Red wonders. Hearing the door jingle, he looks over as another youngish woman walks in. She's wearing a black leather coat with a belted waist and coordinating boots and a black beret seemingly barely attached to her long, massively curly ash blonde hair. All three men can barely take their eyes off her.

"This is my friend Jessica, Red," Eleanor says, gesturing. "Jess, this is Red Tatéweh. He owns the place. And, as far as I can tell, makes a mighty fine espresso."

"Hey there, Red. I'll have a cappuccino for here," Jessica says, pulling out her wallet from her small handbag.

"I got it, Jess," Eleanor smiles, handing Red a twenty.

"Is this here your partner, then?" Red asks.

"Well, not exactly a business partner. Just one of my oldest and dearest friends. Visiting from New York. She's helping get the studio ready, watching the girls, stuff like that."

"Neat little girls. Sure are well-behaved, look at 'em, sitting over there so calm and focused," Red observes. They all glance over to see it's true.

"Yeah. Lucky. They are good girls," Eleanor acknowledges. Red gets busy with the cappuccino for Jessica.

"You got a husband then?" Richie asks.

"You aren't supposed to ask that, Rich! That's too personal!" Barney laughs, hiding discomfort. "You could at least introduce yourself first!"

"I'm Richard Redding." He holds up his mug as if to cheer. "Local old fart. Nosy busy body." He put his mug down, then continued, "I'll have to go home and fill in the wife, and she'll want to know all the details. Especially if you want me to get her to come and do your yoga."

"Well, Richard, nice to meet you. What's your wife's name then?"

"Mary. But she probably won't come. She doesn't need to exercise. She spends a lot of time taking care of the grandkids."

Eleanor takes out a couple cards and hands them each one. "Here's my business card, just in case. It has all the classes listed on the one side there, and the number to call if they want more info. You'd be surprised how many seniors, especially women, are realizing the benefits of yoga, guys. You should think about it yourselves. It would help your golf swing. Do either of you golf? I didn't catch your name," she says, looking at Barney.

"Barney Gaines. Wife's Betty. I'll make sure to give her your card. But no, we don't play golf. We're lucky if we get ourselves out in a fishing boat these days without capsizing and drowning." He laughs, and Richie laughs too.

"Well, keep an open mind, you two."

"What's with the foggy windows?" Richie asks. "We can't look in now."

"That's the point. I like the natural light, but I don't want everyone being self-conscious, knowing the whole world can watch them," Eleanor smiles.

"It's a beautiful studio, guys. You should come over and take a look," Jessica adds, taking her frothy mug from Red.

"Yeah. Maybe we'll do that sometime," Barney says. "Not today, though. I'll be shoving off pretty soon. It's already getting late."

"I'll be over for sure," Red says. "And you don't have to do it now, but I'd love to meet your daughters. I love kids. Never had any myself."

"Well, you better watch out, Red," Eleanor warns. "They lost their grandpa not too long ago, and they're looking for a new one."

"Oh, that's too bad. Was it your dad, then?"

"Yeah. He died about a year ago. They never knew their grandma. She died before they were born. Both heart attacks."

"Oh, man. Sorry to hear that," Red frowns slightly.

"Yeah," Eleanor nods, agreeing.

"Well, you come in anytime, bring those girls in, and set them right up here at the counter, and I'll be happy to keep them busy. I mean it."

"He has a way with kids, Eleanor. My grandkids love'm."

"Mine too. Watch out, though, don't get him started on all his stories," Barney smiles, looking at Red. "He can go on for hours."

"A storyteller. Hmmm," Eleanor smiles at him. "Well, I'll definitely be back, and I'll make introductions before we leave. No time like the present. Jessica and I are gonna go over business stuff, so don't mind us. Though I might be back up for a refill or two."

"No problem."

They pull up a table next to the girls' coloring. They admire several colored pictures before they settle down to discuss business. Richie leans over and talks lowly to Barney, "Well, she's got good looks going for her, that's for sure."

"I'd say. The both of um—lookers. Who knows? I hope it'll make it. It'd be nice to see a young gal like that be successful around here. I wonder if anyone told her she might do better in the new part 'a town."

"Seems like she could probably figure that out for herself if she wanted," Red comments, leaning his head down toward the two of them. "I think it might be good for downtown. Bring some people in, get 'em over here drinkin' coffee. I might have to get some more exotic teas. Things might be lookin' up, 'ey boys?"

"That's the way to look at it. . . . Well, old gents, I gotta hit the dirt. Told the wife I'd pick up some ice cream on the way home. Ben and Janet are comin' over tonight for cards. Betty's bakin' an apple pie. Gotta have the ice cream." Barney stands up off his stool slowly. "See you next week, ya old farts." He pats Richie gently on the back. He turns, and they both pat each other's shoulders briefly, the old man version of a bro hug. Barney heads for the door, stopping to turn and give a final salute as he opens the door. He pulls his fur-lined earflaps down over his ears as he goes out, and a sobering blast of cold air rushes in.

Bleak sunlight sneaks steadily across the room, infusing the air with warmth and deepening the aroma of coffee. Sluggish winter's late afternoon is like a magical sedative, lulling the whole world, it seems, into womblike serenity. Eleanor takes a huge breath and lets out a long sigh, business details finished, finally able to give in to the mellow mood.

"I was so freaked when I saw how much I had left to do. I was probably driving you crazy. Sorry. I know I've been un-calm because I've been biting my nails to shreds." She holds up her hands. Jessica grabs a hand to look.

"That has to stop! How long have you been saying you're gonna break that habit! All is well. Jessica is here. Jessica to the rescue!" She smiles and takes Eleanor's hand up to kiss it.

"When we get this all done, the whole thing: the schedule is smooth, the space is complete, the people are coming in droves, I'm no longer taking money out but finally putting money in. Then I can relax."

"You can relax *now!* You're doin' it, girl! This is your dream! I'm here for two weeks! I know I'm not your big man-stud who sweeps in to save the day, but I'll have to do until he arrives, right?" She wiggles her eyebrows at Eleanor.

"*No comment*," she smirks slightly. "I'm just saying, when—if—I finally get in the groove, we're going on vacation. You may have to take more time off work. We need a vacation."

"Well, work isn't exactly spectacular right now anyway. I've been thinking about quitting. I've been waiting to tell you this, and I guess now is a good time," she takes a deep breath and looks up at the ceiling briefly before she spills her guts. "I'm thinking about moving back." Jessica looks at her, blinking. There's a disbelieving pause.

"Really?" Eleanor smiles huge. "Really?" The girls look over at Eleanor, hearing her voice go up. They pause until coloring and giggling resumes. Eleanor says a silent prayer of gratitude that they are so compatible and easily occupied.

"I'm starting to hate it out there," she lowers her voice. "I'm sick of everyone I work with. I'm sick of Michael. We're going nowhere. And what about 9-11? Something's been lost forever. Do I really need to linger around more tragedy in my life? The whole city is a morgue. I feel like I'm living in a funeral. I'm sick of it, all of it. I feel myself starting to get ugly."

"Ugly?" Eleanor can't imagine.

"I don't know, bitter? Pissy. Not happy," Jessica waves her hand around. "And I can't breathe there. No one can. The whole place is toxic."

"Yuck. Really?"

"Oh, I come home at night and have a layer of soot on me. My skin is aging by the second. Everyone has a cough."

"Well, God knows you're not ugly. Everyone was staring at you when you walked in. You have big city glamour. But wait, what are you thinking exactly? Are you going to move back *here*, like Minnesota? The Twin Cities?"

"I don't know. I'm toying with it. I need my life to change. I've been doing the same thing, hanging out with the same people, for like fifteen years. I moved away when my parents died, and I never came back. I feel like I ran away. Now I feel like I have to face down some of those old feelings and get rid of them all for good. New York makes me anxious. I *need* to come back here; I miss the lake. This is where I grew up. I want to be here," Jessica shakes her head slightly and looks down. Pain passes across her face briefly. "I think I'm lonely?"

"Well. Let me just say. You can move in with me. You *know* I would love it. We can be two lonely old maids together. Let the whole town think we're lesbians. That should bring lots of business!" Eleanor giggles. "You can be my business manager. I can't pay much, but God, how much would I love someone else to do that part for me?"

"You know I don't need money," Jessica glances around to see who might be eavesdropping. "I want to become a teacher. I don't know. I'm not sure yet what I'll do. I feel like I want to come back. Give my life a jolt."

"The blast of arctic air when you stepped off the plane wasn't enough?"

"Hah. Yeah. No. It's not much colder here, really. I want space. I want the clean wind on my face. I want to go sailing. Remember your little boat? How much fun did we have on that thing? We didn't even know how to sail till you taught us."

"I don't have a sailboat anymore, Jess."

"Well, you wanna know who could go right into a sailboat store and buy one whenever she wants to?" Jessica raises her eyebrows. "If I come back, I'm buying one. And you're gonna go out on that lake and sail it with me."

"I haven't sailed since then," Eleanor almost whispers.

"Well, see? Then it's time," Jessica pauses. "You're doing this," she gestures across the street with her hand. "It's inspiring. We can't fuck around anymore. We have to get our lives the way we want them to be. What am I *doing* out there? I'm closing in on forty, and I feel empty. I'm pathetic."

"Stop. If you're empty, what am I?" Eleanor wonders. "You at least can form relationships with men. I haven't dated. For years."

"I can't believe that."

"Jess. I'm not kidding. I haven't been on a date since the girls came. I'm not interested. I'm like a nun or something. I haven't *seen* an attractive man in years."

"Well, I hope you have a good vibrator then." Jessica mumbles.

"Shut up! That's disgusting." They giggle anyway.

Jessica leans closer in, muttering. "I'm, like, in a mid-life crisis thing. I have to do something with all this money. It's just *sitting* there," she uncurls her hand, opening her palm. She adds quickly, "and I've been having weird dreams."

Eleanor shakes her head, closes her eyes, and lifts her face toward the ceiling. She can't talk. There's too much on the table.

"Mommy? When are we gonna go? I'm getting bored," Hope has shut her coloring book and is sitting with her hands on her lap. Eleanor looks at Jessica, silently telling her to *hold that thought*.

"Real soon, Hope. Do you want to go to the counter and get a sandwich?" Eleanor points at Red, "I bet that man can make a really good one."

"Will you come up there with me?"

"Me, too, Mama. I want one, too."

"Come on, let's go up there. There're two stools. One for both of you." They get up to the counter, and Eleanor helps them get up on the stools, and they lean over the counter like they're at home.

"Red? You make sandwiches here, don't you?" Eleanor leans over to get his attention. He's down below the counter digging for something. But he stands up momentarily and comes over to where they are.

"You betcha. I got the best homemade raspberry jelly in the world. Now, who are these two lovely young ladies?"

Eleanor gestures with her hands, "This is Joy. This is Hope. They're twins. Girls, this is Red."

"Like the color?"

"Yep. Exactly. Like the color."

"Is that your nickname?"

"Nope—my real name. Well, it's Redmund, actually. But no one calls me that."

"You have real long hair," Joy notes. "How come you don't cut it?"

"I like it this way," he feels his hair, "and I don't like haircuts."

"Me either. But I don't cry. Joy cries when she gets her hair cut."

"I do not!"

"That's okay. What's wrong with cryin'?" Red has gotten the bread out, and he's making the sandwiches on the counter right in front of them. He's got chips and apple juice as well. Warmth for this old man she hardly knows comes over her. He exudes strength and comfort. How lucky he's right across the street. And he's stocked with PB and J, a standard in her house. She could cry at how easily he welcomes them. Like he's been waiting for them all along.

She gestures to Jessica to come up, and they both lean over the counter on either side of the girls, biting bits of the sandwich. They are surprisingly good and small-town cheap, and he just keeps making them. Eleanor feels a rare excitement, something unfelt for years. She glances at Jessica, and they trade smiles born in the moment.

CHAPTER 10

Love, Love

Margaret and I had a stroke of good luck when Jan, who makes the schedule, graced us with a day off before the Fourth of July weekend hit. She was probably trying to get us not to hate her for scheduling us three days in a row, including the actual Fourth. Three brutal days of getting our asses kicked by the hugest crowds of the summer, and I was somewhat bitter. I, my spoiled little self, had never worked on the summer holiday before, and I knew I would be missing lots of family fun as everybody was up for the long weekend, and many events were planned. Margaret told me to get over it, as she had worked lots of holiday weekends in her life, and she didn't much care about family hullabaloo. So, I adapted, and it ended up being okay because we worked the day shifts, and we didn't have to serve the late-night drunks who forgot to tip. We ended up making huge cash. I met Neal's sister that weekend, and I got to go to a bonfire with him that night. The fireworks were particularly fantastic that night.

We planned our day off on the lake. If it was windy, we would sail; if it was calm, we'd take the little nine-horse out for a day of reading and sun-tanning. What ended up happening was neither, and it started with a knock at the back cabin door early in the morning. I thought it was my mom coming to check on us, though she wouldn't usually knock; she just entered unannounced. I went to the door in my tank top and underwear, thinking my mom had reformed and finally considered my privacy for a change. I was shocked to see Blake Crandahl standing there in his tennis whites. I hid behind the old wooden door and peeked my head out.

"Hi, Blake. We're still sleeping."

"Well, get up. I want you guys to come play tennis. My whole family's gone. I got the place to myself. A friend of mine's here from college, and we want to play some doubles. He's adorable, Ellie, and completely single."

"Yeah," I shut my eyes tight with a slight headache. "I'll talk to Margaret. Give me a minute."

"I'll wait."

You do that, I thought to myself, shutting the door in his face. He leaned against the railing and ran his fingers through his great hair, looking toward his house. I crept up to Margaret's bed and lifted up the covers, shoving her with my knee.

"Margaret, move over." I crawled in, and she began to stir.

"What time is it?"

"No idea. Blake is standing outside the door."

"What?" She sat up. She looked over at me and smiled, "Nice hair. You went to the door like that?" She laughed.

"Oh, you're funny," I try to smooth down the frizz. "He wants us to come over and play tennis."

"Oh! Awesome. Let's go." She begins moving the blankets. I continue not moving.

"No. Really?" I sighed. "I thought we'd hang out *without* Blake Crandahl today. He's always around, Margaret. For God's sake."

"He's so cute, Ellie. I was just telling him how bummed I am; he hardly knows you—you being my best friend and all. He said he'd like to get to know you better because it matters to me."

"I was wondering why he wanted *me* tagging along. I did find that part a little strange," I grumbled, taking note of my headache again.

"Come on. I want you to get to know him better too. This is perfect. We'll play tennis. It's early. We can still go out on the lake. Come on, please?" She stuck her face down close to mine and made a goofy look. "It'll be fun. I promise."

"Margaret . . ." I really wanted to kill him, not get to know him now.

"Please? You'll love him once you get the chance. He's so adorable and sweet."

"You're in a permanent state of insanity, Margaret," I moaned, not at all up for a game of tennis. Margaret scurried over me to the door. I heard her sickeningly sweet voice, followed by a silence that probably meant kissing. Then I heard his footsteps departing.

"I told him we'd be over in fifteen minutes," Margaret announced as she came back. "His friend, Tony, is an average tennis player, so we may kick their asses."

"Fifteen minutes?" I groaned and covered my head with the blankets.

"I know. I owe you, *please?* I need you, or it'll be weird. Me, him, and his friend."

"Fine, but we're outa there in ninety minutes, Margaret, or I'm kicking your ass."

"Ninety minutes. Okay." She walked into the dining room and grabbed her watch off the table. "It's nine o'clock. I promise we'll be back here getting ready for the beach by eleven."

"That would be two hours. I said ninety minutes."

"Fine. Ninety." She walked where I was still sitting on her bed. "Here, you can wear my new tennis skirt."

"You're wacko. I'm not wearing a *tennis skirt*. Besides, Blake bought that for you. I'm not a moron who wears something he bought for you."

"You're gonna have fun. What if his friend's adorable, and he digs you?"

"Well, there's this guy, Neal? I'm not sure if you met him before? I think you have, but maybe you were drunk and don't remember?" I looked at her like she was disturbed.

"I know. I'm just *saying* it could be fun. Just to flirt. I know you're completely intoxicated by Neal. And I love him, too. God, don't get me wrong," she was practically dancing around the room, brushing her hair. I started getting dressed. "Where is Neal, by the way? I was wondering why he isn't part of the agenda today."

"He's going to the Cities to pick up his sister. She's staying a week. I don't know how much I'll see him while she's here."

"We'll get to meet her, right? We should do something. Let's make a plan."

"He said he'd stop over later. He doesn't know what time they'll be getting here, though. He has to work the first tour tomorrow, and we're on first shift, so he may not come if it's too late."

"Well, maybe she'll come to the View."

"I'm sure she will. She'll probably go on a tour." I was finishing putting on my tennis shoes but slowing down purposely to delay the inevitable.

The transition from our lawn to theirs amused me. Their grass stood firm, thick, and even, while ours exhibited dried patches, exposed tree roots, and bumps. As we approached the side door, Blake came out through the terrace entrance. He held two frosty glasses, ice tinkling as he walked toward us. He handed one to me and one to Margaret, gently putting his arm around her as she took the drink.

"Greyhounds," he smiled. "Come in and relax a minute before we hit the court."

"Sure, get us drunk so you think you can beat us," Margaret teased. She had played a lot of tennis by this point in the summer, and her game had improved amazingly. She was hard to beat, and she knew it. Blake could not stop looking at her. He was almost dazzled to stupidity by her.

Sitting on one of the wicker chairs was Tony, his college friend. Striking indeed, in a very preppy, clean-cut, tall-dark-and-handsome kind of way. We cheered our greyhounds, which were quite tasty. Blake went to the stereo and slightly turned up the volume as a live version of "Peace Frog" by The Doors was starting. It was one of my favorite songs of the time. I wondered if he liked The Doors too or if he knew I did.

"Margaret, I had to get you this," Blake grinned. He went over to the bar where he had a white box tied up in a plaid bow. I suppressed the urge to make puking noises. Inside was a cool, incredibly soft, tie-dyed scarf, probably from a pro shop.

"I thought you might want it for the boat later. I want to take you guys to lunch by boat. We should check out that new place, the Lighthouse. You been there yet, Ellie?"

"Nope. Never been there."

"Well, lunch is on me if you guys are up for it."

"Sounds like fun," Margaret gushed nauseatingly, wrapping the scarf perfectly around her hair without a mirror, looking even more like a movie star.

"We'll see," I frowned at Margaret as she ignored me.

Blake and Tony hit the bar to refill. Blake explained, "We're celebrating. Tony got into the U of M Law School. He starts this fall."

"Nice!" I held up my glass to cheer. "Where'd you go to undergrad?"

"Carleton, same as Blake. That's where we met."

"Since I'll be at the U of M Business School, we're gonna room together this fall."

"Really?" Margaret smiled hugely. "Congratulations! Wow."

Blake smiled. "You have to come down weekends and keep me company."

"I will. We will, right, Ellie?"

"Where do you guys go to school?" Tony asked.

"UMD, Bulldogs. Senior year, and man, I'm not looking forward to another January in the arctic."

"Coming from farm country, I like Duluth, with all its hills and pine trees—way more interesting," Margaret said.

"Where're you from, Margaret?" Tony asked.

"A little town called Sleepy Hollow, like the famous story, but not the same place. That Sleepy Hollow is out east somewhere."

"Hah, Sleepy Hollow. I'm from Blue Earth."

"Really? Did you grow up on a farm?"

"No, actually, my dad owns a bank in town. You know the Southwest Banks? I think there's one in Sleepy Hollow."

"Yes. There is. Across the street from my old grade school."

"Alright. Enough small talk. Let's get down to business. How should we play, girls? Tony and Ellie against Margaret and me?" Blake said.

"I say girls against boys." Margaret squinted at Blake. "What do you think, Ellie? Think we can take 'em?" I tried not to scowl at her, smiling weakly instead.

"Well, I'm warning you. Tony and I played tennis in high school," Blake said. He played tennis in college too, but I didn't care if we got our butts kicked. No matter what, I did not want to be Blake's partner, and my care to win decreased with each loud sip of my greyhound.

Margaret and I would play Blake and Tony. Blake wanted to play three sets, but I told him he was insane. I didn't intend to spend the day sweating on asphalt. It was a memorable game, but what I remember didn't have much to do with tennis. Blake and Tony were great partners, and their antics were as good as their backhands. Blake could smash a wicked serve with his eyes closed, and we both scrambled to return it. Though we got beat, if either one of them had really tried, they could have humiliated us. Luckily, they decided it would be more fun to have fun, and I spent much of my time doubled over laughing or with my jaw gaping at their athleticism.

The best of Blake came out on the court that day, and I finally saw and had to acknowledge what Margaret fell for. It was his charm. It's a cliché, I know, but there's no other way to put it. He flew through the air to return a volley like a dolphin out of water, yet he was silly. He would fool you with his seriousness one moment, and the next, he was doing a flip in mid-air after running across the court for a seemingly impossible shot that he answered with his perfect forearm. He would exaggerate a reach for a shot, then pretend to be falling and do a somersault, all without getting hurt or ever landing on the ground with a clumsy thud. All along, adoringly gazing at Margaret, making sure she was watching. Making sure she was aware it was all for her.

His eagerness to make her laugh pried opened my heart. The arrogance I thought he had morphed right before my eye
into a boyish hesitancy,
a vulnerability and humbleness to what he knew was Margaret's strength, her authenticity. She did not project a persona. She had no idea how to. Her self-concept was too intact. Blake had been so adept for so many years at projecting his cool party guy image, but when he was around her, he seemed to revert to the little boy he was before he lost track of himself. She was so real, she could accept nothing less from him, and he had to unmask a part of himself that rarely got exposed. The freedom of it unleashed his sense of humor. Of course, greyhounds combined with the hot mid-morning sun had an effect too. But his real boy self was definitely cute.

Despite their attempts to lighten the game, I was proud of how Margaret and I played. Margaret had the elegant long strokes and the poise of a ballerina. Her long legs and hair moved in sync, and her beauty distracted even me. I had to use speed, and, coupled with my alcohol-induced loss of inhibition, I made some wild, seemingly impossible shots to stay in the game. I played probably the best game of tennis I would ever play in my life, and I remember Blake seemed to appreciate me for it.

Back at the house, Blake headed for the bar again, and Tony followed, carrying our glasses in from the court, which they quickly refilled. Margaret took the three or four steps up from the sunken living room and headed for the kitchen. I followed her because I didn't want to stand there looking stupid.

"Margaret, we're not going out to eat with them, are we?"

"Come on, Ellie. It'll be fun. Isn't Tony adorable?" She turned on the small side tap over the sink and began filling a large glass for me and then one for her with distilled water. "Too bad you have two gorgeous guys to choose from."

"Please. I wouldn't go that far. Tony is gorgeous, but he's hardly interested. And I have to say it's mutual."

"Oh, he might like you if you liked him back. But forget it. Of course. Neal is beyond gorgeous," She began drinking her water.

"I guess we can go to lunch," I stopped to guzzle. "I doubt Neal will get here 'til late anyway. Why waste a good buzz, right?"

"There's the Ellie I love!" She gave me a mini-hug.

"He's adorable. There. I admit it. And now I have to accept that he's brilliant too, if he's going to graduate school."

She sighed, shaking her head, then finished her water. "Come on. Let's go be adorable too, and get a free lunch."

"Now you're talkin'!" I finished my water and put the glass in the sink next to hers. I wondered where the maid was. We went back to the porch. Tony was sitting at the bar, and Blake was standing behind it. Fresh cocktails waited.

Blake looked at Margaret. "Are we doing lunch?"

"We're in. Thank you for your generosity," Margaret stepped up and leaned over the bar as he leaned in for a kiss.

"Least I can do after kicking your cute ass," Blake smiled at her through half-closed eyes. I wondered if he was also purring.

"Blake, where's your family?" I had to ask.

"Wedding. They're gone till late tonight. I got out of it because of dear Tony here. Thank God. I hate weddings. Especially this particular cousin, she's a total bitch."

"Let's go, what d'ya say? I'm starving!" Tony passed his half-drunk glass across the bar for a top-up. Blake filled everybody's glasses to the rim, giving Margaret and me mostly ice, informing us that he knew we were lightweights.

We teetered into Blake's clean, shiny speedboat. He had a portable staircase for us to step down into the boat at the dock. The seats were comfy, the ride was slick, and the lake was flat and windless, as I recall. The water reflected a cloudless sky so deep blue it pulsed, and the sunlight fell all over us. As I gazed over the water, I thought of Neal and wished he were there. But I had to focus on the fun of getting lunch at a new lakeside restaurant. Luxuriate in being served rather than having to serve for a change.

Except for Blake's adoration of and doting over Margaret, which caused me, and probably Tony too, unnecessary nausea, lunch was uneventful. We had a few more drinks to snuff out the annoyance of being forced into a pseudo-couple situation, and I was quite tipsy by the end of lunch. Margaret and I hit the bathroom before getting back on the boat. I actually splashed water over my face. I did not want to be so drunk so early. I was worried about being wasted in front of my family and, worse, having to meet Neal's sister. I didn't want to walk off Blake's dock to find Neal and his sister standing there, with my family behind them, looking at me inquisitively and embarrassed. I envisioned myself tipsily stepping off the dock and plunging into the shallow water, hitting the hard sand on my back and looking extremely uncoordinated. That would not have been good. Luckily, Margaret asked Blake to take the scenic route back. He readily complied, though he said his boat "doesn't like to go slow."

When we got back, it was exactly as I envisioned. Neal and his sister Jessica were on our dock with my sister Julie. I was careful not to fall off Blake's dock as I made my way over. I struggled to keep my level of intoxication masked. Neal's sister was as breathtakingly gorgeous as he was, only her hair was darker, and her face was slightly more child-like, rounder, and with bigger eyes. She was a bit shorter but had the same blue-green eyes, intense and sparkly. I didn't have to think about whether I liked her or not. Like Neal, it seemed she had been part of the gang all along.

Blake offered to take everybody skiing. Definitely a first and only in Marlow–Crandahl history. I enjoyed watching everybody ski, especially Neal because he had such physical strength with his tan, perfect body. I played the spotter because I worried I'd hurt myself if I tried to drunk ski. I told everyone my lower back hurt from all the tennis earlier. It was a golden afternoon. A gift of a day when everyone soaks up the good weather and only good things happen. A day for the memory books.

We all went our separate ways for dinner, and at the table eating with the family, the subject of Blake Crandahl came up.

"How did you end up hanging out with *Blake Crandahl*, of all people?" My brother asked as he passed the butter so I could drizzle it over my corncob.

"Don't ask me." I nodded my head toward Margaret, "Margaret here is head over heels for the guy."

"Hey! Wait a minute. You can't possibly not like Blake anymore. He's not so bad, is he?" She looked intently at me. This was a moment of truth for her. She didn't want him to be the rich asshole next door anymore. If I admitted that much in front of my family, she had made real progress in the Blake campaign.

"Well, he paid for lunch. He took everyone skiing. I guess he's not such a bad guy. Margaret brings out the best in him."

"Really? Hmmm," my brother frowned, trying to imagine it, then took a huge bite of his corn.

"Well, I'm not totally convinced," I conceded.

"*What?*" Margaret said. "Ellie! What else can the guy do to win you over?"

"Well, that's just it, Margaret. Why does he have to try so hard?"

"Why do you need to judge him?" She almost pleaded.

"Alright, ladies," my dad picked up the vibe. "Let's enjoy the meal, and . . . Mom made homemade ice cream."

"Mom, thank you!" My brother gleamed. "I'll get a bonfire going; what do you guys think?"

I glanced at Margaret. She looked wounded. I was afraid he would hurt her, but here it was me. I would apologize later. First, I had to figure out why I clung stubbornly to my judgments. I could not give up my animosity even as it began to feel unfair. I appreciated his devotion to Margaret and his generosity that day, yet his motives still seemed cloudy to me.

CHAPTER 11

Vaporizing

Flames seared, and wood snapped as kids huddled around the campfire. A summer breeze romanced the shushing waves along the shoreline as lake and moonlight danced. Nature harmonized in what seemed a once-in-a-lifetime perfection, yet this was a common Quartz Lake evening. No wonder people have been drawn to this place since the dawn of human time. Time is timeless on nights like these.

The stars have witnessed people around campfires along shorelines,
all around the world, like this, telling stories,
since language began. And people have
witnessed the stars, too,
blazing across the night sky, millennia after millennia.
Only
the details
change.
Kin gather for this kind of leisure whenever they
can. It tucks neatly into the folds of memory,
saved for future days
when age and grief leave a person
beaten and grasping at just such recollections
for a little comfort.
And, oh, how the memories do
change and grow,
expand and contract
as we age. Sometimes they're cyclical like seasons; sometimes, they're anchored in a time, place, or person.

Sometimes our minds distill our memories into wordless sensations of comfort with even the most obscure visual trigger. A butterfly. A champagne cork. A penny from heaven. Or a smell, like hot coffee, or cattails, or burning. The unique smell of a particular body of water, person, or place. Or a sound, like a loon's call echoing over a lake, or someone's laugh. A song and a particular way someone sings it. A whistled tune.

Is it from over-remembering or being deeply affected by our memories that they become tied to symbols and triggers?

What happens when we rarely think of a memory? Is this when it becomes splintery? When all we can really recall of the memory is the sensation or a few vivid details?

What makes a memory's value in our brains? Why do we spend so much of our living time in our memory time?

Sometimes memories cause pangs in the heart that feel like real stab wounds. Sometimes memories flood us with and inform us of our destiny and place in the world. Sometimes memories are too painful to talk about. Does that mean we shouldn't? Maybe memories teach us to be better. Some say memory imprints in our tissues, our DNA.

Memories help bring history into community and help establish and maintain community. Memories unite and distinguish us. Memories help create love, and sometimes they hold us in place when love is lost. Sometimes memories help create such a deep love that the love holds out, even if the memories do not.

Is your mind remembering,

thinking about all this?

What takes you back?

and where do you go?

Here is a memory,

torn and worn,

weaved with a story, timeless and true . . .

fade-in to a big multi-family dinner where each family has contributed: grilled meat, corn on the cob, baked beans, enormous bowls of various salads, coolers of soda pop, and homemade pie and ice cream.

Could this be your family or a family you know?

Envision a picnic table, or three, filled with food, and people of all ages and sizes milling around with plates, grazing. From hours of swimming and sunlight, appetites growled to the brink of insatiable, and enormous amounts of food and drink disappeared in a blink. After the meal, grown-ups claimed the porch for conversation and shooed the kids out. They'd play horseshoes in the sand, throw rocks in the lake, or lie on the dock, digesting. Dusky shadows arose and crept out from under the pine trees, signaling the moon's imminent arrival

when the whole scene went quasi-psychedelic.

The big kids called the game of the night: kick the can, ghosts in the graveyard, trench, capture the flag, sardines, one never knew. Then running, hiding, screaming, giggling, whispering, shouting, and sneaking around ensued. Shadows would loom out at you, and the boogie man was real, in just a harmless kid way, when we played those games. We were baby-stepping the periphery of fear, which most kids associate with thrill, up to a point. Soon, would come several warnings that went something like this: "You kids are too loud, you sound like a bunch of banshees! Now, knock it off, or you're coming in!" Which never happened because the adults were enjoying themselves too much. Eventually, and inevitably it seems, someone got hurt, and the raucous games halted. Or someone broke down crying from too much physical excitement. Then it was campfire time.

Already, someone had been down to the fire pit on the wide, sandy shore to pile up logs and set the kindling. When the kids took their seats, the fire starter baited the dry pyre with a seed-sized flame so all the kids could watch the thing grow into blazes. Stumpy logs for sitting rimmed the fire and often there were marshmallows, but sometimes it would be too late, and the group went right to storytelling.

"You know the story of Raven's Point, right?" came the voice of whoever felt inspired. Murmurs and giggles, someone pushed someone off a log, and more laughter. Everyone knew the story, but no one protested because each storyteller had a different way of telling it.

"This is a story your dad's friend (Remember that guy with the really long hair?) used to tell us when we were little, right?" Gazing around the circle, eyes were sparkling with the reflecting firelight, and faces were lively. The speaker begins . . .

. . . A long time ago, when the Dakota lived here, their village was right over there, along that sandy strip where it thins out. You can practically throw a rock from the Quartz right into Lake Erma; it's so narrow. Remember when we used to stay at Sandy Shores? It used to be a Dakota settlement, over a hundred teepees. Way before resorts. Great Grandpa Aloysius remembered seeing a dozen teepees or so when he was young. But probably the Ojibwe were living there by the time he came around.

In that Dakota tribe lived a very beautiful girl. She was the twinkle in her father's eye, and he was the chief. 'Wind Soaring Eagle' was his name. She was called Raven Girl because they were her favorite birds. She had the most radiant deep, dark eyes and the longest, flowing, black hair. She was the pride of the tribe, and all of them, young and old, adored her.

"But the most amazing thing about her was her ability to talk with birds, or so it seemed. The story goes that on the day she was born, a flock of ravens ringed the teepee, standing at attention. As she grew, it wasn't long, of course, before she had a pet raven. That raven followed her wherever she went. And he wasn't the only one. She could stand at the shore, and a flock of birds would swoop down from the airy heights and surround her, stand on her head, and perch on her outstretched arms. She was a bird whisperer. They would brush themselves along her cheeks like a cat would, and coo and chirp, or caw, and she would sing melodies in return as if they were in conversation. She would dance and sway her arms, and the birds would flutter and glide in sync around her. She could tell her father where the elk herds were, where the tribes could find beaver, and where the thickest beds of wild rice could be harvested. This worked well for the tribe. There seemed to be an understanding that the tribe did not harm or kill any birds.

"Well, one day, Raven Girl was out on the point. It was a little ways from the village, as you know, probably a mile or so. She was picking raspberries and blackberries. In those days, the point was full of berry shrubs, not sand like it is now. She–"

"How'd it get so barren?"

"I dunno. You guys tired of this story? Should I stop?"

A string of "No, no, no's" and a few "shut ups" flew around in reply, and everyone settled in a little more, as one person dropped more logs into the fire and another

          stirred, poked, and stoked with a long, burnt-tipped branch. Bits of glowing orange cinder

          floated up with the smoke and

          disappeared into the black star-speckled sky.

The fire snapped and hissed.

". . . Well, as I said, she was berry-picking, and she carried a basket on her head. Her parents had no fear of letting her go alone, and she often went to the point by herself."

"How old was she?"

"How old? Oh, I'd say she was about thirteen or fourteen. They probably believed bird spirits protected her. That was before they had much contact with the voyagers, the loggers, and the trappers coming down from Canada and coming up from the booming Twin Cities. Wars were on the way, as you all know. But that's another story.

"So, there she was pinching handfuls of berries, her pet raven floating around overhead.

"Well, it just so happened, a pair of logger scouts were coming up the river, scrutinizing land for thick tracks of white pine for the lumber industry. They came upon the point, not only captivated by endless wood, which they calculated into dollar signs, but also by the beautiful Native girl frolicking along the shore. They observed she was alone and plotted her capture. It wasn't long before they landed their canoe and chased her down, pulling her by the long hair into their canoe, tying her arms and legs, and binding her mouth to silence. The raven repeatedly dive-bombed them and pecked at their heads, shoulders, and arms until they struck it down with a large rock. The last sight Raven Girl had, as the canoe pulled away, and the mask was tied around her eyes, was her beloved raven, lifeless, tipping back and forth in the waves lapping the shore."

Some littler cousins were worried, but older cousins whispered words of encouragement to keep on listening; it would get better.

"As the canoe crossed the bay, heading north, Raven Girl could feel her village receding. The scouts had no idea what they were getting themselves into. When Raven Girl realized she might never see her family again, she cried. Up until that point, she had been angry and defensive and didn't want to appear weak in front of these strange, powerful men with sharp, heavy tools."

"What about her bird? Wasn't she sad about him?"

"Oh, of course, but actually, she probably couldn't even think about her favorite bird, sacrificing his life to try and save her.

"Well, like I said, it was all too much, and she started crying. Tears streamed down her face, but she couldn't wipe them away, so they dropped off her chin and blew into the lake. Pretty soon, the lake began to change. A storm brewed quickly and darkened the sky. The men had to beach their canoe—across and not too much further north from Raven Girl's village. While they prepared their tents and campfire, the lake really began its magic. Now, all of you, go back to the dying bird, rocking in the waves."

A brief pause fell over the group while the storyteller took a sip of a drink, rattled the ice, and sent one of the kids into the house for a refill. The storyteller resumed. "Okay, as I said, back to the pet raven, left for dead. As the waves gently rocked the bird, you'd think they'd've slowly drawn it into the water to sink down into the depths and be lost forever, but!

Not so!

"Instead, the bird's eyes fluttered! He found he could move his wings, even though they were wet, bruised, and limp. And he rustled himself up onto his talons. He looked around and searched with his beady, bullet eyes for his beloved friend. And he realized what had happened. He teetered and tottered along the shore,

willing himself to fly.

Before long, he launched, weakly soaring up and up, along the treetops. He flew unsteady, and to make things worse, the storm had come up, and the wind was raging. Waves on the lake roiled and crashed, gigantic and menacing. Still, somehow, through it all, the raven flew up the shore, scanning the darkened trees for his girl.

"It was so dark. The bird flew until he could fly no longer, and he collapsed, distraught that he ever lost sight of her. The next day, the logger scouts broke camp early and got right back in the canoe with their captive, heading still further north. They tried to talk to her, but mostly they just made fun of her and poked at her, trying to get her to eat and accept her fate. They were hoping to use her as a guide, a hands-on naturalist who they figured knew the lake. And at this point, they were coming into the narrows where the channels are, and you know there are long, windy channels all over the place, some lead to dead-ends. There are lots of little lakes to get lost in. Raven

Girl refused to utter a sound, and, of course, they kept her bound up so she wouldn't try to escape.

"The raven, too, woke with the breaking dawn. He did not give up his search, and under the clear blazing sun, he spotted the girl plunked down in the middle of the canoe with a captor on either end. He avoided flying too close because he didn't need to raise suspicion. He was a smart bird; they say ravens are one of the smartest birds of all, and they're as old as time.

"So, he trailed them through the day's journey until they settled for another night. When they pitched their tents and sat around the campfire, they tied Raven Girl to a tree. They proceeded to drink whiskey, laughing and poking at the fire, and her until they stumbled into their tents. Raven Girl, tied and defenseless in the wide-open night, had to fend for herself. As she pondered her plight, crying quietly, staring at the dying fire, she began to shiver." The storyteller paused for effect. Only the fire talked for a moment.

"And you know what happened next?" The audience stared, waiting.

"A giant turd fell out of the sky!" Someone had to say.

"Yeah. Haha. Very funny. No.

"All of a sudden, she was shocked to see her favorite bird, dropping out of the black sky, to land softly at her feet. He wanted to gnaw at the rope where her hands were bound behind her back, but Raven Girl had a different idea. 'Go to my people, my beloved friend, tell them where I am. Lead my father to me. Tell him he must not come alone, but he should come prepared to fight these men who possess weapons I have not seen before.' Raven did not want to leave, but as Raven Girl sat in the cold sand, she leaned her head down and brushed her cheek along his back and the top of his head. When she did this, Raven, who had been flying despite his near-death experience and bruised wings, and crushed feet, was suddenly healed, as if he had never been smashed into the ground by a rock.

"This pumped him up, and he fluttered his wings above her head for a moment. She felt a warm burst of air hit her face and spread down her whole body before he flew away into the night. Somehow, she stayed warm and safe in the cold darkness.

"Now, Raven flew with great gusto back to the village. He didn't wait until morning to awaken the tribe. He fluttered around and around the teepees to get everyone's attention. Then he just dive-bombed into the side of the chief's dwelling, breaking a hole with his sharp beak. He landed right on the belly of the big man, and he began cawing excitedly."

"What was he was saying?" someone blurted out.

"Oh, something like, 'Come! Come! No time to lose! You must go quickly to save your daughter, who moves into the distance while you sleep.' And it didn't take more than a moment before Wind Soaring Eagle clued in, his grief punctured by this information. He roused the whole camp and created a search party by dawn."

Suddenly, a parent called from the porch that so-and-so had to come now; it was time to go home; it was getting late. The storyteller yelled back that the story was almost over and could we just have another ten minutes? And when there was no reply, it was taken as affirmative, so the story went on.

"Well, you can imagine, they got in their canoes and paddled hard through the waves to catch up to the men who stole their most beloved maiden. They followed Raven, who kept to their pace. They approached at nightfall when the scouts were occupied with fire starting and food preparation. Of course, their strategy was carefully planned and carried out. They beached their canoe down the shore and snuck through the deep woods in their silent, calculated way. It wasn't hard to subdue the two thieves. They were completely unaware."

"You'd think those men would have thought about it, kidnapping someone and not even being sneaky or anything," someone noted.

"Yes, well, they were about as experienced with Natives as the Natives were with them, I guess."

"So, did the tribe kill them?"

"Oh . . . No . . . Believe it or not. They had a more creative solution to the problem of what to do with them."

Everyone subconsciously leaned forward. Sometimes they did kill the bad guys. Endings varied.

"Well, while the scuffle ensued, Raven Girl was able to free herself from the tree, and she rushed to her father. She hadn't eaten for three days, and she was weak but full of excitement. Then she held her arms up to the sky and looked for the beloved bird who saved her life. Before long, he floated down and perched upon her shoulder, rubbing against her ear with his shoulder-like wing.

"The chief bound the kidnappers just as they had bound his daughter, and they loaded them into the canoes to head home. Can you imagine what the bad dudes were thinking at this point? Were they going to be scalped? Burnt alive? Not even! The rescue party found a perfect place to stop for a rest, but it really wasn't a rest. It was Rock Island. You guys know where Rock Island used to be?

"A great nesting ground for creatures of all sorts. In particular, huge snapping turtles used to nest there. How'd you like to come face to face with a giant snapping turtle?" Lots of appropriate groans and jaw-snapping imitations, and attack noises followed.

"Well, that's exactly where they left 'em. And one more thing: they brought all of the kidnappers' stuff, but they didn't unpack it before shoving off. No one knows if they kept the stuff or dropped it in the middle of the lake. They left the two men, hands still bound, so they couldn't swim after their canoes and try to sink 'em. The pair sat desperate on the slippery rocks, pleading and wailing for mercy.

The tribesmen did not look back."

"What's mercy?"

"You know, asking to be forgiven or pardoned for what they had done and not to be left there to die."

"Were they left to die?"

"No one knows for sure. The story I heard is that the Natives could see swarms of ravens circling Rock Island for a few days after that, but who knows for sure."

"The lake knows!"

"I think they got eaten by the giant snappers."

"I think they tried to swim for shore and drowned."

"Yeah, and then the big muskies ate 'em!"

"Well, I doubt they survived. How they died probably wasn't very pleasant."

"Maybe they swam to shore and tried to attack the village? But they got shot by poison arrows."

"Could be. Raven Girl's village did face an attack some years later. More tribes pushed into their territory from the East because settlers robbed them of their homelands. Thousands of tribes were forced to migrate westward. Fighting happened with those Indians who came from the East; they were either Ojibwa or Iroquois, probably both. Raven Girl was Dakota. That little strip of land there was ideal, and everyone wanted it. It's got access to two lakes, and it's nice and flat and sandy."

"Now it's a highway."

"What happened to the bird?" The campfire began to break up, and some began to drift away from the subdued fire. A few of the still curious remained.

"Well, that's how the point came to be called Raven's Point. When Raven died, he went back there to rest in peace, where he once got smashed by the giant rock and didn't die. Raven Girl turned into Raven Woman. She always returned there to visit his spirit and for berries. She wasn't afraid of getting captured again, even though, as she grew up, she saw many of her people killed in the territory wars."

Now more listeners fell away. No one wants the really bad news.

Her tribe was mostly slaughtered even though they were gallant warriors, but she and her young family—because she had grown up, gotten married, and had kids by the time the Ojibwa came—survived. Along with a couple of other families, they were pushed to relocate, first to the west side of the lake. They lived somewhere just across the inlet from Raven's Point. Then further west after that.

"Maybe she and her family had special protection from the ravens, and that's why they survived," someone theorized.

"Who knows what finally happened to Raven Woman and her children."

"Maybe some of her ancestors still live nearby."

"Tell us about the big wars. Tell us about Battle Cove."

"Oh, we'll save that for another night. Some a' you look pretty sleepy."

The few lingering listeners kicked sand on the fire to extinguish it, but the memory of the story,

the memory of Raven Woman,

the memory of the fire, the memory of my dear ones' faces, of the emotions, the circle, the food, the stars, the shushing chorus of waves, indelibly fortifies the rememberer. The witness. The one who is present.

Nature weaves every memory through the body into the soul, strung by wind and water, held by neutrinos,

bequeathing an infinite, universal, invisible periplus with which we are all meant to sail,

the *galaxseas* of our here and now

Memory holds the then, and the them,

the me and the you,

in our place,

precisely fixed among the stars.

We are here! We are there!

We were fated to be, to live and to die,

to make memories and to remember.

We are of something greater than our tiny, fleshy selves,

interconnected, immortal

here today

gone tomorrow

never again

but for forever.

CHAPTER 12

Wind of Time

Sitting at the table one early morning, gazing out at the lake, with a full spread of pancakes before us, my family and I were startled by the telephone ringing. It so rarely rang that when it did, a surge of adrenaline hit us with the sudden authority of it. I got up to answer and discovered my cousin, Chris, on the line. He was desperate. Could I possibly crew for him today in the Regatta, and did I have anyone else to bring along?

We had just been discussing the Regatta, and my parents were preparing to take the boat over to watch the races. My sisters and I planned on going along. My brother would be sailing on an E boat with a couple friends who lived across the lake. Throughout the years we spent our summers at Quartz Lake, all of us had raced in the Regatta with one cousin or another. My dad's sister's family raised a handful of sailors, and though we'd never had a racing boat, we loved to race. I told Chris I'd bring a friend, and we agreed to meet at the yacht club in an hour.

Margaret was Blakeified for the day. On a whim, I called Neal at the Harbor View. I looked outside. The waves were picking up as the wind grew in strength. A good day for sailing, and I hoped a not-so-good day for touring. Though scheduled for two more tours, Neal used his male wiles on Gina, the owner, and our manager Jan's boyfriend volunteered to take the tours, so she let Neal off duty. I was ecstatic—we were in the race.

When I arrived at the yacht club, the wind raged, and the sky looked overcast, but sailors busily spread out their sails, checked their equipment, chatted with crew, drank coffee, stuffed donuts, and gazed at the lake, calculating.

I caught up with Chris on the dock. His boat *Nimbus II* was tied near the end of one of the long sections, and it bobbed anxiously back and forth, up and down. Chris had a fellow with him I didn't recognize.

"Hey, Ellie! You made it. Come on, help with the sail!" Chris shouted over the wind. "I brought my neighbor. This is Ben Rysland. Ben, my cousin Ellie."

I stepped onto the boat and shook his hand. He remarked, "I know, you're probably wondering what the hell, right? I don't look much like a sailor." In fact, he looked like a linebacker.

"I know you are monstrously heavy, Ellie," he teased, "but I didn't think me, you, and Neal would be enough for this wind," Chris glanced at the lake. "Ben has weight, and we're gonna need it."

I thought of the small cockpit of the C Scow sailboat, which is more flighty than its longer "stepped-up" version, the E Scow. I was used to sailing on the longer E boat, because usually I was there just as weight on a really windy day. I wondered how all of us were going to squish in there. C Scows are comfy for two, acceptable for three, but tight for four. Still, the wind had its say. Better to be squished and safe than roomy and capsized.

"Ben'll literally just be there for weight, Ellie. I'm hoping you'll do the storage bins, seeing as you're the nimblest. And you're gonna man the foresail. Neal's gonna have to be the grunt. I hope he can take it."

"I can take it," comes a familiar voice from the dock. "I can eat it with whipped cream and a cherry on top, oh captain, my captain!" It was Neal, of course. We had just finished pulling the mainsail up to its full height as his gray shadow, dimmed in the muted cloud light, fell across the broad white sheet luffing recklessly. More introductions were made, and Chris gave us life preservers and the prep-and-pep talk. He said he just hoped we'd finish the race; he knew we were green, especially for the conditions. He won races regularly, so I figured he was giving us a line to make us feel better. The guy was competitive. I knew he was out to take the trophy, even if he wouldn't say so.

The wind whipped a fierce gust. The boats tied to the dock yanked like brash ponies. The dock shook beneath us. It was time. We had to take a deep breath, let loose, and get out in the big water.

Neal was a novice, but Chris was psyched to sail with him. They met at our bonfires and were kindred spirits; both preferred to go through water without an engine. When Neal sailed our Butterfly, he had a natural grasp of balance, wind, and speed, but the *Copper Clipper* was simple compared to a C.

Excitement mounted as more boats gathered, tossed roguishly in the waves, trying not to sail away. I counted eleven C scows crowded around the giant pink buoy that marked the starting point of the race. We maneuvered and tried like hell not to crash into another boat. We ducked under the fidgety boom and avoided stepping on each other's feet. We listened for the third shot, which would mark the start of our race. First to start were the M–16 boats, then the J boats, then the C, and then the E, all about six minutes apart. The catamarans shot out last, but most of the E scows and the "cats" hadn't yet left the docks—too many boats in the stew already. The cats were the favorite to watch, and the spectator boats floating around in the bay typically peaked when the shot announced the start of their race.

We, but really mostly Chris, calculated our position so as to cross the buoy at the exact moment our shot rang out, and we succeeded. According to Chris, this is the moment of truth. It's hard to win without a precise start. It would dictate the rest of the race. Chris was pumped. One buoy down, three to go. He manned the tiller, his wristwatch, the buoy markers, and the conditions. Neal worked the main lines and handled the boom, while Ben and I provided weight and kept an eye on other boats, both ahead and behind. I also had the foresail line, called the jib. I had to draw it in and let it out by pulling and releasing a rope through several pullies, then snap the line down to its designated clamp. It wasn't hard because the jib was relatively small, and it didn't pull beyond my capacity to hold it. In a pinch, I could summon Ben. I just had to be fast-moving from the low to the high side and keep my head out of the way of the boom. Any time we changed course, made a turn or altered the angle of the boat in conjunction with the wind, sails had to be optimized. If we got going too fast with the adjustment, and the wind blasted the sail, and my weight wasn't there in time to hold the boat down, we could instantly capsize. We could capsize anyway, but I didn't want to be the reason.

Because of our accurate start, we took the initial lead, and Chris preferred to keep it. With Neal, Chris calculated all factors affecting our pace, and their movements synced. We were cruising. I heard the mast humming and watched every wrinkle in the sails stiffen out. The lines drew uber-taut with the wind force. I wished I could close my eyes and get lost in the sound of the shushing water as we cut through it—a quintessential rush, so worthy of ears alone.

I tried instead to focus on the rise and fall of the boat through the troughs of the waves and to not fall into the trance of staring at the whirling water splashing over the bow of the boat. I was able to eye the shoreline through the first leg of the race, which kept me grounded. The first leg went smoothly, and we had witty bits of conversation. The energy was high but harnessed. Ben sat between Neal and me, a good thing, as I already had plenty of distractions.

We were quickly blown to the middle of the open bay, rounding the second buoy into the second leg. We shifted directions, which amplified the waves, and we had to adjust. The sails were at a wider angle, and I had to keep hunched over to avoid the boom and watch the competing boats. The water was such a pretty, translucent, seafoam green; the color of it in that moment is easily summoned to my mind, even years later, even with that relentless breeze trying to claim the day.

As the second leg progressed, a couple of other boats edged in to overtake us. Chris constantly recalibrated the tiller, yelling and pointing at the sails, maximizing the peak but steadily shifting edge of the wind. All the while, the four of us leaned our weight out to stay on the brink of not tipping. Chris maxed out the tiller extension arm, and he admirably balanced off the side of the boat, steered, and stayed ahead simultaneously. Staying hiked out and not slipping off was a feat. The entire surface of the boat was slick with rogue water. My eye was keen on the western horizon, where thick clouds were stirring up nastiness. We sensed it coming, and it looked to hit hard and fast before the race finished.

As we came about to make the last leg at the third buoy, the rain hit. The wind rose, enraged. I had never felt such a mean wind. I held onto the boat with stiff wrists; my fingers were sore and cold. Blisters wore through on my palms from rope handling. I dug around for some gloves in the cubbies and found a pair for myself. I vowed to find some for the others. I tried to breathe calmly. Chris and Neal seemed oblivious. Ben, however, had a pasty fear creeping in on his face, which felt somehow comforting. At least my rising panic wasn't solo. Yet, when I tried to see ahead, it loomed like a tornado. Great billowing clouds seemed to be spinning along and drawing more power and energy as they came. We could hardly see ten feet past the bow. Everything was dark and murky like we were caught in a furious battle between wind-breathing and water-breathing dragons.

Chris was steering from memory and sensation, not from any tangible landmark—his own version of dead reckoning. His experience and knowledge of the lake were my only hope.

Behind us, we could hear and see glimpses of two boats trailing by about half a boat length; this was the phase where distractions caused defeat, and strategy mattered most. No one spoke; the wind and rain pelted. I crept around, pulling out more rain gear and helping Neal and Chris put theirs on; neither of them could have both hands free at the same time. Chris shouted commands.

"Tie down that mainline!"

"Get down!"

"Watch your head!"

We all kept low, and we felt jolted and yanked at times like the wind was merely toying with us. On that boat, shrouded in gray, I felt tiny and fragile, on the brink of nothingness. If the storm wanted me dead, it would come to that. Moments stood out, but the rest was an out-of-body experience, like giving up on time and place. Feelings of regret and self-doubt came over me. I wished I had not picked up the phone that morning. I wished I had hugged my parents before I left. I thought of Neal maybe wanting to hug his parents too. I wondered why I ever thought I was any good at sailing. I vowed never to get in a sailboat again.

I was overtaxed, like a rope coming unraveled from being pulled too hard. Heavy thoughts flew off me in chunks and seemed to get eaten up by the atmospheric electrical charges all around me. I felt lightning snapping like the jaws of a beast, biting at but just out of reach of the flesh. The piercing sound of the snap seemed to shock the eardrums. I wondered what it meant to lose your mind. What if you just can't keep control of all of these thoughts and where they take you? What if you hit that cold hard water and never come back up? What if I just start crying uncontrollably and shaking with fear? Luckily the buoy appeared to signal another change, and I forced myself to focus on that buoy and what it was going to take to get around it. I couldn't disappoint the others who were with me on the boat.

On the last leg, the wind came at the back of the boat as we headed downwind. Normally sailors used their broad, colorful spinnakers, like a bonus sail. Yet, I saw no pretty spinnakers in that wind. No chance. Our mainsail was far out to one side, and we all had to cleave to the rear of the boat, so the stern didn't fly up. Chris steered the tiller at a strange, unnatural angle with one hand as he balanced, practically hanging off the back of the boat, his ass rocking in the air, holding on to the edge with the other hand. At any instant, he looked like he might get launched right off into the storm soup. Unbelievably, he looked to be enjoying himself. The boat's extreme rocking meant that at any second, we could hit a wave trough at a bad angle, lose control, and smash over sideways, as the next wave came along and finished us off. We balanced off the high edge of the boat, heels tucked under the cockpit precariously. To say I held on for dear life is no exaggeration. And I waited for Chris to scream something to do next.

We could not use the wind to its max because we didn't have enough weight to keep the boat down against its full force. It was gusty and feisty. Chris constantly readjusted. Every upward launch on a wave followed with a giant drop and a loud banging noise as the front end hit the bottom of the wave. Then a rush of water surged all down the boat, drenching everything. It felt like we were barely moving, trapped by one wave after another, bobbing in a water globe. But watching the other boats, I saw none going any faster than we were. I knew we were moving only because the last pink buoy faded away, though the distance was nearly impossible to grasp.

Somehow the lightning stayed at bay. Maybe the clouds were too heavy for lightning. Could that be? I sometimes think about that storm now and it doesn't seem like it could have been real. Still, today, when I watch a storm come across a lake while standing on the shoreline, I can remember the fear of the tentacles of that storm. Maybe we zig-zagged through those tempest canyons unscathed out of pure chance and luck. Maybe Chris and all of us had Poseidon's blessing on that day. Maybe the lake wanted me to see her dark side while her little Limnades held us safe. Whatever the reason, the race officials never sounded a forfeit-the-race signal. What would we have done anyway? It was too late; all the boats were in the belly of the lake and halfway through the race before the storm hit. We had no other strategy than to finish the race. I did hear later that a few racers did turn back mid-race.

Several E boats passed us in the final leg. Their longer torsos cut a little more smoothly through the choppy water, and the crews were five to seven,

so they had weight to balance the heavy wind. At least three boats tipped, one
of which had turtled, completely upside down. The crash boats, volunteers in
their speedboats who patrolled the perimeters poised for rescue, were all busy.
C boats were the final cluster to round the buoy corner and head for home.

Waves rolled along like monstrous boulders
> bumping
> > down a hill.

We plunged up and down while we dangled
> by our heels.

Storm clouds lurked
> above our heads like over-filled water balloons, morbidly obese
and groaning with indigestible thunder. Their dark gray color made everything
eerily dim and smeared. I felt like I had reading glasses on while trying to
look far away. Fat, heavy raindrops thwapped the top of my head and made
deafening popping noises on the deck. The boat stuttered
> like an engine
> > running out of gas,
over and over, and at times the sail came within inches of slicing into the water.
Everything
> flapped grumpily,
soaked and slippery.

I could barely wipe my eyes dry long enough to see Neal or Chris.
I could feel Ben next to me, but all of them were mostly big misty blurs.

In conditions not even as malicious as this, I had seen sailors suddenly
lose hold, slipping off without a sound, disappearing into the wet wildness.
It meant solemn defeat for the captain. He'd be disqualified if he finished the
race with one less crew on board and didn't loop back to rescue the one now
"loose in the stew" and flailing. Looping around in these conditions would be
near impossible. Well, no matter, it wasn't going to be me; I held on tighter.
Neal and I glimpsed each other, and he grinned. I grinned back as a reflex.

Chris shouted at the wind. Grappling with the mainline, Neal's palms bled.
At times, the boat felt out of control, like at any second, an ill-patterned wave
might pick us off, and we'd lose the lead or the boat itself. I didn't want to think
about all of us pitching into the stew.

Teetering along the wind's edge gave me giddy motion sickness. Two boats
clung with us neck and neck, gnashing through the water with the same zeal.
Unyielding determination gripped Chris's face as he held the finish point,
transfixed. Neither of the other boats could quite push ahead. The last balloon-
like buoy bobbed into view, a sporadic fuchsia dot, iridescent in the gray slosh.

We passed the finish mark first, never having let our initial advantage slip.
We won by half a boat length. Waking me from my daze, the gunshot signaled
the finish.

Chris kept us straight for the yacht club, and the shore came into a misty view. As we got closer, it sank in—the race was over. My shoulders dropped with relaxation. Chris asked if we wanted to jump in. We were already soaked, and the water was warm compared to the whipping wind, so Neal and I went for it. Other boats were shoring up to get out of the storm, but we leaped off the sailboat and began swimming in our long raincoats in the stormy waves, which was not easy. We managed to catch the painter and let the boat glide us through the water toward shore. I touched down like a water bird, first dragging, then placing my feet on hard sand. Then Neal and I walked the boat to shore as Chris and Ben pulled the mainsail down. Other sailors called out to us. "Good job, hot stuff!" Some tipped their wet hats or saluted. Chris high-fived several sailors who streamed by, and he received several hard pats on the back and the top of his head.

Chris got back to work then; he pulled the sail down and detached it from the boat. He set equipment bags on the shore. We plucked everything off the boat, stuffing it into big canvas sacks. Drying out would come later. The sails would get rolled up, but they would need to be unrolled again very soon and dried out.

We stepped onto the hard, water-soaked grass and stopped. The ground felt enormously solid, unmoving, and secure. It was an odd sensation. I had to stand still, but it took me a while to feel like I wasn't agitating. We all shook hands and hugged and beamed into each other's dripping wet faces. I had a combined feeling of nausea and euphoria. Chris and Ben began walking up the hill to go inside, but Neal grabbed my arm. The churning clouds made the light around us gray and surreal like we were in a bubble.

I can still picture it all so clearly. Yet, I remember nothing as clearly as I remember his face and the impact of his smile as it crinkled around his eyes, eyes the exact same gray-green color as the lake, illuminated and sparkling. Those amazing, camouflaging eyes are permanently seared into my mind's eye. Always the eyes. Neal's were as serene and inspiring as cathedrals. As wild and unpredictable as a storm over a lake. So much *part and parcel of God.* Powder-white, jagged spokes spiraled out from the pupils, like lightning coming out of a black hole, kaleidoscoping his gray-green-blue irises into shards, glinting like a pair of wet jewels, holding me helplessly captive.

"My God, Elle! Unbelievable!" He shook his head. "Thank you! Thank you for letting me sail with you," he was sort of shouting through the rumble. He held my arms hard by the elbows, then pulled me close, hugging me tightly. With intensity, he gushed, "I'll remember this . . . the storm . . . the race . . . you, here on this day, with me . . . for the rest of my life!" He pressed me to him so tight I couldn't breathe.

"Me, too!" I sputtered. I wrapped my arms around him. Even sopping wet, he was warm. He kissed me, a heart-stopper, soft but enthusiastic. I kissed him back, several soft quickies. We could've started making out right there . . . but the crowd . . . the weather. I fell limp just for a moment, and I let him hold me up. It would have to wait. We squish-squashed up the hill toward the yacht club.

Inside, the kegs were flowing. The place was heaving with sweaty bodies and damp gear. Margaret stood next to one keg, and behind her hovered Blake; both were armed with full beers. I didn't know she would be there. She plowed straight toward me.

"Wow! Look at you! That was some race!" Margaret exclaimed, staring as if she saw me anew. She pulled me. "I brought some dry clothes for you."

"Margaret! My hero!" I replied, snatching her beer. I wanted to slam it, and I was not normally a beer slammer. Nothing looked more delectable than that cold beer at that moment. Neal stood behind me and asked someone at the keg for some glasses. "Plenty of beer for the winners!" Someone shouted, and two beer glasses passed into our hands. We cheered, we made everybody at the keg cheer, then cheers passed around the room. Revelry resumed. I followed Margaret to the bathroom, and Neal took the sail bags and went to find Chris. He had clothes in his car. We agreed to meet back at the keg. The merriment radiated, and I absorbed it like the sun's heat. I was alive. I had survived. I was a part of this victory.

The bathroom, marked "Gulls," overflowed with she sailors changing, brushing their hair, and putting on make-up.

"Margaret, you would *not* have believed that race! I don't know if I've ever been so scared. Did you see us?"

"Are you kidding? Of course! It was the same for me, watching," she said. "We're with two of Blake's buddies and their girlfriends. Luckily, we had the boat canopy because they all wanted to come in when it started rainin'. I put my foot down, though, and I'm afraid those girls don't like me much. Oh, well. . . . Did you see us?" She handed me clothes.

"I was oblivious. Those waves were intense!" I pulled off a layer. "I couldn't see anything!"

"I know! I was scared shitless. Blake was driving like a total maniac, and he and his friends were laughing their heads off."

We headed back out to the main room. A fire snapped in the stone fireplace, and tables of finger food, coolers of soda pop, and a wine counter framed the room. We hit the keg and refilled our glasses, and found Neal, who was with Chris and Ben. Ben was trying to find someone to get him a ride home. He was a young father at the stage where he preferred to be home with his new baby rather than out partying. Neal offered Ben his car since he was going to be drinking and unable to drive it home anyway. Neal and I would ride back in the whaler with Chris, with the *Nimbus II* towed behind, then I'd drive Neal to Ben's to get his car whenever the buzz wore off. I was going to be with Neal the rest of the night, so I was happy as could be.

We made our way to the big front windows overlooking the lake. The view was almost panoramic as the clubhouse was elevated and the shoreline curved out; it was almost a peninsula. The rain subsided, but clouds still hovered thick and low in the sky. The waves had lush frothy edges like whipped cream waterfalls rolling up the shore. We downed several beers, offering toasts to each other, to *Nimbus II*, to our good fortune . . . our courage . . . our strength . . . to Neal's cute ass . . . it went on and on.

Blake and Margaret and his friends were there too. "It must have been beginner's luck that brought you the win!" Blake suggested, pleasantly conversant, referencing Neal and Ben. "Here's to beginner's luck." And everyone's glass went up.

"Actually, it was hardly beginner's luck," I said. "Chris has won like seven of the last regattas. Here's to Chris!" Glasses sprung up again.

"Well, it's not whether you win or lose; it's how you sail the race," Margaret wagged her finger. She went on, "Okay, you guys sailed like Zen masters! Zen, but *insane*."

"But it is about winning, right, Chris? Would you do it if you didn't have the chance to win?" Blake wondered.

"I don't know. I'm not *obsessed* with winning," Chris grinned, "but I do prefer it."

"The best fun is victory, I'd say," said Blake's college friend, Zack.

"Well, I personally am not in it for the victory, really. I'm in it for the thrill. The winning or losing is a by-product," Neal said.

"You probably don't win much, huh?" He laughed. Everybody laughed.

"Well, in the big picture, it's better to enjoy the process more than the result. What good does all that winning do you on your death bed?"

"Well, you can look back on your life and know you played on top. You may get rich in your victories, and have a luxurious life, and travel, and enjoy great food and scenery—and chicks—all because of your ability to be competitive."

"But what good does all that money do you on your death bed?"

"Well . . ." Zack looked at him like he was an idiot. "You can rest assured you left your family some dough to live safe and sound in your absence."

"You sound like a life insurance commercial." Neal was so serious. He suddenly didn't seem like the Neal I knew. I almost saw a dark wound in him, the wound of his parents' death and all his sadness. It was just there, in the corners of his mouth that normally always curved up. They were flat, and he was holding them taut.

"Hey man, no need to freak out."

"I'm not freakin' out. I'm just saying we're different. You want to win; I want to experience."

"You can't do *both*?" He stared at Neal as if he were an oddity.

"I wonder . . . because it seems to me if a person is so worried about winning all the time, how can he be enjoying himself?" He shook his head a little. He seemed to be trying to shake the whole conversation.

"You're *fuckin'* stupid, man," Zack erupted. All of us were half in the bag, and emotions were a little frayed. No one wanted a fight, so people started breaking away from the keg.

"Come on, Neal. You gotta help me with that sail," Chris took his arm.

"Sorry, man," Blake mumbled as they walked away.

"No, I'm sorry. I wasn't trying to start a fight," Neal turned back and said to them. He followed Chris out the side door.

"That dude thinks too much," Blake said to his buddies, and they all laughed. I didn't know if Blake knew I was dating Neal. It seemed obvious to me, but I'm sure he took no interest in my social life. I'm sure Margaret must have filled him in at some point, whether he cared or not.

A short while later, Zack cornered Neal to egg him on about his "contentedness to be a loser." Neal avoided him, saying stuff like, "Look, Dude, there's no point in getting into it. Just let it go."

I was annoyed. I didn't want this great day tainted by a fight. It bothered me that Zack singled out Neal. I was sad for Neal and thinking about him missing his parents. Neal appeared unfazed, but I couldn't believe he didn't care. *I* wanted to set the guy straight.

Someone rigged up a stereo, and it blared eighties dance tunes. The Human League crooned, asking, *Don't you want me, baby?* The middle of the room was a dance hall. Partiers raged for about two hours unchecked, and two fights broke out. Drunken sailors with past grudges don't do well together, and Blake's friend Zack prodded the drunks into fighting. I watched him work his way through the crowd. He would observe people, figure out how to get them going, then pit one against another and retreat. Then he and his other buddy, a guy named Slater, would sit back and laugh at all the foolery. I never saw either of them with their girlfriends, but Margaret pointed them out to me, sitting in a corner, smoking and looking critical. Eventually, someone weaved around dropping the word "cops,"

and the crowd faded.

Blake didn't hang with his friends much that day, and I was glad. I didn't want a reason to hate him; I was trying to like him because I saw Margaret might not be just "a passing thing" for him. He lingered at her side all during the party. He followed her as she congratulated all the winners, and he seemed happy to ditch his troublesome friends.

I look back on that day and think one reason he chummed at her side was because, other than his two friends, he didn't know anybody. This was not his crowd. In all the years we lived as neighbors, I never saw him get in or even around a sailboat. He was into fishing, skiing, and racing his boat against his friends' boats. That day was the only time I ever saw him at the yacht club. None of his family hung out in the sailing circles either.

So much of our lives center
around circles . . . eyes and irises . . . ripples
going round and coming round.

When they passed us in the speedboat on their way home, it was just the two of them. I don't know what happened to the entourage. As we slowly traversed the lake, a clear sky busted through and dispersed the storm clouds. Margaret smiled and waved in the golden afternoon light, her hair flowing long behind her. Blake looked relaxed and relieved to be in his boat. Speeding down the bay with his gorgeous babe at his side, he ruled, a more familiar realm for him, for sure.

We could have gotten home sooner if we'd ridden with Margaret and Blake, but we went with Chris. It seemed right to go with him in his whaler as he towed the *Nimbus II* back to his dock. His cabin was not far from ours.

As the late afternoon sun appeared on the horizon between puffy, crimson clouds, thick brushstrokes of reddish light fanned across the lake. The water softened and blushed in hues of pink and red as day relaxed into twilight. I remembered the old adage: *Red sky at night, sailor's delight*. It couldn't have been truer than at that moment. Earlier, I had sworn to myself never to step foot on a sailboat again, but there I was, already longing for the feeling of the wind and the shushing sounds of the boat gliding through the water.

Nothing feels better than accomplishment, except for, maybe, love. The two together, a great combo, a total blast for the heart and soul. I got to see more depth in Neal's soul that day, and his heart felt fragile, as far as my heart could tell. I wanted to treasure his heart. I wanted to spend my life treasuring experiences like Neal did. I wanted to experience the rest of my life with Neal's life; I knew it that day. I wished his parents could have been there to see what kind of a man he was becoming. Maybe he had been thinking of them that day, too. His grandparents were so proud when we recapped the race for them later. We had more fun telling it than we did living it; our joy of surviving smoothed our moments of trepidation. In fact, we could laugh at our fears.

Neal must have yearned for his parents' presence, but he never said so. Maybe it was his youth, his inability to even know what words to assign to such deep chasms of emotion. I know I wouldn't have been able to choke out any words. It takes time and life experiences to fill us up with the words we need to understand ourselves, and it's an ever-evolving process. Just when we think we understand ourselves, something happens to show us otherwise. I knew one thing clearly that day, that as he got older, Neal was going to get even more amazing.

The whaler's steady hum and the gentle rocking in the waves floated us down from the beer and adrenaline. As we tooled along, we traded grins, glimpsing the gold trophy on the floor. Chris would add this one to his collection, and the memory of the storm and the race would stay with it. I couldn't stop staring at Neal, and at times he nodded off to sleep, and his head would bob in his seat, briefly, then he'd wake up again, only to drift off again. I saw there, in the young man, the little boy he had been. I saw his breathtaking potential and humility. Neal was the embodiment of a dream come true that day. He seemed to glow in the fading sunlight, surreal; his physical body's outline faded, revealing an electrifying aura. How clearly I can conjure him there in my mind that way, a pearl in my strand of memories held most dear.

CHAPTER 13

Aeration

Eleanor drives the long, winding, private road leading to the imposing fortress with the circular driveway. She parks along the edge of the blacktop, out of the way, noting three other cars parked in front of the four-car garage. She grabs her bag and slams the trunk, heading up the fat stone stairway to the dramatic front door with the round arch and leaded glass windows framing the large oak door. As she approaches, the door opens, and a tall, thin woman stands smiling warmly.

"Hello, Eleanor. We're raring to go, so get your tush in here."

"Hey, Victoria! We going outside today? It's so beautiful!"

"Yes! Absolutely! Come on in. Use this dressing room right here," she says, opening the door for her as if she didn't know which door it was.

"I see three cars. Is everyone here?"

"Absolutely!" She blings. The dressing room is a large coat room, with a dozen coat hooks, shoe bins, wooden benches, and two large closets on either side of a large full-length mirror. It's mostly empty and amazingly clean. A skylight brightens the room, but Victoria flicks on the light switch anyway. "Hurry now."

Eleanor lets Victoria shut the door behind her, then she looks at her watch as she takes it off. She's not even close to being late, so she shakes off Victoria's rush-rush vibe and unzips her black workout bag, and changes into her black stretch pants and black jogging bra. She ties her hair back into a binder as she looks in the mirror. She makes a face like a stodgy, old lady for a quick moment before shoving her clothes back into the bag. She opens the opposite door that leads into a small bathroom and splashes water over her face a couple of times, not bothering to wipe away the water. She tosses the bag onto a bench then heads into the foyer. She hears echoes of the women chattering at the front of the house and goes to meet them.

"Hello, everyone. Nice to see you this morning. You all look radiant! Are you ready to stretch?" Three women sit on purple paisley couches, and they watch Eleanor enter. The house is poised for a party, as usual. On alternating Tuesdays, Victoria hosts the book club for lunch and discussion. Four ladies do yoga before the others arrive. They come the other Tuesday mornings too, but only for yoga, no book club. Maybe lunch. Eleanor wasn't sure what they did after yoga, if anything, on those non-book club Tuesdays. She was only there for the yoga part.

From the sunken great room, Eleanor looks into the dining room, where the table is set with fine china and wine and water goblets. Two beautiful flower arrangements anchor the long white tablecloth on both ends, and five tall, white candles sitting in gold candlesticks of varying lengths, line the center of the table. Eleanor breathes in the fresh flowers. She hears activity in the kitchen, someone getting the meal ready.

"Let's go outside, shall we?" Victoria leads the way out the glass doors toward the huge deck.

"Oh, I have to get my mat. I left it in your bedroom. I'll be right there," says Jeannette, Victoria's best friend. Jeanette is always the first to arrive, so they can discuss Victoria's latest home-making endeavor, window treatments, hand-painted walls, new furniture. Victoria has done all the decorating in her house.

Eleanor loves Victoria's house. It is an environment she knows she could never create in her wildest dreams. She has no decorating skills whatsoever and has no idea how to coordinate wallpaper with fabric. Her idea of a great find is a twenty-dollar desk at the thrift store. Victoria is always gracious, and her decorating is always explained with astonishment. *I know! Can you believe this fabric? I've never seen anything like it in my life! I just had to have it!* And on and on it would go about weave and thread count and Italian markets. It quickly got too complicated for Eleanor to follow.

Jeannette also decorates, so they often bounce ideas. Jeannette also has an impressive mansion to fill with beautiful things. Eleanor knows because, occasionally, they do yoga at Jeannette's house.

The four students roll out their mats to face the lake, in a row arms' length apart from each other. Eleanor takes her spot facing them. "Welcome, Victoria, Serena, Jeannette, and Allison." She looks at each student. "Namaste." She lowers her head slightly. "Stand up tall with a nice straight spine, strong legs, and an open spirit. Let's start in Mountain Pose." Eleanor demonstrates the pose as she talks about it, and they follow along. "How great to stretch with the lake to inspire us. Relax your face and your eyes, and free your mind of clutter and distraction. Let's breathe." Eleanor places her interlaced fingers under her chin and models proper inhalation and exhalation as the four follow along.

As Eleanor moves them through the poses, she is sometimes doing them too and sometimes checking theirs. She turns an elbow, lifts a chin, or straightens a bent knee. She reminds them not to hold their breath but to let it go. Be with it as it moves in and out of their bodies. She adjusts her energy output for this small class. It is different from how she teaches her studio classes or the community education classes, which often contain as many as twenty-five students. She teaches at three resorts that have spas or fitness centers, too, which is where she met Victoria. As a teacher, her favorite feeling to witness is the excitement students have when they breakthrough in a pose, attaining a higher quality of balance, strength, or flexibility. Usually, a similar breakthrough happens in the mind and spirit. Body, mind, and spirit are connected personally, interpersonally, and globally.

She slowly paces around them in a circle, occasionally weaving between them as she winds down the class; she talks with acceptance and affirmation of them, their journeys, and struggles. Modeling compassion. When people improve themselves through practicing yoga, they improve the whole world. This is one key part of yoga she tries to convey. Learning to accept one's body, strengths, and weaknesses, with grace and compassion helps expand compassion to others.

Yoga encourages letting go of superficialities, but this doesn't always happen. Eleanor knows full well. It encourages people to learn more about themselves, and some people are deeply afraid of what they think they will find. This prevents them from ever trying to look. Yet the truth is, doing yoga can lead to more truths, which always empowers, even if those truths are sometimes scary.

Truth. Hard to decipher, this is. She thinks about Yoda and how close Yoda and yoga are as words and in other ways, too. Baffling stuff to contemplate, Eleanor thinks, observing her thoughts flow. So interesting to see how one thought flows into the next; what links them? Where is the mind trying to go when it's thinking, and why does it want to go there?

The foursome has arrived at the final pose, "corpse," where they lie flat on their backs and remain still. This is the sweet spot for Eleanor. Class is mostly over, and everyone is feeling good. Now, the quiet opens up and reveals the subtle accompaniment of the world, in this instance, the quartet of wind, water, insects, birds. A wind chime can be faintly heard. *Such a treat to do yoga outside*, Eleanor thinks, gazing at the lake. A stabbing sensation strikes. The lake is stunning; it's just *there*, so big and amazing. Thoughts and memories radiate out of it. It inspires but also brings twinges of sadness. How does such a thing—a place—do that to a person? Then her ears pick up a plane rumbling high overhead. She thinks about progress, pace, and movement. A sudden sensation of hurling through the air by jet propulsion comes up, and she feels it in her body. Ah. A human sensation, grounded in the body—what an amazing thing to be human. To have a body and a mind and a heart and a soul. To be able to feel and think. *It's no wonder we seek and find comfort in things and places that are always mostly the same—because, as we live, life moves and changes. We've got to hold onto something steady. When tragedies hit, on any scale, we need nature more than ever. In nature, we see how we have changed and how some things never change. It is there. I am that.*

Today the sun shimmers and shifts restlessly, and Eleanor feels like that skittish light. She's bright and blazing but with no mooring. Free, but loose. It's unsettling; this disparity between how she projects herself and how she is inside. She feels like a hypocrite. Her eyes mist, but she turns the feeling over in her mind, replacing it with the cheerful thought of her friend finally coming to stay for good in a few months. This thought's uplifting feeling rushes in so fast that tears well in her eyes. A tiny relief overtakes her. She thinks, *I won't always feel this aloneness anymore! I will soon have her! Friends, too, are a landscape for us to find some steadiness.* As the ladies sit up, using their hand towels to wipe their faces, Eleanor stands abruptly, wiping the extra water from her eyes. Quickly, conversation drowns out the quiet.

They chat excitedly after class, directing questions at Eleanor about how to fix a kink in the neck or a tight hamstring. Then they go inside, and Victoria pulls out sets of towels for her guests, and each moves off to a bathroom to shower and get ready for lunch. Victoria detains Eleanor before giving her a crisp one-hundred-dollar bill. Always a cleaning lady or a "kitchen lady" bustles in the background with laundry or cooking.

Eleanor takes the cash and changes in the dressing room without showering. As she goes out the front door, she hears the shower go on in the bathroom off of Victoria's bedroom. As she approaches her car, she notices a flat tire. She has no spare. She closes her eyes tightly for a moment, sighing slowly as she bends her head back, face to the sky. She lets out a swear word in a long, drawn-out whisper to herself. Was it low when she drove here, and she didn't notice? How did it go flat so quickly? She doesn't want to disturb the ladies' luncheon, but she isn't sure what else to do. As all the other book group members drive in, it will be a topic for discussion at lunch. What is that rusty old Honda doing out there?

Luckily, the girls are in school all day, and she has no immediate plans. Hesitantly, Eleanor goes back up to the front door. It has locked behind her, so she has to knock. The kitchen lady appears, wiping her hands on a white apron.

"Yes?"

"I can't believe this, but my car has a flat tire," Eleanor looks down, shaking her head. "I guess I need to call someone."

"Come in. Of course. Follow me." The woman proceeds to the kitchen and directs Eleanor to a little nook with a desk holding a bright red, old-fashioned, dialing telephone.

"I think I need a phone book. I'm going to have to call someone to come out. I don't have a spare," Eleanor says, more embarrassed and irritated by the minute.

"Hmmm. I'm not sure where she keeps the phone book," the woman says as she begins opening cupboards in the little nook area.

"It's okay. I can look. You've got other things to do," Eleanor remarks, nodding her head at the kitchen.

"Yes, you look. Let me know if you can't find it. You can always just dial information." She walks away. Eleanor doesn't know what to look up, even if she does find the stupid phone book. She finds it momentarily and is paging through the Yellow Pages under "auto" as Victoria comes by with a towel twisted over her head.

"Eleanor. Are you okay? What's going on?"

"I've got a flat tire. I'm calling a service station to come out and put a spare on for me. I don't have one."

"Oh, my God. Well, forget the station. Gerard can help you. He's our driver. He's right outside above the garage. Reynold is a car freak, you know. I'm sure we have a tire in that godforsaken garage out there that'll work on your car. Don't call anybody. Hang on, sweetie!" She crosses to the kitchen, picks up a phone handset on the wall, and presses one number. She taps her foot as she waits for Gerard to answer. Eleanor considers protesting, but something tells her resistance is futile.

"Gerard, my yoga instructor has a flat tire. Can you meet her in the drive and put a spare on?" Pause. "She doesn't have a spare. I'm sure we have one that will fit somewhere in the garage, right?" Pause. "Sure." Pause. "Okay. I'm sending her out. Meet her right away, okay?" She hangs up tersely.

"Okay, Eleanor. He's going to meet you outside by your car. He'll get you fixed up and ready to go in no time. Let me know if you're still having trouble. I've got to get ready now. The ladies will be here any minute! Oh, my! Such excitement! It's good I'm all calm from the yoga!"

"Oh, thanks, Victoria. I really don't mind calling a service station, though. Gerard doesn't have to be inconvenienced."

"What? Are you kidding? What's he doing right now? Probably watching soap operas. He doesn't have to do a thing until four o'clock when he has to pick up Reynold at the airport! He's probably bored out of his mind and dying for a chance to be someone's hero today!" She laughs.

"Well, thank you."

"Really. No big deal. This'll be faster." Eleanor figures Victoria is embarrassed to have a broken-down car in her driveway in front of all her ladies. *The sooner she gets me out, the better!*

She goes outside to wait for Gerard, but he's already there. They discuss the situation, and Gerard begins to jack up the car to take off the tire. As he takes it into the garage, he tells Eleanor he'll have no problem and to go on back inside; he'll find her when he's done. She doesn't want to go back inside. Already one car has arrived, and the fancily dressed lady stares at her as she heads to the house. Another car is coming down the driveway.

"Gerard, I'm going down to the lake. Find me there, okay?" She slips off her shoes, dangling them in her fingertips. She sweeps her bare feet through the soft, cool grass as she crosses the wide expanse of fine green lawn. She walks to the end of the dock and sits with her feet dangling in the creamy water. Listening to the methodic gurgle of the water under the boatlift, she floats off, entranced.

Shortly, the dock wiggles as the kitchen lady approaches. "Ms. Victoria requests you come inside and join the luncheon, miss." Her manner, a mix of servitude and formality, makes Eleanor uncomfortable.

"Gosh. No. I wouldn't dream of it," Eleanor replies. "I'm not properly dressed, and I don't know anyone."

"She insists. If you don't come, she says she'll come down here herself, and then she'll be real mad to leave the table. I recommend you come."

Eleanor reluctantly follows. They enter the house with lots of laughter coming from the dining room. The kitchen lady turns, "Perfect timing. The party is sitting down to eat. A place is set for you."

She goes to the table where the empty place is. It's at the opposite end from Victoria. There are thirteen women, including Eleanor now. The table is enormous, and Eleanor suppresses shock at how elaborately it's set, just for a luncheon. She doesn't have much time to marvel before Victoria stands.

"Ladies, we have the good fortune to welcome a new face to our table today. This is Eleanor Marlow. She is my yoga instructor, well, our yoga instructor. Her car is stranded in the driveway with a flat tire, and Gerard is coming to her rescue. Please, sit, Eleanor. Let me introduce you to the ladies, some of whom, you, of course, already know." She proceeds through a short introduction around the table, saying lovely things about each friend in turn. Then she turns to Eleanor and says, "Now, can you repeat everyone's name?" Everyone laughs.

Eleanor, who's been listening intently in order to ignore the staring, has put each woman's name to memory, and she does go around the table and recite each one as if she knew it would be required.

"My God, you're fabulous! Yoga does wonders for short-term memory, too, huh, Eleanor?" Victoria laughs. The focus changes, *thank God*, Eleanor thinks, as salad plates arrive for each guest. No one moves for the fork until all salads are in place. Then almost in sync, they pick up their shiny forks and begin eating. Eleanor feels big and clumsy next to these elegant women wearing expensive jewelry and modeling trendy hairstyles. Several times she makes loud, out-of-place clinks with her fork against the fragile china, but the women are either oblivious or courteous enough to ignore it. The conversation is mostly out of Eleanor's league, about the Minnesota Orchestra and the summer concert series,

the latest travels to New York, San Francisco, Milan, Scotland, the stress of traveling in the heat, and

how little time there is to spend at the cabin,

land and property purchases,

their college-age-plus children and

what they're all doing over the summer,

their husbands, and

where they're off to or returning from,

the wonderful food, and

the great new spa that just opened.

Eleanor mostly listens, not having anything to add from her own simple life and not knowing any of them.

The conversation lulls as the servant parades in with a salmon dish. As with the salad and the soup appetizers, the kitchen lady holds the plate next to Victoria and displays it as she explains what they're about to eat. "The main course today, ladies, is salmon with citrus avocado salsa. The salmon is grilled to perfection with a touch of Tuscany olive oil," she continues describing all the items on the plate, which is neatly decorated by the food. As she explains, the helper delivers two plates at a time, one to each guest. After all the main courses are out, the speech is perfectly timed to end, and the ladies reach for the second fork. The display dish isn't even one of the plates to be served. Eleanor watches the kitchen lady take it back behind the scenes, hoping the woman intends to eat it herself.

Eleanor has begun feeling slightly out-of-body at this point like she is watching herself in some sort of movie. She keeps waiting for someone to crack a joke, or drop something, or sneeze, or burp—something to break up the formality, but nothing comes. She blurts out, "So, what book are y'all reading in your book group?" A short but heavy pause follows.

Victoria answers, "Oh, we've just read Jane Austin's *Pride and Prejudice*. We certainly have lots to talk about there, don't we, gals. But, we make it a policy *not* to begin discussing it until after lunch."

"Oh, sorry! I was just curious," Eleanor blushes.

"Oh, that's fine. How would you know? We don't post the rules anywhere, do we, Jeannette?" They laugh.

"Eleanor, how long have you been teaching yoga?"

"About five years now. I've been doing yoga for over ten years, though, so it seems longer," she sits up straighter.

"What made you want to become a yoga teacher?"

"Well, I was tired of my real job and paying money for classes at a yoga studio, so I decided to get certified and open my own studio and get more immersed with yoga."

Another woman tosses out a question, "Where is your studio?"

"It's right in downtown Horton, along the river. The corner of Fourth and

River Street. It's called 'Currents.' It's a neat space, an old warehouse."

"Oh, yes. By that little coffee shop? I think I've seen it. You didn't want a more prominent spot, like the newer part of town near the highway?"

"I like being in the backflow, so to speak. Plus, rent's cheaper."

"You'd get more business if you were more central. People probably don't know about your studio. You'd get summer people by the highway."

"Yes, you're probably right, but I like the space. And if people want to do yoga, they come."

"Well, Eleanor, that's what I don't understand. You do these community ed classes, practically for free, I'm sure, and the people who attend pay, what? Five dollars a class? Why would I come to your studio if I can do yoga at the community center?"

"I know what you're saying, but actually, it's a good way to bring business to the studio. It's good to get out there. People who take community classes probably don't have money for studio classes. Most community ed people are seniors on a fixed income. And they love yoga. It's so good for them."

"It doesn't seem wise to me. You'd make more if you did more private lessons. Or more lessons at all the spas opening up around here. I mean, you make a hundred dollars an hour, and you only have four people. And you get to go into people's homes."

"I want to offer lots of options," Eleanor concludes, "I guess I'm not much of a business person."

"Well, I don't know many who could make their businesses profitable or long-term with your strategy, but I won't complain. You're a great yoga teacher, and I *am* glad to have you." Victoria holds up her glass of wine, "A toast to you, Eleanor."

The ladies hold up their glasses, and Eleanor wants to crawl under the table. She looks down at her hands and wonders why she can never get her fingernails to grow out. "Well, thanks, Victoria. I love coming out here. You gals are so sweet!"

The kitchen helper comes out and speaks to Victoria in a low whisper. "We're just about ready for dessert, gals, and, Eleanor, you must stay. It's our favorite, tiramisu. It's Bella's specialty, isn't it, Bella?"

"Yes, ma'am!" She bows her head to the group. "We'll bring it out momentarily."

"Your car is ready to zoom off to the wild blue yonder, Eleanor. But do stay for dessert, won't you?"

Eleanor prefers to dash for the door. Holding her own among these women is exhausting. But she can't think up an excuse. Surprisingly, the party stands up abruptly and moves into the sunken great room, finding seating around the room. Eleanor could have made an easy exit if she'd have known. She would have said, *"Oh, really, Victoria. I must be going now, but I do so thank you for the lovely meal."*

But now she's stuck with more pleasantries and smiling. Desserts are delivered, and they eat daintily, holding the little dishes in their hands. It seems so informal to Eleanor, compared to the luncheon, but she isn't about to question dessert protocol. She's busy trying to find a spot to sit and seeing a wingback chair unoccupied, she makes a beeline. It happens to be next to the couch, where three ladies are sitting, and another is on a floor pillow, having set her dessert on the coffee table.

Eleanor is mostly left out since she doesn't know anyone very well. She pretends to be really into her dessert, studying it with undue attention, admiring the cute dish, then desperately looking around, staring at a photograph of Victoria's family, while she listens half-heartedly to the nearest conversation.

". . . I propose we invite her in. I feel so bad for her." A woman named Joan is speaking. Eleanor knows nothing about her other than what she's deduced from lunch: she's lived in this town for years, but only as a summer and holiday resident. Like many of these women, she is active in the theater and the arts scene; she's on the board for the botanical gardens, and she dabbles in local politics.

"I don't know why you feel bad for her after what she did," replies Serena, one of the yogis.

"What? What did she do? I thought *he* was having an affair," Allison, another yogi, adds.

"No. *She* was having the affair," Joan says. "And when I tell you who with, and everything else, you're *not* going to believe."

"What! Do tell," Serena bubbles.

"Alright, but you have to play dumb," Joan warns, wiggling her finger. "She's going through hell. She's moving to the lake house permanently with Lexie. Zack's keeping the house in town. I don't know what she's going to do here all winter long, but I—"

"Cut to the nitty, Jo. Who was she diddling?"

She sing-songs, "You won't be-lieve it!"

"Who! Come on!"

"Blake Crandahl." Silence follows, except for the odd gagging sound coming from Eleanor's mouth as she accidentally gasps at the same moment she swallows the last of her tiramisu. Everyone looks at her just as she drops her fork into her lap, dribbling down her shirt on the way. Luckily, she snaps her legs together to catch the delicate plate before it splatters on the plush carpet. She looks up and smiles awkwardly at the women who are observing. She knows she has to speak before they let her off the hook and go back to their conversations, but she has to cough hysterically. She stands and holds her hand up in a gesture of "excuse me, please!" as she bolts up the steps to the one area of the house she's comfortable in, the changing room near the door.

She goes into the little room and coughs brutally for at least a minute straight. After she coughs the tickling burning sensation away, she goes into the bathroom and sticks her head into the sink for a big slurp of water right off the tap. *Did I hear that right? Blake Crandahl? I wonder if the Zack they're talking about is his friend. The one I met so long ago. It can't be! How many Blake Crandahls are around here? I gotta get more of that conversation!*

She makes a wet wad of toilet paper and hastily dabs at the tiramisu dribbles. Finding the wastebasket under the sink, she drops the squishy wad, hearing it clunk to the bottom. She sneaks back to her chair, expecting to have to provide some explanation for her abrupt departure, but everyone is engaged. A few more ladies have joined in about the affair.

"... and if you can even stand it, it gets worse ..." Joan leans forward and exaggerates a whisper. "Lexie's not Zack's daughter."

"No! Joan! You're making that up! You have to be making that up!" Allison responds, seeming angry but really gushing. "You're getting this from your soap opera!"

"I don't watch soap operas. Why do I need soap operas? This is better than any soap opera!"

"How do you know this, Joan?" Serena demands.

"She *told* me herself," Joan replies. "She told me Zack told her he knows Lexie's not his daughter. Did you know he had testicular cancer in his twenties? He's infertile."

"You don't necessarily become infertile from testicular cancer," Allison points out.

"Well, she says Zack told her, get this, he knew he was infertile since before they were married. He *never* told her." She pauses, then adds, "Until now, that is."

"So, she had the kid, and they've been pretending she's Zack's the whole time?" Allison looks shocked.

"No! Not both of them! Just Zack. He's known for six years Lexie's *not* his daughter. He just never told her."

"He's such an asshole!"

"What do you mean? She's the one getting pregnant by his *best friend!*"

"No. Wait. There's more. She's not sure it's Blake's even. She was fooling around with her old college boyfriend at the time, too."

"You really have to be kidding now."

"I'm telling you, I'm not!"

Eleanor can no longer pretend not to be riveted. She has to get up. She's slowly ambling around the couch, pretending to look at the artwork and photos, staying close enough to hear. She's mildly shocked that all that prim and proper conversation at the dining table just got sloshed over by all this gossip.

"And it gets worse for poor little Lexie. Zack has cancer again. It's come back, or maybe it's a new cancer, I don't know. But *I think* that's why he flipped out on Lydia. She's really hit rock bottom."

"She sounds like a total slut to me," Allison says. When they all stare at her, she adds, "Sorry. I don't really know her, but I mean, come on!"

"Zack treats her like crap, you know," Joan defends her. "I'm sure he's had plenty of his own affairs and probably not even discretely."

"Well, why wouldn't he? He's supporting and pretending to be the father of his wife's illegitimate child! Geesh!" Her outrage seemed mixed with delight.

"Is she still seeing Blake Crandahl?" Serena asks. "I wonder how his poor little wifey feels about that."

"She's not saying. She said it got ugly when Zack came to the cabin when he was supposed to be away on business. He found them bare-ass naked in their bed!"

"I wonder where Lexie was."

"Who knows. You know what's sad? He'd just found out about the cancer. He canceled his business trip to come and tell her and be with her."

"God, that's terrible."

"Well, really, how happily married could they have been? Why would he expect her to console him? That's probably a ruse. He probably was hoping to bust her."

"Who knows? Maybe he was freaked out. I mean, what would you do if you found out you had cancer?"

"Yeah. Right. I don't know what I'd do."

"Apparently, Zack attacked him. Literally went after him. Punched him and knocked him down. Lydia was screaming. I hope Lexie wasn't there."

"God, sick story."

"And you want this woman to join our book group?"

"Allison, my God. Have some compassion. She hardly knows anyone here. If she's going to live here, it'll be a good way to get to know some of the year-rounders, like Monica and Shelly."

"Well, it'll make our discussions livelier. I'm sure she's got a unique perspective on relationships."

"Ha. Ha. Funny. We should invite her in. Joan, propose it. I'll back you."

"Well, I just want to know one thing. Did Blake Crandahl tell his wife? I'd love to be a fly on the wall for that scene."

Words that could have come from Eleanor's own mouth. Yet, as much as she's eager to hear any smearing of Mrs. Crandahl, she's spent too much time examining the artwork, lamps, and feigning interest in Victoria's family photos. All the chatter has soured her stomach. *Wouldn't it be perfect to get the runs right about now?* She has to make her excuse to leave before Victoria calls the book club to order or whatever she does. It would be so embarrassing to be asked to leave. Especially since she's been itching to leave the whole time. It seems about the right timing—the coffee cups are coming out. The kitchen worker has brought an enormous tray with a beautiful stainless-steel coffee pot and a tray of assorted coffee cakes and finger treats. Eleanor sneaks up to Victoria as she's about to cut her conversation short to prepare everyone for the coffee. She butts in quickly before this happens.

"Victoria, I'm gonna sneak out now."

"Yes, fine, Eleanor," Victoria looks at her, smiling. Then she briefly looks around at the group before turning to Eleanor to add, "It was so nice having you. You're a breath of fresh air."

"Oh, yes. I'm sure." Eleanor laughs lamely. "Well, I'll just sneak out now." As she ascends the steps, Victoria says, "Ladies, I have a fresh bottle of Bailey's here, if any of you are interested."

She grabs her yoga bag and quietly shuts the front door behind her. She looks at the new tire on her old car, wondering if she should pay Victoria for it, or at least offer to. But she doesn't have any money on her, except the one-hundred-dollar bill she just got from Victoria. She looks around to thank Gerard, but he is absent. She'll bring it up next time because there's no way she's going back in there. She gets in her car and drives it down the long driveway, far, far away.

The lake blinds her with the reflection of the full afternoon sun, and the interior of her car is hot. She rolls down her window to fill the car with fresh air but can't stop tossing the gossip around, thinking about people she hasn't heard or thought about in many years. She can't say she's happy to hear about the sorry state of their lives. She wants to laugh and gloat fiendishly or cry hysterically; she can't decide which.

CHAPTER 14

Tamarack Tryst

We agreed to meet at the fire ranger tower, a familiar landmark for both of us. Neal was bringing his family horses, and we were finally going riding together. My excitement tinged with nervousness—I did not consider myself even an amateur horse handler. I was a greenhorn, but I didn't want it to be obvious. I sat in my car, examining my teeth in the rearview mirror when I heard the gravel grinding as he drove up in a big truck hauling the horse trailer. He jumped out of the cab and came up to my door. I was tying my shoe when he approached.

"You ready?" He raised his eyebrows, flashing his grin.

"Yes! So excited! Come on, introduce me to your horses!" I followed him to the trailer. He opened the door and led one, then the other horse out. He tied them to two little hooks at the side of the trailer and got busy saddling them up. I tried to be helpful, but he worked efficiently on his own and seemed to want me out of the way. He talked to them, telling them who I was and how much he missed them as he got them ready and patted them and pet their glossy coats. Finally, he turned and grabbed my hand. He led me to the first horse and patted the horse gently as a way of introduction.

"This is Shimmer. We call her Shim. Isn't she marvelous?" He stroked the side of her long shiny neck. She stomped a foot and her tail swatted behind her. Both horses were solid reddish-brown and mostly identical from my initial observation. "She's getting mellower with age. You'll love her. She's gentle but strong and very eager to please. Put your foot right here and swing your leg up and over. You know how to do that, right?" I did as he instructed and got up, luckily, on my first try, with a huge boost. I took the reins.

"What's your horse's name, Neal?" I asked, trying to hold steady on Shimmer.

"This one is Twinkle. Or Twink. She and Shim have been friends since they were fillies." He threw his backpack on and tossed himself up over the saddle. He turned Twinkle and took the lead. "Let's take the trail to the lake. You know the one. You've probably hiked it a million times, right?"

"Oh, yeah. But never on horseback. I was hoping you'd take me to the land you're thinking about for your horse camp."

"Yeah, we can do both. I've got us a picnic, so we can sit at the beach and eat, then we'll hike back up another trail, and I'll take you to my favorite spot in the woods." He kicked his heels into Twinkle's sides, and she picked up her pace to a gentle trot. Shimmer followed right behind. I didn't have to do anything. It was much easier than it looked.

I'll never forget that ride that day or the gusty wind. It was early August, but the weather felt like fall. The wind had a chilly edge, and it pushed big gusts around urgently like it was running out of time. It was sunny and mostly warm, but white clouds had been billowing and strolling across the sky all morning. At times the air held still, but then a blast hit, swished the trees and whistled that change was coming. On the horse, I found I could be more observant than when on foot. I felt like I was floating among the tree branches rather than under them, scuffing through the rocky dirt. It was heavenly. I got to watch Neal's curly blond hair flow in the wind, and I teased him about how long it was getting.

"It'll all be cut off soon when I start teaching," he said. "Did I tell you my parents were teachers?"

"I think you did. Your mom taught social studies, and your dad was a college professor, right?" I looked ahead in anticipation of the lake, but I couldn't yet see it. We sloped down, but I knew we would hit a rim, and it would get steeper. "I bet they'd be happy to know you're a teacher now too."

"It's weird, but I never thought I'd be a teacher."

"What'd you wanna be?"

"It may seem strange, but I remember the first time I rode a horse, I was eight. I loved it so much; I knew I wanted to work with horses when I got old enough."

He wanted to be a cowboy and loved Gary Cooper movies like *High Noon*. He and his grandpa still regularly watch old movies together. He said it was a way he could feel a sense of his parents being around him. They were all old movie buffs. He said he handled his grief of his parents' car wreck by getting lost in a plot with the likes of Betty Davis, Barbara Stanwyck, Cary Grant, and Jimmy Stewart. Cooper was his all-time favorite, and Neal seemed to try to live out a similar sort of graceful gallantry in his own life, which endeared him to me and made me so sad for him.

"And you will. Your horse camp will be spectacular! It'll be perfect here."

"Teaching'll be good. Yeah. I have all the experience I need with horses; now I have to get some with kids." We hit the ridge, and Neal started down the hill making switchbacks. I felt like I could pitch right off the front of the horse, but I held on and faked calm. I squeezed Shimmer's big body with my legs to hold myself, but I didn't know if my legs could hold out. I had to focus on something else, so I looked up and saw the lake. The view appeared out of nowhere. I took a big breath, exhaling luxuriously. Soon the trail eased and got wide enough that we rode side by side.

"You're great with people, Neal. You're gonna be an amazing teacher."

"Yeah, I guess. I'm excited," he looked over at me.

"I hope you won't be so busy you don't write me letters."

"Letters? Daily, my dear. And I'll be calling you so often you'll be sick of me," he held eye contact for a moment with an unusually straight face. I felt a wave of fear come from him like he might lose me too.

"Not possible," I looked at him with equal seriousness. "Do you think we'll see each other much?"

"Your school is only like an hour and a half away. I can come on weekends and vice versa?"

"You promise?" I felt a jolt in my heart at the thought of not seeing him every day. "I hope some other woman, some young teacher, doesn't come sweep you off your feet."

"I'm already swept off my feet, Elle," he shook his head. "I love your whole family." And I was glad he had fit so easily into my world.

"Me, too," I admitted. "I almost can't believe it."

"I know. It's crazy. But, really . . . I think I knew it the moment I saw you."

"Same for me. I was electrified by you on the dock that day," I smiled with the memory. The trees tossed and rushed and mingled around us, and we were alone together in the beauty of it.

"I pretty much thought I'd be single my whole life. I never thought I would feel anything but grief," he admitted. "I never thought I'd meet someone like you. You're so one-of-a-kind."

"I think the exact same thing about you." I wanted to kiss him, forget the day.

"Come on! It flattens out here; let's run the horses to the beach. They love this. Hold on!" He clicked his tongue, and before I knew it, Shimmer took up a gallop. I almost tumbled off the back, but I held on with a gasp. It reminded me of the jet ski ride earlier in the summer when he hit the throttle, and I had to grab on before I toppled off. My head floated in the clouds when I was around him.

I remember very little about lunch. It was rushed due to the cold wind. But I remember talking about Margaret and Blake because Neal's perceptions were eerily spot on with my own and bothered me. As we settled onto his big Mexican blanket, the horses lingered where the sand met the woods. His backpack was filled with goodies that he pulled out one little surprise at a time, which is how he seemed to do everything.

"So, what's the deal with Margaret and Blake?" Neal asked, handing me deviled eggs, one at a time.

"When did you have time to make deviled eggs?" I had to ask.

"Oh, this morning. My grandma helped. She loves making food. Deviled eggs are one of her specialties. And she loves making picnics. It's fun for us; we get to hang out in the kitchen, you know." He shrugged, looking cute.

"Tell her they're delicious!" I ate another one. "Margaret and Blake, yeah. Weird, huh? I don't know. I'm not sure what she sees in him. I think he's a bore."

"More than that, he's so not good enough for her. He's so self-absorbed. How can someone as cool and amazing as Margaret find that attractive?" Neal wondered.

"I know! He's so full of himself. But, one thing is, he totally dotes on her. He hangs by her like a loyal pet. He worships her. He does seem to get her awesomeness. Ya gotta give him that."

"What do they have in common, though?"

"I know . . . I know. I don't know," I stammered, puzzled. "They're both super jocks? I mean, they both love tennis and golf. They're both competitive. He spoils her. She loves it. Maybe what they like in each other are their contrasts."

"Well, they're a weird pair to me," Neal concluded.

"Me, too. I can't imagine it'll last forever. Margaret's gonna want to live in the country or a small town. He's, like you said, a city boy. I hope he doesn't break her heart. We'll be going back to school. He'll be in the Cities. He's going to grad school at the U this fall."

"So, he'll make the big money he's supposed to then. But if anyone gets a broken heart, it'll be that poor loser. He'll never find anyone like Margaret. He'll spend his life realizing that when it's all over. The only chance that guy has for a real life is to latch on to her."

"I hope I don't have to console her too much when they break up."

"You won't. Here," he handed me the next course, a pita sandwich. "Remember, you have to hang out with me on the weekends."

"I'll be pissed if you *don't* come! It'll be easier than me coming here. Are you going to be living with your grandparents still?"

"Yeah. It's easier. I can keep an eye on them. Help Grandma with the grocery shopping, help Grandpa with shoveling and raking, stuff like that. Plus, I can save a lot of money."

"Will it be weird for me to come and stay?"

"Not at all. I have the whole basement to myself, as you know. My grandparents love you." He glanced at me. "But it'll be more fun to come see you. Are you in a dorm?"

"God, am I a total nerd? Nobody lives in the dorms their senior year. Did you?"

"No, but that's the U. Nobody lives in the dorms."

"Margaret and I have an apartment near campus. I have my own room. Come *every* weekend."

"I'll have to—to beat away all the guys trying to date you."

"Haha. You're funny."

"Well, it's true. I know a catch when I see one." He smiled, taking the last big bite of his sandwich, sprouts hanging out the side of his mouth. I laughed. He made a face. We both started laughing. He almost had to spit out his food. He kicked the backpack off the blanket and grabbed the edge, curling it around him as he rolled into me and rolled us both up in the blanket. We were laughing

until we could barely breathe.

It was warm, all rolled up from the wind.

When we finally did uncurl ourselves,

we had crumbs in our hair, and my shoes were full of sand.

We got on the horses so he could give me the tour and lay out his vision for the horse camp. We trotted up and over the hill that held the basin of the lake and crossed a trickily stream where the trees got bigger and thicker. We strolled through a valley and over rounded hillsides and came to a circular clearing rimmed with clusters of Tamarack trees. I felt myself becoming a real horse rider. I didn't really have to think about it much. Shim and Twink seemed as happy as we were.

Those sensuous trees swaying and shaking in the fall-like breeze did fill me with longing—for what, I'm not exactly sure. Maybe a longing to stop time. The air was a little misty, and, at times, I would feel cold water particles hit me in the face, like fairy showers in some fairytale forest. The ground was soft and mossy, even squishy in certain spots, but we found a nice dry, flat section. We let the horses linger around us, munching on clumps of grass, swishing their tails. We lay on our backs, looking through the spindly trees whirling in the infinite blue sky.

"I want to tell you something," he rolled his body toward me. "But I don't want it to change the way you think of me, which I know sounds sort of stupid."

I looked at him carefully, blinking. "What?"

"I lied before when I said I didn't have a lot of money," he took a deep breath before he continued. "I know you don't like rich people." He put his hand on my side, and it radiated heat. I held still. "I'm not *from* a lot of money, but for most of my life, I've been really good at saving every penny I got my hands on. I invested a pile of it when I was a junior in high school. My economics teacher told me to buy stock in medical technology, so I found Medtronics, a Minnesota company. It turned out to be a great tip."

"Okay . . .?" I felt butterflies in my stomach, not sure where he was going with this, but I wanted to hear more.

"When my parents died, my sister and I inherited their life insurance." He rolled over on his back again. I felt a hint of the enormous grief he must have harbored when he sighed. There was a deep pause. I waited. "I have enough money right now to buy this land outright." He clasped his hands together and held them to his mouth for a moment. I watched his arm muscles flex as they lay on his chest.

"Is it for sale?"

"Not exactly. But I found out who owns these two hundred acres. I've been researching. He won't be selling soon. Which is fine because I'm not ready to buy anyway."

"So, we're trespassing then?"

"Yeah. Oh, yeah," Neal's eyes twinkled. "But I've talked to the guy several times, and he knows I'm interested."

"Can you even start a horse ranch here? Are there regulations for land use and shit like that?"

"Yeah, I checked, and luckily that's not an obstacle. But I wonder about the acreage next to this section, the stretch that runs along the shoreline. Someday it'll be for sale. Land around here is getting snatched up. Have you noticed?"

"But it's state forest. It's been state forest for a long time. People will want to keep it that way."

"But everything has a price. It might not happen for a long time, but it could." He sat up on his elbow, looking around. "It's such great beachfront, I can't imagine some investor won't snap it up and sell it off, bit by bit, for lake homes or worse."

"Well, keep on saving. If or when it goes up for sale, you'll be able to buy it. What would you do with it?"

"Leave it. Use it for trail riding. And picnics." He gave me the eye.

"Perfect," I concluded. He lay back down, putting his arms behind his head.

"Well, that's why I'm telling you all this. I'm not the guy who wants a lot of nice things or to be with someone who wants a lot of nice things."

"You don't even have to say it, Neal."

"Well, I just figured I'd better."

As I began to know him, I realized he had a serious side. I wondered if he always did or if it came after his parents died. A side that has to deal with death and loss and uprootedness. He kept this side hidden most of the time, but it was always there a little bit. It made him more mature than most people his age. And I understood why I never saw him at parties. He had a serious desire to be home. He was not a traveler; he was a homebody who loved to have people around him he loved. This is what had been taken away from him, and like most people, he sought what he had lost, or at least a chance to recreate it.

"Are your grandparents doing okay financially?" I asked abruptly, then felt stupid, so I added, "Not that it's any of my business."

"Well, that's it. I *want* it to be your business. I don't want to burden you with it, but I want you to know what I'm up to." He took my hand then, and he played with my fingers. His hands were soft and warm. All of a sudden, I felt strangely like a grown-up. Talking about grown-up things. "My grandparents are going to be okay. Grandpa has his retirement, and they got the money from our house. They have medical bills, but Grandma is a penny pincher, so they'll be okay. That's why it's good I'll be living here. They need looking after. I don't know if Jessica will ever come back here."

"We're probably going to sell our cabin soon," I clutched his hand tightly for a moment. "My parents have been helping us with school tuition, and the taxes are getting huge."

"It's okay though if that happens, right? You'll always have this place, one way or another. Even if it's memories," he smiled gently. It didn't feel okay, but I had him, and that helped.

I leaned up onto him and kissed him. Then he pulled me in and hugged me, and we rolled over the soft moss. We did a lot of rolling that summer.

I whispered, "and by the way, all this, what you've been telling me, only makes me *more crazy* about you." I kissed him again. "I don't care about money. You gotta know . . . I—"

"Shhh . . ." he whispered in my ear. "Listen to the wind. Sounds like a storm's comin', doesn't it?"

"Yeah," I whispered back. "It's starting to feel chilly."

"Well, I know a good way to warm up," he warbled, and he squinted at me devilishly.

Then the trees hummed.

CHAPTER 15

Advancing
the Aqueduct

Two little girls, school-wizened but still completely impressionable, settle
eagerly onto their usual seats at the bar of the coffee shop. Their mom is off
sweating in the mirrored room. This is their time to drink steamy hot cocoa
and eat sugar cookies. More importantly, it is story time with their favorite
grandfather, "Big Red." Red, with his towering physique and his long gray
braids, displays his Dakota heritage, but it is his storytelling that blazes his
legacy. Sometimes his stories are funny and light. Sometimes they are about
courage and bravery. Sometimes they are about violent encounters and brutal
endings. Many would have his stories pulled from the repertoire, preferring
to save children from aspects of the big picture that prove horrific and
unsettling. Some will deny they are relevant or real, but stories have a power
all their own. A good storyteller knows this. These girls sit rapt with attention.

Though his stories sometimes come out in little bits and segments,
because coffee has to get poured, and money has to be exchanged, Red gifts
the little ones with his truth, history as he has seen and been told it. Every
living being over half a century is a living, expanding library. And as Red long
passed fifty, his hindsight flourished. He honed his stories not to trim the
truth but to enlighten it. Brutal as it often is, Red generously weaves it with the
best ingredient: hope.

"... The canoe travels slowly as it slides through the tall rice stalks,
and the soft breeze gently wrinkles the water,
causing the lanky reeds to sway.
The woman in the front, with her strong bronze arms, reaches
out and pulls her tightened fist along the stalk, and with nimble fingertips,
releases the rice kernels into the bowl that she holds below with the other
hand. Many in her tribe use two sticks to loosen the rice, but she does it faster
and more efficiently with her bare hands. The man, her husband, who sits
in the back, steadies and paces the canoe as she grasps and pulls, grasps and
pulls. The rice falls with a subtle rattling thump. In the early morning sun, it's

pleasurable, musical, and relaxing to gather wild rice in this unhurried way. Swish, zip, rattle, thump, swish, zip, rattle, thump."

"How did they do it, Red? Show us."

He gives them the hand gestures, but it's not as cool seeing it without wild rice paddies or stalks to enhance the motion. He goes to make an espresso shot and steam up some milk, then he comes back.

"This dance, of sorts, goes on until ten bowls are filled; then they stop and empty them into two side containers in the back of the canoe. The floating containers are on both sides of the birchbark, tied in along the top seam of the canoe.

"The side bowls are not full until the woman, let's call her the mom, because, well, she is a mom and—"

"Let's give her a name, how 'bout?"

"Okay. How about Raven Wing? That was her name. When she was little, she was Raven Girl, but she grew into the Raven Wing because she seemed to have the ability to talk to and fly with the ravens."

"What exactly are ravens, Big Red?"

"Well, you wouldn't know, now would you, because they aren't around these parts anymore. But they were around when Raven Wing lived here a long time ago, at least one hundred and fifty years ago. I actually think they disappeared right around when she did."

"What happened to them?"

"I really don't know for sure. I'm sure some of them flew off to other places. I hear they're common down south. Many died out, like most of my people who used to live around here."

"Do they look like blackbirds?"

"Mostly, they do. Their beaks are bigger, and they have fluffy necks and bigger tails. They're really smart, too. Smarter'n blackbirds. They make neat 'caw-caw' sounds, and they make a call that sounds a little like a drop of water plunking in the sink. Do you know that sound?"

"A-huh. But I've never heard a bird make it. I wish I could see a raven!" Hope clasps her hands.

"Okay. But let's get back to the story, Big Red. Tell more about Raven Wing. You said she could fly like a bird,

like a raven. How did she do that?"

"I'm not exactly sure. I don't mean she could put out her arms and float through the air. I mean more like in a spirit sense. Like she could fly where the birds could fly, when she was asleep, like in a dream."

"Why does that matter? I can fly in my dreams too."

"Sure, we all can. But she could fly and see specific things. Things the birds would show her. Like where to find game so her tribe could hunt. Where to find the berries to harvest and the wild rice paddies. Stuff like that."

"I guess it was a big deal then, huh?"

"Well, it was a way she helped her tribe survive. She held a high place of respect in her tribe because of her insights—you know, what she could see and stuff she knew."

"Alright. Did she look like a bird too? Did she have one of those pointy noses? Was she pretty?" Joy raises her eyebrows with curiosity.

"Oh, yes. She was beautiful. She had warm, loving arms. She was just the kind of mom anyone would wish for. She had long dark hair. She was thin, tall, and airy, like a bird's wing, which is maybe how she got her name. Can you picture her?"

"Yes. She's like a Disney princess in my mind."

"What about the dad. What was his name?"

"He was Wind in the Reed. He was born on a very windy day, so—"

"Wait. What'd he look like?"

"Oh. Hmm. Well, he was tall, too, but not as thin as Raven Wing. He had big shoulders and strong legs. He had long dark hair, too."

"Did he look like you?"

"Hmm. Well, yes, I guess, maybe in a way, he did."

"Only his hair wasn't gray like yours, huh?"

"Haha," Red laughs. "Yes, exactly. He was younger. Hardly old enough to be a dad. But he was . . . raising his family and helping his tribe."

"Okay. Keep going. What happens?"

"Alright. You have to be patient, then, and try not to interrupt and ask so many questions, right?"

"Yeah, be quiet, Joy. Let him tell the story, okay?"

They take careful sips of the hot cocoa and bites of the cookies. Red makes a few more trips back and forth behind the counter, then he comes back.

"So, Raven Wing and Wind in the Reed turn the canoe around and head for home, paddling in sync to keep the heavy canoe steady."

"Are you talking about Quartz Lake?"

"A-huh. Across the lake from Raven's Point. Has your mom ever shown you Battle Cove?" He raises his eyebrows.

"Yep."

"Hope! Now, who keeps interrupting?"

"Sorry. Keep going, Big Red."

"Okay. So, they get home and hit the shore, and as the tip of their canoe wedges into the sand, it lurches to a halt. Hearing the dull thud, an older woman, the grandma, emerges from her teepee and comes up to them. I know, I know." He stops and holds up his hand, "I'll be right back. Then I'll tell you her name, too."

He had to go in back and get a loaf of bread and fill a big lunch order, so it took him a while. Then he had to give the two girls peanut butter and jelly sandwiches. Finally, he got back to the story.

"The grandma, her name was Stands with the Sun. Let's call her Grandma, though, alright? She was a very happy, cheerful person, which is why they gave her a name with the sun in it."

"What does that mean, Red?"

"Oh, you know, she had a bright outlook on life. She was light, like the sun. She was liked by everyone in the tribe, too. She had a beautiful round face, I'm told. Oh, and she was a good storyteller, I might add." He hands over a couple of damp napkins, observing the sticky mess forming on their fingers and cheeks.

"Grandma wades into the shallow water and unties the thick cords holding a basket. She lugs it up onto the beach. Wind in the Reed unties the other basket while Raven Wing holds the canoe, then she grabs the front end and pulls it up and out of the water. She joins her mother, taking the baskets back to the teepees set back in the trees. They pour the rice out onto flat mats and spread it in a thin layer to dry in the sun. Several other villagers, too, are busy doing stuff, getting ready for the fall harvest celebration.

"Some were boiling birch sap syrup with rocks heated by fire; some skinning rabbit and deer pelts. Others were winnowing batches of roasted rice grains by tossing them up in big, flat sheets of birchbark. This is how they loosened the rice chaff, the little jacket keeping the rice warm, and released it to the wind. Some were cleaning fish at the water's edge; others were smashing raspberries and blackberries into big wooden bowls. Little kids were runnin' around pickin' wildflowers and reeds for bouquets."

"Did they go to school?"

"Joy, it's still summer," Hope sighs in exasperation. "They were still on summer vacation, right, Red?"

"Well, it was late summer, yes. But they didn't go to school the way you two go to school. They learned from their elders.

Their school was the wilderness.

They learned about nature and how to live in harmony with it."

"That sounds so fun."

"You'd probably get bored, Joy," Hope said.

"Neither of you would have been bored. Trust me. . . . I doubt they even knew what boredom was. . . .

"So, Wind in the Reed pokes his head in Grandma's teepee and goes in. Two babies play on a blanket on the dirt floor. He picks up the baby boy and kisses him on the cheek. Raven Wing comes in and takes the other baby up in her arms. Grandma comes—"

"Can we call her Grandma Sun? I like that better than just plain old Grandma, don't you, Hope?"

"A-huh." She nods. "Call her Grandma Sun."

"Okay. So, Grandma Sun comes in and begins to make breakfast. Neither Raven Wing nor Grandma Sun does much talking as they work, but a bad feeling, like an invisible fog, starts floating in around them, even though they're excited about their party coming up. It's a feeling so delicate it can't be put into words. Have you ever had that happen to you?"

"Oh, yes. I know what you mean exactly. One time, I had that feeling that something bad was going to happen, and then it did. I fell off the swing at school and got a big scrape on my knee, and I ripped my pants and everything. Remember that, Hope?"

"Yep."

"Exactly. And that bad feeling is around the tribe, too. Only I hate to say it, but what happens is a lot ickier than a scraped knee."

"Keep going!"

"Well, both Raven Wing and Grandma Sun feel it, but they don't know what to do about it. How many others had a bad feeling that day? I sometimes wonder that. How many of us know when a pivotal moment is coming in our destiny? I'm just asking that for you to think about. You don't have to answer now." Red leans forward and talks quietly, signaling an important part of the story is coming.

"Then it came, a monster-loud crashing noise. It wiped out the harmony of that dream-like day. A party of warriors comes barging in from the deep forest to take down the little village. They come swinging their weapons and clubs; they come kicking and choking, pummeling and smashing. They kill every living thing in their path. Seconds before, there had been a group of people, you know, maybe fifty or eighty of them, and a dozen teepees. One minute they were getting ready for their harvest party. The next," he snaps his fingers, "buckets of rice were spilled and trampled.

Red berries and blood stained the sand.

Screams echoed over the water and

into the sky.

Then chaos

faded

to whimpers.

And every last whimper is snuffed out with a blow;

nothing left but raw silence."

"Everybody dies?" Joy is horrified, scowling, and angry.

"Wait and listen. I know. It's terrible. But—" he puts his hand on her head.

"Did it really happen? For real, Big Red?" Hope wonders.

"I'm sad to say it did. I don't want you to be sad, though. It's—"

"But those were rotten, mean people! Why did they have to kill everyone? What about the little babies and the kids? Why did they have to kill them?"

"I hear ya. I know—it was wicked mean. The babies and kids didn't deserve to die. No one ever deserves that kind of terror. That's how life is sometimes, though, right? Bad things happen, and all we can do is try to recover and go on as best we can. But hear the rest of the story, okay? It's not all bad. Some of the villagers did survive."

"Wait! How come the ravens didn't warn Raven Wing? You said they always told her stuff, so she could help her tribe. Why didn't they 'caw-caw' and tell her?"

"That's a great question, Hope. I don't know; maybe they did try to warn her. I bet some ravens tried to peck at the attackers."

"I don't like this story, Big Red. I wish you didn't tell it to us." Hope sighs deeply and looks distraught.

"Well, hang in there, and listen to the end. Like I said, some of them survived. *Raven Wing* survives. Don't you want to hear about her? The worst part is over. You'll want to hear the rest."

"Okay. Fine." Joy puts her head down on her arm, which she has stretched out on the counter. The cocoa, cookies, and sandwiches are long gone.

Red can't explain the full details about the ideal and romantic memory of tribal life that lingered in the minds of the few survivors of that tribe. It existed in the minds of the slaughterers, too, before they, in turn, met the ground with a finalizing thump.

Before the wars,
     and the traders, settlers, and land prospectors
          filled their lungs with the pine-fresh northern air,
             that romantic, harmonic world was palpable.
It did exist. Life was not easier then. Not at all. But humans had a humbler relationship with the rest of the living world, and human consciousness lived in a more prayerful state, a sort of ecological reverence with nature. Somewhere within the human coil of memory, it is there.

The wielding of a sharp spear shattered it all.
          It was over so soon,
             almost like it never existed.

Raven Wing's village was prime real estate, an alcove sheltered from harsh weather but positioned to provide a tactical advantage against incoming hostility. The backdrop of the cove was thick with pines and shrubs, excellent hunting grounds, berry harvesting, and firewood supply. How the villagers were unaware of the attackers can never be precisely understood. One might theorize the tribe was having too much fun for their own good. The enemy timed a lucky strike. Whatever the case, fate spoke. The carnage became clear within minutes. Most were dead instantly, not even a scribble in the scrolls of history. Broad details can be found in the record books. But their names and faces are lost. Many believe the meek shall inherit the Earth. Some grander scheme is at play, the full roundabout, we know not.

Yet the hard facts are that a small village of Dakota Indians
was ground into the dirt to make room for the Ojibwa.
But the Ojibwa, too, watched their tribes diminish,
ground into the dirt the same way. Pioneers
manifested their great divine destiny.

The Dakota once roamed Minnesota, Wisconsin, the Dakotas, Iowa.

When the Ojibwa were shoved westward, like shields for the settlers, they
met arrows and rocks and clubs,
cunning and greed and survival instincts, and
war was their destiny. The tribes fought it out, leaving room for the
next wave.

One event dominoes another:
genocides,
relocation programs,
reservations,
boarding schools,
casinos,
drugs,
disappearing girls
—endless layers of loss,
poverty,
the kind that smothers a mother's,
a people's

breath
away,

spliced into Earth's flesh, weaving a bloody smear through the
delicate destiny of humankind. Generational trauma makes heavy the blood;
it endures time.

Red gives the girls the resin of hope that remains; it falls out the bottom
of the story like a sinker takes a fishing line down to catch the fish, and most
of the facts are grim. The man, Wind in the Reed, lies mortally stabbed,
crumpled, and bleeding at the entrance to his home. He dies trying to prevent
brutal killers from entering his sacred space. The two women, Raven Wing
and Grandma Sun, though struck and trampled, have fallen face down and
gone into stillness, shock, and trauma-induced paralysis. All around them are
dead.

Within the wrinkled circle of the soft dwellings, the smoldering light
recedes into steel twilight when Raven Wing feels one of her babies, clutched
in the wrap that held him to her waist, stir and cry out. She startles back to
life and, by instinct, stands up feebly. Her body, bruised and stiff, somehow
moves, and she holds her baby with a talon grip. She squirms and fights her

way out of the collapsed shelter into death's epicenter. Smoke and fetid air hover. She begins to feed him when her heart lurches to see her mother lying near her. Her eyes are open, not in death, but watching. They come together, mourning. The other baby wrapped to his grandmother does not move, no matter how many tears they leave on his soft round cheek. The smell of burnt everything permeates the stillness, and in the deepness of the dark night, they pack what they have left. They kiss their lost ones, and, somehow, they drag themselves away. They must leave before the marauders come back to pillage and claim their stakes. They limp noiselessly away in the night, struggling through the brambles.

They meander west, hoping to find a small village of their kind. And when they do, they stutter their story and hold out their arms for mercy, to be embraced and fed. What they know becomes tactical intelligence in the attempt for survival.

The onslaught of progress nearly wiped them off the pages of history entirely, if not for their gritty endurance, their ties to ancient visions, and their tears. Grasping to hold on to each other for hope, such fortitude foments reckoning. The day of redemption may remain unwritten in the digital calendars of the technologized world, but that does not invalidate its coming. On the contrary, it wields no digital weight, nor has it a need for such substantiation. It floats in the blood, streams invisible, and the dream of it is more important than the existence of it, but it's out there, nonetheless.

Some of the babies grew up, and they remembered the stories as witnesses and through the memories of their elders. They know their history within their cells,

just like the sediment at the bottom of the lake knows,
and the swirling ripples on the sky-reflected surface know.

The landscape of today is not the landscape of the future, nor is it
the landscape of then.
And somewhere in the wretchedly pillaged
waterways,
Gitchi Manito,
sacred god of rice,
wanders still.

CHAPTER 16

Frilly Rills

One busy shift deep into happy hour, with the lake splashing giddy waves across the docks, Margaret bee-lined over to me at the bar as I set drinks on my tray. She grabbed my elbow and leaned into my ear. "I've gotta talk to you," she muttered. Then she trotted off to take an order. I had seen her talking on the phone behind the bar. I suspected it was Blake. We met in the salad prep area.

"What?" I asked, sprinkling bacon bits.

"Candice is back in town."

"Who?"

"*Candice!* Blake's old girlfriend?" She stared at me incredulously. "She's home from Europe. See those two guys at the bar?" I didn't have to look.

"Yeah. They're loaded."

"I heard them say she's having a party at her house tonight. A sort of 'Welcome Home' party for her and all her friends."

"How do you know it's the same Candice?"

"They said Candice Comoro. I heard it loud and clear." She loaded her tray with four dinner salads. I grabbed dressings from the cooler.

"Is Blake going?" I drizzled deep red French dressing.

"No, so he *says*. He's going to a bachelor party tonight. Some friend of his is getting married."

"So . . . " I started saying, not sure where she was going with this. She started walking briskly away.

Tipping her head back at me, she whispered, "You and I are goin' spyin' tonight!"

I stared back at her, wondering what she was talking about, as she dropped into the crowd. The buzz of happy hour must have gotten to her. But then, I got excited. Spying on rich people while they party? It did sound like fun. God knows, from next door, I had witnessed enough Crandahl bashes throughout the years, but usually, it was the older crowd gettin' down over there. Watching people my own age would be interesting. I wondered how different it would be. I was sure there would be handfuls of younger versions of Mrs. Crandahl in sexy cocktail wear, done up from head to toe, swishing martini glasses, and not eating the finger food.

I had sometimes snuck out on our dock, lying low, observing with a unique view while they entertained. I remembered being privy, more than once, to some distinguished gentleman stooping to make what looked to me like "a pass" at Mrs. Crandahl. She kissed a lot of men on her dock, and never once did I see that one of them was her husband. He probably had his own scenarios going on somewhere else. Mrs. Crandahl liked moonlit water. I'm sure it made her skin glow just right. I hated picking up soggy cigar butts that drifted to our beach the next day.

I wondered what Margaret hoped to accomplish. It couldn't be simple curiosity. We discussed it further at the end of our shift while we rode our bikes home.

"I think he's freaked because she's back," Margaret explained, her face tightening as she leaned over the handlebars.

"When did she get home?"

"I don't know exactly, but he's, like, pulling away from me a little bit. I had no idea she was back until I heard his friend Chad bring her up a few days ago. He said he was over at her house, and she was looking hot. It was awkward because Blake didn't say anything back to him. Then they sort of exchanged this look. They didn't say any more, and I didn't get into it. And my God, his mother brings her up every time I'm over there. I think *she's* in love with the girl. I think she wants Blake to marry her or something."

"What? No." I shook my head. "I'm sure she loves you more. You kick ass. Although I do agree, she *is* a bit out there."

"I'm telling you, she doesn't like me. She thinks I'm a hick. She has this critical way of looking at me. She analyzes what I'm wearing all the time."

"Don't worry about her. She's a superficial, empty-headed bimbo."

"Yeah. Well, she has a lot of influence over Blake."

"I truly doubt that. Blake is way smarter than his mommy." I looked at her, but she wasn't smiling. "You think he's going to the party?"

"I hate to say it, but yes. Did you see me on the phone? He called to tell me he was going to be out of the picture tonight and that I shouldn't try to catch up with him because of this big bachelor party. He doesn't usually have to emphatically tell me to leave him alone. I don't sit around and wait for him to get home at night, ya know?"

"God, Margaret. Forget it. He's a moron. You are so *not* a cling on."

"Then what's with that phone call? Calling me at work? Making *specifically* sure I won't try to find him? Does he tell me she's having a party tonight? NO, I hear it from two drunks at the bar!"

"Maybe he doesn't *know* she's having a party."

"Yeah. Maybe. That's what we're gonna find out. We have to go there tonight. Do you know how to get to her house by car?"

"God, yes. Her house is massive; you can't miss it. It's all marked off with a stone wall, and there's a huge bronze elk with a big rack at the entrance." I huffed up the last hill before we glided down into our driveway. A doubles match was in session on the Crandahl's tennis court, Mrs. Crandahl and three of her posh lady friends. They all had cute coordinating skirts and tops. They moved in a polished sort of way as if they were more conscious of what they looked like as they swished their rackets than trying to play real tennis. It was a beautiful afternoon—light breeze, sunlight reflected on the transparent blue-green water, and it radiated invitations *come swim, come swim, come swim* with every shimmer on the horizon.

I envisioned us getting busted by Candice while hiding in her bushes, so I decided we'd better get a little drunk before we went in, or I would be totally embarrassed if we got caught. If we were drunk, we could just say someone at Harbor View told us about it. I told Margaret my idea, and she heartily agreed it was a good cover. Part of me wanted to throw an 'I told you so' out there. In a low place inside, I was hoping a little bit for some concrete proof of his asshole-ness, some affirmation of what I felt I had known about him all along. Blanketing that thought was how Margaret would feel, and I already wanted to punch him.

Neal was not available that night, so I could gladly devote myself to Margaret and our adventure. He told me during my burger delivery that he intended to go out just before dawn in his kayak to see the sunrise from the sandbar at Raven's Point. He'd never known any history related to that part of the lake until he started doing the boat tours, and he felt a communion with the place. He wanted to be there to sit quietly and see what kinds of feelings or sensations may arise. He loved to do stuff like that. I had never seen a sunrise from that spot, and neither had he, but it was one of his goals for the summer. He had only a one-seater kayak, so, for the time being, he would scope it out himself if the water was calm that morning.

But I was a girl with some of my own dreams and ideas, too. I hoped we would go out there for a sunrise together, and he might give me a ring or something. I wasn't hung up on getting married, but I did imagine us together in the future. I felt sure we were already bound to each other, so I was in no hurry. I had my year of school yet, and he had his first year of teaching coming up.

I wanted to collaborate on his horse ranch for disadvantaged kids. I wanted to make a mark of some sort, too, a positive mark. He deserved a chance to see his dream through, and I admired his vision. It may have been a byproduct of his grief, but it may have been innate from the start of his life here on Earth. He might have been born *that* good. It's hard to know how much we are *born* good, and how much what we do with our choices and the time we are given *makes us* good. Or bad.

I figured I could at least help with the business and promotional side of his dream. I knew we both loved Quartz, and it would be a part of us and our story forever. That part made me the happiest. To have such a love for a place in common. It proved an ample base. I believed our time was coming. It was a nice fantasy to think about being proposed to at Raven's Point, a place full of memories and love, in the middle of a sunrise with so much promise in the air. I was so young, and love had turned me to syrup.

I played it out in my mind as my arms swung up over my head, one, then the other, pushing the creamy water behind me with my cupped hands while I did the front crawl down the shore. Emotions charged me as I envisioned it; I felt like a bionic woman cutting through the water. I felt I could have swum the entire perimeter of the lake that day. I didn't realize I left Margaret behind until I drew up to our dock and stood in the waist-deep water breathing hard. She was three docks back. I stretched while I waited for her. The idea that I could join my destiny with Neal's, this beautiful, unique spirit of a companion, made me feel like I was in free-fall. I felt fluid, as though I might morph into the water, all my molecules

melting into the big lake,

to flow into the wide ocean someday. It's like I had a deeper knowledge of it, had already experienced the whole of it, the whole life of us, and it floated in a timeless, perimeter-less state within me, and what came through, what resonated, what pulsated, through the elastic grid of my body, was the emotion of it. Almost like it was already a memory. It made me soft and mushy, permafrost. I barely stood solid in the water. I felt not only waterlogged by the water, my fingers wrinkly and soft, but the liquidity embodied me in the floaty qualities of the water itself, water and blood merging. I wish I could have held my sensations captive in a bottle. Then I could use that captured, charged energy like a drug. But even more, I wish I could have known that such feelings sometimes signal the coming of a transformation or a shift in the scaffolding of one's destiny.

CHAPTER 17

Casting Karma

The water seems dormant, still, and flat like mercury, a mirror of the gray-domed, dawning sky. The girls climb sleepily out of the wagon as it draws up to the edge of the hill, where the staircase leads down to the beach. Eleanor searches for a light spot, some weak point whereby the sky will crack under the hammer-like pressure of the rising sun and break into fluffy white florets. All three of them are wearing shorts and sandals, but she's wondering if she was too optimistic about the day's weather. Luckily, they've brought jackets. She scans the silver plain for a boat. She listens for the sawing hum of a motor, and, sure enough, far up the shore, just coming round the point, is the boat, the only one in sight. The little Alumacraft is towing another small boat about the same size.

"Mama, why'd we have to come so early?" Joy turns toward her mom and grabs her free hand. "I'm too tired. Will you carry me?"

"Oh, it's gonna be fun! Let's get your life preservers on, quick, before Red gets here. See his boat down there?" She points. They all stare for a moment.

"Yes! Yes! Hurry. Here he comes! See him, Hope?" Joy begins jumping in anticipation, hardly seeming sleepy. She holds out her arms to slip into the life jacket. Eleanor zips up their windbreakers. Then she clips one girl, then the next, into their complicated life jackets. She grabs the soft cooler with the lunch in one hand and holds Joy's hand with the other. Hope trails behind; she is scanning the cloud dome also.

Down on the dock, they watch their friend Red Tatéweh coming closer. The girls are waving their hands somewhat frantically when Eleanor tells them to calm down.

"Remember, girls, Red is a grandpa. He loves kids calm and cool. Be cool, okay? If you wiggle or go nuts in the boat, we'll tip over." Not likely, but Eleanor knows they don't know this.

"Why's it taking him so long?"

"Why's he got two boats?"

Eleanor squats and looks at them steadily, raising her eyebrows. "Well, you don't know the adventure you're in for, do you?"

"Come on, Mama, tell us!" Joy is jumping again.

"Well, if I knew, I'd tell you!"

"How come you don't know? Why are you taking us on an adventure that you don't know what it is? What if it's dangerous, and we get killed?"

"Come now, you know Red. Would he do that to us?"

"Huh uh! Big Red is fun! I do wish he'd *hurry up!*"

As he approaches, Eleanor sticks out her leg to brace the edge of the boat from knocking the dock. Red flips the engine into neutral and grabs hold of the post. He says, "Turtle rescuers, step right up. All aboard!" He stands and holds his hand up to stop Joy from leaping aboard. "Enter at your own risk! Oh, and be careful." He grabs her hand like he's grabbing a princess's hand and helps her jump down steadily onto the middle seat. "Joy, you and Hope sit up front. Eleanor, you sit in the middle." He winks at Eleanor.

He's wearing a windbreaker that matches the dark gray shimmers in the water behind him. His long, mostly-gray hair, which he has pulled back into a ponytail, is just the color of the lighter gray tones, blending him with the water. His brown skin and wrinkling, twinkling green eyes, framed by his wire-rim glasses, are vivid in the crisp morning air. He seems to carry a light aura, maybe because of how his hair matches the light in the clouds, or maybe it's something else that gives him a special brilliance. A seeming angelic timelessness or a living history. Eleanor's eyes are held by the sight of him and the peace and strength he brings. She begins to understand the treasure of being in the presence of elders, like being with her parents and grandparents, whom she misses so much.

"Big Red, are we gonna rescue a turtle?" Hope asks, her hands snug in her pockets.

"Well . . . not technically *a* turtle, but turtle *eggs*. Lots of 'em," he explains. "See those buckets?" They look back to see a collection of old white buckets, the kind used to hold paint, with thick metal handles. "We're gonna scoop up as many turtle eggs as we can, and move 'em to a different part of the lake."

"How come we had to get up so early? Can't we do that any old time?" Joy asks.

"Not exactly. Turtles around here only lay eggs during early summer, and unfortunately for the mamas, where they normally nest is getting all dug up. The eggs are gonna get crushed or buried, and the baby turtles won't hatch."

"Why?" Joy leans against the boat. "Will the mamas know where the baby eggs are going?"

"That's the tricky thing. The mamas won't know. We're going from one end of the lake to the other, a long way. But the momma turtles don't worry about the babies once they're born. Turtles aren't like humans. Moms don't raise baby turtles; the babies fend for themselves once they hatch."

"Where're we going, Red?" Eleanor asks. "Is it where I think?"

"The channels. They're filling in the first channel and building up the shoreline. That corporate retreat center? Deconstruction has begun. Wait till you see."

"How can they fill in a channel? I mean, really, how do they do that?" Eleanor's voice rises with an edge. Both girls check out of the grownup talk, leaning down over the seat in the space between them. They had stashed little toy ponies in their pockets, now they're trotting the ponies back and forth, making whinnying sounds and chattering.

"Hmmm . . . how do I begin to answer?" He replies calmly. "You know a lot of money changed hands. How it passed an environmental impact study and community uproar is beyond me, but all proper signatures appeared. It's a done deal. They started moving the next day. Now, all we can do is do what we can, right? I remember a fortune cookie I read once, the night I met my wife, in fact. It said: 'The greatest mistake is to do nothing because you think you can do only a little.' I'm getting too old to strap myself to the bulldozers, but I still got some fight."

"Yeah, you do. Thanks for taking us along." She could berate herself for not being part of that community uproar, but since she was a kid, she witnessed the relentless mechanisms of progress transform the lake from wilderness to tourist mecca; she had no hope for any protest.

"I can't imagine how much money they're literally *sinking* into this project," Red continues. "I don't think a structure will last fifty years before its foundation collapses. But who am I to say? Let 'em do what they want and figure it out the hard way, I guess."

"You mean because the ground is so unstable?"

"Exactly. I can't believe there's enough sand and dirt in the world to soak up the water reserve there. It's a spring! For the whole lake!" He breathes heavily. "Enough to build a structure? Especially one as big as the gig they got planned? I tell ya . . ." he closes his eyes. Eleanor doesn't say anything. She doesn't know what to say. Red is rarely speechless.

"When I get too old to do this, I've taught you and yours what to do for the next time," he smiles, raising his bushy eyebrows above his glasses. They've been crossing the lake, heading to the channels, an area loaded with memories for Eleanor.

Eleanor says. "Why let it get the best of us? My dad always said 'time marches on.'"

"Indeed, it does. Still, I don't see how things can keep going the way they are. You can't drink your own piss and survive for long, now can ya? It's a question of—"

"Grandpa Red, you said a bad word."

"Sorry, Joy," he grimaces. The morning sun has eased up over the trees in the east, and the clouds have begun to break into soft round rosettes, and rosy hues emerge against the vibrating blue. It's a moving painting. The water, still flat, dances with streaks and shimmers of gold and pink. The girls look up every so often to gauge the boat's progress and gaze in trance-like silence at the colors playing with the water. Suddenly, Hope pipes up. "Big Red, you still haven't said why we had to come out so early. I don't see any other boats. Anywhere."

"That's it—this is a secret. I don't want anyone to see us."

"We're not doing something bad, are we?"

"No, not bad at all, but something that certain people might want an explanation for, and I don't wanna have to explain. To anyone. Do you?"

"No—you can do the talking. If we get caught, I'll just sit here quietly."

"Good for you. That's exactly what you should do. But no one's going to catch us. We have to get to shore and dig up the eggs and quickly put them into those buckets before the workers come to work for the day. They might not be happy we're walkin' around where they work, see?"

"What if they come while we're there?"

"Well, I've been watching for a couple days. They don't come to work until nine o'clock. We'll be long gone by then. I want you girls to help me scout out the nesting spots. I watched the mother turtles lay the eggs, and I drew myself a diagram so we could find them, but you think you can help me look?"

"Oh, yes! Mom says I have a keen eye!" Joy says. "How many are there?"

"Good question! I don't know for sure, but I only have ten buckets so I hope we can get 'em all. I don't think there are more than ten batches, but I'm not sure."

"When will we be there? I'm getting bored. Will you tell us a story?"

"Not right yet. Maybe later when we're crossing the lake. That'll take a while going this speed." He looks at Joy; she's waiting for more, her expression expectant. "See, right over there, next to that big bluff? That's where we're going. Let's make sure we approach quietly in case a few mama turtles are swimmin' around still."

"If we see one? Can we catch it?" Hope asks. "Wouldn't it be nice if we could catch the mamas and take 'em to the other side with the baby eggs too?"

"It sure would. I don't know if I can catch the mamas. They're pretty fast, and I didn't bring a big net."

"They can swim across the lake anytime. They'll be happy to know their babies will survive in a better place, away from all this construction."

Eleanor wonders about this. She wonders what a mother turtle would feel about this situation. *She seems stoic, to my stupid human eyes, but is she? Would she see the greater good going on? Was the greater good going on? Or would she see stupid following stupid, or would she see evil? My heart tells me we're doing right, but how does a person truly trust the heart? Was what felt good to me really what was good for all or even the mother turtle? Do I have a right, or an obligation, or a fifth sense that justifies my getting involved? Why do we second guess advocacy? Don't so many of us wish we would have done more when we look back in hindsight?* She wishes the turtles would tell her. She hopes for a sign.

"Look, I see the channels," Joy points. Sure enough, the ground underwater has risen up and become visible as they cross over the shallow bed that creates a perimeter around the channels. Eleanor's mind drops back in time. The memory dial spins to a classic summer day at the lake. She and her sisters, sitting in the old rowboat, her brother maxing the throttle of the little fifteen-horse, clipping through the chop, hair flying, spray flying, the nets and oars rattling against the aluminum sides. They'd take turns standing up while racing along, wagging their arms as they'd yell and whoop, even though they knew they weren't supposed to. And they'd snort and cackle at their silliness. Her brother, rolling his eyes and trying not to laugh, and all of them singing. Remembering, her heart crinkles up like a smiling face. Then as they begin to tool through the tall green reeds, another memory rolls in of a dark and grim late summer day, lying curled up in the bottom of a canoe all by herself, floating to nowhere. She turns her head sharply to realign with the moment at hand, her girls, her friend Red, and the turtles.

First, she notices the tree stumps, the vacant ghostly feeling of the gaping hole where the giant fir trees had recently stood. Pine sap scent fills the air. Like blood oozing, like flowers around a coffin around an altar. The pile of dead tree trunks stacks high like a dent in the scene, a poorly angled backdrop. It looms over the top of the hill, quite a distance back, but dominating the scene in a macabre sort of way. Next, she observes the bulldozers, three of them,

fat, hideous, mustard yellow brutes, menacing and abnormal amid nature, even in their resting state. Mechanical hounds, here to do the master's bidding. All over the hill are shards

of trees,

branches, bark, pine needles,

scattered, frayed, disheveled.

Only the red blood is missing.

Red maneuvers the boat, landing smack in the middle of the new beach. A narrow beach had already existed, but the chopping down of at least two-dozen ancient trees has expanded it. Transformed it into an entirely different place, really. As the hill has been sliced into, the incline has become steeper. A giant boulder tier system that is beginning to take shape remedies the angle. Piles of new soft sand and separate piles of big rocks sit here and there, waiting to be placed: a layer of rock wall, another cut into the hill, a level of soft brown sand, another layer of rock wall, another cut into the hill, another level of soft brown sand, and finally a third tier. The new shoreline stretches two hundred feet across and at least as far back, stopping abruptly on both sides with the untreated steep hill and thicket of pines.

One side weaves around into the big bluff, upon which three new mansions have been dug into the hill. The structures, too, feel abrupt, distinct by their clean-cut corridors, glossy cathedral windows, tidy new brick, zigzagging steps, and electronic trolley lifts. New metal docks protrude from the bushy edge. Boat lifts sit on both sides of the docks, holding an assortment of speed boats, pontoons, whalers, fishing boats, and jet skis.

The other side of the new beach stretches out straight for a half-mile or so, then takes a distinct curve, coming together with the opposite shore, narrowing and forming a natural channel that leads into a round inlet where the Harbor View Inn and a busy public boat launch is located. Soon, boat traffic will emerge from that opening, and she feels urgency.

She kicks off her sandals and climbs out, helping the girls. Red cautions, "Now be careful! Don't run on the sand here; there are little nests everywhere!"

Red rolls up his khakis, though they're already wet past the knees. Then he's back behind the engine, untying the towline of the second boat. He turns and throws the line to Eleanor, who takes the front end and lifts it; her heels sink deep into the new sand as she pulls the boat up until it is secured. Red does the same with the first boat. Eleanor calls the girls over. They climb all over the piles of rocks.

"Hey, you two, get over here! The last thing we need is an avalanche of big rocks, and one of you lost underneath. Come 'ere!" They scamper up to her. Red has the buckets and shovels. He gestures for them to come over and hands Eleanor a shovel. He says to the girls, "Now you two, separate these buckets and set them in a straight line, right here. We have to be as quiet and as fast as we can."

"Like 'Jack be nimble, Jack be quick,' right?" says Joy, jumping and flapping with excitement.

"Exactly. Nimble and quick! The turtle nests will be the candlesticks. We have to make sure we step over them, not on them. Okay?"

"But where are they?" Hope looks around. "I don't see any eggs anywhere."

Red turns and observes the shore. He walks to an area next to a pile of rocks. "Come here. Look." He squats down. Everyone gathers. "See this small indentation. You can barely see it. That's why we have to be careful *not* to step on them. We have to be like Jack. Look at this little gap. If I dig into this, there will be eggs here. I drew a map, see." From his windbreaker pocket, he pulls out an impressively detailed sketch, including where the tree stumps had been before they were extracted. Who knew he was a sketch artist? They stare at it for a minute, a little in awe, then he hands it to Eleanor, who notes it's been dated. "I watched for days until they came. They were late this year."

"My God, Red. You're a fanatic." They grin at each other.

"Well, come on, let's start digging!" Joy leans down to start. Red grabs her hands.

"Wait! Listen. The digging part is your mother's and my job," he looks intently at Joy. "You and Hope get the buckets ready, so we can drop the nests in. We have to use shovels, and we have to try to get the whole nest, making sure the eggs stay surrounded by sand. We don't want to expose or crack the eggs. They need to feel safe and warm in their little pile of sand. If they get out, they could get too cold or exposed, then the shells might break, and we have no baby turtles. You see?" He looks over at Hope, then back at Joy, still holding her hand.

"As I dig 'em up, you have to be right here with a bucket, waiting for me to gently put the sand in. Then I'll carry it back to the boat, and you get ready with another bucket. BUT! Here's the tricky part for you, little girls. You can't be running up and down the sand here. Look around. Do you see?" He starts observing the landscape himself.

Joy is eager to begin helping. "Is that one over there?" She points. Red looks.

"Yes, maybe. You may be right about that. Let's get this one here first, then we'll go over there and check it out," he stabs his big wide shovel into the sand, in a perimeter around the little groove. Sometimes he stands on the back edge of the shovel base to push the shovel deeper down. "Sand is kind of tricky, girls. It doesn't want to stay where it's put. It wants to slide around. That's why we have that big round shovel your mom's holding there. After I get through loosening up the sand, your mom's gonna scoop the whole thing with her shovel, and then, I'll show you what to do next." He keeps digging out around the hidden nest. "Like I said, we have to gently get the whole pile into the bucket without disturbing it too much. Watch."

"That looks like a snow shovel," Hopes notes. "Like for a giant!"

"You're right, young lady. It is!" He finishes his parameter dig. "You'll see how perfect it is for scooping turtle nests, too." He trades shovels with Eleanor, who is quietly observing and having doubts about how well she will be able to scoop sand without letting it all sift out. Red adeptly digs out a little opening and wedges the scoop shovel into the sand at a wide-angle, into and under the dug-out circle. He slowly and steadily pushes down and forward, rotating the snow shovel's handle back and forth, moving the hidden nest and all its sand onto the base. The big sand pile settles, nicely intact, on top. "Take the bucket, and hold it sideways, see, like this," he turns the bucket horizontal and sets it next to the scoop shovel, the handle of which is horizontal, almost level with the sand. "Hope, hold the bucket steady, lean on it a little, so it doesn't move."

He points to the flat shovel, "Eleanor, while I lift with this shovel, use that shovel to stop the sand from falling off the front. Hold it up against the front rim until I can tilt the scooper back slightly." They work together; as he lifts and slides the scooper up and out, she uses her shovel to support and hold the sand in place. Then he turns the scooped-out sand, heavy with the nest of turtle eggs, and gently places it inside the bucket. Once the scoop is inside the bucket, he looks at Eleanor, "Before we tip the bucket upright, let's pile more sand in there, as much as we can, really, without making the bucket too heavy to carry." She scoops sand into the bucket while he loosens the scooper out of the bucket until the bucket is ready to be tipped up without upsetting the sand.

"Big Red, I didn't see any eggs in there. I don't think there are any," Hope shakes her head reluctantly.

He leans down close to her face and says in a loud whisper, "That's exactly what I want to hear. Trust me, Hope. They're there. I've investigated turtle nests. I know what I'm doin'." He smiles at her. She smiles back. "We don't *want* to see the eggs. If we see one, that egg might not make it! Let's try to get all the nests out without seeing one egg!" He holds up a finger.

He stands up and carefully tips the bucket upright. The sand settles without too much disturbance. "Here we go, bucket number one! I'll drop this in the boat, and we're ready for number two!"

"I kind of want to see one. I want to see what they look like."

"I know what you mean. They do look pretty cool."

"Are they white like eggs we eat?"

"Are they pink, purple, and yellow like Easter eggs?"

"Not exactly. They're a lot smaller and kind of yellowish-brown. We could probably dig them out with a spoon. They'd fit nicely on the round part of a teaspoon. I'll show you a picture in a book, okay? Remember, our goal is to NOT see one, right?"

"Yep!"

He picks up the shovels and hands them to Eleanor. He grabs the bucket and walks toward the towboat. He turns his head and says back to them, "most of the nests will be up along the hillside. So, you can see why we had to get here quick." He drops the bucket into the boat and grabs another. "We'll find a nest or two down here, but they seem to prefer plodding up an incline before they dig. This area is perfect for nesting. I guess I should say it *was* perfect."

"Here, look here, Big Red. Remember where I said? Is this one?" Joy is standing in the spot she identified. He goes over and looks down. "I think so! Good job, Joyous! Let's dig. Here, you hold the bucket. Hope, you go scouting— be extra careful now." Hope tiptoes exaggeratedly away as they begin the process to fill bucket number two.

They work smoothly. Hope makes a perfect scout; she is more patient, observant, and calm than Joy, who is the designated bucket fetcher, a job she relishes because it involves a quick relay to and from the boat, and she gets to be right amid the action of the digging and scooping. For over an hour, they work non-stop, and every bucket is filled with sand, and some with dirt too. Every so often, the girls wander off and explore. They have to take breaks, but they do make the process faster, so Eleanor often calls them back.

Soon, the whole beach is pocked with holes amid the construction. Red and Eleanor use the shovels to dump sand into each hole, and stomp on it, to level it out. They sweep their shovels over the top to smooth out the sand and eliminate big footprints. Here and there, they use their hands and shuffle their feet, to sweep and scatter sand to make it look even and undisturbed.

Eleanor helps Red shove the towboat out into the water; it's loaded down and heavy with the buckets. The girls jump in, and then Eleanor pushes them out, and Red gets in, holding the towline for the second boat. Eleanor holds the front tip of the boat, standing ankle-deep in the cold, mushy sand, waiting while he re-ties the two boats together, and they get the second boat positioned out of the way. Red pulls the starter cord and revs the engine slightly. Eleanor gives a last shove off for the motorboat and hoists her knee up on the tip, swinging her other leg around to climb aboard. After so many years of jumping on boats, it felt good to be doing it again, even if circumstances had changed.

"Good job, Mama!" Hope smiles broadly at her. Eleanor smiles back and pats her head as she steps over the first seat where the girls are sitting. She holds out her hand flat, and all three give her an energetic slap. She sits as Red steers the boat around to head back south across the lake. They are so loaded down, the engine sputters slightly, and Eleanor says a quick prayer that the motor, and the girls, for that matter, hold up for the long trip. But she's got food to while away some time. Never underestimate the pleasure of a picnic. She pulls the soft cooler onto her lap and unzips a pouch with four slender water bottles inside. She hands them out, hearing the ice in them clinking.

As they get underway, Eleanor looks back at the old nesting ground. She scans the area for anyone who may have observed their doings, but all around is eerily vacant, even as the morning gray gloom has been replaced by bright sunshine. She feels like crying, thinking of the old trees and the mama turtles. But the puttering boat and the gulps of cold water going down her throat lift her up, and she turns to look on the wide-open lake before them.

In the open bay, boaters are popping up on the water everywhere. Most of them are fishers, but some are already out joyriding in the glory of the morning sun and rising temperatures. None are close to them, so they probably don't have to worry about getting caught, but Eleanor knows Red will hug the shoreline, and the chances of having to explain will be minimal.

They munch on fresh fruit, carrots, cheese and crackers, and muffins. Red has a thermos of hot coffee and a cup for Eleanor. The steady hum of the engine and the sway of the boat, are a peaceful duet. The girls, with bellies full, hold long reeds they plucked from the shore. They pretend the reeds are fishing poles, dangling over the side, and they gaze dreamily into the water.

"So, where are we going with our refugees, Red?" Eleanor says, sipping her coffee.

"I don't know if you've ever been to Green Lake. Have you?"

"Past the entrance to Quartz River?" She squints, trying to picture where an entire lake might be that she doesn't know about.

"Yeah, it's literally at the southern rim. There's a short little channel and it opens into a marshy little lake. It's about the same size as Timmins Lake, by the yacht club, you know? More like a little cove than a true lake, but they call it Green Lake."

"Through that super shallow area?"

"Yeah, exactly," he nods. "You gotta be in a small boat like this to get back in there. We'll get in easily. We have to get around Raven's Point and hope to God we don't run across the sheriff."

"Oh, gosh. Is that . . . likely?"

"Well, you've seen the sheriff's boat around lately, haven't you? They're making lots of money ticketing tourists for not having enough life jackets and for speeding through no-wake zones. Haven't you noticed?"

"Well, seeing as I only have a canoe and I can hardly ever take it out with all the boat waves and drunks everywhere, no, I haven't. We look pretty conspicuous towing this boat."

"Do you think I should cover the other boat? I brought a big canvas." He's considering the idea and looks at his watch. "I actually think I should. Even at nine-thirty a.m., it's already pretty hot. I don't want the eggs overheating. I'll pull the boat up and get in; you keep driving this boat while I do that, so we don't lose time. If we do get pulled over, I'll think of something. I'll say we have buckets of bait for our fishing expedition. Hopefully, they won't wonder where the fishing poles are."

He steps deftly into the back boat. Eleanor notes how big and flat his bare feet are, and though he is big and ancient, he's surprisingly agile. Under the back seat, he reaches down and pulls out a large, dirty white canvas tarp. He unfolds it and flips it out over the boat. He leans across each side, tucking the ends under the buckets. Eleanor tools down the shore. Rarely do they encounter people on their docks, and when they do, they exchange a friendly wave.

Red resumes driving, and the girls are sitting up because they are approaching Raven's Point, and already a smattering of boaters are parked on the sandbar that extends to a distinct point. Several people are swimming; some are listening to tunes, drinking cocktails, smoking cigarettes, and

laughing. They skirt past
undisturbed.

"Big Red, did you know our grandpa?" Joy turns around to ask.

"Yes, Joy. I knew him well. We spent many summers at the same resort. I'm sure your mom told you about Quartz Shores Resort. My dad was the maintenance man there. Your grandpa 'an me were around the same age, and we had lots of crazy times together."

Eleanor looks at Red, remembering when they discovered this weird connection. One day, when she mentioned her father by name, Red gasped with the sudden memory and realization of who he was. He hadn't seen her father for years. They had gone their separate ways when Red joined the military and then became a protestor, and Eleanor's father went to college and on to career and family. Yet, he held that friendship dear, making the protective bond for Eleanor even more tenacious. Eleanor loves knowing he was her father's friend, someone who knew him long before she was born. In a weird way, it makes her miss him, but being around Red makes her feel like she is in his presence somehow, too. Could he have brought them together?

"What was he like, Big Red?" Both girls edge closer, sitting on the middle seat, leaning on their mom.

"You know . . . he was a lot like me. Big and goofy looking. Fun and funny. He liked to have a good time. He was a good storyteller. And he was a good athlete. When the resort finally got a speedboat one year, we were about sixteen then, your grandpa was the first to learn how to water-ski. And he and his brother taught everyone at the resort how to do it. He loved to do that!"

"His brother was his twin, like us!" Joy notes.

"You're right! Isn't that cool?"

"Ah huh."

"Did he teach you how to ski?" Hope asks.

"Oh, you betcha. We used to ski and pull ourselves along behind that boat on anything we could find, long wooden boards, the oars from the fishing boats, you name it. And we used to go fishing and hunting together. Catching frogs and lizards. One summer, there was a rumor a famous criminal was staying at the resort. No one knew for sure if it was him because I guess he was really good at disguising himself and changing his appearance. Your grandpa, his brother Abe, and I decided we were gonna sneak a peek in his window one night to figure out if he really was who everybody thought he was. No one could get a look at him. He didn't come out much during the day, but I guess he'd go out in the dark and hit the night spots."

"Didja see him, then?"

"We snuck up there, alright. I sat on the ground on all fours, and your grandpa stepped up on my back to get a look in the window. There was just a tiny little triangle of open window between the closed curtains; you know, a perfect little peephole. He told me he could see the old guy cleaning his gun, right at the dining room table! Well, of course, I had to get a look, so we rotated places. You know what I saw? When I was looking at him through the window, I swear, he was sittin' at a table, and he raised his hand like a gun and pretended to shoot at me! Scared me so much I fell down. We got up and trotted atta there so fast we almost blew a fuse! We got back to our cabins and laughed and laughed and had the best time telling everyone our story. Of course, we had to describe him, too. Everyone was askin' 'what'd he look like?' 'What was he wearin'?'"

"What *was* he wearing?"

"Oh, gosh. Just what you'd expect a criminal to wear. He had a big wide hat, like a cowboy, and a red bandana around his neck. He wore old blue jeans and a denim work shirt with a collar. He had pasty white skin and a nice mustache. And boy, did he have beady eyes! He had boots on, too. Like he was gettin' ready to go out—at least we thought so. It all happened so quick."

"Then what happened?"

"Well, the next day, you'll never believe . . . the police came to the resort. They arrested him, and he had a buddy hiding out there too. We heard he had thousands a dollars hidden. Oh, yeah, and a pile of guns too!"

"Were you scared he might shoot ya, Big Red?"

"No, we were too stupid and young to think we'd get hurt. I think he was just messing with us. Who knows? He seemed to be smilin' at me when he raised his gun. But I didn't stick around to find out."

"I woulda been scared."

"After he got arrested, kids at the resort snuck into his cabin tellin' stories about him late at night, scaring ourselves and making ourselves laugh silly. We had some great times in those days."

"Mama had some great times too. She tells us about her memories when she was little," Hope smiles as she leans into her mom's lap.

"Well, and here you are, right now, making great memories to tell your grandkids someday, right?"

"Yup. That's right. I'm gonna tell 'em about the time we rescued all the baby turtles and brought them to a new home," Joy looked out beyond the boat. "Are we gonna be there soon?"

"See that opening? That's where we're going." He points straight ahead at a long stretch of shoreline not far ahead. "We're going to put all these eggs in a little lake tucked back in here. It's swampy and shallow, and not many boats go in. At least not right now. Who knows about the future? For now, it'll be a great place for baby turtles to grow up. Hopefully, they'll come here to lay their own eggs one day."

Joy raises her hands in salute. They continue.

"See how shallow it is? You could stand in it, almost. It's good it's so shallow; it keeps big boats out." Red steers straight for the opening. They come up to it and easily go through. On the other side, a small roundish pond, perfect for a hockey rink, many would say, beholds them.

Shallow, reedy grasses rim the entire shore. Red steers to the far end, across from the opening, where a narrow sandy sweep of shoreline rests. It's the only sandy bit of shoreline on the pond, but it appears to be a perfect new home, similar to the previous spot, complete with a hill in the background, though much less steep.

"We've gotta work quickly, girls. We want to be home in time for lunch, right?" Red gets the boat settled; he stands in the water next to the engine, untying the tow. The girls are out and ready to work. Eleanor takes off their life jackets and tosses them into the boat. Windbreakers are quickly discarded too. "We have to dig decent holes because the eggs need to be below the surface, where temperatures stay cooler, and the eggs will be safer. Your mom and I have to do most of the work this time because those buckets are too heavy for you to lift, even if you work together. Can you keep yourselves busy while we do this?"

"Why don't you go up the hill and see what you can see from the top?" Eleanor suggests.

"Yeah, okay! Come on, Joy. Let's find some rocks." They trot off, happy to be let off the hook. They have a pony in each hand, and the ponies are flying through the air via their hands as they run along, making whinnying noises. Red and Eleanor go quickly to work. They start digging holes. Eleanor transports the buckets to the holes then gently tips each on its side. Her hands dig down into the bottom of the bucket and, with her whole arms, scoop to drag the sand in one lump pile forward while Red holds the scoop shovel under her arms to catch the sand and slowly ease it down into the hole. They work until the buckets are empty. Eleanor sweeps the area, gathering the empty buckets, stacking them, and setting them back in the boat.

The girls come down from the hill, reporting that all they could see from the top was the pond and some trees. Red warns them to be careful of the new nests, and he points out several other nests already there, using them as proof that this spot is good for baby turtles to hatch and grow. They spent a few minutes standing at the edge,

tossing rocks into the water.

They listen intently to the plunks,

each having a delightfully different sound.
They relish the warm shallow water, splashing and jumping. Eleanor and Red sit against the rowboat, talking. Eleanor worries the eggs won't make it, that they've disrupted the course of nature, that there may now be too many turtles in this area for successful turtle populations to be sustained. Red nods

quietly and answers each fear with the wisdom of his age and his willingness to be defiant of the ills of progress, and his belief in the goodness of their intentions. He yields, "What else is there to do?"

He stood and turned to look out at the lake. "Now look at that," he says. Eleanor looks up and sees a gorgeous cloud in the sky, somehow set apart from other clouds, almost framed by them. This particular cloud is taking shape like a turtle, wearing a top hat. They all almost gasp to see it so distinctly.

As they board the boat and begin the journey back, Hope begs, "Tell us another story, Grandpa."

"Sit back and enjoy this beautiful morning for a while."

"Aww . . . come on. You have so many good stories to tell," they plea.

"Oh, alright. Where to begin? Let's see . . . you're right, if I think about it, there are lots of stories to tell . . . let me just think . . . that cloud reminds me of the time a turtle saved my life. . . ."

And as the story unfolds through the air into their ears, the greatest part was, as they puttered along the lake, the turtle cloud moved and changed, and as it did so, it tipped its top hat. A dancing bear hallucination, only it was a turtle, and they all saw it.

CHAPTER 18

Reeling Reality

We decided to make a real night of it. Fall was closing in—two weeks, and we'd be packing our bags for school. Margaret was leaving in just one week to go home for a few days before school. We needed to celebrate; we both possessed a plump stack of worn bills, so we splurged on a good meal. We went to Sandy Shores, a family resort just down the road from Candice's house. We could leave the car parked in the resort lot and walk down the road to her driveway.

From there on in, I didn't know what would come next, but I had to admit, I was into the unpredictability. We spiffed up and did our hair, and we had appetizers, steak and potatoes, and dessert, along with a couple drinks. We stopped at a liquor store before dinner, each of us buying the other a bottle of champagne.

After the meal, bellies rounded, we went to the beach and sat on their beach chairs, and cracked the first bottle. We stared out across the lake to the opposite shore.

"It's crazy, Margaret, when I was a kid, those red radio towers weren't there," I said, observing how the blinking red lights undulated upward into the night sky.

"When I was a kid, it didn't seem like anything changed. Maybe I wasn't paying attention. But now it seems like everything's changing faster and faster."

"How do you mean? All the big mansions?"

"Yeah, that, and the gadget fishermen, and pontoon boats, and, I don't know, tourists, I guess. It doesn't seem like anyone cares about the lake; they just want to use it."

"It's like that in my hometown, too. The farms keep getting bigger, big business buying it all up. Town feels like it's shriveling away. People are moving on."

"Moving up here, I guess," I laughed, because it certainly wasn't attracting farmers. More like tycoons, politicians, and movie stars. I thought of the latest celebrity-sighting stories at the restaurant.

"Yeah, right. Well, here's to farmers," she held out her glass for a cheer, a slam, then a refill. We had no problem putting away the first bottle, sitting back in our chairs. Luckily, no other people were down there with us. It was getting late. Our talk turned to serving and some of the mean awful customers we had.

"More like arrogant assholes who don't notice or care that you're a human being."

"Exactly! Like that guy I dripped on?" The infamous drip story. Red wine on white golf shorts during a Sunday brunch. Who drinks red wine on a Sunday morning? Who wears white golf shorts to brunch? A grown man throwing a tantrum, that's who. And it wasn't pretty. We both cracked up, remembering.

"Like . . . listen, do you hear a siren?" We stopped; a siren traveled somewhere down a road behind the lake.

"I swear I used to hear only loons at night."

"You're starting to sound like a loon." She laughed at her silly joke. I laughed too. I sounded old. I felt really old for an odd moment there, like time had zoomed past me in fast forward. I wanted to shake off that train of thought; it felt too negative, too much like the end of summer. It was feeling a little chilly, and I wished I had a blanket. I cracked the second bottle and changed the subject.

"What if you see Blake there?"

"I'm gonna rush out of the bushes and tear his eyeballs out," she replied evenly.

"Oh, God. Are—"

"I'm *kidding?* Is that my style?" She giggled. "It could be funny, though."

"Shit."

"If I see him, I'll be cool, but I'll bait him into telling me about it when I see him tomorrow. If he doesn't say anything, he's history," she said with a flip of her hair. "I'll just brand him with a letter A first. A for 'asshole,' that is."

"You'd just dump him?"

"Well—he'd be a big fat liar! Should I be dating a person like that? Besides, summer's ending, I'll go back to school. He never really talks about anything beyond right now, anyway. He says I'll be coming to the Cities to see him. He never mentions coming to Duluth. He thinks Duluth is for hicks."

She'd used the word hick a lot that summer, I'd noticed. It wasn't a word I'd heard her use before, really ever.

"Hmmm. I don't know what to say to that," I said, thinking I wouldn't be around much anyway. I poured more bubbly. "When we finish this bottle, let's go." I wondered if that would be how it would end. I fumed a little, thinking a guy like him could hurt a girl like her. But I also kept thinking he might *not* be a bad guy. He really could be madly in love with Margaret and not want to jeopardize it. I sat on the Blake fence.

"Yeah. We'll be more than ready," she tipped her glass back. "What about Neal?"

"We'll write a lot of letters. I almost can't wait. I bet he writes amazing letters. I wonder if he'll give me a birthday present. It's coming up, you know, Margaret, hint, hint." I gave her a giant wink and a big smile.

Margaret was distracted and quiet for a minute, and then she predicted stoically, "I think you guys'll make it. You fit together. He is such a great guy. You are *so* going to miss him!" She picked up the bottle, which was emptying steadily. She looked up at me, adding, "Hell, *I'm* going to miss him! *He* can come and stay anytime. I adore him, you know."

"Okay, fine. Then Blake can come and stay too since you have to be so nice about it!" I held my glass out to be refilled. "I don't know if I *can* say I adore Blake. I can say he's grown on me."

"Well, cheers to that!" We clinked. "We may see another side to his character tonight, though," she swallowed hard. We drank some more.

I got up, suddenly feeling the full meaning of tipsy, and she picked up the bottle and got up to follow me. I muttered, "Let's go into the game room, and plop a few quarters into the jukebox, and play some ping pong for a while. It's got to get darker." We needed the buzz to settle in too. "Did you read *Harriet the Spy* when you were a kid?"

"Shit, yeah, I loved that book. I'm going to call you *Harriet*, Harriet."
We started up the sidewalk to the game room. We sat outside to finish the bottle, but we left it sitting with a few swigs on a table outside; we were well bubbling over with bubbly by that point. Or, as some of the older folks at the bar would say, licked. We were falling down laughing while we played ping pong. Margaret was a master at funny faces and physical contortions as she whapped the ball at me. She kicked my ass because I was in hysterics most of the time. Finally, my stomach stiff, I placed my paddle emphatically on the table, "Let's go."

We swerved to and fro as we walked down the road toward Candice's house. Arm in arm, we giggled along, trying not to tip over. We made a plan. We were going to walk nonchalantly down her driveway, and when we got close to the house, we would hide behind the stone wall and see what we could see. As we approached, the driveway was all lit up, the wooden sign over the driveway, with the word "Comoro" elegantly etched across it, was draped with a "Welcome Home Sweet Candy" banner. White Christmas lights framed the big sign. The giant bronze elk was wearing a sparkly gold and silver top hat like it was New Year's Eve.

I pulled Margaret's arm, pointing out the obvious, muttering in an old man's voice, "dees is de place." We giggled at the ridiculousness of the scene and that we were actually in it. We started down the driveway. A row of cars lined one side, packed in tightly. The driveway was long; at least, it felt about a block long. At one point, car headlights stretched down the smooth blacktop from behind us, the opposite of a shadow, sneaking up on you. We both panicked and trampled into the woods. I watched from behind a big pine tree, immediately astonished to note the car, a blue Suburban. It was Donovan's, Blake's younger brother. Four heads were distinguishable through the windows. They rolled slowly down the driveway; none of them even remotely seemed to notice us. We were completely unobserved. We emerged and continued. I was so glad we had run and hid. But I had sticky sap on my fingers.

We arrived at the house. It was the biggest house I had ever come close to. It was actually obnoxious. It didn't fit the woods. It was like someone blew it up like a balloon with too much air, contorted out of its own shape. It was all lit up, and the circular driveway wound around a three-tiered fountain with colored lights flowing from blue to pink to purple to green and on and on. Two young valets worked the wide brick entryway, and one of them got into Donovan's Suburban to take it back down the driveway to be parked.

We jutted behind the nearest car as the headlights swung around at us. Creeping around the car, we easily stole behind the stone wall. Both of us bent over and scurried along the wall, following it toward the lake, and party noises grew louder. A band belted out disco tunes, and waiters strolled around with cocktail trays. Beside the house, on big long tables covered with crisp white tablecloths, were piles and piles of appetizers overflowing on shiny silver-tiered platters. White Christmas lights lined the three terraces, and people were everywhere. I thought maybe one hundred and fifty or more.

We perched in a perfect pocket behind the wall and settled in to see. The terraces surrounded a large, rectangular swimming pool, all lit up and shimmery, reflecting lights all around it. I marveled at the size of the pool, and the fact that it was within fifty feet of their pristine swimming beach, wondering why such a pool was necessary, even legal, so close to the water, but it made a good party centerpiece.

We were completely in the shadows of the woods, two little flies upon the proverbial wall. Within minutes we spotted Candice. She paraded in her white halter-top; her thick gorgeous hair, streaked multi-colored blonde, was pulled back to the base of her neck and tied with a thick white ribbon. She was wearing tight white capri pants, and her ass was perfection. Hours of trekking around Europe, I supposed. She wore white platform shoes that had to have been European because I'd never seen anything like them. Her ankles were thin and tan. She wore her white halter honorably, with tanned, muscular arms and shoulders and perfect round boobs. She was laughing and kissing practically everyone. Her arms flew wildly about her as she told stories in animated speech, drawing out certain words and shaking her head. Tales of Paris, I'm sure. Before I could finish examining her, I saw Donovan and his buddies come in from around the house by the driveway; two of them smoked, little orange lights illuminated at their fingers.

As they crossed the terrace, I caught a glimpse of Blake and another guy coming out the door from the house. My eyes immediately went to watch them. I peered over at Margaret. She saw them, too, and she squinted and studied. She didn't look at me. They traipsed out to the grass and trees nearly right in front of us. I was afraid they would hear us breathe, but, luckily, the party sounds were perfectly distracting. They stood there talking, and we heard every word. Too good to be true, but I worried Margaret might lunge at them, especially as we listened to them talk.

"She's lookin' hot, dude," the other guy remarked, lighting a cigarette.

"Yeah, I already fucked her once tonight, up in her room," Blake bragged, grabbing a cigarette as his friend took one out of the pack for him. I glanced at Margaret. Her jaw was clenched. She didn't move.

"How was it?"

"Well, there'll be more of that later. I doubt any of us'll be sleeping tonight," he fake-chuckled lightly. He didn't even sound like Margaret's Blake.

"Who's got the blow?"

"Zack and I got it for the bachelor party. You in?" Blake flicked an ash right toward the woods where we crouched. "He has a shitload at his house. We can get more."

"You guys drive here?"

"No, a bunch of us came in my boat. I dunno how the guys're gonna get home, though. I'll be doing lots more of Candice. I won't be goin' home."

"What're you gonna say to your girlfriend?"

"Which one?" He flouted. "You mean, Margaret?"

"Tall, hot legs, tasty body?"

"Yeah. Margaret. She's going back to college in a week. I can fuck around with Candice—no one has to mention it to Margaret. What she don't know won't hurt her. I have no intention of getting back together with Candy. She's a bitch, and she'll *pay* for fuckin' with me. All her bullshit about Europe and her new boyfriend? Yeah. Good one." He had morphed into a demon by this point. His shoulders really looked scaly, and his ears, how they did point!

I looked at Margaret. I figured she'd heard enough. Amazingly, we'd heard exactly what he would not have wanted us to hear. But she firmly grabbed my arm and gave me a hard stare. We weren't budging, which was fine. The conversation was riveting, but I kept an eye on her, afraid she'd pounce at any minute, and I wouldn't have blamed her. Part of me now wishes she would have. There were so many things then that might have turned out differently.

"Did you see Suzette Miller? She obviously needs a good fuck tonight, Tommy. Why don't you oblige her?" Blake hissed.

"Yeah, but I'm not sure I could get those big thighs over my shoulders, you know? Give me Amy Pedersen, man. She is hot. She's definitely been working out."

"My brother fucked her, dude. She's got an ass like cottage cheese. Stay away from her. She's super clingy, and she's out for dough." They watched the crowd and criticized nearly every female they saw, observing how each one walked, the hair, the clothes, the faces. Their fuckability. They each had two keg glasses of beer, and as they smoked out their cigarettes and emptied their beers, they started walking back.

"Let's find Zack."

"Yeah. Let's go. I'm gonna fill'er up first."

"Hey, man, not a word about the coke to my brother if you talk to him."

"Does Candice know?"

"Fuck, yeah. She's already blown a whole bunch, and she's ready to hump me for more." They turned their backs to us. "Check her out." They viewed her, and I followed their gazes. She stood on the edge of the patio right by them, hand on one hip, the other hand tossing her hair up behind her head. The white ribbon was history; now, her hair fell all around her face. She must have felt their gaze. She turned away from her adoring crowd and called out to them.

"What're you boys up to?" She sing-songed. "Come 'ere, sweetie." They approached her. She held out her hand to Blake. He transferred both beer glasses to one hand, then grabbed hers. They stopped and smooched. Her peons had moseyed on and mingled. "Did I show you what my daddy brought me from Sierra Leone as a welcome home present?" She teasingly tipped her head. She dropped a hand into her skin-tight pocket and somehow produced a little white leather box, about the size of a tin of breath mints. She opened it for them. I wished I could have seen inside.

"Every color. Every cut. Just for me." She purred. "Go ahead, Tommy, pick one up." Tommy put his big paw in the box and pulled out a nugget. He held it up carefully between thumb and pointer finger against the party lights. It was tiny, not seeable, from where I stood, but it glinted. He whistled his admiration.

"How many ya got in there?" He looked in again. She gave the box a little shake for his pleasure.

"Too many to count, baby." She said the word baby like she stroked him with it. "Now put that one back before you drop it, and it's lost forever." He obeyed. They both looked in one more time as Candice tipped the box slightly for them. Then she snapped it shut and tucked it back in her pocket. Her pants were so tight, I didn't know how she got it in there, but it disappeared somehow.

"Sweet pants, we're going for more *zesty*. You wanna come?" He put his hand on the curve of her ass and squeezed as they started walking away. Their conversation began to mesh with the background noises, but we watched some more. Some older men mingled in the crowd, and as I took it all in, I realized her father prowled around too. An equal number of young females to half-older, half-younger men. Most of the women were adequately hot, along the same lines as Candice. So many trays of finger foods floated to and fro along with the cocktail trays; there was an open bar and at least two kegs going at the same time in two different places. The middle terrace functioned as a dance floor, with older men feeling up the young women and sometimes kissing them like drooling dogs, stealing a quick lick before the swat. I didn't know Candice's mother, though women were there who could have been around her mother's age, but just a few. Maybe all the older women were in the house? Where would they go to escape the hideousness of their slobbering male counterparts?

Margaret grabbed my arm, pulling me. The last thing I saw as we retreated was Blake and Tommy walking toward the wide lawn that rolled down the hill where stairs led to the dock. Candice's shoreline was at least six hundred feet of the most spectacular vista of the whole lake. Up until that point, I thought we had the best view, staring south across the big bay, but Candice's house was on a point where there had once been a mission. Before the missionaries came and re-landscaped, it had been one of the longest-standing Ojibwa settlements in the area. It was elevated and had water on three sides; the view was almost due west, but also south and north. Though I wasn't standing on the edge of the hill looking down, even from where I stood, about a hundred yards back, I felt suspended over the lake, and the shimmering moonlight made the view luminously big, almost in your face. It was lovely beyond a dream; it caused an ache inside me. I didn't want to stop gazing. I couldn't stand that it belonged to a spoiled brat. It just didn't seem right.

Margaret and I didn't talk until we got out to the road. We had both stumbled at times, and I, for one, had more than a few mosquito bites and tree branch scratches.

"A for Asshole, all right," was all I could manage, scratching one particular pink bump of skin on my forearm.

"No! F for *Fuck Face!* Double F's! That fucking *fucker!* I will never speak to that . . . *scumbag* ever again," she concluded. I was amazed she wasn't crying. She was alarmingly calm, albeit pissed as hell. "I had no idea he *smoked!* And he's a *cokehead!* Great!"

"Margaret? Are you okay?" I tried to see her face but
the road was dark where we stood.

"Yeah. I'm fine. I saw it all. What a prick! I hate him. I really hate him. I want to kick him so hard in the balls."

"I think you should," I grabbed her arm. "I'll hold him down for you." We started walking back toward Sandy Shores. I felt sober, but we agreed we'd better walk for a while just to work some of the booze out of our systems.

"What's the deal with that box, I wonder." We needed water.

"Do you know her father owns a *diamond mine* in Sierra Leone?"

"Whaat?" I felt dizzy. Diamonds. A hearty handful of diamonds in all shapes and colors. "She's gross. I thought her dad owned golf courses."

"Actually, she's annoyingly beautiful. Don't you think?" She sighed exaggeratedly. "And he *does* own golf courses. Like six of them."

"That's what I thought. Do you really think she's *beautiful?* I mean, I guess you could say she's 'hot' in a high-class call-girl sort of way," I muttered. "She ain't got nothin' on you, though," I added.

"Whatever. I don't fuck him in the upstairs bedroom during a party, that's for sure, so. . . ." Her eyes flashed, and I saw tears barely contained in the rims.

"Exactly. You're not a slut. You have class, Margaret. So, your father doesn't own a diamond mine or a slew of golf courses. You still make her look like *nothing*. You're respectable. She's rich. So what. Fuck her. Fuck him. They're gross." All the fun fell out of the night. I had a hard time recalling there was any fun. "And sick."

"You think he'll be all normal tomorrow?" She stared up at the sky as she walked and moved with a sway. She was wiping her eyes now; though she wasn't sobbing, it was a slow stream of tears.

"You're not gonna find out. If he comes over or calls for you, I'm gonna tell him to fuck off and punch him in the face."

"I just want to know how stupid he thinks I am."

"I think you should do as you first said, not speak to him anymore. Do you really want to get into a fight over his sliminess? What's it worth?"

"Just satisfaction. Knowing how thoroughly and purely he *is* slime. You said it. You said it all along, Ellie. Why didn't I listen to you? Thinking about him now, after that, I can't think for one *second* what I found attractive about him."

"He has a cute smile," I replied lamely.

"He's scum. That's all." We ripped him to shreds all the way back to the car, where we got out a big jug of water and guzzled, taking several detours around the resort grounds as we drank the water jug, first, to make sure we got in every last insult, jab, and sneer, and second, to pee a few times. When we finally got to the car, I unlocked it; we got in and sat there for a minute in silence. I jingled my keys a little.

"Are you okay to drive?" She asked me. It had been two hours since we emptied nearly two bottles of champagne.

"I'm sober," I proclaimed, though I surely couldn't have been. The events seemed to have slapped me into a different state of mind. "I feel kind of sick, though. I've never seen so much food and booze, God." I put the key in and started the car, but I just sat there, frozen, still shocked at the whole thing. I turned the heat on in the car, and it felt good to warm up even though I hadn't even noticed how cold I was. We sat there for a few minutes, rubbing our hands together and feeling the heat coming out of the vents. I knew he was a jerk, but I had no idea just how much of a jerk. I didn't want to know how he assailed girls, how he dissed Margaret. Why was he such a dick in front of his friends? I couldn't believe it. Why did he have to act so arrogant? So different from the Blake I'd finally begun to warm to.

"Let's go over there one more time and see what's going on now," Margaret said. "Think they're back from their coke run?"

I looked at my watch and moved my wrist into the light from the streetlamp. "It's two o'clock. I wonder. You really wanna go back there?"

"Yes," she said firmly. "Come on, we're going." Then she opened her car door, and out she went. I turned the car off.

I can't believe it,

but we went back. The party was still raging, with about twenty people left, including Donovan and his buddies. A bonfire flickered. A couple of joints passed around. Lights blazed all around and in the house. This time, we saw Blake and Candice upstairs in what looked like her room. When I first noticed them, they were together in an embrace. We watched them kissing. I wondered if they didn't know—or didn't care—that anyone could look up and see them going at it? Then I wondered if that was part of the fun. They got a little more intense, and then they dropped onto the frilly white canopy bed.

At the campfire below, Donovan and his buddies got up and went inside, looking like they were going to leave. Tommy was with them. We watched a couple more cars drive away, and it looked like only the hard-core partiers were sticking around—those buzzed on coke, most likely, the hangers-on from the bachelor party. I smelled pot smoke mixed with the campfire. We left. Enough already. The whole atmosphere and mood were nauseating, a half-smoked cigarette mushed out in a wet ashtray.

Summer was over.

CHAPTER 19

Below the Epilimnion

"Won't you tell us more about Raven Wing?"

"You said they survived, but you never told what happened to them. Where'd they go? What happened to the baby and Grandma Sun?" Hope asks Big Red, trotting beside him as he walks down the dirt road toward the lake. He's taking the twins fishing. Eleanor has a yoga lesson, so Red is babysitting. It's the height of summer, and the sun is in its heyday.

Joy bounds along behind them, carrying the lunch, a beach bag, and her life preserver with the strap dragging.

Red stops and holds up his finger. "I'll tell ya about Raven Wing, but the best part of fishing is watching the sun come up over the lake. We might miss it; you two are so slow. Hop, hop, now!" He resumes walking, but he stops again. "Here, give me the lunch. Hope, you have to carry your life preserver." They switch the gear around and continue.

Joy says, "Boy, you sure don't walk like an old man!"

Red answers, "Well, old's all in your head. I'm not old in here!" He pats his chest where his heart is.

They get to the dock where Red's little boat is tied up. He's got gear neatly tucked along the sides. They step down and get ready for take-off. Red gives the pull starter a good tug, and the engine purrs. He unties the back rope. "Hope, can you untie that rope up there?" When she does, he puts the engine into forward and pushes off with his big hand. As they skirt out around the docks, he tells Hope she can sit up front and Joy can sit on the middle bench. They'll switch on the way back. He hits full throttle, and the rushing air picks up their hair, and the front-end bounces slightly in a nice steady rhythm. The lake is calm and flat, not a whisper of wind. They head south to Timmins Lake, the small round lake used to harbor boats for the yacht club. Perfect for small fishers just learning to fish. The lake glitters from dark gray to fairytale pink right before their eyes as the sunrise infuses it with light, like an enormous paintbrush drenched in fuchsia dipped its tip into the water and color saturates the whole giant bowl.

When he approaches the spot where he plans to stop, he slows the throttle then moves it to neutral. The boat comes to a near standstill. Red turns off the engine. He pulls his anchor out from under the seat and slowly drops it off the side of the boat with a splash. It yanks slightly when the anchor hits bottom.

"Ah. Nice and quiet now, huh girls?" He looks at Joy. She's looking not too excited to do anything at the moment. "What did you think of the sunrise?"

"Magic."

"I'd say. See why I had to hurry you up?"

"Yeah, but that ride made me sleepy. Can I just lay on the seat and look up at the sky, Big Red?" Hope asks.

"Absolutely. Let's sit for a while—so much to see and hear, isn't there?"

"I like how the water looks. It's like a mirror. You can see the trees in it, isn't that cool?" Joy leans over the side and pokes her finger in the water.

"It sure is. Someone once said lakes are the Earth's eyes. Isn't *that* cool?"

"Oh, I think that's true, don't you?"

"I do," he agrees. "But sometimes, I think maybe lakes are just big bowls of water." He grins at his own humor.

"I wonder if Earth likes us floating around and driving our boat all over her eyes?" Hope wonders, staring up. "I wouldn't like that."

"Oh, I bet she doesn't mind much."

"I bet she doesn't like all the gas that leaks into her eyes."

"Yeah. Probably not that so much," Red agrees. "But she's got a good cleaning system. She can take care of her eyes okay, mostly."

"I hope so. I don't like pollution. Do you? Mom makes us pick up garbage on the beach sometimes. We find weird stuff. Once I found a picture frame."

"Did it have a picture in it?"

"Sort of. It was all wet and wrecked," Joy recalls. "Why would someone throw a picture frame into the lake?"

"Who knows why people throw anything into a lake," Red says, kicking back. He props a seat cushion against the side so he can swing his legs up onto the seat. He looks pensively at the trees and sky. All three are quiet. Little bubbles occasionally trickle up from the depths of the water as the slimy green weeds below the surface sway and hold still.

Ripples of the wind's breath
        skitter around
                on the water's surface, pushing the boat around slightly. Cicadas hum and birds flutter busily in the trees, occasionally circling overhead. The cattails along the shoreline behind them exude a pleasant earthy smell in the air around them. Red thinks about how kick-ass cattails are in the field of phytoremediation. Cattails can somehow utilize nasty chemicals and waste in the environment and clean the water. He thinks about all the

engineers itching to build enormous sewage systems when what the whole world needs are more wetlands filled with cattails, reeds, mosses, and other mushy vegetation. They are a part of the Earth's kidneys. Finding enough water to rinse the Earth is getting to be a challenge. It must be acknowledged that plastic is now endemic to water. Red closes his eyes and sits in his own darkness.

After a while, Red stirs. The girls sit up as Red pulls out the fishing poles. They watch as he sets the line, hooks and sinkers ready, and baits the hooks.

"Are those real worms?"

"They are."

"Eeauuww! Yuk. I don't like touching worms."

"You can always use fake bait, Hope. Then you don't have to touch real worms or leeches. But I like real bait."

"I feel bad for the worm. I mean, what'd he do to deserve that? Getting stabbed by a hook, put into cold water, and swallowed by a big fish. Seems pretty unfair to me." Joy shakes her head. "I'm glad I'm not a worm."

"Yeap. Worms have bad lives, rolling around in the dirt, waiting for someone to come along and smush them or eat them," Hope adds.

"Well, maybe so. But worms are important and helpful if they can exist in the right places. All that squirming around in the dirt is good for some soils. Worms clean the earth, did you know that? We'd be hurtin' without worms. They may be small and meek, but they know their destiny. They know their role, and they do it, and we love them for it," he hands over a rod. "Here you go, Hope. Just hold on while I get Joy's pole ready."

After some basic instruction from Red about hook safety, rod holding, and patience, the girls drop their lines in the calm water. Then the fun begins. Within minutes, first one, then the other, has a cute, hand-sized sunny on the end of her hook. Red never stops baiting and releasing fish for the next hour and a half. Finally, they run out of bait. Red hasn't put his rod in, and the girls want to call it quits.

"Mommy's gonna be mad she missed this."

"Well, she's not a big fan of fishing, girls; I hate to break it to you. If you want to go fishing, you'll have to go with me. She doesn't even own a fishing pole."

"We don't care. You'll take us out again sometime, won't you, Big Red?" Hope gives him her sweetest smile.

"For sure, Hope. Besides how fun it is—I get to bring home half a dozen fish. It'll be my dinner tonight. You don't mind if I keep 'em, do ya?" He looked at them, looking a little sad. "You're not gonna say you feel sorry for the fish now, are you?"

"Well, I do, sort of. But I guess it's like you said. Their job is to be food for someone. If not you, then a bigger fish, or maybe a bear or somethin', right?"

"Right." He said, "You just never take more than your small share."

"Well, can we sit here a while, and you tell us more about Raven Wing?" Joy asks, adding, "You said you would."

"Let's go to the channel and see what Quartz looks like now that it's nearly noon. Think there's waves yet? The wind's pickin' up."

"Let's go see." Hope turns to get ready for the ride. Red puts the gear away, pulls in the anchor, and starts the engine, trolling back. They can see the big lake through the channel, and it looks almost as still and calm as where they are. Boats cause a few waves, but the wind is still mild, so Red drives out of the channel. He putters straight toward the middle, then cuts the engine.

"Let's drift a while, girls. . . .

I'll tell ya about Raven Wing's son, Broken Day.

It's cool because part of the story takes place in this bay, right here."

"Oh, boy! I'm gonna listen and not ask too many questions. But I'm kinda hot. Can we jump in first?"

"Sure! Do you guys have your suits on?"

"A-huh!" They start taking off all the layers. Hope wears a little blue and white ruffled swimsuit. Joy has a similar suit, only hers is red and white. They jump eagerly off the side of the boat, their wild curly hair flying out behind them. Red watches as they dog-paddle around the boat a few times. He's delighted they're not afraid to jump or swim in the deep water.

"We do this with Mommy in the canoe all the time," Joy explains, breathing hard as she paddles around. "When we want to get back in, she lets us get pulled by the rope, and she paddles to the shallow water so we can get back in. We're good swimmers, huh, Big Red?"

"Gosh, yes. I'm impressed. You don't need your life preservers."

"The last time we went out in the canoe, Mom said we could try it and see. It was okay. I went first. Joy was a little afraid."

"I was not!"

"Well, you sure don't look afraid now! Look what great swimmers you are!" He eyes them steadily. "Is it cold?"

"Nope!" Joy declares. "It's perfect!"

"How we gonna get back in, Red?" Hope treads water energetically.

"Are you ready? I can lift you out. That okay?"

"Okay," Hope agrees. "I'm ready now." He leans down and scoops her up under the arms like a sack of potatoes and sets her, dripping wet, on the middle seat. Then he grabs Joy and sets her next to Hope. They pull out their towels, and after drying off, they spread their towels on the seats to lie on them and soak up sun. Red studies their round, innocent faces, so young, unwrinkled, wide-eyed, and poised for life. Their smallness is even more pronounced with their hair plastered against their heads. They grin happily as they take in the warmth of the day. Red relishes the gift of them and their childhood, breathing deeply.

Finally, Joy says, "Okay. We're ready. What happened to Broken Day?"

"Let's eat while I tell the story; how about that?"

"Great!" So, they got the lunch goodies out.

"Well, I don't want to give the story away, but let me just say that when Broken Day was a boy about ten years old, he swam across the lake, right here! This big bay? He crossed it by himself."

"What?" Joy gives the bay a good scan. "You kidding? I'm a good swimmer, but I don't think I could do that! Why'd he do it; for fun?"

"I bet someone dared him. Like in school, when someone dared me to jump off the top of the slide. I didn't think I could, but I had to because I got dared."

"Well, you didn't have to. You could've said 'no way!'" Red says.

"I guess, but then everyone'd be callin' me a chicken."

"Wouldn't it be better to be called a chicken than to break your leg doing something crazy just because someone dared you?"

"Yeah. Prob'ly. But I wasn't too scared. I saw someone else do it first. I was pretty sure I could do it," Hope explains.

"Okay, but back to Broken Day," Joy says. "How did he get his name?"

"Well, I'm not one-hundred percent sure, but I think his name came from the day his tribe was attacked. Remember that story? That was a broken day for his tribe. People would take on several new names throughout their lives if certain events happened to change someone. In a way, a new name signifies that a person becomes new again, maybe for the better, maybe for the worse."

"In Broken Day's case, I bet it was for the worse."

"I'm not so sure. Broken Day became very brave because of the things that happened to him and his tribe. I mean, he swam across the lake by himself when he was ten. Isn't that brave?"

"I'd *say!* Now go on. Don't say anything now, Joy. Just listen." Hope says sternly, then takes a bite of her sandwich. Joy sticks her tongue out at her but stays quiet.

"Well, his story begins on a day like today—warm and sunny. Broken Day and his mom, Raven Wing, and his Grandma Sun, as you know, survived the attack on their tribe. For a while, they lived with a neighboring tribe. They had wandered to the south end of the lake, where they found others of their kind. They lived with this other group for about nine years, watching Broken Day grow, and Raven Wing even remarried. She married a man from this tribe. Broken Day didn't remember his birth father or his old tribe and where they used to live. Remember he was a baby when that happened. So, he loved his stepdad, Sharp Arrow. Sharp Arrow was an excellent hunter, and he shot many deer for his tribe. Broken Day, Raven Wing, and Grandma Sun lived well with Sharp Arrow, and everyone was nice and fat on all the meat he caught.

"One day, news came that three other people had survived the attack that had happened at Raven Wing's village. The three survivors were, of course, related to Raven Wing. It was believed it was her sister, her sister's husband, and their son. Raven Wing was so excited. She couldn't believe anyone else survived the massacre. She replayed the horrible scene in her mind to see if she could recall any hint of anyone else being alive that night, but she could not. She had to see them to believe it. They survived because they had been away from the village that morning; no one knows why. But Raven Wing didn't know this at the time. She begged Sharp Arrow to take her to where the other three survivors were reported to have been living. Raven Wing wanted a happy reunion. She hoped to introduce Broken Day to his cousin. So, Sharp Arrow met with the person in their tribe who had delivered this information to find out exactly where the other village was so he could get there. Raven Wing packed. Though her mother was quite old, she had to bring her, even though her mother would make the journey slower.

"Sharp Arrow traded some meat for a wagon from a Swedish farmer who had moved into the area. This would ensure Grandma Sun would make it. He'd never used a wagon before, but he was excited to, and it made Raven Wing happy. When he brought the wagon home, everyone came to check it out. No one had seen such a thing. Many of 'em were in awe, but several of the elders were aghast."

"Wait. What does that mean?"

"Oh, you know, like surprised, freaked out. Suspicious."

"Huh. That's weird. Wagons are cool."

"Well, I agree. But these guys'd never seen one before. It'd be like if you saw a spaceship or something."

"Yeah. Okay, sorry." Hope looks at Joy, who's frowning a little. "Go on."

"Well, as soon as Sharp Arrow parked it outside their teepee, the elders called a meeting with him. They tried to discourage Sharp Arrow from going ahead with it. They warned him nothing good could come from it, and this was progress of the wrong sort. He tried to explain to them that Grandma Sun was too old to make the journey on foot, but they told him to have her ride along on a horse. Pretty soon, Sharp Arrow became frustrated with the old coots. He was mad because they didn't see him as clever and a good problem solver. He refused to give in to their authority, and his stubbornness made them dig in their heels more. Threats went back and forth. The meeting ended in shouting, and Sharp Arrow stormed out.

"The next morning, the wagon was gone. Sharp Arrow, Broken Day, Raven Wing, and Grandma Sun were gone too. Their teepee was gone. Everyone figured they left to find Raven Wing's sister. Many wondered if they would come back.

"Meanwhile, the party of four started on their journey in the wagon. It proved beneficial since all of them could ride. The flatbed had space to hold all of their stuff. Everybody enjoyed riding through the forest, even if their route was restricted because they had to use the rutted roads that ran in the general direction of the other village. Sometimes Sharp Arrow would turn over the reins and run ahead to see about the road conditions to avoid going where the wagon could get stuck.

"One day, while making decent time across a prairie, they saw thick woods in the distance where the road seemed to stop. Sharp Arrow ran up to scout. Raven Wing slowed the horses so Sharp Arrow could return with his report, but he never came back. Night drew up its curtains just as they approached the darkening woods. Raven Wing and Grandma Sun hid their fears. They set up camp, and, after eating, they fell restlessly asleep in the wagon, hoping Sharp Arrow would return before morning.

"But when dawn came, Sharp Arrow was not with it. They packed up, but Raven Wing was not sure where to go. They continued skirting the woods because the road had indeed gotten deeply rutted and tricky to drive a wagon on. They didn't know if they'd gotten off course, and the day stretched out long, and travel was slow. Broken Day sat beside his mother, scanning for the first sight of Sharp Arrow. Another day passed, with no sign of their beloved.

"Certainly, the next day, Sharp Arrow would find them and bring their hopes back into view. Raven Wing cried secretly, worrying about Sharp Arrow and fearing she'd never see her sister again after all. But she kept going, and the journey brought them to a small town with a church and a trading post. The three travelers spoke only their own language and were afraid to talk, but they couldn't go on without asking about Sharp Arrow. Raven Wing went into the church while her son and mother waited in the wagon. She found no one, so she went into the trading post, discovering a young man inside. She tried to convey her questions, describing Sharp Arrow, using hand gestures and body motions, but she couldn't get any info about him. They left more discouraged and feeling like someone, the whole weird little town, was watching. They could only think to continue in the same direction and hope their luck would change.

"Soon night was on them again, and another day had passed without Sharp Arrow. They had a dismal meal and slept in the wagon again. This time, in the middle of the night, Raven Wing woke to the sound of someone gasping and groaning. It was Sharp Arrow!"

"No! What happened? I can't stand this, Big Red!" Joy shakes her head.

"Okay, I'll cut it short; the lake's pretty busy now, too; look at all the boats. Your mom'll be expecting us soon."

"Well, you have to finish the story!" Joy urges.

"So, Sharp Arrow finds them, but he's been attacked and severely injured. He says he crossed paths with a band of hunters,

enemies,

in the woods.

"They beat him and broke his leg, left him for dead. But eventually, he woke and got to work tracking the wagon. He was lame and hobbled for two days and two nights before he found them. Raven Wing was distraught. She nursed his injuries and got him settled in the wagon. He convinced her that they must turn back or the bandits would find them and finish them off for good. So, they turned around and headed for home. For two days, they retraced their path, and on the third day, in broad daylight, they were attacked. It may have been the same group who attacked Sharp Arrow before, or it may have been a new band of thieves. Nobody knows. When they attacked, they dragged Raven Wing and Grandma Sun out of the wagon and into the woods. Sharp Arrow was lying in the back of the wagon, hidden by all their stuff, and the bandits didn't see him at first. He lay low planning his defense. Broken Day was up ahead on the road scouting when he heard the screams. He ran back to the wagon and found Sharp Arrow hobbling out of the wagon. Broken Day clung to his father. His father told him to stay out of the way as he went to try and save the two women. He said," Red whispers exaggeratedly, "'Go lie in the tall grass and play dead, son. Wait there till this danger passes. Wait for me. We have to get to the lake. I was wrong about the wagon. I was wrong! Run,

hide,

play dead, son!'"

"Did he play dead?"

"You bet he did. But when his dad went to save them, he had no physical advantage. He moved too slowly, and by the time he got to where they were, they were dead. One of the bandits saw him, and they killed him too. They stole the wagon and everything in it, vanishing into the dust of the remaining daylight. Broken Day waited a long time but finally got up. He found his family dead in the dark, and he was terrified."

"They all three died? Broken Day was alone now? He was only ten years old! I would die too; I'd be so scared!"

"I think he probably wanted to die. He lingered around them, laying on their dead bodies and crying over them even as they were bloody. He was so scared and alone and hungry. It was probably one of the longest nights of his life. Can you imagine?"

"Big Red, I don't like your stories; they're too sad! I don't want Broken Day to be scared and all alone. I want him to be with his mom! He's been through so much already."

"I know it. But he was strong. He had courage, and he made it through. Don't you want to know what happens to him?"

"I guess." Joy frowns. Hope follows with a similar expression. Their hair has begun to dry in ringlet curls, thick with humidity.

"Well, the next morning, he had to suck it up, as they say. He buried the only three people he'd loved most in the world. He dug shallow graves with his hands. It took him most of the day. Then he really *knew* he was alone. He remembered what Sharp Arrow said and knew he had to try to get to the lake. It was the only thing he could think to do. He had nothing, no food, no weapon, no shelter, but, somehow, he did it, all by himself. When he got there, night had fallen. He was on that side right over there." Red pointed across the lake.

"That's a long way."

"Sure is. And when he got there, he fell on the ground at the lake's edge and cried himself to sleep. When he woke up, it was the next morning. He could see smoke from a fire across the lake. He wasn't sure if it was his village or another village or what, but he didn't know what else to do or where else to go. He studied the shoreline and saw it would take days to follow it all the way round to the other side. He had no food and no way to get food. The only solution he could think of was to swim across the lake. He was only ten, and I don't think he really understood how wide the lake was."

"How wide is it, Big Red?"

"Oh, I think about two miles. A long way to swim, especially for a ten-year-old, for sure."

"I don't think I'd ever do it, even when I grow up."

"I'm not sure I could either, Hope. But he set out to do it anyway. He didn't know what else to do, and he decided if he didn't make it if he drowned, then he would at least see his mother and father, and grandma again in the afterlife. So, he scavenged some berries to eat and geared up for his swim. He didn't know how long it would take, but he didn't want to swim in the deep water at night; he knew that for sure.

"So, he got in, and he started swimming. He was going along fine for a while, keeping a slow but steady pace to not get too tired. He'd rest every now and then by floating on his back."

"Yeah! I do that, too, when I get tired. That's a good thing to do, alright!" Joy says eagerly. "What other strokes did he do? Did he do the front crawl? Mom is teaching us that one!"

"Oh, I don't know how good a swimmer he was. He probably did the dog-paddle, you know what that is, right?"

"Ah hah. I do that one mostly, too. It's the easiest," Hope nods.

"So, as I said, he was going along, trying not to think about how deep the water was. It must have been a day like today, not a lot of wind, and the lake would have been flat and smooth because there were no speedboats back then. He kept his eyes on the point across the lake where he had seen the fire the night before."

All the while, Red's boat has been drifting down the shore, getting closer to Eleanor's dock. She'll be waiting. He has to finish it up quick.

"And there he was, in the middle of the lake, about mid-afternoon, and he starts to tire out. He just can't get his legs to keep kicking. His arms are so tired and sore he can barely keep afloat. He becomes so weak; all he can do is struggle to tread water. He looks up at the bright blue sky and thinks of his mother. He sees her face, and he hears her voice telling him he has to keep kicking. He just wants to stop and slip under the surface, letting it all go, but her voice encourages him. He's struggling, but he looks around to see where he is, and coming up from behind him, swimming in the water, are three deer."

"Deer?"

"Ah huh. Deer. He can barely see 'em, but he can hear 'em breathing, and they sound angry and hungry. He figures he's done for, the deer'll probably come and attack him, drown him, if not eat him! He doesn't know what else to do but watch them coming closer. He can't swim away. He's so exhausted and afraid; he's frozen. He just keeps watching. One of the deer has a big rack on his head, so Broken Day knows he's a buck."

"I didn't know deer liked to swim. Why were they in the middle of the lake?"

"Great question. Who *knows?* I'm sure it was a strange sight for Broken Day. It'd be a strange sight for anyone."

"Did he dive underwater to hide?" Joy asks, eyebrows furrowing.

"Well, that might not've been a bad idea. But that's not what he did. As the three creatures got closer, they headed right for him. And you know what they did? They stopped by his side. He stared into the buck's eyes, and he seemed gentle. He didn't know what to do, but the buck seemed to be offering him a lift! So, Broken Day grabbed hold of his rack and held on. The buck let him ride along on his back as he began swimming again!"

"*What?*" Hope puts her hands against her cheeks in shock.

"Yep. The deer swam alongside the buck as he gave Broken Day a ride. They took him across to the other side. When they got to shore, the buck waited in the shallow water until Broken Day got to his feet. And he stood, though he was ready to faint, and watched the animals leap across the sand into the hills beyond the lake. Broken Day was mesmerized for a few minutes, then he remembered where he was and what had happened to him. He saw the smoke, and he gathered what remained of his courage and made his way to the fire."

"Then what happened?"

"Well, I'll finish his story another day. But he *did* survive. He found someone to take care of him. And there's a lot more to *that* story, but we've gotta get back. Your mom's gonna be worried. It's two o'clock, and I told her we'd be back around noon!"

"But, Big Red! You can't stop there! We have to hear what happens next!" Hope pleads. "Mom'll understand."

"Well, how 'bout when we get back, if your mom's there, I'll tell the rest."

"What if she's not there?"

"Then we have to walk back to your house, and I'll drop you off at home."

He pulls the engine starter cord, and they tool the short distance back. Eleanor is on her chair out on the dock. She stands and waves as she sees them coming. She catches the boat as it pulls up.

"Where've you three been?"

"We've been fishing up a storm, Mommy!" Joy explodes. "I caught twenty-two fish!"

"My goodness! How many'd you catch, Hope?" She puts a foot on the boat to hold it steady while they hop out.

"I caught eighteen. It was so fun, Momma. You have to come next time. Red says he'll take us again."

"You must've been good then."

Joy says, "Red's been telling us about Broken Day, and how he had to play dead, and swim across the lake, but he almost drown, except—"

"—a big buck came swimming by and rescued him! He rode on the buck's back all the way to the other side. From there all the way to here!" Hope points to each shoreline.

"Hope! Quit interrupting! I was telling the story!"

"Well, the story has to wait until next time, girls."

"No, Mom! We have to hear what happens to him, he was practically drowned, and he doesn't speak English! How's he make it when he can't speak to anyone? Can't we just hear the rest?"

"Well, that's funny," Red cocks his head slightly. "You told me you hated my stories just a few minutes ago, out in the middle of the lake."

"I was just kidding. We love 'um! Sometimes they're so sad. I don't like how so many people die in your stories."

"I don't like it either, Hope," Red agrees. "But good stories, like real life, have a mix of good and bad."

"Well," Eleanor pipes in, "I love his stories too. We can sit awhile. Look at this day! You guys want to swim first?"

"Oh, yeah! We're boiling, Momma!"

"How 'bout like ten minutes."

"Hope, let's bury ourselves in the sand. Then run off the end of the dock.

Okay? Wanna do that?"

"Yeah!" They trot down the dock to the beach.

Eleanor calls after them, "Hey, wait! One of you has to first bring a chair out here for Red!"

"Okay!" Joy volunteers. And she brings a folding beach chair for him to sit next to Eleanor. They angle their chairs so they can watch the swimming area and gaze at the neon blue water.

"Well . . . guess what?" Eleanor blinks at him.

"Okay. What? What's the verdict?" Red knows what's on her mind. It's the issue of the six hundred feet of primo Quartz shoreline and the twenty-some cabins, one of which is Eleanor's home, within a three-square-mile plot of land that used to be a logging camp more than a hundred years ago. When Eleanor purchased her home here a handful of years ago, the property was part of a cooperative association of landowners who shared beach access and maintenance costs. In the recent real estate boom, a developer sniffed out the profitability of this gem that still looks and feels like the 1940s. Many cabins, Eleanor's included, still have their original structure and character despite winterizing and updating. Eleanor has spent these years falling in love with her home and reconnecting with the Quartz, a lake she knew well but hadn't seen for twenty years.

"It passed. We're history," she glances back at the hill covered in native grasses, weeds, and wildflowers.

"You're kidding," he scowls. "You've got to be kidding."

"No. I'm not. We got outvoted. The condos are in. I have to be out by the end of September. You just missed Barb. She was just here with the news."

"I can't believe it. What's old McAlester gonna do?"

"I don't know. The man's lived here since World War One. Where'll he go? Where will Luis Wilson go? And Dell Thurman's family? None of those bastards gave a thought to those people, did they?"

"Damn greedy. What a shame. Sorry to hear it," he shakes his head slowly. "What're you gonna do?"

"I don't know," Eleanor clenches her lips between her teeth. "I gotta make some calls. School'll be starting so soon, and my fall schedule . . ." she fades off, overwhelmed. "I've got less than two months to figure out where I'm gonna go!" She blinks hard. "I wanna grab Martha Danders by the neck and squeeze! She hasn't lived here, but what—two years? She's got everybody seeing dollar signs."

"Yeah," He sighs. "Places like this are a thing of the past. There's plenty a people whose necks I'd like to squeeze real tight myself."

"I can't afford lake prices and property taxes. I gotta move to town."

"Well, you'll be closer to the yoga studio and the girls' school. I've got some connections, you know. There's some perfect house waiting for you.

We'll find it." He leans forward and pats her forearm. "I'll check into it. Heck, my friend, Barney's been talking about selling his place."

"It's probably way too huge. Doesn't he have a big family?"

"Yeah. Maybe you're right. Well, don't give away all your optimism. We'll figure it out."

The girls resurface from the swimming area and climb the ladder on the end of the dock. Eleanor hasn't broken the news to them; that's one thing on her afternoon agenda. She doesn't want to do it at the lake, though, because they all might end up crying.

"Never a dull moment, I guess," Eleanor shakes her head. "Well, let's change the subject. I want to hear about Broken Day," she says as the girls come. Eleanor drags her cooler bag out from under her chair. She's got juice and cheese and crackers for everyone. Red starts talking at his slow, even pace, first catching Eleanor up on the story, then continuing where he left off.

"Remember he'd just gotten to the shore, and he watched the buck sprint off into the woods?" They nod.

"Well, he watched for a few minutes. Heck, he may have passed out for a while from exhaustion, but, eventually, he decided to cautiously approach the campfire where a man was lingering around. He was cooking a small carcass and pretty intent upon his task, so he didn't see Broken Day coming up. But when he did see him, all the boy could do was fall to his feet and begin sobbing uncontrollably. The man walked him up to the small shelter he had built upon the hill. He gave him some food and a blanket because the boy was shivering even though the day was warm. Quite suddenly, Broken Day fell fast asleep, lying on the floor of this one-room wooden shack that was the beginning of the St. Christopher Mission."

"Really, Red? You mean right around the point? That's the mission you're talking about?" Eleanor asks. She had been on that property only once, and it had been under disastrous circumstances. She wonders if that land is cursed.

"Yeah. Where that huge mansion is now. Some of the best lakeshore on the entire lake, right there. It used to be an Indian village, but it was flattened in the usual method of a surprise attack and lots of lawless murder."

"How long was it a mission?"

"It didn't last too long; I'd say less than fifty years. There was so much fighting going on around here, and the Indians who did visit and attend school didn't last long. There was a lot of chaos. Trying to subdue and control a people who had always been independent was not easy. And then alcohol came along, and with it came plenty more chaos and violence. Church officials ended up ordering the mission to be moved further north near the Canadian border, but that was after someone set fire to the place, and it was basically demolished anyway."

"Wow. My grandpa said he remembers seeing teepees there too."

"Your grandpa was right before it was ever a mission,
it was a large Indian village. The village
extended all the way down from the point around the bend to where the
highway now comes through. That road was an old Indian trail long before
it was ever a road. When settlers and loggers started coming north, all the
wagons carrying the newcomers drove right through the middle of the Indian
settlements. They had to; it was one of the few solid strips of land between all
the little lakes and marshes around here. But that road was the beginning of
the end for the village. All the travelers coming along got a great view of the
lake. Lake fever began, and it's never slowed since."

"You'd think the Indians would have attacked anyone who tried to
drive through the middle of their village," Eleanor says, and Hope nods in
agreement.

"Sure, maybe at first. But gradually, there were treaties to sign and
agreements made over bottles of whiskey, and pretty soon, there was a road
there, like it or not. I imagine the Indians began retreating away from the road
until the missionaries got a good look at the nice slab of land they occupied
out to the point. Then the same thing probably happened all over again. The
treaties, the booze . . . you know."

Eleanor takes a deep breath and sighs. Red waits a moment for her to
comment, but she says nothing, so he goes on.

"As far as I know, only two buildings made up St. Christopher's mission.
There was the little chapel and the meetinghouse, which was also where
the minister lived. His name was Emmanuel, but they called him Reverend
Manny. He was single when he came, young, as I heard it, like twenty-five
or something. But within two years, he established the school to educate
the Natives. Ironically, many set up teepees by the mission to live there and
get food. Of course, to get food, they had to agree to be baptized and go to
church. Reverend Manny was alone for those first years, but soon he hired a
local school teacher, she was a widow living in Horton, and she had a young
daughter."

"What was her name?" Hope always has to know.

"Oh, the little girl? Elizabeth. She was a pretty girl, like her mother.
They were Irish; they both had dark hair and blue eyes. That schoolteacher
ended up marrying Reverend Manny not long after she got the school up and
running. She was several years older than Manny, but she was happy to find
someone to take care of her and Elizabeth. And they had about six more kids if
I remember right.

"But . . . can you imagine how hard it was for Broken Day, that first day,
coming to the mission? It was just getting started, and Manny had hardly
anything to offer him, certainly not the kind of food he was used to eating. So,

the two of them had a lot of learning to do and a lot of teaching, each trying to get the other to understand his own customs and language."

"I think Broken Day was so brave. I mean, really!" Hope says. "I'd be so scared. If I was all alone and had to go into an Indian village by myself, I don't think I could do it. I'd be *so* scared."

"I agree, Hope. What a brave boy he was!"

"I bet his mom was watching from heaven and was so proud of him."

"For sure!" Eleanor smiles at the girls, recalling conversations they had been having about their own birth mom since they were getting old enough to understand the whole adoption thing. "You know she was!"

"Well, and it proved to be a good thing for Manny that Broken Day came into his life that day, too. Broken Day was a hard worker, and he was good at manual labor. He and Manny basically built the mission by themselves. Even though it was small, it was a neat place. They had a tall fence surrounding the whole flat stretch of land, right up next to the shore. Manny and Broken Day painted the stained-glass windows on the little chapel. Those very windows got moved and are still intact in the mission they built up along the border. I'd sure love to see them. Of course, Manny taught Broken Day how to speak English and how to write it, which came in handy for Broken Day as he got older. It also helped Manny in building relations with the Indians, and Broken Day helped Manny translate."

Eleanor refills lemonade for everyone, not talking but waiting for Red to go on. They all watch a boat zoom by dragging a skier.

"Broken Day lived at the mission for the next, oh, five or ten years. As he grew into his teenage years, he began wandering away, staying away for weeks at a time. He told Reverend Manny he felt like he'd been playing dead too long, and he needed to come alive again. That's why he needed to break free, I guess."

"Maybe he was trying to find his old tribe, or his mom's sister and cousin like he had set out to do with his mom that day."

"I'd suspect that's true. No one knows what he did, but he began having a hard time sticking with the new lifestyle he'd adopted when he found himself an orphan. But then, something funny happened to bring him back into the White man's world."

"What?" Joy sits up a little.

"He came back one day, after a long disappearance, and he saw Elizabeth looking all grown up and pretty. She had been learning at the mission along with the scattered young Indians who came and went. But suddenly, she was a beautiful young lady, and Broken Day fell for her. They wanted to marry, but there was a big struggle. Elizabeth's mother didn't want her to marry an Indian. She wanted Elizabeth to go to the Cities and take care of her grandmother and get more education. Her mother didn't have much control over the situation, though. Plus, she was busy taking care of the other six children she had, all in a short period of time. In fact, Elizabeth had practically been running the school since she was about fourteen, and she herself was looking for a way to escape."

"How could she be teaching when she was just a teenager?" Joy looks puzzled and skeptical.

"Well, age was different back then, Joy. It actually wasn't that unusual."

"So, did they end up getting married then?" Hope asks.

"Oh, yeah. They eloped. Broken Day stole Manny's wagon one night, and the two of them left. They went to Horton and were married there. Don't ask me how, because not too many people around these parts back then would marry a White woman to an Indian. Maybe they had a nice sum of money to offer as a bribe. That'd be my guess. I can't say for sure how they got a marriage license, but they did. Out of curiosity, I looked it up at the county seat one day.

"Then they settled in Pineville. Elizabeth got the teaching post at the newly constructed one-room schoolhouse.

She was the first teacher of Pineville.

Broken Day had taken a new name when he began living at the mission, and that's the name he used on all his records from then on. It was Broden Davis. That's the name he used on his marriage license and on his four children's birth certificates."

"Broden sounds like Broken. Is that why he took that name?"

"I don't know, but it sure could be."

"What did Broken Day do then, living in Pineville while Elizabeth was a teacher?" Eleanor asks. "And did they ever go back to the mission?"

"You know, he opened a grocery there on Main Street. He built it himself with help and direction from Manny. He had such good language skills, and the town was growing so fast that it succeeded, even though many people didn't trust Indians back then. But I know he wore his hair short, and he wore the typical clothing of White people back then. He had two sons and two daughters with Elizabeth. One of the sons took over the store and began selling gas there, after the turn of the century when Broken Day was an old, old man."

"Did Elizabeth ever speak to her mother again?"

"They had a good relationship, as far as the story goes. And they did go back to the mission to visit. They probably first went back to return the wagon they stole!" He grinned. "I'm sure it wasn't easy at first, but Elizabeth's mother loved those four grandchildren. Broken Day continued to help Manny, too, in his later years, when the mission burned down, and they relocated further north."

"Did you *know* Broken Day, Big Red?" Joy looks at him intently.

"Well, you know . . . Broken Day died sometime in the early 1900s, years before I was born.

But guess what?

He was my *grandpa*.

His daughter was my mother."

Everybody looks surprised. Eleanor sits up, "Really, Red?"

"Yes."

"Really?" Joy has to ask again.

"Really. It's true. How else would I know all these things? I'm not a good storyteller by chance. My mother, Rose Tatéweh, was Broken Day's and Elizabeth's youngest child. She was the only one of their children who lived to old age, actually."

"My gosh, Big Red!"

"Rose Davis worked at the first nursing home in the area when she was a young lady. While she was there, she took care of an old Indian. That old man had a grandson named Albert, and that is where he got his first glimpse of Rose Davis. They married and became my parents."

"Wow," Eleanor says plainly. "It's so cool you know so much about your family history."

"Well, it's one of the few things we old Natives can still treasure these days," Red says. He notes the sleepiness of the twins and winks at Eleanor. "I'm glad I have such an interested audience."

"Tell us more when we see you again, okay, Red?" Eleanor stands up and begins packing up the bag under her chair with her book and coffee cup. "We gotta get outa the sun, or we'll all be lobsters. Hope, you definitely look pink."

"I wanna jump in one more time first, Mommy. Come on, Joy." Hope stands up quickly as if charged with electricity, striking a jump-in pose. Joy moves more slowly but gets into a similar stance.

"You've already been swimming!" Eleanor protests. But she can't resist their eager faces. "Alright! One more jump! That's it! Give Big Red a hug and thank him for taking you fishing and for the stories."

After the hugs, Red climbs into his boat, starts up the engine, and Eleanor pushes the tip of the boat away and shoves it off with her foot.

"See you tomorrow morning for tea. I've got an early class. The girls are going to daycare." They watch as he putters away, waving his arm overhead as he disappears into the ripples.

Eleanor smiles at the girls as she pulls off her t-shirt and stands on the edge of the dock ready to dive. She asks, eyebrows raised, "Who's gonna count to three?"

CHAPTER 20

Water's Womb

I didn't begin to know the details that ended my summer until I was already at work for an hour that next morning—when I learned Neal was dead.

As I heard it, my heart combusted, blowing out inside my chest like a shattering light bulb. As the heavy weight of horror moved in, compressing my lungs until I couldn't inhale, I collapsed like a folding chair behind the bar. My hands stuck to the slimy floor. I could not move. I didn't want to be a drama queen, but I froze; not even one muscle could be coaxed even to tremble. That's when they went and found Margaret. I slumped in the corner, blocking the cash register, in shock. I could not believe it. I don't know how long it took for Margaret to show, but the phone cord kept swinging and hitting me in the face. A part of me heard Jan talking to Margaret, explaining that she needed to take me home. That Neal was dead. Neal was dead.

I never went back. That was the last day I stepped foot in the Harbor View.

When Margaret saw me, she started crying. She helped me up off the floor as if I were an ancient, gossamer gown she had to lift out of a box. My last visual memory of the place was Margaret guiding me out the back door. I remembered glancing over my shoulder and out the big windows facing the lake. The tour boat, tied to the dock, swayed slightly, empty and lifeless. Muted sunlight penetrated the gray cloud cover, shimmering all silvery on the surface of the water.

The water . . .

the water . . . the water! I pushed down the urge to run down the dock and go off the edge, to plunge into the oblivious depths, to sink down into the murky mush of the harbor, forever. The only thing stopping me was the lecherous slime of the shoreline by the docks. Years of boat exhaust, dregs, river-esque weeds, and water life mingled together without much cleansing renewing water flow. Jumping in there would be a horrific way to die. This thought hit my head like a brick. Then I thought of Neal, dying in the reeds by the channels. And I was lifted by the thought he had died in the clean, beautiful water, in one of the most delightful parts of the lake. A place filled with good memories. At that moment, I liked to think of him there. I remembered hearing about people who had died in a landslide or even quicksand, and my stomach churned. I felt like I may hurl some bile right out;

maybe it would explode out my eyeballs. I was terrified. I didn't know what would happen to me now.

Everything was blurry like someone tweaked the focus gauge of my eyes. I could not sharpen the images. Margaret drove me to Neal's grandparents' house because I had to find a way to know it was true. When the door opened, it was a neighbor, a middle-aged mom-type. She immediately embraced me and guided me to the kitchen table. She said Neal's grandma was lying down, and the grandpa, I could see, was on the couch staring ahead at the void. So, it was true.

Mrs. Campbell, "call me Sarah," reported she had spoken to the police, and Neal's body had been recovered. She seemed to anchor everyone down with her statement. She explained that the police said he had no outward injuries, but he sustained severe trauma to the head, and his neck had been broken.

"The good news, honey, is that he died on impact. There was no suffering." I gasped. Neal! Neal! Neal. All I wanted was to hold his warm body. Save him. But he had been erased. Dead. He wasn't even in the hospital lying on a bed. He was probably at this exact moment being transferred from underwater to a morgue. No hospital required. How was he being transported? Was he lying on his side? Was he in a bag? Did they take his clothes off of him? Was his hair still wet? What did his skin feel like? He always had baby skin. I had loved his skin.

My shoulders sagged, and I could only think about breathing. I breathed in and out, and I realized that nowhere on Earth was Neal doing the same thing. He wasn't breathing anywhere anymore.

I saw pictures of him all around me. As a boy . . . on his horse . . . with his sister . . . the whole family . . . all the images, all the memories of a life not fully realized, began swirling in a wild blur. I tried to stay focused on what Sarah was saying. Her voice was quiet and even, and she looked at me steadily. Sincere concern emanated from the gentle wrinkles of her face. Her hands were warm. I wanted to crawl into her lap and hide, and tears streamed down my numb face even though I wasn't crying. I was beyond crying. It simply could not be!

He had been struck by a speedboat while he was kayaking. A fisherman called the police about seven-thirty a.m. They estimated he died around five that morning. I know he'd been on his way to Raven's Point. If I just could have been with him! I pictured his face. He was smiling, grinning, of course! We were discussing our plans. That was the last time I saw him. I would never see him smile again.

His body was recovered not far from the kayak, which was battered to pieces at the mouth of the channels. The place where we had coincidentally met and really talked the first time! My stomach churned, and I had to run in the bathroom with dry heaves. I felt hot, yet my body was shivering and trembling out of control. I was learning all there is to know about grief, like it or not. Margaret never left my side, and the knob on our friendship cranked tighter. When I look back on that moment, all I can really feel is my deep love and gratitude for her: her quiet, relentless presence. I don't know how much more warped I would be if Margaret hadn't taken a seat in the background of the tragedy. She was a dim but steady light.

Sarah didn't know much more. I don't remember how I learned what few details I do know and can recall now. I recall anger. It still feels like a toxic rash festering inside. All the unknowns. All that was never to be solved or resolved about how he died. Who was driving the boat that hit him has never been proved. No one has been punished for his murder. The sinister twist of fate that brought Neal's quiet kayak into the path of a humming speedboat will never be clear. How it is he was unable to avoid getting out of the boat's way—I can only theorize, he tried. Or maybe he was oblivious and died before he knew what hit him. I hope for that actuality. My heart still aches. It's a physical and psychological yearning that comes from everywhere and nowhere in the body. Cagey. In a cage with something unimaginable. I have cried and cried out in my sleep, though I rarely know what I've dreamed. My sleep is dry and cracked, like old skin. It has never bounced back. I wake up sometimes . . . often . . . feeling cracked and dry.

When I left his grandparents' house, Sarah was calling Neal's sister to deliver the bomb. I gave Sarah my phone number and asked her to give it to Jessica if she could do it gracefully. I wanted to talk to her. She was the only tie I had to the person who had held my heart. In the days, months, and years that came after, Jessica was the one good thing after losing Neal. We became life-long friends. We would've anyway, so it's not like it was the result of Neal's death, but it's the best I can do. And she, like Margaret, stood there, another dim light in the heavy seas of sorrow. She had now lost her whole family. With Neal gone, her grandparents would be left alone. Jessica simply could not come back. Not for a long time. She lived far away, and, for me, she became the excuse to escape the suffocating monotony of loneliness. When the holidays hit, or a close friend got married, or I lost yet another loved one, I'd get on an airplane and find comfort on the couch of her tiny Manhattan apartment. I offered her the same escape on my couch. We'd hang out together for days, walk along the river, hit museums, go to movies, sit in coffee shops, so many coffee shops . . . and always,

I'd be startled by expressions she had

that belonged to Neal.

But she was not there the day he died. And so much time passed in

oblivion.

When we got back to the cabin, everything was changed. The cabin was old and stale and smelled rotten. My clothes were whirled all over the place. Margaret kept trying to talk to me. I could not speak. I had to go somewhere. I didn't know where, but I went to the canoe. If only we had taken the canoe that morning! Why did it have to be the kayak? Why did we go to that stupid party?

I dragged the canoe down to the shore, packed an anchor and a line, and paddled straight out toward the distant shore. I noticed the Crandahl's boatlift was empty. Their place was deserted. A haunted sensation menaced me. Everywhere I looked, haunted. The trees swayed like giant monsters, the wind whipped like spit in my face. A crackly, scary, witchy voice spoke clearly in my head, "Blake Crandahl did this." I ignored it. I was probably projecting anger from the night before. I didn't know what the hell to do with that. No energy to follow up on it. I couldn't care less whose boat it was, who was driving. Neal was gone. Poof. A blank space showed up in his place. Or was it a black hole? Numbness. Stiff. Like the hammock of life had stopped swinging, the cradle had definitely crashed.

My internal autopilot said I needed to disappear, and the only place I could go was out there, into the water. I could feel Margaret watching as I left the shore, I knew her tears were streaming. I envied her, I wanted to be her, I wanted to be anyone but that shell-girl who was me.

I paddled robotically to the channels, where Neal took his last exhale as he went down. He didn't have to sink far. It was shallow there. I wondered what he looked like. Was he half-floating, legs dragging in the sand, tall reeds all around him, swaying? I had to shake my head to prevent the image from coming. I realized my neck had seemed to seize up, and I asked myself, *oh, what else?* Spasms wracked me involuntarily. The shivering came in waves; my whole body would tremble-vibrate, then it would stop, then it would do it again. My body shook on and off for hours, and for hours, maybe days, my breath was erratic.

In my zombie-esque state, I tossed the anchor out in the shallow waters. I wanted to be where he was. I stared out, around. A silence so profound overtook me; it roared like a vacuum. I was a vacuum. I didn't exist within myself. I was everywhere but inside my body. And somehow, the day bent glorious. The gray dome had risen into high shallow puffs of clouds,
    like spirits,
          wandering with the blue infinity.
        A warm, wispy wind fluttered out of the south
              creating little feathery waves
                    gently undulating the boat.

I curled up on the bottom with the old spider webs and dead insect shells. My head dropped onto my bicep muscle as I took over the fiberglass floor, and I could hear the "plunk, blunk" of the air pockets rolling along the seam down the middle. There I rocked, in the middle of the lake, curled up in a ball beneath the blaring sun. There in the womb of the lake, I zoomed through time into timelessness. I was removed. Before long, bliss came while I was warmed from the outside in by the sun. Neal was there, compassionately cradling me, infusing me with harmony. He talked to me like a faint thunder, a gentle rumble far away in the distance. I heard him, but I don't know what he said; it was just his voice, his mellow tone, his gorgeous smile that massaged the pain away and it did not exist. I think I fell asleep for a long time. I had a brief taste of security, a security I would not feel again, ever. It was a parting gift, his last breath in my ear. Maybe it came from the vapors of the water, from the waves splashing up against the canoe, little swishy kisses, and the boat bobbing massaged me with an opaque transcendence. Maybe, it was an attempt to tuck me back into a cradle of innocence, but I would never fit there again. Still, that canoe on the lake gave me a memory that is warm, stirred in with all the cold loneliness that followed.

When I woke, it was to the sensation of a shadow and a flutter passing over me, and I sat up, startled, inhaling quickly, mystified. I was compelled to look up, and I saw a large black bird fading into the sky, a black dot shrinking into the updraft. I blinked hard, staring at first, trying to see it after it had gone, then holding my eyes shut. My ears were ringing. My cheeks were wet, yet I didn't know that I was weeping. Was it tears or the lake water that had collected on the cold metal bottom of the canoe?

The lake had turned cold. The day was old; the sun was low, and the warm had been snuffed out by a rising wind, and it whistled autumn. I was cold and stiff to the bone, hard with a grief that hadn't even begun to crack. I wanted Neal so much. I wanted his strong arms around me. I looked up to the sky. The bird was long gone. The sky was empty and dull. I whispered aloud in a chant, "Brace me . . . God . . . brace me." Then I paddled back, in a trance-like rhythm, all the while mumbling, "Brace me."

Back at the dock, I landed the canoe and went into the cabin. Margaret had been cleaning and making a meal, but neither of us could eat. What I didn't know at that time but what Margaret told me some days later was that she unintentionally that afternoon had a conversation with Blake.

She was out getting towels and t-shirts off the line when a squad car drove up and around the Crandahl driveway. Blake and an officer got out. Margaret watched. Blake lifted his head, and from across the thick green grass, he noticed her, and their eyes met. He offered no reaction to seeing her. It shook Margaret, and she froze. She watched as he and the officer went into the house. A short while later, Margaret was in the cabin, lying on her bed, staring at the wall, when Blake came to the door, knocking lightly. She recapped their conversation for me.

She went to the door, opened it, and said, "I have nothing to say to you."

As she shut the door in his face, he held out his arm to stop her.

"Margaret, please. I have to talk to you. Do you know what happened?"

"How stupid do you think I am?" She answered. She didn't know what he was referring to specifically, but of course, she knew many things had happened. She stood against the door, not moving her body to let him in.

"I can't believe it was our boat."

"What the hell are you talking about?"

"The boat. That killed that Neal guy? It was our boat. Someone took it last night. It was gone this morning. The cops found it crashed up against the rocks over by the highway."

He was talking about the east side of the lake, about a half-mile down the shore from Comoro's. The Army Corps of Engineers built a retaining wall, using giant boulders to boost the embankment. It was nowhere near the channels, where the speedboat splintered the kayak and killed the most beautiful person I would ever know. How these two details fit together has never become clear. I have speculations . . . but back to Margaret.

"What do you mean? You're telling me you weren't driving your boat last night?" She stood back on her heels, still blocking the entryway. She crossed her arms. "What were you doing last night? I thought you and the guys were going barhopping for the bachelor party."

"We did go barhopping. We went by car."

"You're such a liar."

"What? What are you talking about?"

"Shut *up*, asshole! I know you were at Candice's. Who the fuck do you think I am—a dumb little farm girl?"

"Margaret . . ." he sighs, wiping his face. "We went there after the bars closed. Zack's got the hots for Candice. Which is fine with me."

"You are *such a fucking liar*. Your boat was gone last night before it was even dark. I got home, *here*. I live *next door*! Like I wouldn't *know* your boat was gone? The lift was empty. I know you were out in the boat. I know all about your *bull . . . shit*." Her voice broke. She wanted to slap him silly, and she wanted to make him squirm. Find out more about what he knew. What more lies he was going to spin.

"Okay. You're right. I'm sorry. We did go out in the boat. But that was later. We started out in the car. And we did go barhopping by boat. It was late when we got to Candice's house. I swear." He paused. He ran his hand through his hair, a habit Margaret once found charming, but now she saw it as nervous conceit. "Margaret, someone *took* the boat from Candice's dock. When we tried to leave last night . . . we went down to the dock, and it was gone. I tell you, we–"

"What time was that?"

"I don't know, Margaret. I was a little drunk."

"Oh, and you were planning to drive the boat home? I bet you *were* driving. You were so drunk you didn't know what you were doing! *Until it was too late!*" She felt her voice rising to hysteria, so she forced herself to calm down. "You killed him! You *killed* him! *Didn't you?!*"

"Margaret, I can't believe you're saying that!" He looked at her, pain in his eyes. "Am I really that scummy? You really think that about me?"

"Fuck *you*, Blake!" She was sobbing now. "What!? You're going to tell me some *stranger* walked up--from God knows where . . . *down the shore*, untied your precious boat and got in? This raving lunatic then started it up without your knowing, and went for a little joy ride around the lake in the early morning hours . . . and *you* didn't know about it?"

"Yeah. Exactly. Believe it or not," he held his eyes shut. ". . . I left the key in the boat. Maybe it was somebody at the party. *I don't know.* We'll probably never know. All I know is the boat was crashed up against the rocks this morning. It's pretty much destroyed." He moved toward her.

"DO NOT come in here!" She stepped back away from him. "I really doubt Ellie would want the *killer* of the love of her life," her voice cracked again, "to step foot in her house. Get the hell *out* of here!"

"You really don't believe me?"

"Why should I, Blake? And why do you care? I'm completely *unaware*, right? I mean nothing to you. I was just your little *toy* for the summer. Until your *big* toy came back from Europe. Summer's over, now you can give me the old *heave*, right?" She had both hands balled up into fists. Her arms were seized up tight. He looked startled. He'd never seen Margaret be anything but sweet, and really, neither had I. I still have a hard time picturing her this mad. It's easier to picture her using her racket to smash tennis balls at his face. She, meanwhile, noted the stairs behind him and envisioned herself shoving him backward and, oh,

how far down he would fall.

"Margaret. I care about you! I can't believe you're being like this to me right now. I fell in *love* with you. I—"

Margaret laughed.

"You so did *not*, Blake Crandahl," she shook her fist at his face. "Your saying that to me shows just how truly *fucked* you are," she snarled, shaking her head as if to knock him loose, out of her head.

"I *do love* you. I've never known *anyone* like you, Margaret. I want to spend my life with you."

"Oh, my *God!* How dare you!" Margaret screamed in his face. "You are so full of lies. You are such a liar; you don't even know you're lying!"

He changed the subject. "You don't believe someone *stole* the boat?" Anger rose in his voice. "You think I could do something like that? Come on. You REALLY think I am THAT fucked up?" She said when he said this, it was a plea more than a question. She was shaking.

"I believe you *are* capable of murder. I believe you *are* scum. Now GET the hell away from me!"

Then she couldn't resist; she threw out her arms, cupping his shoulders with her palms, and shoved him. He stumbled back, down a couple steps, but caught the railing and steadied himself. Then he turned and went down the rest of the steps.

"FUCK you then, Margaret," he roared heatedly, turning his back to her.

She couldn't think of anything mean enough to say back, so she said nothing. The sensation of his disturbed aura finally moving out of her space was relieving. She let the screen door slam and blasted the inside door shut behind her. Then she
broke
    down
        crying.
    In the months
        that followed,
            after Neal's funeral, I went back to college, but I also pursued the few threads of the story I had been told about how he died. I went to the Pineville Police Station. I talked to the officer on the case, and I read the file. Blake Crandahl was never charged with any crime from that night, though he had been questioned, as had his brother, Donovan. The papers reported Neal's death; they told of the unidentified driver, who had apparently stolen the Crandahl speedboat. The speedboat held clear evidence, as did Neal's kayak. The two vessels had made uncompromising contact.

No fingerprints were found anywhere on the boat, except Blake's, his brother Donovan's, and Mr. Crandahl's, who all had clear-cut alibis, said the report. Candice and several of the party attendees attested to Blake's consistent presence at Candice's house all night. According to several witnesses, Blake arrived at nine-thirty p.m. and stayed through until morning. Even some of the waiters and a valet corroborated his innocence.

When I told the police I was there, hiding in the bushes, spying, and I heard Blake say he was leaving, and actually witnessed Blake, and another guy, leave Candice's house to go get cocaine, they told me they had no evidence Blake or anyone else at the party had used cocaine. They said Margaret and I were making up a story because we needed someone to blame. The dead boy was my boyfriend, after all. Margaret had been jilted, after all. The chief of police was a friend of Mr. Crandahl's, after all.

I can remember, on more than one occasion, seeing the round-bellied chief, bleary-eyed, hiding behind a scotch glass, comfortably sunken into one of their plush patio chairs. He was such a cliché! He was an obnoxious drunk, often relying on Mr. Crandahl to get him home safely as he was frequently the last guest to leave. Always, a cab appeared in the middle of the night from God knows where. I never saw a cab in that area other than in those instances. The cab thing always puzzled me. His unmarked car sat in the driveway until late the following afternoon. Yes, I knew exactly who he was, and he knew

I knew

it.

He knew I lived next door to the Crandahls. And he knew I had no connections to powerful people or any leverage against his rank and connections. He had no motivation or reason to hold Blake accountable for any of his actions that night, whatever they were.

I know for a fact: he was using cocaine, he'd had sex with Candice and pretended he didn't, and he'd left the premises at least once but very likely more than once, given the gimme-more-now cocaine flush. Maybe he was just posturing when he told his friend he'd fucked Candice when we had clearly overheard him. Maybe. Maybe he was able to curb his urge to go get more coke, but he'd clearly said there was a ton of it over at his friend's place. I just don't believe it.

It seems quite plausible to me that Blake and some of his coked-up cronies took off in the wee hours of the morning across the lake to Zack's house, which, not coincidentally, involved passing right by the mouth of the channels where Neal paddled. In the ratcheted-up hum of their brains, did any of them watch where they were going, cocktails in hand? Were they in such a merry blurry rush to get to Zack's house and back that they were going hyper-speed, so dangerous at such a dim hour? Would any one of them stop and consider what *could* happen in such a state—what *did* happen? Might they even have laughed, or even not known they killed someone, in their oblivion? What would it have felt like to blast into something going at high speed? Did they spill their cocktails? Did any of them bump their own heads? And then . . . how easy would it have been for them to about-face and scream it back to Candice's dock, throw the line to the wind, kick the front tip of the boat away, and watch the boat list off. Then scamper up the steps into denial, into a new made-up reality. I was haunted by the reoccurring vision and imagined sensation of how it must have been for Neal, seeing a speedboat suddenly upon you and then, THWACK, darkness and cold water, loneliness and pain . . . your physical remains now just tatters of memories floating in the water's melody. I hoped his parents' spirits were there, ready to embrace his spirit as it lifted out of the water and into the endless, effortless sky. His life journey ended there, but his spirit soars ethereally now. I must think in these terms. Yet, still, my mind probes. Why does it matter when he will never return? Somehow it does. It just does.

Who had information besides Blake's friends? If anyone saw, no one came forward. How do people live with themselves if they know? Isn't there a knot in their conscience somewhere inside? Could there have been a fishing boat nearby? Was it too foggy in the early hours for anyone to have been seen or heard? Could it have been someone at the party? Maybe thinking it a fun prank to steal Blake's boat? Could it really have been a random stranger? There was no smoking gun, no bloody black glove left at the scene.

There would be no further investigation. There would be no arrests, no trial, no convictions. No resolution. No counter-hammering to the hammering fact that a beautiful and significant person, a person who wanted to make the world a better place, had died. All because he decided to go slowly and quietly across a lake to witness a sunrise. It packed a staunch punch. It ended Neal, and it ended more than Neal. It ended everything he stood for and everything he had been and would never have the chance to become. Like it is for all who die young, and for those who lose someone young, it was beyond tragic; it was the somber and unchangeable truth, a bottomless black canyon ripped apart forever. Its grimness left to pall all over everything. The only, only, only thing to save the situation, the blemish of light in the impenetrable quartz, was that his parents had already crossed through the horizon, and maybe they had found each other out there, beyond. One day, I would too.

Neal's grandparents had no energy or support to muster a case for further investigation. They were battered by tragedies, sea-worn: two boats barely moored in the endless hurricane of despair. Some say God doesn't give people more than they can handle. I say bullshit. Many crumble, crushed by grief. God seems to remain detached.

It took the little energy they had left to linger just a little longer in the world. Staying for Jessica, I'm sure. Yet all they could manage was six months, leaving Jessica orphaned, adopted by my family and me. Jessica had no ability or desire to dwell on the tragedy, to follow up on the crime. It took all her energy to begin processing the loss of her only sibling and last family members. She was a real-life Dickensian orphan, only she lived in New York. The anonymous city provided her a place to be someone else, someone whose family was back in the Midwest, not all dead.

Twice, I went back to the Pineville Police station to try and get a scrap of help in pursuing the crime further, but both times, the scene ended with me screaming and being escorted out the front door, only to fall down on the steps alone and frustrated, crying and hysterical with unharnessed rage. I can only imagine how people of color feel in our white bread legal system, bread that is more like burnt toast. Burnt to a crisp. Charbroiled with corruption, in fact. I don't believe in the U.S. criminal justice system anymore. I'm not sure I ever did. People who believe in it have never had to deal with it personally, or they got lucky. Or they work for it.

I felt like I lived in the real-life version of David Lynch's *Twin Peaks*, a weird but popular TV show that came out after Neal's death. I was addicted to watching it. It was about a small-town murder that no one really cared to solve, and it was all very surreal. Around this same time, the O.J. Simpson trial happened. It, too, offered questionable legalities, oppressed evidence, police bungling, surrounding Nicole Brown's murder. I learned that First Lady Laura Bush killed someone when she was seventeen by crashing her car into another, killing the other driver. She never faced legal consequences. Wealth built connections—connections that formed armor against the arrows of the law.

In the fall-out, anger lurked. So much fury simmered within me that Quartz Lake, my beloved lake, became vile to me. To gaze at it was to gaze upon the grave of love and dreams and hope. To gaze at it was to scan the shoreline and see the mansions popping up. Gone was carefree innocence, happiness, and childhood. The water's depths menaced me. It nauseated me to be in a boat. I got headaches in the sun. The sand was dirty and annoying. Family traditions and history,

held together by memories, were shredded by sadness and bitterness. Yet everything

      eventually settles,

              dark and deep—

                      into the wrinkles on our skin,

                      into the layers of sediment

                          in the waterlines of time.

CHAPTER 21

Haunted Hooves

By strange coincidence, Eleanor clutches four horseback riding passes for a stable about ten miles west of town. She's never heard of the place. The woman, a grandmotherly yogi, talked the place up, and she wouldn't take no for an answer. She said it's been around for twenty years. Eleanor hasn't been on a horse in at least that long, and her memory of horses makes her melancholy. But she decides she'll take Joy and Hope and a couple of their friends.

Riding to the stable, the four girls chat excitedly in the backseat, allowing Eleanor time for her thoughts. She thinks about dreams. What really happens to a dream deferred? Too many other sprouting questions and answers follow. How closely dreams and memories sometimes intertwine as one grows older, she thinks. But she can't go down memory lane today. She's gotta keep her mood light to make this an experience to remember for the right reasons. As she takes that last turn onto the long driveway to the front entrance, she feels like she's treading upon sacred yet empty memories and dreams. It feels auspicious, but she has no idea why.

The dirt driveway is straight and narrow, but both sides are lined with white fencing that hems a beautiful field on both sides, each hosting half-a-dozen grazing horses, tails swishing. The day is young, and the wind is playful, but the heat is notable for early May. At the end of the road is an old-fashioned farmhouse with a barn-style roof and wrap-around front porch. The driveway stops at a row of parking spaces, where three other cars are parked. They step out of the car and are overcome with the smell; it's not horse manure but flowers. A row of lilac bushes at the height of their bloom separates the parking area from the residence. The house is neatly painted, windows glinting in the sunlight. More flowering shrubs and thick masses of sun-colored daffodils surround it. Over-the-top quaint. They walk to the big red barn about two hundred yards from the house. The stable doors are open, and the stalls and bales of hay are visible from where they stand.

Just inside the barn are half-a-dozen picnic tables. There are pop machines, candy machines, a big water cooler with paper cups, and a stand-up popcorn machine complete with a fresh batch smell. The stalls are empty.

A man stands near the first stall, talking with a woman making arrangements about a birthday party. He is scribbling notes on a pad of paper he holds in the palm of his hand. He looks over at Eleanor as he listens, and he holds up his pencil-holding hand to indicate, *I'll be right with you.* Eleanor smiles and nods. They sit down, and Eleanor fills out the forms for the insurance waiver that are sitting on the first picnic table.

When the man approaches, she notices his cowboy boots and baseball cap. He is her height. He holds out his hand, and as she takes it, she feels compelled to look closely at his face. His eyes sparkle blue, friendly, his face is tan and very handsome in that rugged Marlboro Man kind of way. He holds her hand just a bit longer than a usual handshake.

It isn't long before they saddle up, and to Eleanor's surprise, their guide is the man himself, not either of the two college kids who helped get the girls into their saddles and led the horses out to the trailhead. At the front of the trail is the junior guide, who explains the tour to the riders gathered around him as the tour begins.

Eleanor finds herself in conversation with the man while they ride. The girls are in front of her, and the man, who is last, is right behind her, so they can converse easily as they go in single file down the narrow path. At times, the path widens, and they ride side by side.

"Your stables are beautiful," Eleanor feels compelled to say. "And your house—wow!"

"Thank you. The landscaping is my wife's. She does all the gardens herself. She loves it."

"Wow. That's big."

"Yea. She's gone all around the house, the barn, and the entrance gates. Her next big project is wildflowers along the fences."

"That'll be nice. Those fields are gorgeous, with the horses out grazing as you drive up."

"I'll tell her you said so."

"I can't believe I've never seen this place. I've been around a long time. Do you do any marketing?"

"Well, no, I don't really advertise," he looks at her a little funny for the strangely specific question, "we're busy enough. I hire six to eight kids every summer. I got a few permanent workers, that's enough for me. I don't want to get too commercial."

"Yeah . . . that makes sense. I know what you mean. I have a yoga studio in town, and if I get any busier, it'll be too much; I don't want that either."

"Exactly. I got two kids like you, and you don't wanna spend all your time on business; you wanna be with your family and have a life, right?"

"Totally. Yes. I agree. Okay, strike any idea about marketing. I used to write advertising. I'm imagining what I could write about this place to talk it up. I'm picturing a photo taken as you drive up with the horses and the white fences and all the flowers. It'd get the crowds coming."

"It would lose its appeal then, don't ya think?" He glanced at her sideways and gave her a sexy smile. Her heart skittered a little.

"Maybe. These days, with so many tourists, it's hard to keep a family vibe," Eleanor turns her face to catch the light spring wind coming through the budding trees. She catches a pleasant whiff of their sweetness. The moment fills her with a bit of joy, and she smiles, happy to be here. She looks ahead, the girls' heads sway back and forth, taking in the warm hug of the forest. The horses' flanks roll up and down, lulling as a cradle.

"It's getting tougher, that's for sure," he says, patting his horse's sleek neck. "Not only do I have to compete with virtual reality cowboy games—I just got notice about another big resort moving in with plans for a golf course. It's gonna border the entire east side of my property."

"Another golf course? Just what we need. What's happening to your property taxes?"

"They only go one direction."

"And where's that money go? Mega mansions everywhere, owners paying big property tax—where is it all?"

"Hey now!" He says sarcastically, "We got that nice new community center!" He glances at her as she scowls. "Easy, girl!" He winks.

"No, really! We might have to move. I live in an association, and we just got an offer from some development company to buy up the whole lot. It may all get built into condos."

"Really. How big's the association?"

"Like a mile long by two miles wide, pie-shaped, with four hundred and fifty feet of lakefront. The offer is unbelievable—an astronomical figure."

"What's happening now?"

"Well, our officers meet with lawyers, then the members get together to hear the proposal and the offer. It's probably going to get ugly because I don't know how they'd divide the money. Who gets what? Some people have torn down the old cabins and rebuilt, some have more land. I'm just hoping the offer gets rejected, and the big bad developer will go blow houses down somewhere else."

"Wow. That's a doozie. That'll be in the *Horton News*, I bet."

"It'll make headlines, for sure. I can't imagine there's been a bigger exchange of money up here. Plus, the old place is sort of a landmark."

"You think it'll get voted down?"

"I hope so, but I hear mixed feelings. People are nervous about their taxes skyrocketing. They want out while the gettin's good. Even after 9-11, property values are still climbing. I just keep waiting for the crash."

"I know. I don't know how they keep going up and up."

"People are coming from both coasts for what they think is climate security in the Midwest."

"We're beginning to see no place is safe, that's for sure."

"Yet, still they come."

"Plus, I hate to say it, but about half the residents are retired or near retirement. They're happy to take hassle-free money and go away."

"It is hard to resist," he pauses. "So, where d'ya live then?"

"The east shore of Quartz. The old Towering Timbers logging camp. Know where that is?" She glances at him, and their gazes linger. She's thinking about what she finds appealing about him.

"Oh, sure. That's a neat spot. Like stepping off the wheel of time. No paved roads, no streetlights, and no curbs. You love it?"

"Yeah, totally. But the oldness is an advantage for the developers, I think. Our president told me the City of Horton hates our association because it's hard to raise our taxes. We rejected the city sewer and water system. The fire department is upset about that."

"Hard to put out a fire with no hydrant."

"Exactly. And believe it or not, some people get their heat and electricity from generators. One guy I know is for sure off the grid. He's got solar panels and geothermal heat."

"Ah, there should be more a that!"

"I agree! But here we are—goin' the opposite direction. Big condos, big electrical grids, big parking lots. . . ."

"But there's advantages to communal living too."

"Yeah, but here's the kicker for me. We have this great, shared beach. It's never been tampered with. We've got native grasses and natural sand and rock."

"Yeap, that'll change if the condos go in," he shakes his head slightly, "damn shame."

"Heart-breaking," is all she can manage. She finds herself wondering what it'd be like to kiss him. Then she wonders what the hell she's thinking about that for.

"What's the time frame?" He looks at her as if he can read her thoughts. "We'll know end of August." Her face feels red.

"Did you grow up around here?"

"Well, sort of. My parents had a cabin on the north shore of Quartz. So, I spent summers here."

"Oh, I know some people on the north shore. The Crandahls. You know them?"

Eleanor's stomach drops at the mention of the name. She replies, "Yeah. We used to live next door to them." She raises her eyebrows but keeps her expression blank.

"I went to college with one of the Crandahls. Brandy. *Brandy Crandy* we used to call 'm. I think he's the youngest."

"Brandy Crandy?" Eleanor's heart pumps a hard pulse then begins speeding up. "You mean Brandon?" Suddenly she feels the sun beating down hard, and her back is soft with sweat. The trail is mostly shady but for a sliver of sunlight coming down directly overhead.

"Yeah. We called him Brandy. He was quite the partier in college. He'd drink entire bottles of brandy. Don't ask me why."

"Brandy?" She frowns.

"I said, don't ask me why." He laughs. Then she laughs. "Really. It was rather strange."

"Where'd you go?" She squints at him; he's still grinning. A grinner.

"Carleton. Brandy lived on my floor. He was quite a character. I didn't know him all that well. I just used to bum rides with him back and forth to school. He'd be going to his cabin; I'd be goin' home. I grew up in Pineville."

"Wow." Eleanor can't think of anything else to say. Her mind begins spinning. She remembers the letter the girls' mother had written. She mentioned a Brandy Crandy. Could it be the same person? That would mean Brandy Crandy is the girls' biological father? It can't be. Eleanor blinks hard, absorbing the information.

No fucking way.

"Do you know Brandy?" The man asks, drawing Eleanor back in.

"Ah . . . only casually. He was probably about ten years younger than me. He didn't get along too well with his family, as I recall."

"Yeah. You're right. He hated them. He really hated his older brothers. He used to bitch about them all the time."

"What's he up to these days?" Her horse tries to strain and bite off a section of shrubbery, but Eleanor pulls on the reins to keep his head straight.

"Well, he went to law school. Then I heard he moved to Florida. I haven't seen him for years. Have you?"

"No. No. I wouldn't, though." She laughs lightly. "I don't keep in touch with the Crandahls." A silence falls as they go through a gracefully wind-swept meadow. Then they continue talking.

"I wonder if he still lives in Florida."

"Well, I was just at a Carleton reunion thing about a month ago. That's what everyone was saying. I guess he's still single. Never married."

"Wow." Again, Eleanor's mind surges. She's got to investigate. She has another reason to visit Florida now. The first being Margaret, who runs a bed and breakfast in St. Augustine and has for over ten years. Never once has Eleanor visited. The only time she ever sees Margaret is when she comes to Minnesota. Their friendship survives via long telephone conversations. But now, the time may have come. Eleanor takes a deep breath, then asks, "What part of Florida does he live in, do you know?"

"No idea."

"Hmm." Eleanor is quiet, thinking. Wondering how to begin checking up on this Brandy Crandy fellow. She could start with the Carleton Alumni office. Wondering if she should. Maybe she should just let it be. It could be a huge can of stinky worms, or worse. If he is the girls' father and a lawyer, things could get smelly, even rotten. Then she wonders, *is this why I've had this weird anticipation or whatever it is, this odd sensation hanging around me all day?*

Pretty weird coincidence.

"You've seen all the changes on that lake, huh?" He lifts his cap with his fingers to scratch his head. His eyes are so vibrant. *What is it about men on horses?* she thinks.

"What's that?" Eleanor jumps back into the conversation. "I missed that; what were you saying?" Her horse does another lurch for the shrubs, but she pulls the leather straps tight.

"I was just saying how crazy all the new development is around here."

"Like the water parks and strip malls and chain stores?"

"And the golf courses. But so far, I can't bring myself to leave, even though I sometimes hate the tourists."

"I know. I love it, but I kind of hate it at the same time. My parents sold our cabin a long time ago. The taxes shot up so fast." *That'd be the short explanation, anyway,* Eleanor thinks. Eleanor looks ahead at the girls as they approach a wide field. Suddenly her horse is galloping. She sees the girls wild and free. She feels the same exhilaration. Then memory and emotion rush over her.

She looks up at the blue sky and blinks back tears.

How can a person feel happy and sad at the same moment?

She keeps her eyes shut, focusing on the

rhythm of the horse.

Be here now . . .

here . . . now.

The treetops whirl past, and

dust flies up

on the heels of the horses,

and the air

seems to twirl about her head.

Then they slow down, alighting back to the Earth, like letting go of a ski rope and slowly sinking into the water while losing speed.

"Where would you move to, then?"

"No idea. My business is finally making money. I don't want to go back to the Cities, but houses here are outrageous."

"Well, that's true for waterfront, but in town and in some of the outer areas, you can still get a great place for decent money. Just start looking. You'll find something if you have to. But hopefully, you won't. The Cities are no better."

"True. But if we turn down the offer, I'm afraid they'll come back with an even bigger one, and we'll go through the voting thing all over again. I'm afraid they'll get what they want. It's just a matter of time."

"That sucks."

"They keep after it until they break down whatever obstacles exist, then they move in."

"Depressing."

"Yeah. Leaving Pine Hollow—that's what we call it—would be such a drag."

"Especially because it'd be torn down, too, I suppose."

"Yeah. Exactly . . . what's your name, by the way?"

"Travis Grand. What's yours?"

"Eleanor Marlow. I own the yoga studio across the street from Harvest Moon, the coffee shop. Know where that is?"

"Oh, sure. Old Red. Been there lots a times. That old codger is quite a character."

"Yes, he is. My girls have adopted him as their grandpa."

"Does he do yoga at your studio?" He looks shocked.

Eleanor bursts into a laugh. "Red? No way. He thinks I'm a weird, new-agey type."

"Yeah, but he's a little weird himself."

"He's out there; I'll give ya that. But he'd never step foot in a yoga studio."

"I can almost picture it." They look at each other and laugh.

"You should try yoga," Eleanor grins. "It's awesome."

"Na. I'm a horse and barnyard kinda guy. I mean, my parents named me Travis, for God's sake. I was such an anomaly at Carleton. I think that's why they let me in."

"I was wondering about that."

"But they have a great business school."

"Did you experience culture shock?"

"For sure. But I also got a lot of scholarship money."

"That helps." Eleanor tries to entice him again. "You know, if you do yoga, you'll be able to ride horses well into your old age."

"Well, I get my exercise working around the farm. That keeps me able-bodied enough—and busy, I wouldn't have time. And I'd look ridiculous in a leotard."

"Nobody wears leotards!" She scoffs but smiles, thinking about how hard it is to get macho men to try yoga. She changes the subject. "So, tell me about the new golf course. Where will the turn-off be from the highway?"

"Get this. The turn is the same as ours, but just after you turn onto Pebble Creek Road, instead of going straight, toward our stables you take a sharp left, and the road winds around until you come to the clubhouse, which is already plotted out. The whole area is nesting grounds for whooping cranes."

"Yeah? Don't tell me. I don't want to know."

"They're filling in parts of the swamp," he continues anyway. "The DNR plans to *relocate* the cranes. We'll see, right? Lots of us are protesting, but you know how that ends up."

Eventually, the trail brings them to a rolling open hillside. On the brink of turning green, the short grass is just starting to grow. The horses begin trotting eagerly, knowing the stables are close. Eleanor catches smiles on her girls' faces. Hope's hair flies out behind her. She looks at Eleanor with a grin so wide Eleanor beams. She looks over at Joy, but she's busy shouting something to her friend and laughing with her usual gusto. Eleanor holds back her horse as the others go ahead, and the ride comes to an end.

The perfunctory end-of-the-ride stuff and exchanging of gratitude occur, then Eleanor loads the kids into the car as they chatter about their horse's quirks. Travis walks with her toward the car.

"Hey, come back soon, okay?" He says, touching her arm.

She nods at the noisy girls. "You think I have a choice?"

"Well, come back for yourself, too, okay?" He says, eyes piercing.

"Oh, okay," she says with exaggerated reluctance. She tries to deny her desire to come back. And maybe even her curiosity about him. If only he'd have said, *Come back for me.* Now there's a thought.

"I'll be watching for news of Towering Timbers," Travis says as she gets in the car. Then he shuts the door for her as she puts her keys into the ignition. He waves and backs away as she puts the car in reverse and turns the car around. Eleanor finally glances up in the review mirror to see what Travis is doing. He's leaning against the doorframe of the barn, one leg crossed over the other, watching her. *Is he trying to be incredibly sexy? Or is he just like that? I need to get out more—he has a wife, for God's sake. You are imagining things!*

But he's reassuringly real. And she wants to hold onto his image. He holds out his hand, then with his arm, gestures in a sweeping motion at the land, his place, up to the sky, smiling. She holds her head out the window and beams a giant smile back at him, and waves. Sometimes you get a near-miss in the fantasy of fate.

In the long drive down the dirt road, the girls are still high-energy and caught up in conversation, so Eleanor is quiet. The air from the open window rushes in, and sunlight streams through the wake of dust on the road behind her. She remembers the young Brandon Crandahl as she thought of him in those days long ago when they were neighbors. He was always alone, often playing in the sand. He never had friends around and entertained himself quite easily. He and his mom were often on the dock together. She'd be kicked back in her lounge chair, smoking, as he'd go jumping off the dock and climbing the ladder, over and over. Never was he with his dad, who always fished with the older two boys. She used to see him tinkering in the garage. He had a miniature car he'd drive around the driveway. His mom would run out, and though she tried to be subtle, she'd yell at him when he drove on the grass. He did it a lot, probably to get a rise out of her. She'd drag him to the tennis court and force him to play, but he never seemed to play by choice and never with anyone his own age. He was a mama's boy, but he also seemed to torment his mom with annoying behavior. Eleanor wonders how he may have gone from being that ten-year-old boy,

     to hanging out in casinos,

        drinking brandy,

           and hooking up with women.

He did have a defiant streak if she remembers right. Eleanor calculates he would have been in his early twenties, maybe right out of college, when the twins were born. The typical age for one-night stands, but the odds he's the same person, are unlikely. Still, Eleanor's curiosity churns, remembering that little boy and how he used to play alone on the beach for hours. He had Matchbox cars, and he'd sculpt roads and buildings to drive them around, create bridges and tunnels, and dig long, straight rivers down to the lake. He'd stand with his hands on his hips, his bony elbows sticking out like wings, and he'd cock his left foot out as he looked at his sand cities. She sees her memory of him clearly in her mind's eye.

    It unsettles her. A culminating point to a whole day of weirdness.

This is, she becomes aware, disconcertingly similar to a stance both Hope and Joy have. They, too, spend hours in the sand, making little homes for their plastic ponies, with roads, buildings, rivers, and tunnels. They, too, stand back, hands on hips, left foot cocked, to admire their creations.

CHAPTER 22

Wake

The surface of Quartz Lake was still the morning of Neal's funeral. The air was still, the house was still, the blood in my veins was still, too. I had fallen asleep on the dock the night before, the night of the wake. I had become comatose as a result of the attempt at sociability and in the exhaustion of grief, and I was somehow capable of calm breathing only when I had the lake in view. Its ever-changing face kept me enough distracted and yet, dulled, that it was the only place I could tolerate for very long. Everywhere else I went, I could only hover; I could never actually root to the ground, to the present. I was just visible, weakened like a day-old helium balloon. I was passing through the timeframes of life without actually impacting them.

Margaret stayed out there with me until she shivered so much, she had to go in; still, she kept coming out all night long, trying to make me come inside. I felt like I was zipped up all the way in a wet sleeping bag; I could hardly respond to her pleas.

My family tried to dote on me after Neal's death, but I was so sick of everyone; I pretty much shut down the conversation with scowls and one-word responses to the point where my siblings began avoiding me. Margaret tolerated me, and probably only because she knew we were going into our senior year, and she was stuck with the lump formerly known as me for the next nine months.

I didn't like myself either. I tried to figure out a way to escape me, but there I was, trapped inside my head. Everyone else could get up and go off to whatever they had to do, but there I was, choked by the monstrous grief. Holding the proverbial bag. It was enormous and without parameters. I envied the rest of the world for being able to get on with it. I knew I would have to go to school soon and read stuff, and take tests, and write papers, but I really didn't know how I'd pull it off.

That dawn on the dock, long before the sun showed up, I watched the lake breathe wisps of fog that floated along the flat, murky surface. I resided in the sullen stillness, the pervasive chill, and the hovering silence. Occasionally, the long forlorn cry of a loon echoed in from out of nowhere like my inner wail manifesting in the outer world. I wanted to feel something for the loon calling for its mate. But I was numb. I watched the molecules of darkness evaporate into the expanding mist, slowly being replaced by particles of light. It seemed to me that process was like how a person's vital force moves from life through death and into the other realm. The lake allowed me to witness this inner state, and I felt Neal there, invisible in the visible.

I felt as though I could feel his sorrow, not at having died, but at having caused me agony and grief. I contemplated that for a long time through those spikey first few weeks. It was comforting to think that he was okay being dead. I didn't know how that could possibly be true, but somehow the notion was there, in that moment and in the memory it left me. It still has me puzzling over what happens after life.

I lay there curled over on my side, my head resting on the soft bicep muscle of my arm until the sun drove golden rays of light piercingly into my soppy eyes. I pulled myself up to a sitting position just as my mom was stepping onto the dock to make me get up. I had to get ready for the funeral. She wrapped her warm arm around me and escorted me to the back cabin, trying to pep me up so I could dress into some kind of a living, walking, functioning zombie. It felt pretty logical and almost inevitable to just fall asleep there on her warm shoulder and possibly never wake up, but she said, with kindness in her eyes, "It's time for *you* to stop being dead now." Then she launched me up the steps to the back cabin door, and I was soon enough out there in the big bad world navigating again, which I found entirely unrealistic.

The entire day played on in a predictable blur—a slow-moving hallucinogenic horror show. It rests in my memory only in little visual clips, like a movie trailer—a grim, gothic tragedy, of course. I can vividly recall the physical condition I seemed to have developed. A nervous pit in my gut. My torso was a black iron cauldron where I was bubbling lots of murk. Somehow, it steamed out invisibly through the top of my head, and occasionally, I could feel something heavy like tar turning to ash, tingling out through my pores. The thick, molten resin of grief gyrated down deep in my potbelly. It slowly stiffened into a mass as the days flipped by. If my grief could be described in physical form, it would be a giant brain-like shape. It was splotchy, darkly-colored petrified wood, unbelievably heavy for its size, hideous, and all banged up with scuffs, dents, scabs, and jagged scars. I only know this because for several months after his death, I had an intermittent, reoccurring dream where I found the thing perched on the shoreline in my path, and I had to lift it with heroic strength and roll it out of my way before I could continue.

Finally, after I truly don't know how long, in one dream, I became so frustrated with the repetition of finding the thing in my way once again that I picked it up like you would attempt to lift an old sleeper couch and somehow staggered out to the end of a random dock and foisted it into the water. It made a stupendous splash, almost sucking me in with it, but it disappeared

in the dark depths. I began to feel better, slowly, after that particular dream, but I can easily drum up the vision of the thing and its weight, even these many years later. I don't like recalling it, and when I do, I remember the part where I released it, too afraid to let it linger long in my head. I also began to emerge from the sudden bouts of nausea that used to hit me for no apparent reason.

But on that day, the day we had to say goodbye, my arms, legs, mouth, and head seemed to be wired-on appendages doing things and saying things completely outside my control. I went through the motions, as people say they do when they experience something so grievous. I know I seemed and looked odd because I got many strange looks and plenty of whispers from all around the church, and probably for months, who knows, maybe even years afterward.

The church ladies, the ones who always show up to handle the lunch in the basement after the Mass, looked at me with such deep sorrow, I've often wondered how they, who were the funeral people, processed the tragedy of Neal's life and those lives he left behind. Did they know how young he was? Did they know how he died? Was he just another day at work for them? Their faces displayed an understanding, in a non-intellectual way, of the depth of the loss, even though they never knew him. I wondered how they willingly put themselves in the midst of grief—but maybe it actually fuels them, somehow. To be able to actually *do* something productive in such circumstances would maybe feel empowering.

The funeral was, everyone told me, so beautiful, and the church was stuffed full of people. I remember looking around at one point and seeing people standing two rows thick all along the walls of the church, all the way from the back up to the altar. Two busloads of students from the university had come up the night before to attend the wake and pay their respects. Neal had so many friends, it blew me away. The priest at St. Francis Catholic Church, where Neal's grandparents had been parishioners for years, had allowed the students to camp out under the pine trees in the big chunk of land between the church and the graveyard. I met Neal's roommates, his study partners, and a couple of student teachers who did their practice teaching at the same school as Neal. I met a couple of the professors who had him in class.

The wake the night before was something no one in the entire town had ever seen. The line of people waiting to pay their respects to Neal's grandparents, Jessica, me, and my own family, went out the door of the church, down the block, around the corner, and past the bakery and video store. People in town wondered what celebrity had decided to be buried in their humble little graveyard; though Neal was not to be buried there, he was to be cremated, and his ashes would be set free.

The wake was supposed to end at nine p.m., but we were all still there at midnight when Jessica finally had to excuse herself and her grandparents, who were actually physically falling apart by that point. His grandmother's face had fallen in with weariness, her pale blue eyes, saggy, tears dribbling steadily out the bottom rims. My brother almost had to carry Neal's grandpa out to their car and set him in the backseat. I don't know how he managed to look so clean and stand up so straight the next morning, but he did, probably purely out of respect for the young man who had devoted much of his life to caring for him and his dear wife. I could barely look at them, but I do remember the warmth of his grandma's soft and tiny hands, one hand's bony grasp held my hand on the one side, and Jessica's on the other, through most of the ceremony. I used my other hand to continually hold a ball of tissue up to my eyes, soaking up the tears that flowed with no effort.

Mr. Dale, Neal's supervising teacher when he did his student teaching, spoke about Neal during the Mass. I couldn't even absorb all the amazing things he said about Neal. He remarked about how truly unique Neal was. It seemed his every word crushed my heart more and more until I felt like it couldn't get any more pummeled. Words of praise, admiration, love, loss, encouragement, perseverance, and gratitude flowed and flowed regarding Neal and his presence, his aspirations, and his impact on this world. I didn't know how I would ever let go of him.

Neal's body was cremated, and his ashes were placed in a cold steel urn. Though some of his friends made giant boards overflowing with pictures of him displayed throughout the basement of the church for both the wake and the funeral, I could not look at them. When I tried, I would begin hyperventilating and gasping, and I would nearly faint. I could not look at his face and see his young, vibrant body. It stabbed me. My heart would momentarily stop, then pound real hard once or twice as if attempting to make up for the gap in rhythm. I heard occasional hushed laughter from some of the people who gathered around the pictures, but when I came around, the laughers stopped, and some would cover their faces with their hands to mask their tears.

Neither Jessica nor I could participate in the myriad of conversations that surrounded the picture boards or contribute anything by way of pictures, stories, or mementos. Our sadness was paralyzing—such things were futile as an attempt to capture what we had lost. I had no idea how I could ever pay tribute to him or the role he had played in my life. I still don't. No picture board or eulogy could touch it.

It hurt, too, that I didn't know any of his friends. I had just barely gotten to know Neal. We hadn't even had time to blossom. Margaret was my only friend who knew him. Our separate sets of friends couldn't know each other's grief, much less our connections to Neal. Why we all loved him so. I ached that the world would never know I was his girlfriend. I didn't get to be introduced by Neal to his friends. His friends and teachers never knew us together. I never got to see him in the classroom with his students or brag about him to really anyone. The only friend I had who could link pre-Neal me to post-Neal me was Margaret. It's made the whole thing seem phantom.

I never got to see him again in his flesh form since the last day we were together when he told me he was going to kayak to the point to watch the sunrise. I remember his fully animated expression and that cartoon-sized smile that crinkled his whole face. He was so excited about the days ahead, his new teaching job, coming to visit me at school, planning the purchase and design of his horse camp. He had nothing but full steam ahead enthusiasm for everything that came his way.

I still feel an unbalancing, gravitational suction toward the ground, so heavy and strong, when I think about how wrong and messed up it is that he died with so much life left to live. I find myself captivated by the colossal mistake of it all—how could anyone say this was fate? . . . and it hits me suddenly, wherever I may be standing and whatever I may be doing. I am too familiar with the sick sensation, like having breathed too much car exhaust when I come up against the hole in the atmosphere where his spirit used to be.

I have hundreds of pictures of him stored in boxes, but there's only one picture of him I can actually look at without feeling an ache and deep sadness. It's a picture of him wearing a hat, something he didn't do much the whole brief time I knew him. I knew him three months—not even. A handful of days. So few days, I won't even let myself count how few they actually were. And yet, I never overcame those handfuls of days. What an insultingly short blip of time to be undone by. I could relate to those people who commit a crime in a flurried instant and pay for it the rest of their lives. Cuffed by a moment, out of life's fruition.

In the picture, he's standing on my dock looking out at the water, and I can't even see his face all that well. It's mostly in profile. But he's squinting, and I can almost imagine him older, grown-up all the way. His curly, white-blond hair, sticking out from the sides of the hat, can almost look like white, old man hair. I like that he's looking out at the world and not at me. I can handle that. If it were a shot of him looking at the camera, his eyes would bear into me like searing radar beams, and it would hurt too much to see him there, trapped in a little square shiny photograph. Frozen in an image left for a memory.

But looking at him looking far off and away, I feel he is still dreaming, visualizing, plotting, and concocting. He still exists in my thoughts in this way. Only now, he's an angel and can spin his dazzling eye wheels ever so slightly to tweak circumstances, to somehow still affect the world, even if he didn't exist within it anymore. I liked to think of his eyes having that power. They still resonate in my mind like a pulsating chakra.

Throughout the predictable funeral proceedings, the priest droning on about his life, the professor speaking about what an honorable and dignified student he was, his roommate talking about his sense of humor and zest for life, I kept staring at the urn that held his ashes. I tried to picture Neal's essence somehow being contained in the hard but shapely contours of the thing, being stupefied by the idea of it.

For years after his death, sometimes I would enter a room or turn a corner, and for a brief second, I'd see that urn sitting there, oddly out of place and alarmingly scary and vivid. Who had set it there and why? Then it would disappear, of course. It was never there at all. I'd be rattled, my pulse and breath completely out of kilter for an hour or so afterward, like a bad drug hallucination full of diabolical imagery.

And I did wonder how badly my brain had frayed and feared I would continue to spiral downward into an asylum. The loss of him did threaten to undo me completely. I am a drama queen, I guess, since some would say, look, it was only a matter of days . . . and somehow that made things even worse. I did fear I could die of grief. And it would take apart my mind on the way down. It was not pretty.

And yet . . .

a candle lit amid this darkness,

a friendship ignited between Jessica and me. I remember walking in the back doors of the church with my family, Margaret at my side, just before the wake began. Jessie was standing at the altar with her grandparents, admiring all the flowers, and when she looked back from where she stood, she saw me. She turned her whole body and bolted in a full sprint down the aisle to where I wobbled along. She grabbed me and hugged me so tight I felt my lungs collapse, and I couldn't hug her back tight enough. I dropped my purse, and Margaret picked it up. Jessica began sobbing hysterically. Her long wavy hair was wild and unmanaged, falling all over my face and shoulders like an old shredding blanket. We both cried hard. My family continued down the aisle to console and support her grandparents, but we stood crying and hugging for what seemed a long time.

Margaret just stood there beside us, waiting and contributing her presence without asserting it. When Jessica finally let go, my collar was wet and covered with black smudges. We looked at each other, and suddenly we both let out a quick, sullen little laugh as we realized we had both just ruined our make-up, knowing it was inevitable. What a stupid thing it was to put on make-up at a time like this. Margaret handed us a big stack of tissues without saying anything. Jessica glanced at Margaret and squeezed her arm, clenching her lips together in an attempt at a smile, then she grabbed my arm, and we walked down the aisle together, mopping our faces into balled-up snot wads. Margaret followed, her head bowed, silent and grim.

As the funeral lunch began to wind down and people had mostly cleared out of the church basement, the church ladies kept busy in the kitchen cleaning the coffeepots and tying up the giant garbage bags. Jessica, Margaret, and I sat at one of the round tables covered with a paper tablecloth. I kept looking at a run in my black nylons and wondered how long it had been there. I said something like, "I can't believe it's over." And they echoed their disbelief. My parents were taking care of Jessica's grandparents while my siblings helped carry flowers out to the cars, picked up the box of cards and other small tokens of grief people had left on the table near the box where the cards went. Luckily my sisters and brother were there to pick up the loose ends. Neither Jessica nor I lifted a finger.

I think I may have drunk some horrific black coffee out of one of the tiny Styrofoam cups, but that and a few chunks of broccoli were the extents of what I had consumed for nourishment. Jessica had put her head down on the table, and within a matter of seconds, she seemed to have fallen asleep. Margaret and I discussed how we'd get back to the cabin, and she agreed to drive my car, and we'd give Jessica a ride back to her grandparents' house.

But somehow, when we finally tore ourselves from the table, we didn't want to leave. Even though it had been a thoroughly exhausting day, and the place was hardly comfortable, it was the last place where we were still with Neal. We didn't want it to end. That would mean a new day would have to start, and that day would be empty of Neal. Yet, somehow, we got in the car, and Margaret drove Jessica home. When Jessica got out of the car, she turned and leaned down to speak to me; though she could hardly get the words out, she was so tapped. I was in the backseat and didn't have the energy to move up to the front seat when she got out.

"Elle, I want you with us when we spread his ashes. You'll be there, won't you?"

"Please, God in heaven, don't let me miss it!" I sobbed. "No matter what, call me, and I'll be there. Just like James Taylor, I'll be there." We smiled weakly at each other. I slumped over onto the door.

"You're my family now, you know," she choked, leaning on the car door.

"You're mine, too. Promise you'll call me!" I yelled, suddenly charged with a last bolt of energy. I leaned up over the front seat as she stood up to shut the door behind her. "Call me every day. Every. Single. Day."

"I will. And if for some reason I don't, promise you'll call me. Okay?" She started crying again as she began to walk away. "Don't let me forget him, Elle. Don't let me!" She raised her voice, alarmed and almost panic-stricken at the idea of it.

"We'll *never* forget . . . never . . ." I choked and began crying again. She waved her hand as she dragged herself up to the house, but she didn't look back. I could tell she had the other hand covering her mouth, probably stifling a scream.

We didn't scatter the ashes during those weird days surrounding Neal's death and funeral. None of us had the energy to do it with any sort of dignity or ceremony worthy of Neal and the occasion. We decided to do it the following summer, hoping we'd be in better shape by then, but that plan never came to pass.

The day after the funeral, Jessica came and stayed overnight, and she probably would have permanently suctioned herself to my side, except she didn't want to leave her grandparents alone during the remaining days she had before she needed to get back to New York.

The night she stayed over, Margaret stayed busy cleaning the back cabin, packing, and calling her folks and some of her friends back home, basically trying to stay out of the way, allowing us space to grieve and bond. Jessica and I sat in the sand, right at the shore, our butts wet. It felt soothing to burrow our feet in the cold, wet sand, listening to the quiet lapping of the feeble waves.

We talked about everything except Neal. Whenever the words started to wander in his direction, we both managed to steer away from it. We just couldn't talk about him. Still, we can hardly bring him up, and neither of us can say his name comfortably out loud. But she told me all about school in New York. She was going to be a sophomore, studying art history, and hoping to get a job with one of the New York museums after graduating. She was so young to have lost her whole immediate family. I always made myself think about *her* chasm of pain when I started to feel sorry for myself. I worried about her constantly, and I hounded her with phone calls for a long time after Neal died. She would always be my connection to him, rooted in that summer, symbolically sealed that night.

We talked deep into the blackest hole of night. Until
        the faintest rim of light appeared on the eastern shore,
           even as the loon calls
ricocheted over the water like sad thoughts
        grasping for the receding dark or the last musical chair.

Light continued anyway. We never moved from the edge of the water, and the craziest thing happened while we lingered, too tired to accept this night's defeat. The day dawned despite us.

Jessica blurted out, "I don't *ever* want to forget him, Elle. I need something—a sign—or a message! Something *from* him, like a reminder he's still here, around me," she sucked in a gulp of air. "He is, don't you think?"

"He is. I know he is! I do believe it," I looked around the atmosphere and felt him there, right then. I said, "Sometimes I feel him around me. He comes and goes. Sometimes it's so strong tears come to my eyes. I feel his warmth. Something will happen to you like that. You *will* know he's here."

She rooted her toes deeper in the sand, almost in desperation, like she was digging for something to rise up out of the sand.

Then something did.

Her toes stopped digging. I watched her struggle with her foot to get a feel of it. We both leaned forward.

"What is it?" I looked at her face, barely visible—her features ghostly gray in the airy darkness. "Is there something there?"

She kept digging with her foot, then she stuck her fingers in the sand and began scratching at the thing.

"Oh, my God," she said, wiggling it out. She held it up, and we stared. Then we stared at each other in the surreal twisting light. Unbelievable.

A *horseshoe*.

CHAPTER 23

Destiny's Delta

Humming neon bulbs framed the giant casino, sending waves of light particles staggering into the midnight sky. Their momentary but continual radiant presence held the darkness at bay, rhythmically releasing tiny, illuminated notions of possibility, out across the parking lot, over the land, like stardust in the eyes of gamblers, gold-rushers making their way toward the double glass doors. Opening into the unforeseen universe of so-called chance, those transparent doors could lead to a dream come true with the simple pull of a lever, the quick pop of a quarter into the magic slot.

Trudging through the heavy snow, a youngish woman, swamped with ideas of transformation and life anew, stepped onto the dry, cement entryway, stomping out her boots and irritation before plunging ahead. She readjusted her scarf and flipped her shoulder-length hair out, then she pushed the door open, stepping into the dingy, sporadically lit interior.

Instantly assaulted by aggressively lingering cigarette smoke, she rubbed her eyes and looked around for the bar. Though she'd been here not long ago, her recollection of the layout was foggy. Spotting the familiar grounds, she bee-lined it up to the bar and wedged her way slowly into a stool. She studied the bartender and, feeling a stroke of good luck, realized it was the same fellow tending the bar as it was that night six months ago. The bartender eventually made his way over to take her order, but noticing her giant protruding belly, he hesitated.

"It's okay. I'm not drinking anything hardcore. Just get me a Coke, okay?" She smirked at him. He moved away without comment, shortly returning with the tall icy glass of Coke.

"Hey, do you remember me?" She asked, looking hard at his face, trying to get him to look at her face. His shaggy, tangled, gray-brown hair gave him the appearance of an old dog, and his squinty eyes, bad posture, and meaty complexion didn't help. But these traits made him memorable; the woman indeed remembered him; he served her and her friend several rounds. He had interjected strange comments here and there throughout their stint at the bar.

"No." He answered.

"Well, I was here, like six months ago? Me and my friend? Her name was Jean. We were having a great time until her *boyfriend* showed up, and those two got into a fight, a screaming match, really. Remember?"

He stood there stiffly, his head angled down. She leaned in, slightly, toward him to check for signs he was listening. She wasn't sure he was, but she continued anyway. "They, of course, *made up* and took off to hit the hotel room that *me and* my friend were supposed to be *sharing* . . . and I was stuck with nowhere to go. So, I sat here till like two a.m."

"Were you playing the slots?" He made his mouth into a tight straight line, barely glancing out from his curtain of hair.

"What? Was I using the slot machines?" She wondered why this mattered, but she answered. "Yeah. Here and there. But then I met this guy. Here, at this bar. You . . . you waited on us. I was ordering rum and Cokes. He was drinking brandy. He had brownish hair, brown eyes. Good looking. He was pretty tall, taller'n me, anyway."

"How much didja spend? On the slots."

"Man, I don't know. Fifty bucks? Why does it matter?"

"Why're ya askin' me if I 'member you? Am I s'posed ta? Did ya shoot someone while ya were here? Did ya shoot cher friend, for makin' up with 'er boyfriend, and leavin' ya with no room?"

"No. No! That's not why I'm asking. I'm wondering because I'm trying to find the guy. The guy I met here, at this bar—a night *you* were bartending. Maybe he's a regular? Do you remember? About six months ago? Remember us drinkin' here? We were laughing and having a great time until like two in the morning."

"Did ya leave with the guy?"

"Why? Does that matter?"

"Well—you after the guy cuz 'a that then?" He pointed with his head at her rounding belly. "Is that why yer tryin'd' find 'im?" He rubbed his eyes.

"I guess, in a way, yes. I *more* want to find him because I think we're meant to be together. I think he left me a note. He may have left it here at the bar, with his number—his contact information. In case I came looking for it." She took a deep breath, then a huge sigh, then began talking again. "Ya see . . . I left his room in the morning . . . in sort of a hurry. I called my friend in *our* room, from this *guy's* room, and she was all uptight because she and her boyfriend were—look, his name is Brandy Crandy. That's the name he told me. I can't say for sure it's his *full*, like, *legal* name. Did he—"

"Hold on a sec, wud ya?" He moved slowly away to help another customer, washed a few glasses, filled the nut bowl, took a phone call. She took the opportunity to look around the bar. It was sadder and dingier than she remembered. The others at the bar looked about as forsaken as one could possibly imagine. Every one of them exuded deep aloneness. Each one drooped over the glass, hardly bothering to be aware of the surroundings.

Before she could say anything, the dreary bartender returned and spoke. "The fact he made up some weirdo name like 'Brandy Crandy' aughda tell ya he pro'bly didn't want ya t'find 'em, ya know."

"Well, he *told* me that was his nickname. He told me everyone calls him that. He said he'd leave word for me at the bar. Here. Right here. Can't you just answer me? Do you remember me—us, being here?"

"Lady, I work here 'bout every night a' the week. I serve hundreds a people drinks, every day. You don' strike me as partic'larly unique, 'cept a' course for ya bloomin' belly. Ya got twins in there?"

"Ha. I don't know. I actually think I do, yeah. And I'll be quite honest with you. They are Brandy Crandy's twins. Okay? Do you get it now? That's *part* of why I need to find him. He needs to know I'm carrying his child. Or children, actually, possibly. But I also just want to *find* him. I really do think we're meant to be together."

"Yeh. You said that."

"You must *know* who I'm talking about. He had money. He tipped you well. He told me he'd been comin' here a lot. He wasn't exactly happy about it, but he was going through a rough time. He said he liked coming here because he could be unknown. It was away from the places he normally went, where his friends went, and everybody knew him."

"Don't that make ya think maybe . . . he didn't want whacha might call a *long-term* entanglement, then? If he was, like you was sayin', doin' the anonymous thing, or whatnot?" He stuck his chin out at her slightly.

"No. *No!* He *said* as I was leaving his room the next day that he'd leave word, like how to get in touch with him . . . here, at the bar!" She frowned at him.

"Well, I don't have no notes back here, anywheres," he glanced up and down the underside of the bar in a sort of attempt to back up his statement.

"Do you *know* the guy?" She sort of pleaded. "Does he still come in here?"

"No. I don't know who yer talkin' bout, lady. I never heard a Brandy Crandy," he shook his head slowly. He reached for his dingy bar rag and resumed pushing it around.

"Yeah. *Okay.* And if you *did* know him, would you tell me?" She smirked at him. "I don't know why I bothered to tell you the whole story. Is there a manager around, or anything? Could you just look in your lost and found bin, see if there might be a note, an envelope—or something? Or ask the manager to come over here so I can ask him?"

"Manager's a her. She's not around right now. She only works till eight. Then she's off. She'll be back at nine t'morro mornin'. Wait, no. Tomorrow's Sunday, so she's not in on Sundays. You can talk to her on Monday." He blinked at her. She wanted to stand up and smack him with the broad side of her palm so hard he'd fall over. But she feared she might lose her balance, so she held her fists tight to herself instead.

"*God!* I can't believe I wasted my time here! Talking to *you!*" She leaned sideways and slipped off the barstool. She left the half-drunk Coke sitting in its watery ring and didn't leave any money.

She walked away because she didn't know what else to do. She couldn't look at his face one more second. She began wandering up and down the rows of slot machines, not looking at anything in particular, lulled by the monotony of bells shrilly jingling. The place was mostly empty, but the machines made the flurry of activity and jingling money sound relentless like the place was crowded somehow. She consciously had to focus on not throwing up.

She'd thrown up so much in the past few months, it seemed a natural, functional response these days. Anything that struck her as annoying, sad, or frustrating seemed to be accompanied by retching. And the belly . . . growing and growing. She was so huge, at six months pregnant, she could not see her feet. She could set stuff on the top curve of the protrusion now, no problem. She knew, pretty much for sure, though she had yet to go to a doctor, she was carrying twins. She felt two separate sets of feet kicking her, sometimes at the same time, a duet of seedling spiritual vivaciousness coming from within. A not-so-meek notification, something like *Hey, you out there! There are two of us in here, see? Feel that? And that? Ya ready for us?*

She held her belly protectively as she stepped hesitantly up to the bill-changing machine she happened by on the way in. She cashed one of the two twenties she had in her coin purse. She got two rolls of quarters and began mindlessly plunking them into one slot near the bathrooms. It kept her from needing to hurl. But it only halfway suppressed her thought waves which spiraled round and round, same old stuff . . . her beleaguered life story, her predicament, her inability to scratch-out a clear action plan, or even a first step toward a plan, any plan, out there, somewhere.

Desperation, loneliness, fear, and anxiety had rudely moved into her little one-bedroom basement apartment. Those mean emotions stood in the corners; they hid on the bottom shelf of the refrigerator. They dallied in the dust along the tile trim in the bathroom. The dingy living room blurred with a menacing unseen *something*, and it sucked up the air. It came to a point she had to get out. It seemed to push her out.

She didn't know where to go; she just got in her little Mazda and started driving. She came up with the idea she should find Brandy. He was the only thing, or person, to give her hope—or a memory of joy—commonality, something. The casino where they met was a three-hour drive from the Cities. It was the only place she could think to look. Maybe he'd even be there, sitting at the bar by himself. Luckily, she hit the freeway after rush hour, and the drive proved calming, giving her time to think outside of her little box while sitting inside another.

She had tired of searching faces for real human contact. Everybody seemed caught up in their own drama. She didn't know or remember anyone she could contact or count on for kindness. Her life played out like the cruelest game of musical chairs, but the simile was real. The music had definitely stopped. No chair in sight. She had tried to get in touch with her sister a few times, but that seemed like her last straw. Her sister didn't bother to reply the last time.

Day after day, she put off the reality of the pregnancy. She would get up and struggle for about an hour with the temptation to walk down to the corner store to buy cigarettes and booze. Why did there have to be a liquor store a block away? She did give in, often, in the first few months, but then, she'd pass out, and the headache and heartache became too much to bear. It became easier not to go, especially when the money ran out.

Most days, she'd at least get up to go for a walk. Enormous hunger growled in her belly. She'd walk to the little grocery store and buy herself a can of soup, or tuna, or a loaf of bread and some ham, then walk home and make some lunch and fall asleep on the couch watching her favorite soap opera. Some days, she'd visit the food shelf and eat whatever she could until she satisfied the relentless hunger. Then she'd buy a paper and search for job listings in the want ads. She didn't have the internet or knowledge of how to use it to find a job. Rarely she had the energy to type a letter and copy her résumé and get it all in the mailbox with an actual stamp on it, but those days were becoming rarer. Jean, her one last friend from the days when she had a normal life and worked at the airline, never called anymore. She and the boyfriend moved in together, and their lives were meshing fine without her.

So, here she was, wandering friendless in a casino, wildly pregnant, without a partner, lonely beyond pain, and so sick of herself she didn't care if she woke up ever again. When her legs felt too heavy to lift and continue moving in the forward motion, she would put her hands on her belly and remember she had to carry on because she had two people depending on her. She rallied.

She cashed out her winnings (she was ahead by three bucks) and straightened her back, slipping the heavy coin pile into her coin purse. She sniffed hard, still trying to overcome her chronic drippy sinuses, and made her way to the hotel lobby. She went down the dark, narrow hallway connecting the two buildings, and as she came to the hotel entrance, she looked up at an old black and white photograph
 of a Native American man
  standing next to a lakeside teepee.
The photo had been blown up to poster size, so it was somewhat fuzzy, but it was displayed in a heavy, dark wood frame, uniquely hand-carved.

"1927" had been hand-written at the bottom of the photo. She studied the man because he seemed to be looking right back at her. He looked ancient yet timeless, as it was impossible to guess how old he was in 1927. He still seemed alive through the eyes of the photograph. He was wearing full Native tribal clothing, from the elaborate eagle-feathered headdress down to his beaded moccasin-fitted feet. He wore a necklace with an enormous, round medallion of shiny silver with a dazzling turquoise fish in the center. Behind the fish was a sun with rays crackling out from the center to the edges. In his left hand, he held a wooden tool, what looked to be a smoking pipe. His face proved the most interesting of all the many details in the photo. He attempted a smile, but behind his eyes, and within the lines of his grin, sadness rested. He seemed to be trying to look happy for the photographer but suppressing discomfort. His eyes were deep, dark. . . .

Aged, ageless, intriguing.

His brow, nose, and jawline were broad and strong.

It looked like a hot summer day, and he looked warm in his outfit. His cheeks were somewhat shiny. In his eyes,

she recognized

a familiar feeling of isolation.

She wanted to know him. She imagined he was kind, giving, and wise. She reached her hand up and touched the glass where his face was. His expression made her want to cry. Here she was, alone. There he was, alone. They were alone together but not really. How

depth-defyingly

depressing.

She took a long deep breath and sighed, then turned to pull open the heavy door to the hotel, glancing one last time at the old man's face before she went in. He remained there, frozen in the frame, while she moved on and away.

After she interrogated the hotel desk clerk and he offered no knowledge of the alleged Brandy Crandy, she realized she couldn't suppress the puke any longer and left quickly. She had to stop twice on her way to her car to throw up in the snow. The sight was so horrible she kicked snow over it to cover it up. Then she arrived at her car, and she stood leaning on it with her palms, arms taut, head down.

The thought of getting in and not knowing where to go made fear shimmy up her spine again. She pushed off with her hands and stood back, kicking snow at the front tire, half-heartedly. After a minute of that, she noticed a couple, teetering, arm in arm, down the row where her car sat. She quickly backed away from her car and passed the drunken pair as she headed back into the casino. She would gamble for a while. She stood three bucks to the good; maybe she'd hit a jackpot.

Two hours of machine entertainment later, all her quarters were gone. She switched machines several times, but her coin supply only every now and then increased. It mostly steadily decreased until no more. She considered cashing the other twenty for more quarters, but she couldn't find the bill-changing machine. She felt nauseated from the damp, smoky air and thought she'd step outside to clear her head, then return to look for the bill-changer. When she got outside, though, the air felt good, and she didn't want to go back inside. She walked to her car, feeling the chill of the darkness, the reprieve, and the reboot of the fresh night air.

She settled down into the driver's seat and started the engine to warm up. The dashboard clock said 2:11 a.m. She had nowhere to sleep and no money to get a room. She had the twenty in her bag. The remnant of her unemployment money for the month. She shivered when she remembered there weren't many months left of her unemployment income. What was it, two? She held her eyes shut tight and changed the subject in her mind. Luckily, she had filled her gas tank. She decided to hit a drive-thru for a coffee, and she'd just drive around, drive until she could find a good spot to watch the sunrise, then she'd head home. Maybe driving would help her come up with a plan.

She drove for a while and found a great road; it was a two-lane and completely empty of cars. It wound around a giant lake, up and down small hills, around curves, and through giant pine forests. She had to go slow, which was exactly how she wanted to go. She had her radio playing softly and kept one eye on the road and the other looking out the window. *When it all goes crazy, and the thrill is gone. . . .* Firefall sang softly in the background. The coffee did its trick, and she was wide awake and actually a little happy, or at least content, alone in her car. The heater was warm; the dashboard lights were cozy.

She couldn't see much because the road had no lights, but every now and then, the road ran right up along the shore of the lake. The moonlight tiptoeing on the lake stirred her with a measure of starry glee. As she'd come around a curve into a wide-open stretch, it just poised there, the moon, waiting to be seen, like a special beacon just for her. Already fall had become snowy, blustery winter, but still, it was only October, so the lake was nowhere near frozen. Her watery surface pleated with the wild winds, and it waved the moon's dazzling beam like a wand, casting a rosy, sparkly, spherical spell round the rim of her eye and through the translucent air and out through time.

The temperature lifted, and
               as the sky began to blink
                       awake in the east; the woman pulled over.
A decent shoulder separated the road from the ditch, and she could park without worrying about getting smacked by an early morning driver.

She sat in her car, watching, drinking the last few sips of cold coffee. She blinked slowly and found herself dozing off for short periods of time, but she was warm and content. She let the morning come to fruition while she vacillated between nodding off in a dream state and waking up feeling lazy but comfortable despite the belly being tight up against the steering wheel as she leaned back in her seat.

After a while, she noticed the clock said 8:44. The sun, beaming over the lake, warming the day, invited her out of her car. The snowfall from the past few days stood diminishing before her eyes, melting into little streams and puddles. Her door squeaked noisily as she cranked it open and leaned on it to pull her awkward mass up and out of the car. She carefully made her way down the sandy lip of the shore and put her fingers in the lapping water, noticing it was barely above freezing. But it felt good and clean, and she wiggled her whole hand into the sand under the shallow water. Then she cupped the water with both hands and splashed it over her face. Though she was bending at the waist, relatively balanced, she dribbled some water down the front of her jacket. It didn't matter. She did it again and again, letting the freezing water dribble down her face until her cheeks began to feel numb. It made her wake up; it pushed back any idea of crying, though she had all kinds of sad thoughts.

What the hell am I doing? What the hell am I thinking? I just made the biggest idiot out of myself. Why did I go there? I didn't even bother to leave my contact information! What if he comes looking for me there? Yeah . . . like he gives a shit! I'm such a lame-ass! Splash. Splash. I'm not going to make it through this. I'm always going to be alone. I'm never going to amount to anything! Splash. Splash. And the dreams! Those terrible . . . dreams! Stop! Stop! Just stop it! You've got to pull yourself out of this! Stop it! Come on! Get with it. Come on! Splash . . . Splash . . . Splash . . . Splash.

She suddenly thought of the old Indian.

He stood tall and proud, a chief somehow.

He may have been thought of as a prop, but he held his dignity. He had to have been a man of authority in his tribe, even if the photo tried to make him look like a roadside attraction. She stood up straighter than she had in months, maybe years. Her spine lifted, and she felt tight, snug inside her body, and physically strong. She felt the weight of her protruding belly. She gazed out over the lake, and new thoughts came rolling in.

Think you're all alone? Everyone's alone! But you're not going to be in a very short time. You are going to give birth. You will have babies to take care of. You have a life. You are somebody. You matter. Take charge of yourself! Rise up! Wake up! Come on! I'm with you!

She didn't know who "I" was, but she had a sense of someone or something boosting her. A wave of inspiration, a flood of clarity. Origin

unknown. She moved with a different focus back to her car. She opened the door to the backseat and grabbed an old notebook sitting on the floor. She climbed in, shut the door, and turned on the ignition to warm up. She wiped her face on the back of a mitten she'd left on the passenger seat, then reached over with great difficulty and pawed through the glove compartment for a pen. She had the first step to a plan. She needed to write some letters. She needed to acquire some peace,
        like the man in the photo
holding the peace pipe seemed to have.
Exhaling, fluttering
                puffs of smoke
                        out and away,
                                easing pain with every whisp.
                                        Gray Eagle
relit the pipe, slowly
                beginning his daily ritual, inhaling deeply and meditatively, blowing the smoke down over his blanketed lap. He stirred restlessly in his wheelchair, working his rickety spine and restless legs. While he waited for Rose to return, he mumbled to himself the old prayer he'd been saying since childhood.

I will live a long life,
        and he thought of each of his family members. He looked out across the terrace at the navy-blue water in the lake below and sighed long. He summoned their spirits to join his spirit. He began with his birth family, his mother and baby sister, whom he'd grown up with and loved dearly.

He recalled the spirits of his father and two older brothers, respected warriors in his tribe who died fighting the frontiersmen in the Minnesota River Valley in the 1850s. He remembered the way his father wore his headdress. And his huge, broad hands, usually cut up and scabbed, but strong and warm, always. He looked at his own hands and saw they were the same hands he remembered as his father's hands.

Gray Eagle held the pipe firmly in his hand, the same pipe his father had smoked with his people. The pipe his father had made. He ran his fingers across the figures carved into the narrow neck of the pipe. The belly of an eagle formed the bowl of the pipe; its wings and curved head and beak formed three knobs on the end, perfect for gripping and passing. In its talons, the eagle held a gopher, and below that a rabbit, and finally, a fish, whose wide tail fin formed into the broad mouthpiece. He'd had a gift with wood; he was able to whittle spirits out of the fibers, revealing the wood's nature, creating amazing trinkets and tools.

His brothers used to take him fishing, but they delighted in how well he, himself, Gray Eagle, could fish without their help. He had that gift. He beamed with pleasure, even on this day in his wheelchair, at the fact he could provide his family with food at such an early age. He remembered the words of the elders at his naming ceremony. They told him he had the fishing skill of the eagle, but rather than focus on his skills, he must focus on the rewards of the fish, the blessings of the bounty, words he recalled throughout his life.

He loved to talk about that part of his life, his golden childhood, before the killings. It lingered in his mind, with blood-sepia nostalgia, as the romantic days of old, when the men he knew and looked up to, stood on the soft earth: strong, independent, and free. Unaware of the future, for the most part. He remembered it in his mind; he never saw it captured on film anywhere. It was a whole different orientation to reality. A way of being on the Earth as an integrated part, not as a conqueror or visitor. He wanted to have grown up with that relationship to the Earth. He knew people thought this was trite now.

But today, he wanted to tell Rose about the second tragedy, the one that befell him in his teens. He had to get around to discussing his grandson with her. There needed to be a memory of family history, a telling of the family story. This was the way to win her heart; he knew this. This was the way to reel this fish in.

She'd be back; she just had to wheel a few other residents out for their after-lunch fresh air. She always came back to sit by him, to hear his stories. She was a Native, too, and she had recently lost her aged mother, who, she had said, was a great storyteller. He loved Rose's long dark hair and subtle greenish-brown eyes, her thin arms, and her elegant aura. She exuded an inner beauty, and her name, Gray Eagle realized, was a perfect fit.

"Mr. Belmont, how is your pipe today?" She came up next to his chair and knelt down beside him, her arm resting on the back of his chair. She spoke formally to him, not sure how his mind would remember her. It was a caution she learned from working with the elderly. "Are you getting inspired? Is your mind sharp today? I'd love to hear a story."

"Rose . . . yes. I have a story in my mind today. It's another sad one, though."

"You're not going to talk about your son killed in the war. You already told me that one. That one's too sad to hear again." She smiled, sitting back on the short stone wall that bordered the terrace, her back to the lake. "Tell me about when you had your sons. You must have been happy then, right? What did you do as a young man—as a father?"

Gray Eagle took the last puff and rested his hand on his lap, holding the now lifeless pipe. He wanted to tell about the years when his sons were born.

His life glowed with happiness every day. They were farmers then. He had taken over the land of his stepfather. But to get to that part of the story, the happy times of his early fatherhood, he had to tell about how he acquired the homestead.

"Rose, when I was a really young man, I found myself running a farm and raising my two stepbrothers. I knew nothing. I had mostly helped my stepfather in the fur trading business. It was my mother who grew the food in the field out behind our little shack. My mother made the meals and fed me and my brothers. Of these things, I knew nothing. Yet there I was, thrust into a situation without a guide."

"But you told me you had a sister. I bet she knew something of how to grow food and make the meals and raise children."

"Yes. I did have my sister, Citanwin. She did come to help me quite often. But she had married and moved onto agency land. She had four youngsters of her own to take care of, and her husband drank, so her life teetered with its own hardships. But my dear Citanwin, yes. She was a great help to me in those days."

He thought of her in her last days upon the Earth, before his son had taken him away to the old-age home. Gray Eagle had trudged across the agency land to see her before she had taken flight into the spirit world. She had been alone in her hut, passed out on her couch with the little radio playing classical music in the background. His heart throbbed, remembering.

He had gotten there at the moment of her death. He was so glad he was holding her hand. Or had she waited for him? He had retraced his steps that day and wracked himself for all the stupid divergences he'd had that day before he finally showed up for that moment, at exactly that moment. These are his thoughts these days: how long had she hovered there in her body before he had arrived to hold her hand through the invisible gateway to the other side? Had she been in that death state all day, lingering, or had she fallen into it suddenly? He doesn't know the details of her cause of death, other than to say she died of old age, but she hadn't been that old.

He thought of her four children; two had been randomly killed in their childhood by a group of traders, who opened fire as they rode by in their wagons, just for fun. The other two still lingered around the agency, lost in their sorrows, pointlessly battling the reservation and its restrictions. He sat silent for a moment, forgetting his train of thought. Trying to remember when the boarding school came.

"So, what did you do then, Gray Eagle?" Rose asked, bringing him back to the terrace. He gazed out again at the cold, blue waters. Though his eyes were old, they were still sharp, and like his mind, they kept him alive while his body softened and hardened, deepening negotiations with age. It was a blustery fall day, and the wind jittered about nervously, mucking up the surface of the lake. It was an unfamiliar lake, but still, it breathed, and he preferred its dynamic vista to the dull brown walls of his room. The sun shone brightly against the back wall of the residence, and though it reflected warmth onto the patio, Gray Eagle appreciated his blankets.

"Well, we made do. That is all. My stepfather, John Belmont, was a trader. He married my mother, as I told you, after she was widowed. They moved from the river valley. John made a good living as a trapper and trader, and he trained me. We worked together, and John bought land on the shore of the Nokissasa, one in the Quartz chain. Do you know it?"

"Yes, in fact, I do. I live over that way myself," she smiled.

"Then you know how nice a lake it is. You can imagine how pleased we were to live there. We lived through much fighting by the Minnesota River when I was very young. I was glad to be away from that. And I was a good fisherman. We lived happily, and my mother had three more children with John, two sons, my stepbrothers, Walter and Leroy, and then a daughter, Ana.

"Then, one day, it came to a sudden halt. I had taken my brothers to the lake to catch fish, but when we returned, the homestead was quiet. I did not let my brothers enter. I went in and smelled the blood. I saw my mother and baby sister dead. They had been badly stabbed and slashed. Baby Ana was just a few years old. It made me sick. I made my brothers go off to find John, and while I dragged their bodies out of the house and tried to clean up the blood, my heart went stiff.

"When my brothers returned, they said they'd found John, but he had been struck down and killed. He had been beheaded. My brothers were crying, and they took me to see. It was gruesome. I am most sorry that my young brothers had to see such a thing. We buried them all together behind the shed."

"Oh! Oh, my . . . Gray Eagle!" She blinked, and tears fell out of her eyes. She looked at him with such empathy, his heart crackled with her warmth. She urged him to keep going and patted his arm a little, resting her hand there for a minute.

". . . I think they were killed in a raid on the agency by the full-bloods, enraged by the cheating and so many unchecked crimes of the agency officials. I went to the agency a few days after their killings. I found many of those living at the agency had also been killed. There'd been a raid. Confusion and fear gripped so many full-bloods that they took their rage out on the mixed-bloods.

"My stepfather had been a fair and honest trader, but many of the non-agency Indians hated traders and their families, anyone who mixed with Whites because they were blamed as the root of the problems. Many traders took entitlements from the Indians to pay debts they said Indians owed for their trades. Agency Indians always lived on the brink of starvation—more and more with each passing season. Yet the agency was passive to their plight, and the traders kept doing business, gathering more riches while the people scratched around like rodents."

"I know a different version of the same story, Gray Eagle," Rose concurred.

"We made it through, somehow. I raised Walter and Leroy. When they were big, they both went to the city. They cut their hair short. Walter married a White woman, and he ran a store down there—his wife's family store. He left in his late teens, and I never saw him again. He sent me letters, he still does, through the agency. Leroy joined the Native alliance, and he traveled into the Dakotas. He was killed not long into his life. I do not know the details of his death or how he lived once he left the homestead. He was a good man, though, and I know he died bravely."

"I'm glad you still have Walter, at least. How did you meet your wife? Were you alone on the homestead for a while?"

"It was Cetanwin who arranged my marriage to Waziwin. She had been orphaned and taken in by Cetanwin's husband's family. She came to my homestead when she was only fifteen, and we were married. We had three sons, as you know. She was a beauty, like you, Rose. And she had many gifts. She could work the land and raise food on it. She made beautiful jewelry. We sold many of her hand-crafted pieces in our teepee booth."

"You had a store then?" Rose crossed her legs and turned slightly, so she could look out at the lake. Some of the other residents, who still had their ability to hear and be entertained by listening, had moved closer. Gray Eagle tended to draw a crowd. It may have been his even, steady voice, deep and lulling but captivating at the same time.

"Well, when my sons were all still young, the government men came and took our homestead. I had no way of proving my stepfather had purchased the land. I did not know if he had a deed or where he kept the deed, though Waziwin and I searched everywhere in the shack. They say we were not entitled to the land because it was to be turned into a state forest. This was untrue, of course, because now, you know, there is a resort on my homestead. But we were moved to agency land and given a hut. When that happened, we struggled.

"We did not have land to grow our food, and Wazi was very sad. She did not like living at the agency. She was constantly afraid of raids and waited for death to come to our family. I hated living there too. We were surrounded by disease and sadness. Many of my neighbors drank whiskey and were idle. They took kids away from their families and tricked them into the schools.

"But I remembered the words of my elders back in the tribe of my birth. I continued to bless my bounty, and we all worked to stay together. I fished, and we lived on fish and what I could hunt. I refused to drink whiskey. I saw what it did to Cetanwin and her family.

"Soon, the agency men approached me. They knew I spoke English. Some remembered John Belmont, and they asked if I wanted to open a trading booth. And that is how I started selling. We sold many things but not on the agency land. No one there had money to buy anything. After a while, I moved my teepee booth out to the road. I made friends with a tavern owner who used to buy from me. He knew John Belmont, and he allowed me to put my teepee on his property along the side of the road. We did much better then. We had many customers coming in their wagons and, eventually, in their cars. I had a nice view of the big lake there. I was happy.

"The tavern owner ran a gambling business in the saloon, and sometimes his customers won big money over the cards. They'd spend some at the teepee. I saved and saved the money we made. Wazi's jewelry made us lots of money. We sold wild rice and dried corn. I sold many items from our younger days, many I wish I had saved, but I wanted money. I learned my English well, and I knew good business skills. I had the greedy eye for a time. But what I wanted more than money was to buy my own homestead again and get off the agency."

"Did you do it?"

"No. I never was able to leave the agency. I lived there with Waziwin until she died. She died of grief. When our first son, Harmond, was killed in the war. She died a little bit the day he left to enlist, and when we heard he'd been killed, her spirit took on a layer of earth. She stopped making necklaces. My second son, Albert, was a gifted woodworker. Northern Lights Lodge hired him to make a totem pole. They paid him to go to the Pacific coast to apprentice with a famous old Chinook there. Albert made his way as a craftsman, but he took to drinking, and he vanished too, not long after Waziwin became a spirit. He was not that old. All I have left is Arnold. What money we saved I gave to Arnold."

"But now, your son, Arnold, also has an Albert, right? His *son*, Albert? Hasn't he been here to see you? Right?"

"Oh, yes. That is right. You met my grandson, Albert. He's a handsome one, isn't he, Rose? And you know . . . he is not married," his eyes twinkled at her. "He plays the saxophone."

"Yes. I have met him, Gray Eagle. He is a fine man," She smiled back. "Is your son, Arnold, still alive?"

"Arnold is still alive. But he's ashamed of me," he sort of chuckled. "He has not been to see me. He drove me here. He took me away from my hut, and he's never come back."

"That can't be true. Why would he be ashamed?"

"Rose, he is. He could not accept my actions. He doesn't know how my bones ache. He thinks I gave my soul to the White man."

"But how could that be?" Rose looked confused. They both sat silent a minute, gazing out at the lake, now fully blown-up with the brilliance of the afternoon sun. Its shimmer caused them both to squint. "No matter what, a son loves his father."

"When I gave Arnold the money, I also gave him what I had left from my booth. I was too old to keep it going. I could not get around to my friends to get the wild rice to sell. I did not have Waziwin's jewelry. I'd run out of trinkets. Arnold worked for a lumber company and bought some land, but not near me. He married a White woman, and he had his two children. His boy, Albert, and his girl, Mary. All this, and Arnold still never comes. I was always lonely.

"I kept going to the tavern because I didn't have anything else to do. I sat there during the day because home on the agency was too sad for me. The tavern owner convinced me to dress in my best clothing and wear the headdress of my father, Tatéweh.

"I had John Belmont's name, but I was still my father's son. I gave my sons my father's name. It was written on their birth certificates. I had saved my father's headdress, and when I wore it, I felt my father's spirit. Soon the cameras came. People offer me a penny to be photographed with them or just standing there by myself.

"One day, Arnold came in his wagon. He heard his father was giving his spirit away to the White man. When he came, it was a bad day. A crowd of tourists was there. They were laughing at me. Arnold was mad and dragged me away. He tried to make me stop going there, but I counted my coins every night. I was still making money, and the tavern owner fed me. I did not care that the tourists found me funny."

"What made you stop?" She felt a chill and realized she needed to get everybody back inside before the temperature began to drop. She stood up and went over to pat his arm. He clutched the pipe absently and didn't respond. The afternoons slipped away so quickly sitting with Gray Eagle. She could listen to him for hours; something about the old man was so enthralling. Maybe it was his serenity; even as he told of all the heartbreaks of his life, he was living proof of endurance and fortitude.

She wanted to get Gray Eagle off his train of thought, so she said, "you must've found something else to do, huh?"

"I didn't stop going to the tavern. Not until Arnold came and packed me up and moved me here." He lifted his chin to catch her eye as she wheeled him around, and they began heading back inside. Another nurse had come out to help bring in the residents. She flashed Rose a frown, but she didn't say anything. She knew Rose had a thing for the old Indian.

". . . and Rose," Gray Eagle held up his hand, to reach for Rose as they rolled along down the hall toward his room. Rose stopped and came to stand in front of him as he grabbed her hand. "I still have that headdress. I'd love to show it to you."

"Oh, I'd love to see it. Maybe I should arrange to have it hung on your wall, so you can see it every day. Would you like that?"

He didn't answer her question.

Instead, he said, ". . . and those bags of coins? I still know where I buried them, Rose. There are quite a few." He squinted at her, his gray eyes watery and saggy, and still holding her hand, he pulled at it to get her to stop. Then he continued, and his eyes perked up a notch,

"When you marry my grandson—"

Rose laughed. Then they both laughed a little together. She didn't think the idea was too far-fetched, actually. Albert had caught her eye the very first time he'd been in to visit Gray Eagle. She loved the way he always grabbed hold of his grandfather's hand and held it while they sat together talking and laughing on the terrace. She loved that he took the time to know this ancient gray birdman.

"You'll have to invite me to sit down with you two then, the next time he comes to visit!" She winked at him.

She bent down and took his grisly, talon-like hand up to touch her cheek.

Her smooth skin against his hand sent warmth
straight through his arm to his heart.

Their laughter echoed down the empty hallway as it began to grow dark with late afternoon, still,

the energy from their laughing radiated into him
like the brightness and heat of midday,
and Gray Eagle's rugged heart . . .
fluttered.

CHAPTER 24

Xeriscaping

Margaret was giddy that last day at the lake, but I was the polar opposite, so we had to stay out of each other's way. She was going home soon. I had no home. And with all her hard-earned summer money, Margaret arranged to buy a little Toyota from Gina, the owner of the Harbor View, and I agreed to drive her over to the restaurant to get her new wheels. She had all her bags mostly packed and sitting in the kitchen of the back cabin, waiting to load into the new car. She was eager to spend Labor Day weekend with her family and friends. We didn't start classes until the third week of September, so we wouldn't be seeing each other for a few weeks. This was good and bad news. Good, because her happiness annoyed me, but bad because her happiness kept me alive. I am sure she needed to escape my ornery scowls and anger, but I feared even further loneliness at the thought of her driving away in her new car, radio blasting, on her way to freedom—freedom from me.

She managed to contain her joy as we drove to Harbor View. She had all her cash in a big envelope, ready to make the exchange. When we pulled into the parking lot, I wanted to throw up, but I vowed I would not enter the building. I told Margaret I'd wait in the car. In a matter of minutes, she came bouncing out the back door, the car's title dancing in her hands.

You'd never have known she'd just recently had her heart broken by a complete schmuck. She covered her sadness well, or she knew how to live in the moment, anyway. She still had her interludes of grief, but she was not entrenched with it the way I had been. I tried not to let that bother me. I had enough to be bothered with already.

She opened the passenger door of my car and hopped in. "Elle, drive down there; it's at the end of the lot, in that row." She pointed, smiling broadly as she jingled the keys. "Come on . . . you gotta be a little bit happy for me? Just a little?" She raised her eyebrows. I smiled for real. She wouldn't be contained. We drove down to the end, and there it was. A bright red Toyota Corona, four-door. It was clean and shiny. I double-parked, and we both hopped out. Gina had been kind enough to make it sparkle anew only for Margaret.

"Wait, Elle!" She unlocked the driver's door. "Pull into this spot. We've got to take it for an inaugural drive, okay?"

"Yeah. Let's take the lakeside drive!" I grinned. "See if you can get a speeding ticket!"

"Ha! I'll leave that to you," She pointed at me. It was well-established I was a habitual speeder. We monkeyed the cars around and then peeled out of the parking lot. The lakeside drive was a two-lane road, full of hills and rounding curves, at times paralleling the shoreline, giving spectacular views of the broad bay. Fall was in the air, but the noon sun was bright and hot. We had the windows rolled down, and the tunes cranked. We didn't talk for a while, and it felt good to escape and let the wind mess up my hair. After a while, we turned around and headed back, and the mood changed.

"Isn't it weird . . . the Crandahls have completely disappeared," Margaret said, breaking our silence. "Not that I care, but I never saw them packing or anything."

"Yeah. That is weird. My mom heard they went to California for *a little vacation*. She saw their housekeeper packing a bunch of stuff the day of the funeral, and they had a conversation out at the mailbox." I added, even though she didn't specifically ask about Blake, "apparently the whole family went."

"Huh," was all she could muster.

"Did you want to see Blake again?" I wondered, keeping myself neutral.

"No, not at all. But, ya know, after our big blowout? He didn't even *try* to see me again." I didn't say anything. I was thinking.

"I mean, not that I wanted to talk to him. Believe me, I've never despised anyone more than him, but you'd think he'd be somewhat contrite, and try one more time. . . ."

"Margaret, you give the guy so much credit. He had you fooled, but he never fooled me." Realizing that sounded harsh, I added, "Sorry. . . ."

"I just can't believe it. I just *still* can't *believe* I fell for such an *asshole!*" She shook her head and stared out the windshield, her face rigid. "I mean, how stupid am I?"

"You're not stupid! He's adorable. He's fun. He charmed the heck out of you. He charms everyone. I've just known him a long time, that's all. You could never have known him the way I know him—his whole family, for God's sake. But now you do."

I gazed out the window.

"I just feel so . . . *stupid* . . . " she chokes with emotion. "God, I'm so awful, Elle. I'm so sorry. I feel like I betrayed you . . . and you're my best friend in the whole—"

"You didn't betray me! You could *never* betray me, Margaret!" I clasped my hands together. "You aren't that kind of person, and you're not that kind of friend!"

She just shook her head and blinked back tears, still staring out the windshield.

I continued, "I mean, Margaret, look at me. *I'd* be dead if you weren't here, propping me up, keeping me from slumping away," my voice cracked, "into oblivion."

"You're not that bad! You're going to be *fine*."

"I really . . . don't know." My turn to shake my head. More silence.

"You know? He's *more* than just an asshole. He's a *criminal*. A *murderer!* I fell for someone who should be in jail!" She put her hand up to her face, pulling at her right eye, so the tears would stop.

I took several deep breaths. I didn't know what to say. The whole thing overwhelmed me. Finally, I said, "I know. It freaks me out so bad. I hate him. I don't want to hate anyone, but I do. I hate him."

"I just wish he would have come over one last time to try and apologize again. Just because I want to slap his face!" She tensed her jaw. "I mean, really. I visualize myself beating the shit out of him. I mean, kicking, pounding. . . . I want to spit in his face."

"I'd help. I'd hold him down so you could get some good kicks in, preferably in the balls. Then we'd scratch the hell out of his face." We looked at each other. We didn't laugh.

"God. We've got to stop this! I can't live with all this rage!" She slowed down as she realized she was really speeding, and she looked over at me. "You can't live like this either, Elle."

"We can be mad for a while, Margaret," I frowned. I liked her being mad with me. "I think we can. I think the situation calls for it."

"Well, then I think about him. God—he's gotta be suffering. He ended someone's life."

"And we don't really know that for sure," I'd tried playing the devil's advocate in my own head, round and round for hours. "Someone else could have been driving."

"You know it was him, Elle. You know he did it. He never lets anyone drive his precious boat."

"Maybe he was passed out, and his friend took off in the boat."

"Maybe. But remember: they were all coked up. Nobody sleeps on coke. You saw yourself they were planning a jaunt across the lake. We heard them. He truly *killed* someone. How could you live with yourself?"

We made the turn into the restaurant parking lot and pulled up to my car.

"I don't know. *That*, I really don't know," I blinked and shook my head slowly. "But I think if anyone can do it, he can. He doesn't seem to have a conscience, Margaret. The truth will come out. The cops will find some evidence, and he's gonna go down hard."

"I still can't believe it. I just want to wake up and—" she let out a sob and put her forehead on the steering wheel, crying and mumbling about how stupid she was.

I just put my hand on her shoulder. I started crying myself. We just sat there for a minute, the car idling. I listened to cicadas humming, transitioning into the soundtrack of late afternoon, a prelude for fall.

"We're screwed, Ellie. How are we going to meet new people and get on with our lives?" She continued as she cried. "I thought this was going to be the best summer of my life? Now it'll be the summer I wish I could forget . . . all because of him."

I just kept muttering, "I know, I know." I felt so guilty about all of it. I was the one who had talked her into being at the lake all summer. I wanted and claimed all the blame. I didn't have anything else to offer. We watched a group of middle-aged women walking together across the parking lot toward their cars. "We'll be like them someday, Margaret. We'll be laughing with our friends, and all of this will be behind us." I shocked myself with this realization. It felt weird to think such a thought, and I suddenly opened my car door and stepped out. Before I shut the door behind me, I leaned in and said, "I can't imagine it, but I have to believe it's true." And I choked back a sob.

She sniffed and rubbed her eyes. Leaning back and looking over at me, she nodded slightly. Taking in a deep breath, she said, "Yeah . . . you're right." She let the air out, "You're amazing, you know."

"Please!" I smiled a little. "I think *you're* amazing."

"Okay. We're *both* amazing!" She smiled. She put both hands back on the wheel and turned back to look out the front windshield. "I'll follow you." I shut the door, then she leaned out the window and added, "But take it easy, Mario."

When we got home, I helped load her car, and my mom and I stood in the driveway and waved as she drove away. Then my mom said I should give Sarah Campbell a call. She was Neal's grandparents' neighbor, the one who had been so nice to me the day I found out. I called her, but she wasn't in, so I helped my mom go through the linens and dishes and things, packing, cleaning.

Everybody else in the family was back in the Twin Cities, but my mom and I stayed through the week. The whole family would be up again through Labor Day weekend, but then, we'd all be saying goodbye to the place for good. I'd go home to the Cities for a few weeks before school started. My brother, Frank, landed a banking job in Chicago, and my parents planned to drive down with him and help him get settled. My sister, Julie, started graduate school for psychiatry, and my younger sister, Nancy, started her second year at Winona State University. All of us being busy with new things helped take the edge off losing the cabin.

I am grateful for those five days I spent with my mom. Though I moped and crabbed a lot, Mom stuck with me. We ate our meals together, did a little school shopping in Horton, and stayed up late together, reading and watching old black and white movies. Our favorites always included Barbara Stanwyck. Her sassy resilience offered a tendril of hope. We laughed about memories we had with our family things as we packed them away. We talked about all our framed photos and got a chance to know each other a little as grownups. I had distanced myself from her over the past few years, but Neal dying, and selling the cabin, made us raw and exposed, and we appreciated leaning on each other as we put one foot in front of the other.

Amid my grief of losing Neal, I had a chance to make real and lasting memories with my mom, and though I was down and out, I cherish that time. I pull it up in my mind when I get low. I couldn't know she was going to have a heart attack and die just a few years into the future, but I sometimes wonder if Neal had that knowledge somehow, and from his ethereal sphere helped make that last remnant of time at the cabin with my mom happen. It buoys me from the weight of the memory I have of Neal's room the last time I was there.

On the Saturday of Labor Day weekend, after talking to Sarah Campbell, I went to visit Neal's grandparents. My dad and brother were taking the dock in, and my sisters and mom were loading the moving van, so I snuck out for a few hours. I stopped at the mailbox at the end of our driveway and checked the mail for the last delivery we would receive at our lake address.

One white envelope sat inside. It was a letter to Margaret. I knew Blake's handwriting all right. I wanted to rip it to shreds, not even tell Margaret about it, but I forced myself to stuff it in the glove box. She'd been so upset that he didn't at least give one more shot at an apology. I vowed to give it to her when we got back to school. When I pulled up behind the garage at Neal's, Sarah Campbell must have been watching because she crossed the lawn and met me as I got out of the car.

"Ellie, I'm so glad you could come over. They're so *terribly* lonely. Even though Jessie calls them every day, they just miss you and Neal," she grabbed my arm and gave it a squeeze. I loved to hear my name linked to Neal's like that as if we were a real couple.

"Sarah, I'm glad you called. I've been meaning to come and visit. I guess I've been avoiding it. But we're moving, too, so I've been busy packing with my mom."

"Oh, that's a lot. Are you going to come and visit every once and a while? I know Herbert and Kate would love if you did."

"I will, for sure. I hope maybe they'll let me stay overnight once and a while. I'll come visit while I'm at school. When Jessie comes for holidays, too, I'll come up and stay a few days," I smiled, thinking of that.

"I've talked with a social worker," she paused. "You know I'm a nurse, right, honey?" She walked with me up the steps to the front door. "I'm happy to look in on them every day, but they may need some extra help with all this. They don't like to feel like they're burdening me, though I'm telling you they couldn't possibly be a burden." She gave a little laugh, adding, "Since my kids are all grown now, it gives me something to do."

"Thank God for you, Sarah," I patted her arm this time. "I'm with ya on the social worker. I feel better knowing you're next door, and you know what to do."

"Oh, heavens, honey!" We stepped up to the threshold and knocked. "Don't worry about it. You're way too young to have to handle such situations. You must try to enjoy your last year of school." I looked down at my feet, waiting, without comment.

"Well, you make the best of it, anyway," She patted me again. So much patting. "That's all any of us can do . . . and you know, I'll be praying for you!"

"Thanks, Sarah," I said. How are some people so good-hearted, like to the core, and others so rotten? I felt nausea coming on. The door opened, and his grandma stood there, just about ready to burst; she was so happy to see me. We sat in the living room for a while and talked. "Grandma Kate," as I called her, eagerly served me an egg and cheese sandwich and a big mug of root beer. After eating, she asked me to go into Neal's room and pick out things I'd like to keep. Anything I wanted, she said I could have. She didn't tell me what she was going to do with all the stuff I didn't take. Then Sarah took Grandma Kate to the grocery store. Herbert decided to take a nap, so I had the place to myself.

Crossing the threshold into his room, I began shaking. I sat on his bed for a long time, looking around at all the stuff on his walls, on his desk and dresser. I lay down on his twin bed and smelled his pillows, his sheets. I surprised myself by not crying. I felt mostly numb until I glanced over at his nightstand and saw a picture of the two of us in a frame. I knew the picture. I remembered when we took it. We had been at the beach all day. We were on my dock, and the sun was setting. We were sunburned and waterlogged, and our hair was plastered to our heads, but oh, we look so happy. We both had enormous grins, and our heads were touching, our eyes at the same level. Neal's one arm was draped over my shoulder, the other arm reached out, his hand holding the camera.

I stared at it, then I grabbed it and held it to my chest. I rolled over on the bed and just started sobbing. I worried I might wake up his grandpa, but I knew he was hard of hearing, and I didn't think he'd come in the room anyway, even if he did hear me wailing. I cried for a long time until I actually fell asleep. But when I woke up, I noticed only about twenty minutes had gone by on the clock.

I sat up on his bed and put the picture into the box his grandma had given me. I sat some more and looked at all his posters. He had a couple of posters of Bob Marley and the Wailers and Jim Morrison and The Doors on his walls. He was a fan of Earth, Wind, and Fire, too. He had several pictures of his family there. The four of them horseback riding, snorkeling, riding bikes, and wearing formal clothes at someone's wedding. In one especially handsome photo of him, he and Jessica are standing on a football field after a game. Neal's all scuffed up. He holds his helmet tucked under his arm; his wild, white-blond hair, long and shaggy, framed his wide and golden smile. He was such a dream.

All I could think about was how much his mom must have cherished him. I took that photo off the wall and kissed it, then tucked it in my box, but I promised myself to talk to Jessica about it. I would rather have her keep it, but I wanted to make sure it didn't get forgotten. I loaded up all the pictures I liked, which were most of them. In many of the pictures, he was much younger and with his parents. They all looked so much alive! He looked so much like his dad. His family was always smiling so big and bright! What a happy, perfect little family! They smiled the way people do—having no idea what's coming. A happy family crushed in accidents with speeding vehicles. I stared at their faces and thought about that. Perfect family, except they don't exist anymore. Not so perfect.

How I wished I could go back, have my face look like it looked when I didn't know what I know now. How I wished we all could go back. The words to "Photographs and Memories," came floating into my head, and I heard Jim Croce's voice singing to my heart, and the tears just ran down my cheeks.

I learned a lot about him, looking through his drawers and bulletin boards, and closet. His mom had made him a beautiful "My Son Neal" scrapbook. He excelled in track, competing at state as a pole-vaulter and hurdler for three years in high school. He played football all four years of high school and went to the state tournament his junior and senior years. He played for three years in college. He was a wide receiver and had lots of awards and newspaper articles singing his talents. I wondered why he didn't play his senior year. Maybe it was his parents' death. I puzzled it for a minute, then tried to remember to ask Jessica if she knew why. He never talked about his football days either, like guys who play football do. I wondered why. This only added to the puzzle of him, the one I would spend a long time trying to put together even after I ran out of pieces.

He played the accordion. *Who plays the accordion?* He had a high school sweetheart named Jane, lots of cute dance photos of them together. They looked so innocent. He looked great in a tux. I didn't meet Jane at the funeral, and I wondered why. He never mentioned her to me, so I made a mental note to ask Jessie about her, too. He had a pen pal in Peru, a boy his same age. There were lots of letters from Pablo. I took one with a return address and thought maybe I'd write to Pablo and fill him in on what happened.

He had taken several art classes in college and seemed to prefer metal sculpture as his medium. There was a neat photo portfolio of some of his artwork, and, as I flipped through it, I realized I had to ask Jessica where this art had gone. I wondered if I could get my hands on some of his work.

I took several of his sweatshirts. I took some papers he wrote in college. I took many of his albums, our favorites. I took his alarm clock. I took a baseball cap and all the little notes I had written to him over the past three months. Happy little love notes, full of smiley faces and chit-chat about where to meet me and what time. How much I couldn't wait to see him. Embarrassingly gushy, I was.

I didn't recognize the handwriting anymore. Some old me, long gone now, had composed them. He had them all together in his top drawer, hidden under the socks and underwear. I took his key chain. I took his driver's license and college I.D. After a little while, I just piled in random stuff without even thinking about it anymore. I wanted to load up his whole room and swallow it, contain it within me forever. As it was, the room already looked empty of life, like a flower stalk with all the petals plucked.

Outside, the trees buffeted in a gathering wind. I glimpsed a twinge of orange in the maple across the lawn, and I realized fall was sneaking in.

The light stretched long across the front yard outside his window. He had a view of the lake from his room in the basement. I saw a kayak down on the shore. I thought about asking if I could have it but realized I had nowhere to store it, much less use it. Anyway, it wasn't Neal's kayak. His had been destroyed.

I lay down again on his bed, holding his pillow and listening to the quiet. Listening for some notion of Neal, but I heard nothing for a long time except the hum of crickets. I was so sad he wasn't there. Gradually, I became aware of footsteps crossing the kitchen, and I heard Sarah's laugh. I knew I had to go, but I didn't want to leave. I knew I'd never come back. I didn't want his grandma to come down to see how I was doing, so I sat up and swung my legs down to meet his floor. I thought about his feet having been there not so long ago. I whispered to the emptiness of his room, *"I love you. I love you so much."* I sort of hugged myself but felt stupid and awkward, so I stopped. I didn't want to start losin' it again, so I stood up. I picked up my box of Neal and walked through the door. I stopped one last time and turned back to look inside. I caught his eyes staring out at me from one family portrait when he was probably twelve years old, still left in the room. He smiled at me so big and bright I just had to smile back at him. I whispered, *"I'll never love anyone like I loved you."* I propped the box on my thigh so I could wipe away a tear from my eye.

I turned and leaned against his doorway, becoming aware of the dust particles suspended in the long, sullen rays of the late afternoon sunlight cutting across the room. Time seemed suspended in that moment. I felt weightless as I considered those tiny dust specks floating along in space aimless and meaningless. Everything felt so random and infinite. No parameters. No limits. I felt as though I, too, might dissipate. Then I snapped out of my trancelike state. There was no other choice. I walked slowly up the steps into the warm kitchen.

I visited his grandparents a couple times that fall and attended their funerals the following spring. They died within months of each other, and I thank God for that living angel, Sarah Campbell, who helped Jessica and handled most of the details.

My parents put our two cabins up for sale that fall. They sold in a week for just under two-hundred thousand dollars, which seemed like a lot for the late eighties. To our disgust, in January of the next year, the purchaser sold to the Crandahls for just under two-hundred-and-fifty thousand, an offer too hard to refuse.

The Crandahls tore the place down and built a new home for Angelique before the next summer peaked. It was as if our little cabins and the Quartz Shores Resort itself had never existed.

Eventually, the three older Crandahl children had cabins, in addition to their parents', on that serene land on the north shore of Quartz Lake. It's valued in the millions now.

It was excruciating to part with the place where our family made so many memories and loved life so fully, but it would have been impossible, for me anyway, to continue living next door to the man who killed Neal and tainted my life forever.

The money my parents made from the cabin helped pay our tuition, and my parents paid off their mortgage on the house in the Cities. Dad went into semi-retirement, and they traveled. When Mom died, we could look back and accept, with better clarity, why selling the cabin had been good. We hoped, someday, we'd be back.

We couldn't fully acknowledge that Labor Day weekend was the last time we'd be together at the lake. A page had turned in our family history book. That realization dawned on us gradually, as only such truths can.

We weren't real estate hounds, so we didn't know that lake land in Minnesota was skyrocketing. Millionaires had found a new playground. The last decade of the twentieth century was too early in my and my siblings' work years to be able to buy lake property. By the time any of us were in a position to put a little money down on a lake place, the Quartz lakeshore was already one thousand dollars per foot. The price of any existing structure was also a factor, but most buyers did not see old cabins as assets. They quickly tore them down to build modern luxury spaces.

It was only in brief encounters that any of us, me, Julie, Nancy, Frank, or Jessica, experienced Quartz Lake in the years that followed. Dad had a brother who had a small place on one of the chain lakes, and he spent a lot of time there. My siblings and I would stay with other relatives once and a while, but the deaths were too much in the forefront for me. To be there was painful and not fun.

My sister told me she saw Blake one summer day when she was walking the back road we used to know so well. He didn't acknowledge any recognition of her, but she said he looked "weary." He was by himself, driving uncharacteristically slowly, in a purring silver sports car. She said he had a sad, lonely expression.

I can't imagine how, or if, the lake changed for him after he killed Neal. He never tried to contact Margaret again, and we only heard general news of him and his family. It wasn't like we sought to know. The fact they owned the land we once loved grated our hearts. Sadness replaced the neighborliness that had once been there; no opportunity came to try to salvage anything.

Angelique and Donovan had children early on. Their parents still had big parties; they still knew lots of people in high places. Their first lake home eventually disappeared, and a cathedral-sized manor took its place. It's a castle on a sweeping estate now.

I remember that Monday evening when our cars were all loaded up, and my brother, sister, and parents left. Nancy and I were to drive home together. Nancy went down the road to say goodbye to the cousins, but I begged off. I sat in the front yard leaning against the old oak tree instead.

This was the tree we played kickball with.

It was first base. It was the home base for trench and ditch.

It had held a rope swing for a while and one end of a large hammock.

I knew its music well,

how it creaked in the wind

and rustled proudly in the summer breezes.

I knew the cracks and bumps in its bark, and it felt like an old, comfy chair against my back. I thought about Steinbeck asking, "can you live without the willow tree?" At that moment, I didn't think I could. And my sobs wrenched me to the core. We all have our recollections of how we said goodbye to this time and place in our lives; they're swaddled like babies in our memory banks. My sister said my dad cried in the tool shed. Frank cried at the firepit. I know many, many souls have mourned at the water's edge.

As I remember it, the lake was calm and quiet that night. Many summer residents had taken down their docks, and the shoreline looked vacant and felt ghostly. I gazed out at the translucent pink, mirrored water; it was ablaze from the sunset, so glorious! So spectacular! So extravagantly performed! Tears drizzled down my face as I felt the urge to applaud. My heart gave a standing ovation: a lone girl under an oak tree witnessing the performance of a lifetime, and she was weeping with joy and grief.

I gazed up through the tree limbs at the purpling sky beyond, scattered with torn, cotton-ball clouds. I wasn't hysterical. I wasn't angry. I was blown away by all of it—this—this wildly generous and enormous finale, all for me. I stared and stared into the lake's infinite belly, vowing I'd never forget the way the water appeared to me at that moment. I attempted to absorb its psychedelic fluid essence internally, eternally. And whenever I cry, a little lake water trickles with the tears and sloshes around inside.

When we drove away, each passing mile scratched a deeper gash, deepening my sadness. Then just like that, the lake became past tense.

I turned to the present moment; Neal and the lake were gone with a glare. But I don't begrudge that glare. It burned and replaced the passion of love, however feebly, to motivate me. I managed to finish my senior year, though it was a blur and did not include fantastic and bittersweet memories that usually accompany a person's last year of school. I was pretty anti-social and camouflaged myself in the library most of the time.

Luckily, and often without fail, if I want to hear Neal's voice in my head, I pick up Thoreau's *Walden* and read a few pages. It takes me back, always, to that day on the bridge. The golden day that was. It mixes with Thoreau's words in my mind.

One day along my new life route, I found a good writing job, and my life managed to get on, for a time, in some remote way, despite my soured soul.

And what of Quartz Lake? The lake, too, has changed irrevocably. How could she not? Zebra mussels and other invaders arrived. They take hold relentlessly. The water grows clearer. Does that mean cleaner? And the neon green slime weaves layers into the bottom. What's happening to the fish, the turtles, and the ecosystem? Does anyone know?

The lake reflects and delights, as it always has. Tourists still enjoy her surface beauty, but all the powers that be, the DNR, the EPA, the media, the resorts, the corporations, the local, state, and national governments, the homeowners, the business owners, the outdoor enthusiasts, all those who claim to care about the lake and the future, seem full-on engaged in smoke and mirrors. Denial drums a deft beat.

The birds, animals, plants, and water cling to life anyway.

The train of progress has been going too fast for too long, and the rails it traverses are worn and rickety. We passengers on the journey have begun to feel the inescapable swerving and veering, wielding out of control, yet we know not how to slow down, get off, or correct our course. Everyone thinks someone else drives the train, but the conductor's seat may be empty and dangerous to occupy. It's been hollowed out by fire and storms, mental and physical illness, rising temperatures, misinformation, and denial, by pain, suffering, injustice, imbalance, and greed.

The cold, rotten truth is no one is driving the train, no one at all.

CHAPTER 25

Alluvial Anguish

Eleanor stands at the counter in her yoga studio, having just said goodbye to the last person to leave from the seniors' class. The studio is empty and so quiet that Eleanor feels she can hear the plants breathing. Abruptly, the door to the street opens, and a man steps in, looking down at his feet. He wipes them off on the mat, though they don't seem to be dirty, then he steps out of the way of the door, and turns to shut it with deliberate gentleness. As he turns to face her, he lifts his head, and they look at each other, and for a moment, Eleanor's heart stops. It skips way too many beats as she realizes she's looking at Zack, long lost Zack of the Blake Crandahl era. She blinks hard and takes a deep breath, "Can I help you?"

"You own this yoga place, right?" He asks, coming toward her.

"Yes. Yes, I do. You interested in yoga?" If he doesn't know her or pretends not to know her, she can do the same.

"Not exactly. Eleanor. I came to talk to you," he puts a hand on the counter in front of her. She doesn't know what to say. She stands there looking at him.

"I'm Zack Slavin. You probably don't remember me, but I was a friend of Blake Crandahl's. I met you a few times one summer, a long time ago."

"Yes. I remember. I try not to, though. On a daily basis."

"I don't know what to say, exactly . . . but I'm here to say something."

"What? What then?" Eleanor sputters awkwardly. She wants to be nice and invite him into the back room to sit down, have a cup of tea, relax and spit it out, but she more wants to be mean, to not give him one inch of slack. She pretty much hates him, after all. And who knows what he's really up to.

"I—I dunno. I—" he squeezes his lips together and looks up at the ceiling. "I came here with something to say; now I don't know how to say it." He sighs. "It's so complicated. It's—"

"Here, come inside, here," she can't help herself. Her good-heartedness takes over. She sees he's hurting; he looks terrible, yellow and frail. How she recognized him at first glance is puzzling. He looks nothing like the hearty jerk he once was. "I have to pick up my kids soon. So, whatever you have to say, you better do it quickly."

She goes through the beads dangling over the doorway and into her back room, where she has the tea and a little kitchenette. It is also the teacher changing area, and there are a couple couches, which is where she goes and sits down. He follows, sitting on the other couch. Jessie continually sends her loads of fabric and collectibles from India via New York City, so the whole room feels like it should smell like incense, except Eleanor never burns incense. The smell gives her a headache. She prefers the fresh, conservatory-like air created by her large and ever-growing collection of plants. She observes him observing the room, waiting.

"Do you remember that summer?" He looks at her, pain in his face.

"You're really asking me that?" She looks back, annoyed.

"Sorry. Yeah. I guess that's a stupid question." He puts his hands in his windbreaker pocket and throws his legs out in front of him, leaning back slightly against the couch. Then he sighs loudly. "Man, I don't know where to start. I thought when I finally saw you, I'd just know what to say. But . . . I don't . . . ah. . . ."

"Start at the beginning."

He takes a deep breath, letting it out slowly as he speaks, "Okay. Ah . . . hmm . . . Here it is. I have cancer. Stage four . . . and . . . ah . . . it's really . . . throwing me for a loop. I hope I don't die from it this time, but . . . I've started looking at my life."

"Okay . . . ?" She's still waiting, listening.

"My life's all fucked up. I've been keeping secrets my whole life . . . and . . . I'm sick of it. I think secrets turn into cancer in your body. That's what I think. Especially if the secrets are horrible and involve people dying and getting hurt."

"Still not sure where this is going, but—" she looks at him blankly.

"Alright. Wait. Just . . . let me talk, I'll try to get it all out. I feel like I'm at confession or something. This isn't something I'm used to doing, so I'm on some weird-ass turf," He looks at her, grimacing, pleading for grace.

"When your friend died." The room got sullen. "I know some shit about that night." He shook his head. "I didn't say anything. I kept it in. And not long after, I got testicular cancer. Now, what is it—twenty years later? I still know these things. And now I know *more* things, and I still haven't said anything, and now . . . cancer again." He straightened his spine a little and took another deep breath, letting the air out with a shuddery rush.

"I gotta say something *to you*. So . . . here it is." He pauses. "I was in the boat when he was killed. Blake was driving. Blake ran him over." He stops suddenly, taking another shuddery breath, and puts his hands to his face, covering it. He holds his face in his hands for what seems like a long time.

Meanwhile, Eleanor thinks she might faint. She can't breathe. Everything she's known in her gut is coming to the surface. She's shaky and buzzed like she's had too much caffeine, as if she might lose her cool and start screaming. All the buried anxiety sits down there, about to boil out any second. She squints against the ringing pain in her ears and feels a monster headache coming on. She doesn't know what to say. She just sits there, breathing, trying to stay upright.

"We were stupid. It was an accident. A *terrible*, tragic accident. We were partying way too hard and . . . we just didn't think." He looks at her. She's a statue.

"The love of my life died." The words come out robotically. She doesn't realize she has spoken them. "His name was Neal."

Zack takes a long, deep breath. "Neal. Yeah. Right. I know. . . . I'm . . . I'm sorry. I am so *sorry*, and I really hope you can try to understand." He stammers, pausing and waiting for her to interrupt, but she doesn't, so he just keeps talking. "I'm sorry I didn't speak up sooner. I'm sorry I was so selfish . . . and immature. I'm sorry I'm such a lame, pathetic idiot."

"Why should I believe you?" Her eyebrows arch.

"I don't know. You don't have to. I just . . . had to say it. I have to come clean." He stammers. "It may not mean anything to you, but I . . . have suffered with this secret . . . every . . . day of my life. Really suffered. I—"

"You know what? You don't have to tell me about *suffering*. I *know* all there is to know about *that*." Eleanor can hardly restrain her hostility. It seems to come out of nowhere. She blinks quickly, suffocating tears that try to form in her eyes. *Here's your chance! Find out all you need to know, ask him!* Her mind spins. She says in a gruff voice, almost gritting her teeth, "Tell me about that night. Tell me everything."

"God. Where do I begin? Ah—"

"Why don't you start with Candice's party? I know you guys were there. That *asshole* lied to my friend Margaret. But I know you *were* there. I know you guys were on coke. I know you were all trashed!" Her voice rises, even as she tries to control it, as she accuses him.

"Yeah . . . Okay . . . right. We were there." He sighs big. "We had hit a couple bars before we got there, but yeah, we were there. We were definitely partying big time. Blake didn't tell Margaret because he loved her. He didn't want her to know about his dark side, his partier side. She was so wholesome and clean. She'd never have gone to a party like that with him. She would never have let him go."

"Whatever! She didn't *let him* anything. Does that give him an excuse to lie to her? He's such a *fucker*. I really hate him. And I hate you. I hate all you assholes! You—"

"I know. I know . . . we're assholes. But you also gotta know . . . Blake really loved Margaret. He was a mess when they broke up."

Cutting through the thickness of their conversation, the phone's shrill ring startles them both. Eleanor moves across the room and out the beaded doorway to answer it. Zack looks down at his fingernails and begins cleaning the dirt out of his thumb until he notices some skin that needs trimming, and he starts biting at his index finger.

"Hi, my dearie!" He imagines her smiling. It must be someone she knows and has been waiting to hear from. Eleanor mumbles to try to keep the phone call somewhat private, but Zack can hear her side of the conversation anyway. She uses a lighter voice with this person, sounding upbeat and encouraging. "I'm leaving in a few minutes to get them, then we'll be on our way." She pauses and laughs. "I'm fine!" Pause again. "Really!" More laughing. "My voice is not *strained!*" He realizes she definitely is straining her voice, trying to mask the stress of his presence. She continues, "Alright, well, I'm in the middle of a conversation here so I gotta go." Pause, listening. "Yeah. Very. I'll call you when I'm driving down." Pause. "Why? You can't get reception on the plane?" Pause. "Oh." Pause. "You got the tickets?" Pause. "The girls'll be ecstatic! I'm gonna tell 'em when I get home . . . okay?" Pause. "Oh! You better believe it, honey! I already got sunscreen!" She laughs a little. "A-huh." Pause. "Okay. Yeah. Talk to ya then." Pause. "Bye."

She passes through the beads again and looks at Zack, "Sorry. I had to answer that call."

"That's fine. We were talking about Blake and Margaret."

"Oh, yeah, right," she's back to scowling.

"Blake was under a lot of pressure in those days. He was practically forced into getting back together with Candice."

"Please! That's bullshit. No one could *make* him get back together with her. And, if that's the case, he's pathetic!"

"You don't know his family. His mom—"

"I lived next door to them, did you forget? I know all about them. If he didn't want to, he wouldn't have married her, Zack. I'm not stupid, and neither is my friend, Margaret. And I know he *fucked* her that night. Was he thinking about how he loved Margaret while he was with Candice?" The bitterness came right out, no effort at all.

"Do you know his mom told him he'd be out the inheritance from his grandma? And they threatened to cut off the money for grad school if he didn't manage to work it out with Candice."

"Right."

"I'm really not kidding. Blake's dad basically got a free golf course out of the marriage. Like a . . . what d'ya call it, a . . ."

"Like a dowry?"

"Yeah! That. I mean, it's old-fashioned, I know, but that doesn't make it less real."

"Whatever." But her curiosity gets the better of her. "But why? What's so great about Candice?"

"Candice?" He pauses. He looks up at the ceiling, formulating what he wants to say about her. "Well, she's from one of the richest families around, man. I mean, Blake's parents have a lot of money, but these people, the Comoros, I don't know. . . . It elevated the Crandahls to a whole new playing field. And Blake's mom loves Candice's mom, so it was practically an arranged marriage if you ask me."

"Well, they seemed perfect for each other," Eleanor says flatly.

"I'm not telling you this to defend him . . . ya know? I guess I want you to tell your friend, Margaret, if you still talk to her. He was never the same after she broke up with him."

"You think she'd keep dating the person who killed her best friend's boyfriend? We *saw* him with Candice at that party. If he loved Margaret, he wouldn't have lied to her."

"You don't get it. You don't want to get it. It's like you need another reason to hate him."

"Him being a murderer is plenty reason to hate him. What he did to Margaret only adds to the picture of perfect *scum*." She practically spits the word at him.

"Well, his three-million-dollar inheritance was tied to their marriage license. I don't know, if you ask me, his mom wanted him to end up miserable."

"Yeah. She couldn't stand that he dated a farm girl and had a chance to be a real person with her."

"Yeah. You're exactly right," he looks astonished at her summation. "His mom's a trip, that's for sure," he took a deep breath, "he never could've married a farm girl. That makes sense. I didn't know she was from a farm. His mom would never accept that. Think about it. Oldest son?"

"Again. Whatever." Eleanor holds her palm up and clamps her lips together tightly. She doesn't want to hear any more about Blake and Margaret. She closes her eyes tight for a moment, then changes the subject. "Why were you guys in the boat at five in the morning?"

"We never slept," he answers quickly. "We were buzzing out of our brains. I had to work a long shift the next day. Blake was supposed to go to some shindig with his parents all day. We were going back for more coke. My next-door neighbor at the cabin was a dealer."

"God! I so knew it! My God!" She springs to her feet on impulse and starts pacing the floor. Zack still sits on the couch. His hands press so hard into his pockets they act as weights, keeping him from getting up. "I'm so infuriated! I could kill you! You fuckers killed a beautiful young man on the brink of his life! He was going to be a *teacher*, you know that?" She involuntarily gasped and whimpered, "I loved him. . . ."

Zack groans. "I'm sorry. I knew this was going to be impossibly hard."

Eleanor shakes her head back slightly to get the hair out of her eyes.

There's a clock by the tea kettle, but she doesn't look at it. "So, what happened after you got in the boat? Didn't you all know you were too drunk and stoned to be driving a speeding vehicle? Did any of you stop and think about that?"

"It was just me and Blake. And, no, we didn't stop for even a second. We figured, hell, it's five in the morning. Who the hell is out in their boat before sun up? Who the hell would be out paddling around, practically invisible, in a *kayak*?" He's waving his hands around nervously now. "We were just laughin', drinkin' our drinks, and cruisin' along. We were goin' fast, way too fast, but we weren't thinkin' about it. It was still practically dark. You know, when it's all dusky out? Everything was shadowy. The whole lake was calm. And it was foggy. Neither of us ever even saw him. We didn't hear him or see him. You'd think he'd've had a light or something. You'd think he'd've heard us comin' and got the hell out of the way."

Eleanor interrupts, outrage boiling over at the way Zack puts the blame on Neal. He didn't have a light? He should have made himself heard or seen? "Neal's kayak had lights on both ends!" She screams into the air. "How do you know he wasn't paddling like hell

to get out of your way?"

"I *don't* know. That's the thing. My guess is he heard us long before he could see us. In that fog? I'd say by the time he saw us, it was too late. We were goin' along, I thought we were both paying attention to where we were going, but . . . we were . . . looking off ahead . . . trying to spot the shoreline where my house was. We weren't looking at the water right in front of us. Then we just felt this huge impact. A horrendous . . . cracking sound. The boat sort of swerved hard, and both of us pretty much fell over out of our seats. Then the engine quit. We looked around to see what the hell we'd hit, and we couldn't see anything at first. We didn't hear anything. Then we saw something floating. It was probably his kayak, but . . . we thought it was a buoy. . . . Neither of us had any idea we'd actually *hit* someone. We—"

"It wouldn't have mattered, though, would it? You still wouldn't've stopped."

"I don't know. I can't say that for sure. . . . We laughed. We were so relieved when the engine started right up. I'm ashamed to say. We thought, 'what the hell's a buoy doing out here?' I mean, we were near the channels, but we weren't *that* close. We figured one of the buoys came loose and floated out where we happened to be going by. We really didn't imagine there was a *person*."

"Then when did you figure it out? Why did you let the boat loose off Candice's dock?"

"Well, we went to my house, tried to get my neighbor to hand over some more coke, but he was out cold, and he was pissed we woke him up. We were freakin' because we knew we had a hellacious day ahead of us and no coke. We headed back to Candice's because we knew she had a coke connection, too. We were clinging to the idea she'd score us some before we had to get home. I had to work at like eight o'clock that morning. Blake had to show his ass up at home sometime around then, too. We took the boat all the way back to her house, totally avoiding the area where the accident happened.

"When we got out of the boat at Candice's dock, it was the first time we noticed the front of the boat. It was tweaked. Blake didn't want any trouble with his dad for smashin' up the boat, so he shoved the boat off. He figured he'd say someone stole it for a joy ride from the party."

"When did you figure out you killed someone?" Eleanor folds her arms over her chest.

"Blake called me at work. We never did score more coke. Candice had to drive us home. My car was at Blake's. She bitched at us the whole way. They got into a screaming match in his driveway at like six in the morning. I can't believe you didn't hear it from your house. It was ugly."

Eleanor's mind spins back to that night, with no recollection of the sleep, the moment, or the night when it happened and shortly after.

When she and Margaret got back to the cabin, they both collapsed into a post-drunken stupor. She didn't hear a thing, nor did Margaret, nor did anyone in her family report any goings-on in the early morning hours of that dark day. She wished she would have been woken up by Neal as his spirit left the living world like some people say they experience when a loved one dies. People knew their loved ones died in the wars, in the 9–11 tragedy, in the Fukushima nuclear disaster . . . the list goes on . . . way before the official report are given. Some have dreams, some have sensations in their bodies, some cry uncontrollably for no known reason until it soon becomes clear.

Maybe he tried to wake her, and she was too drunk. The idea kills her. She can't go there. She thinks surely a spirit can overcome a drunken sleep. Maybe he, too, was too heartbroken to do it. She doesn't know. She only knows it didn't happen, no message dream. When morning arrived, she left for work with a mighty hangover, and Margaret was still asleep.

Zach lurches her back into the conversation.

"The cop who took the report got ahold of the head of police who happened to be at the same brunch where the Crandahls were. I don't think they'd found Blake's boat at that point. It was just news of a death on the lake. Blake heard his dad talking to the chief about it, and he panicked. He called me and told me to keep my mouth shut and that I'd probably be getting a visit from the cops."

"Did they find you then?"

"Oh, hell yeah. Later that day, we all got questioned. A bunch of us had to go down to the police station. Everybody from the party. I got fingerprinted. . . . I just went with Blake's story. We never left the party; the boat disappeared off Candice's dock sometime in the middle of the night. Didn't see anybody or hear anything."

"How could the police not suspect you when there were no other fingerprints in the boat. *Anywhere!*"

"I don't know. I guess we had enough witnesses verifying that we never left the party. Maybe they thought the people who stole the boat were smart enough to be wiping their fingerprints. Or wearing gloves or somethin'. I don't know. Believe me, I never asked. I just shut my mouth, kept my head down, and prayed like hell for the whole thing to just go away, or blow over, or whatever."

"Why are you telling me all this now? Why do you care?"

"Well . . . like I said . . . I'm sick now. I keep having nightmares. I'm sick of hiding the truth. I have to get it out." He pauses. "Eleanor, I didn't kill your friend. I was in the boat, but I really didn't know what happened until it was too late." He hung his head. "I didn't want to go to jail. I didn't want Blake to go to jail. I knew it was an accident."

"You should have told the truth then!" Eleanor has tears in her eyes. "I just wanted to know *what* happened. We all did."

"No. It would've gotten ugly. It would've been in the papers. Blake would've gone to jail. Or worse, he could've blamed me. Said I was driving his boat, and I would've gone to jail."

"You deserve to go to jail! Because of your stupidity and carelessness, a young man died!"

"I didn't do it!"

"How do I know you weren't driving? What makes you think I won't go to the police and tell them what you've told me?"

"Go ahead, Eleanor. I throw up my hands. I'll tell them what I told you. They'll go to Blake, or maybe they won't. He seems to have immunity to criminal convictions."

"So, he's out there committing crimes, still?"

"How do I know?" He waves his hand in exasperation. "I'll say this, though. I hate him. He's ruined my life. And that's about all I can say about 'm. I thought he was my best friend, but in actuality, I have absolutely no idea what true friends are. I don't know if I have any true friends." He blinks hard at the reality of his statement.

"Why don't the cops give a shit about him?" Eleanor realizes she knows the answer to her own question. She holds up her hand. "You know what? Never mind. I know why." She concludes abruptly, "I have to go pick up my kids, Zack."

"Sorry to dump all this shit on you, here in the middle of your normal day, your normal life. I realize it's selfish. But even though I did it for my own sake, I still thought you would want to hear it."

"I do. I know I should say thanks or something. But I really just feel like slapping you." She looks at him hard. She's nowhere near him, and she can't imagine actually slapping him, but she feels like it would be justified.

"You can. You have every right. . . . I know I don't deserve forgiveness, but I really am sorry. Sorry for all of it. I wish I could redo the whole night. I have never been the same since." As she starts for the beaded door, he gets up to follow her out. When they both get near the door to the outside, Eleanor crosses her arms and stands back on her heels.

"You know what, Zack? If you see Blake Crandahl, tell him to burn in hell." This is all she can think to say. She wishes she could say something more forceful or threatening, but nothing springs to mind. She's not sure at all what she'll do with this information, but her first thought is to call Jessie back. She might not have boarded her plane yet.

"Hey. I'd be happy to. I doubt I'll ever speak to 'm again, though. He's been fucking my wife for the last—oh—*ten years* or so . . . but *whatever*—he's probably had more sex with her than I have."

"*Nice*. That's a detail I'll be sure to hold on to." She walks up to the door and opens it, waiting for him to go through it so she can slam it behind him. "I'm sure your feelings for Blake have made it a lot easier for you to come out and say, 'he did it,' too, huh?"

"I'm sure it hasn't hurt." He looks at her hard for a second, then drops his head.

He walks through the door out onto the sidewalk as she says, "Have a nice life, Zack. Hope that cancer works out well for ya."

"Wow. Okay. Well . . . despite your hostility, I . . . hope you'll be okay, Eleanor. I hope you find peace with all this, somehow."

"Yeah. You, too . . . I guess."

She shuts the door quickly before he can say anything else. She looks at the clock behind the counter. So many questions are spinning in her head. She has to get home right away. She can't even call Jessie back to spit this all out; they're waiting. They're old enough to be left for a few hours with a teenage babysitter, especially when they have the option of hanging out in their pj's watching their favorite Saturday morning Looney Tunes cartoons with Senator Foghorn Leghorn and the gang. Still, they get nervous waiting if she's late.

This afternoon they're driving to the Cities to pick up Jessie from the airport. She's coming for good this time. Getting her own place and a job. It had been a long four years since she first mentioned wanting to come home. If she hadn't met Ben, who distracted her until he broke her heart, she'd have come back sooner. It was the news of Eleanor having to move away from the lake again that finally put a big enough boot in her behind.

After doing her own moving, she weirdly agreed to help Eleanor carry out the enormous task of packing and moving a household. And they have less than a month to do it. Eleanor hopes Jessie isn't too fried from her own packing ordeal. But luckily, Jessie hired movers to do all the lifting and a driver to transport her large moving van to Minnesota over the next week or so. Everything would sit at Eleanor's new residence along the Crow River until they return from their visit to Margaret's, and even more importantly, for the girls at least, to Disney World.

Little did she know when, months ago, she made the plan with Margaret for the first three weeks of October that both she and Jessica would be in the throes of moving. It would be chaotic and unsettling, but at least there would be several relaxing days at the Atlantic Ocean. Eleanor has one other item on her agenda for her Florida visit, but she's keeping that a secret from the girls, at least for now.

She hopes Jessie'll be happy living in Minnesota, but she's not convinced the exciting pace of The Big Apple has entirely left Jessie's blood. Can she really adapt to living in such a small town as Horton? Can she find a way to make it? She's a great painter, but who wants hand-painted walls in Horton, Minnesota? Eleanor needs someone to manage her books, and they've agreed Jessie will do it for a while, but they've also been toying with the idea of expanding Eleanor's yoga studio to include an art studio so Jessie can begin teaching art classes. They haven't had any luck with the landlord, though. They need to kick out the next-door tenant, an insurance company run by the landlord's long-time friend. They've considered relocating altogether, but Eleanor hates the idea of leaving the coffee shop across the street and the dear old man, though he'd hardly disappear from their lives if she were to move her studio. Too many things to figure out for right now.

She rushes around, grabbing her stuff and digging for her keys. She's flustered, scattered, and unable to figure out what she's supposed to be doing. Very un-yoga-like. She tries to focus on the excitement of moving and Jessie's arrival, but it's impossible. Finally, when she gets into the car, she wants to start crying, let it flow out. All she's known for years! All she tried to validate but never could! Her eyes sting when she shuts them, but she holds them tight for a minute anyway, thinking what to do. Trying to get with the agenda. She feels swollen and numb. Her lips tingle like after a trip to the dentist. All she can think to do is call Jessica. Or call Margaret. But she doesn't have her cell phone.

She starts her car and begins driving home, but at the last turn, she finds herself robotically going straight down the road to the beach instead of turning right to her little bungalow. She drives like a zombie all the way to the shores of the Quartz. Plenty of packing awaits, besides getting ready to drive to the Cities, yet here she is. She parks and looks out at the lake from her car.

It's a breezy, gray day at the shore. It felt warm in town, but out here, by the open bay, with the wind coming from across the lake, the wild air is chilly and heavy with humidity. Though it's only September, it feels like November. She rolls her window down all the way even though it's freezing, and listens to the water rushing, crashing, churning. She looks down the shore to the south; a few docks that are still out are drenched from giant waves. The dark gray troughs of the waves make her a little motion sick, and she realizes her head is pounding. Her thoughts are raging too.

Goddamn it. Goddamn this lake. I hate this lake. I am sick of feeling all this shit. I am so weak. God! I'm such a mess! Why can't I just get over this? I just keep going over it and over it and over it . . . why won't it stop!?

She slumps sideways in her seat, sobbing uncontrollably, gasping for breath, squeezing her fists so tight together that the tendons in her wrists feel like they'll give out.

Neal! Where the fuck are you? Why don't you ever come around? I need to know you're around. I'm sick of being here alone. I'm so frickin' alone. God, I hate you! I hate you, Neal. You fucking deserted me. You left. You left me! You had to be the big kayaker man! Why did you have to go out there so early!? Why did you have to die? Fuuuuck! You were supposed to be here . . . with me. We were supposed to have a life together. I can't take this anymore. I need something good. For once in my goddamn life, please God, make something good happen!

She cries her eyes out until the tears stop coming; a good, solid five minutes, maybe ten. Then, still, she sobs, but without tears, heaving and moaning until she begins to wind down, bled of energy, too taxed to keep it up. She's bent at the waist, lying across her front seat. The emergency brake is relentlessly jamming into her ribs until she finally notices the physical pain of it, and she has to right herself. She sits up, her head pounds, and her temples throb.

Raindrops start hitting the windshield and then dropping in through the open window onto the inside of the door, bouncing off the vinyl onto her arm. Her face is hot, so she leans over to the opening to let the cold rain hit her face. The drops are big and fat, and they sting, but she just sits with her face leaning on the window ledge, and the drops smack again and again. Inside her chest, her heart pounds with exploding grief. Sharp pains ripple through her heart so hard she pushes against her ribs with her hands. *Stop it. Just stop it now.* Exhaustion rolls heavy over her. *If only I could just go to sleep for a long, long while . . .* she thinks, as she sort-of drifts out of consciousness for a minute or two, or four. . . .

Slowly, she comes back to her senses, starting with her ears. She hears the waves crashing along the shore again, loud hammering and pounding. *The lake is angry, too,* she thinks. *Well, you're damn right!* She tells it in her mind. *You killed my best friend, you fucker. I can't like you anymore. You don't deserve my love. You never deserved my love. You betrayed me! You both betrayed me. Even if I wanted to, I can't stay here.*

It was just a few days ago that she and the girls were swimming and jumping off the dock, floating on their little rafts, laughing, and having so much fun in the warm waters of the peak of summer. So much had changed.

She had been shutting down, burying her love for the place the day she began packing. Wait, maybe it was more like the day she found out she had to move away. Again. It was hard enough to leave back when she was twenty. She had thought she was so grown up then. Now, in her forties, she felt stupider and more vulnerable than ever before.

How did I get so raw? What the hell is going on with me? I don't even know who I am anymore. Here I am sobbing about something I should be long over. I've spent years . . . meditating, doing yoga, praying . . . trying to cast off the bitter, solitary person I don't want to be. Will I never move forward? Am I stuck in hell forever? Who am I, some old spinster, dwelling on a tragedy that happened in her youth?

She looks up at the swollen sky, oozing with the cloud cover and a mean storm. She gets a wild notion to go spit in the lake. She could imagine spitting in Blake Crandahl's face. It would be a feel-good ritual, she thinks, a way to mark the finality of this rage. Put it to rest for good. In a few weeks, she'll be permanently removed, she hopes, disengaged from this place forever, settled into her little nook by the brook. This may be her last chance to give this lake a piece of her mind, her pent-up emotion. She gets out of the car and flings the door shut, heading for the stairs. She decides to go to the end of the dock to hock her spit-wad of hatred. *You fucking lake!*

She gets there, walking too fast along the wet wood, and suddenly her feet slip out from under her, and she goes plunging into the water, hitting the dock with her elbow as she goes down.

It's cold outside, and the rain is still pelting, but the water actually feels pleasant for the few seconds Eleanor drops underwater. It's not over her head, and the bottom is sandy and smooth. She puts her feet down and stands up. She looks to see if anyone might be around to have witnessed her klutziness, but the coast is clear. She looks down at her yoga clothes, sopping wet, and she feels a laugh coming. She rubs her elbow a little, laughing, imagining what her falling into the water must have looked like. Here she's all angry and punchy, gets to the end of the dock to hurl a spitball, and wipes out. What a complete moron!

Suddenly she's smacking at the faces of the incoming waves, laughing and saying in her head, *Yeah! Take that! . . . and that! You, stupid waves!* Then the heavy cold hits. She struggles to pull herself up on the dock, but she can't do it. She's exhausted and has no arm strength, her elbow's bruised to boot. She has to trot along with the pushing waves to shore. As her ankles clear their last steps of the shallow water, the cold wind sears through her. She races up the hill and plops into the driver's seat, quickly rolling up the window. Inside, the car is drenched. She shivers, thinking she'd better strip off all her clothes. First, she starts the car and cranks the heat. Her yoga bag is in the trunk of her car, so she jumps out to grab it, hoping by some weird chance she has extra clothes in there, which would be unusual.

She could just drive back down the road, she's not far from home, but she's shivering uncontrollably now and can only think about warmth. As she opens the trunk, she sees her old purple and white Mexican blanket tucked way up inside. It's the one she and Neal used for picnics. They'd lie on it and roll themselves up in it, laughing and smothering each other with kisses, until the urge to tickle each other got too strong, and it turned into a sort of wrestling match. She'd have to try to escape while he did his best to tickle her to death. She smiled, remembering his laugh. It came into her head so perfectly clear and musical right at that moment.

She almost forgot she was freezing, but then the shivers got through, and she reached down to pull out the blanket. Now it was just something to warm her up; it didn't have any other significance anymore. It'd been sitting in all her different car trunks for years, unnoticed and unused. She could never bear to replace it all these years or throw it away.

It's dirty with old trunk gunk, but she quickly takes it out and shakes it furiously in the air, snapping it to fully unfold it. It's still raining, so she does this quickly to keep it from getting too wet. She hops back in the car, looking around one more time, then takes off her clothes, dropping them into a pile on the floor of the passenger seat. She takes the grungy Mexican blanket and drapes it over her body, covering her chest and legs, tucking it in neatly along the sides. It's scratchy and not at all soft, but still, she begins to warm up quickly underneath it.

She puts the car into gear, glancing at the clock. She's so late, and she steps on the gas, wheeling her car around. She slows down a little to pass a man in a raincoat. With one hand, he holds an umbrella, and with the other, a leash attached to an Irish setter, urinating on a wooden fence post. He begins frowning as he looks into her car, seeing her bare shoulders, and wearing an old blanket. She gives a little wave, starting to smile as she drives past.

She glances at the rearview mirror. The man still watches her drive away. All of a sudden, she begins giggling. This is exactly wacky enough, something just like he would do, go swimming in his clothes in the fall, during a storm, then strip naked, and wrap a blanket around himself to drive home. For a brief, sensational moment, she feels like he's there, sitting next to her in the passenger seat as if they had gone swimming together, pulled off some great but meaningless caper. And suddenly, she's going way too slow, but she doesn't care; just for a minute, she wants to feel this feeling. The radio weirdly happens to be playing an old favorite Doors song, "Touch Me," and she turns it up to sing along. For a few seconds, she remembers what it used to be like when the grungy purple blanket had a purpose. She feels like a warm, sticky blob with this flood of good feelings having taken over, as if being in the arms of someone hugging her.

Then she pulls into the driveway at home. She looks down at herself and her condition. She catches her face in the rearview mirror as she reaches down to grab her wet clothes. A little giggle escapes as she sees her face; exaggerated dark circles from washed-out mascara make her look like a zombie. It'll be a little weird trying to explain to the teenage babysitter why she's wrapped up in an old Mexican blanket, dripping wet and naked, a half-hour late and scary looking, but somewhere out there, she can hear Neal laughing.

CHAPTER 26

The Ethereal Estuary

Eleanor wakes to the unusual sound of silence and, for a split second, can't imagine why it's so quiet. She opens her eyes to blinding brightness streaming through the yellow curtains, and she remembers she is sleeping in the luxury suite of Margaret's Bed and Breakfast in St. Augustine. She peers at her watch, and it's almost nine-thirty. What? She gets up quickly and grabs her robe, opening her door to step into the hall. She pauses, listening for a minute to hear if the squirrely noises her girls make are happening somewhere in the house, but the place is quiet.

Eleanor rounds the banister and goes down to the kitchen to find Margaret. They barely had a chance to talk the night before when Eleanor and Jessie and the twins pulled in close to midnight, after their long drive. They had driven to Florida in a rented mini-van to do a little investigating, a little visiting, a little sight-seeing, and a little touring.

She walks into Margaret's elegant and large country French kitchen. A youngish couple sits at a parlor table having coffee and muffins. A girl from the kitchen staff is working the espresso machine. She looks at Eleanor as she approaches, nodding toward the machine, wondering if Eleanor may want a shot.

"I'd love one. Add a little cream." They smile at each other. "Where's the woman of the house?"

The girl nods at the backyard, "Garden."

Eleanor lets herself out the French doors onto the terrace leading down a few steps into a dreamy garden. She sees Margaret snipping dead Zinnias. The yard is ablaze with flowers, lush green shrubbery, and a trellis covered in Clematis. Green grass, thick and dewy, covers the ground, but it's curved and angled to highlight the swelling flora.

"My God, Margaret, are you getting ready for Adam and Eve? You are too much." Eleanor says as she walks up behind her.

"Oh, stop. It's easy to grow things here; it's Florida! It's always sunny and mostly warm every day," she turns and stands up, wearing an apron of sorts, dirt on her knees, and gardening clogs. "Come on, come sit over here with me; I've been waiting for you to wake up!"

"It's past nine—I mean, what the hell? Where is everybody? Where's Joy and Hope?"

"Well, my friend, you slept so long, I wouldn't let them wake you up. They took off for the beach with Jess."

"Oh . . . bummer! I would've helped them pack up and had breakfast with them."

"They went in your room several times, hoping you'd wake up, but you were sound asleep. I figured you were exhausted. You drove like a wild woman. That's a long jaunt!"

"Oh, man! But we had so much fun!" They sat on the white wicker chairs, and the girl brought two café au laits in giant white cups. "That mini-van has a movie player. We had no trouble keeping those girls occupied! Jessie and I were gabbing away the whole drive down here. It was a lot of fun."

"Well, I hope you're staying the whole week. The couple in the kitchen are leaving today. The inn is empty except for us for the whole week."

"God, Margaret, you didn't have to do that!"

"Well, we've got a wedding here on Sunday, so I'll be pretty busy all day Saturday getting everything ready."

Eleanor gazed around at the beautiful garden, noting the sign on the side of the house where the gate from the front yard opens into the back yard. "So, *Greta's Gardens*. Greta's your grandma, right?"

"Yeap. Of course, you know that. I've been running this place for almost ten years now, Elle! I'm mad you never come to see me!"

"Hey! You've been busy as hell, too. You and Paul are always off somewhere. Theo is so busy with all his sports, my God! How do you find the time to do all this?"

"Well, I finally just hired a kitchen assistant. Now I've got four employees, well, Paul and I do. Two maids, the gardener, and now my kitchen girl. Tessa is a great help. She pretty much runs breakfast now for the guests, so I'm off the hook."

"How old is Theo?"

"He's a senior!" She shakes her head. "I think he wants to go to college in Minnesota. We're looking at St. John's. Paul would be so happy if he went there."

"And how's Sandra?"

"Fine, she's got the teenage attitude thing. And a boyfriend. I'm a nervous wreck."

"I'm not looking forward to that phase. I'm glad I have a few years."

"Yeah. You'd better enjoy it now."

"Well, I love Sandra. She's a mini-you, for God's sake!"

"Oh, I know. I adore her. You know that. I just don't like her yakking away on the phone all night when she should be doing homework."

"You'll be an empty nester soon enough."

"We can still have babies, you know, Ellie! We're really hardly into the forties! I could still have one. You could too, you know."

"Oh, for God's sake Margaret," they look at each other, grinning. "You're crazy."

"Well! We could. What if you see Brandon Crandahl and you fall madly in love."

Eleanor almost chokes on the hot coffee. "You're insane. Me, marry a Crandahl?"

"You said you don't think he's married! Stranger things have happened."

"I pretty much guarantee that's *not* going to happen. Besides, he's almost a decade younger."

"But it'd be so cool. What if he is the father of Joy and Hope? Wouldn't it be cool if you got married? They'd be with their dad."

"You gotta stop smoking the crack pipe, Margaret. You're so out in la-la land."

"Okay. Well, I can dream, can't I?" Margaret takes a sip of her coffee. "I want you to be happy. I don't want you to be lonely. I want you to find someone and make the rest of your life an adventure."

"My life *is* an adventure. I just drove here from Minnesota! I love being a mom, Margaret. It's enough. Really," she has herself convinced. The layer of loneliness has lain so long it's normal.

"I know. I know you're happy. But I still wish that for you. You can't stop me, you know." She adds with a wink, "And I know the perfect place for you to get married."

"Alright, you. Let's change the subject. Where do I meet him? You said you know where this place is, right?"

"Yeah. It's easy. You can walk. It'll take ten minutes. St. George Street is a no-brainer, but I'll draw you a map. When you get to St. George, just keep walking and watch for it. It'll be on the left side. The street is the main shopping spot. No traffic, just walkers. So cute. You'll love it."

"I hope he shows."

"He will. And he'll fall madly in love with you," she grins. "It's touristy, so you have to deal with people, but that could be a good thing. You'll have to remain calm, right?" She tilts her head slightly.

"I will," Eleanor frowns. "What? You think I'm gonna start screaming or something?"

"Well, ya never know. I mean, it's weird how he might be the girls' dad. I mean, isn't that weird?"

"Ah. Yeah. I'd say. But he might not be. It would be a *pretty* strange coincidence."

"So, Jessica said she'd be at the beach all day with the girls. When you get back from your big meeting, we can drive and hang at the beach with them. It's a gorgeous day, huh?"

"Surprise, surprise," Eleanor smiles, raising her eyebrows, appreciating how Margaret so easily works out plans. "So, you do weddings here, huh?"

"I make more renting the place for a wedding than as a bed and breakfast. And anniversary parties, graduation parties. It's more an event space really than a B and B. People like it because it's full service. Did you see how big the dining room is?"

"No, not yet. I haven't seen anything. Wanna give me a tour?"

"Yeah! Come on. I'm so excited to show you! How much time do we have before you have to go?"

"I'm meeting him at noon. High noon at the St. George Café."

"Hah. Funny. Hey, maybe we can get a power walk in before you go. Are you getting all spiffed up, like showering and the whole thing?"

"I guess. But I'd love a walk. Give me a walking tour of the town."

"Oh, good! I am so happy to have someone to walk with! I usually walk by myself. We can walk right by the café, so you'll know exactly where it is."

"Okay, give me the home tour, and then I'll get dressed. I can be in my p.j.'s, right? There's no one here?"

"Right. Okay. First, before we start the tour, I gotta show you some 'before' pictures Paul and I took when we first got here. I loved my grandmother dearly, but she had been living here alone for so long, the place was a little forlorn. When we were young, we'd come with my parents, and my dad would work the whole time. We'd be off playing at the beach, and he'd be here fixing stuff. But he inspired me. I understand now why he had such a furious need to keep it somewhat in order. It's so great."

"It really is spectacular. You seem really happy," Eleanor hooks her arm in Margaret's as they mosey up the stone walkway toward the terrace.

"Yeah. We are. I thought I'd miss the Minnesota farm country, but I haven't. It's great to wake up every day with a warm breeze and the birds."

"It suits you."

"I'm so glad you finally came for a visit!"

They head into the big kitchen, and Margaret pulls out a three-ring binder to show Eleanor a series of photographs of the place from ten years ago. There were no gardens around the front of the house, the steps at the front entrance were crumbling, and the whole outside of the house was gray with red trim and needed a paint job. Now, the place is painted a soft yellow with white trim, there's new gray Spanish tile roofing, and all the windows have been replaced. The gardens are extensive in both the front and back yards and a small private patio on one side of the house connects to what Margaret designates as the honeymoon suite. A white picket fence, covered with vines, makes the backyard private, and many couples use the trellis to say their vows. Connecting the front and back yard on the other side is a large, flat, open space of grass. It had held a gardener's shack, but the structure was too decrepit, and they tore it down. Margaret uses this area for a large, white tent for wedding and anniversary celebrations. Her calendar of reservations books solid through the spring and summer seasons. Fall is mostly booked too.

The business, which includes eight private suites, each with its own private bath, works well for Paul and Margaret. Margaret had been a horticulture major in college, and she managed a large greenhouse in southern Minnesota after college. While handling the flowers for a wedding, she met her husband, Paul, who managed a formal wear business in the same small town. Paul had a degree in business management and marketing, so when they had the chance to purchase Margaret's grandmother's place, Paul was eager to turn it into a bed and breakfast, handling the books and promotions. Margaret also did all her own decorating and renovating. Margaret and Paul, with their two kids, Theo and Sandra, live across the back alley in a home they purchased when it went up for sale in the first few years they renovated Greta's Gardens.

"My God, Margaret, the place is like a compound or something," Eleanor gushes.

"Alright, enough," Margaret pushes her arm, "Come on, let's get our walking shoes on. I'll meet you at the trellis in five minutes, okay?"

"Perfect."

A few minutes later, Eleanor is tying her shoes under the trellis as Margaret walks up, saying, "So, what's the juicy news you said you're dying to tell me that you wouldn't tell me over the phone? Is it more to do with the girls and Brandon?"

"No. Not at all. It's about Blake Crandahl. Remember him?"

"Very funny." Margaret frowns at her, "Be serious."

"Oh, I am! You are not going to believe who walked into my studio the day before we left to drive down here."

"Who?" Margaret waits, but Eleanor doesn't say anything. "Don't even say it was Blake!"

"No, not Blake. His friend. Zack. Remember him?"

"Oh. My God. No way!" Margaret stares at her with her big brown eyes as Eleanor smiles enormously.

"Do you still have that letter he wrote you, by the way?"

"No, you know I burned it years ago. Don't you remember?"

"No. I was comatose those days after Neal died."

"I read you the letter before we torched it. I can't believe you could forget it. Don't you remember what an ass he was? The whole thing was about him. It confirmed everything for me. He never gave a shit about my feelings. He wrote it to try to relieve his guilt," she pauses. "I couldn't care less about him, Elle."

"Well, you have to hear what Zack told me. You won't believe it. And *your* name came up, a lot."

"Okay," She gives in. "Spill it." They walk through the trellis down the alley to the sidewalk. Eleanor begins recapping the whole conversation she had with Zack, most of it still vividly scripted word-for-word in her memory. They rehash the story—all they can remember and all they had once felt and still feel about what a pivotal point that summer had been in their lives.

Margaret had gotten over Blake fairly quickly and had a new boyfriend by Christmas of her senior year. They dated a few years but broke up when Margaret was swept off her feet by her amazingly brilliant and handsome now-husband, Paul. She harbored no lingering love or attachment to Blake. Her re-assessment of Blake, his inability to do the right thing and be an honest man, though it shocked her, continued to stick throughout the years, but she confessed it took her longer to forgive herself for having fallen for such a loser, for having made such a gigantic mistake in not perceiving his true character.

She feels bad about Eleanor not being over Neal and the hostility she carries around, but she keeps working on it with her. That Eleanor can say Neal's name without choking up, and talk about the whole incident with some amount of humor, has got to be a good sign. But over the years, Eleanor had not met anyone significant or formed any relationship with another man. She'd had a couple boyfriends in her late twenties, but they never amounted to anything long-lasting.

Margaret puzzles over just what it is that fails to ignite. Is it Eleanor's own heart, too shattered to ever work right again? It devastates Margaret, and she can hardly think about how it must feel for Eleanor. She can't imagine life without her husband and kids. She doesn't want to believe Eleanor has gotten used to it. Eleanor admits, after so many years of declaring herself "just fine" as a single mom, that, yes, it has been lonely. This is why Margaret secretly hopes the encounter with Crandahl the younger will be the beginning of something significant. The timing seems perfect. She hopes, if there's a wedding, she won't have to host the whole Crandahl family. She would do it for Eleanor, but she decides she'll push for elopement if the love story develops.

After they finish their walk, Eleanor gets ready for her big meeting. Eleanor had found Brandon Crandahl's law firm and all necessary information quite easily through the Carleton Alumni Office. What astonished her even more was how near it was to where Margaret now lives. She had not seen Brandon since that summer, when he was still just a boy, and she couldn't imagine what he was like.

When his secretary answered the phone, and Eleanor gave her name, explaining she wanted a personal meeting with Mr. Crandahl, the secretary put her on hold. She had braced herself, expecting Brandon to get on the line, but the secretary made the appointment without further questions. She hoped he wouldn't cancel or find himself too busy when the time came. The secretary asked if she preferred to meet somewhere other than his office since it was a personal matter, and Eleanor agreed, thinking a neutral location was best. She explained to the secretary she would be in St. Augustine, and the secretary suggested a nearby coffee shop.

Eleanor carries a thin manila envelope under her arm as she enters the place. The crisp aroma of rich chocolate croissants is overwhelming, and her stomach growls. The place is busy, with dishes clattering and the comfortable sound of the espresso machine launching a new, steaming shot for the next drink. A line of patrons waits to place their orders, and most of the dozen or so booths and tables are already occupied.

In the folder is the letter that was written by the girls' birth mom, the adoption papers, a couple of baby pictures of them when they were very small, and a recent picture she took on their first day of second grade. The folder has begun wilting as Eleanor begins sweating, realizing she doesn't have much evidence. She hopes he's kinder than she predicts he'll be.

As she scans the booths, she notices one toward the back has only one person sitting in it, a youngish man, head bent down, reading. He has blondish-brown hair, a little longer than expected for a lawyer-type, but he is wearing a collared shirt and tie. As she approaches, hesitantly, he lifts his head, and they look at each other with instant recognition. She knows instantly he is the father of the twins. His eyes are unmistakably similar. He has the same nose and chin. She knows it intuitively. And even more weird is he looks more nervous than she is.

"Ellie Marlow?"

"Ah huh. You're Brandon, right?"

"Gosh," he flashes a gorgeous smile, and she thinks he must be the best-looking man she's ever seen, at least, in twenty-some years' time. "Sit down. Please. They've got waitresses here. The line's just for people ordering to-go. Here, sit. Sit." He moves his papers and a black leather document bag.

"Okay," Eleanor sighs, feeling drained, hoping she'll get a double espresso to the table quick. "This is weird. You don't look how I remember you at all."

"Really?" He smiles again; she can see he's nervous too. "You look pretty much the same. Your hair's shorter. You're still as pretty as I remember."

"Hah. Well, thanks," She looks down, then puts her hair behind her ears.

"Are you hungry? They have great deli sandwiches here," he hands her a menu. He already has a coffee, so she scouts out a waitress and orders her usual. They have a pleasant introductory type of conversation; Eleanor explains she's visiting Disney World with her two girls and a friend. Brandon says he's lived in the area for about five years, bought a house on the coast, how relatively inexpensive the housing prices are in this area, but how much of the population is retired. They order lunch, and Eleanor notes he does not wear a wedding ring.

Eventually, it's Brandon who strikes out on a shaky limb by saying, "Ellie, I know why you wanted to see me. Everything's exploding back in Minnesota. You want to see what I know, right?"

"Ah . . ." Eleanor squints. "Not sure what you mean."

"Well, I know you hate Blake. I get it. Believe me. I mean, I know *you know* what happened. You want to see if I know anything, right?"

She decides to go with it, "Sure. I mean, I'm not sure we're thinking about the same thing, but—"

"Neal. Your friend. About the night he died?" He looks at her with his clear brown eyes, and the dizziness begins.

"Okay . . ." she waits for him to go on. "You know about that night?" She has to pause a second to absorb this. "I mean, you were only, what . . . ten?"

"I was twelve, actually," he smiles, tilting his head sheepishly. "Well, what did you want to see me about then, if not that?"

"Actually, I'm curious to hear what you have to say about the whole incident. I do have other stuff I want to talk to you about, but first, tell me what you know."

"I know a lot. I know it all, pretty much," he sits back a little. "But I'm wondering what you're gonna do with the information."

She sighs deeply. "I'm not sure. I want to know just for my own sake. I live on the Quartz, you know. Well, actually, I did, until just a few days ago. I had to move because my house is being destroyed for some corporate condos."

"Yeah. I know all about it. You live in the old Towering Timbers, right?"

"How'd you . . . know that?" Their sandwiches arrive. They're both eating the veggie Ciabattas.

"When you called my office, I was pretty freaked. I hadn't heard your name in years. I had no idea why you'd want to see me, especially when you tell my secretary it's personal. She's got the whole office abuzz thinking you're my new girlfriend," He laughs. "But I did a little investigating and found out where you live. Your web page on your yoga studio needs some work, though." He teases.

"Nice!" She laughs. "You're right, though, I know. I have a friend helping me fix it up." She smiles, thinking of her first "to-do" item for Jessie.

"You live where Blake's company's new condos are being built. I figured you might be putting together a case against him or something."

She doesn't want to give away that she had no idea Blake bought out the association. She feels anger coiling up between her shoulder blades at the enormity of that detail, at her lack of insight into the whole situation. She shut down when she heard the verdict on the sale. Brandon's suggestion she might be building a case against the evil Blake had not occurred to her until this moment, but it quickly takes hold. She thinks Brandon's not a very good lawyer, giving information freely to the opponent, but she begins to see his angle as their conversation continues.

"Well, you couldn't be more right about how much I hate your brother. But I don't intend to use anything to blackmail him or anything if that's what you mean."

"Not blackmail, exactly. I mean, it's probably way too late in the game for you to get anywhere legally. Like trying to send him to prison for killing Neal."

The words come out so matter-of-fact.

"How do you know that?" Eleanor can't tell whose side he's on. He seems to be on her side, but that doesn't make sense.

"Do you know the whole story about me and my family?" He wipes his face with his napkin. She's startled to see he's sweating.

"I'm not sure. I guess I don't. I mean, we moved after that summer. Your family swooped in pretty quick and demolished our old cabin," Eleanor swallowed hard. "I had a lot of feelings to deal with about everything. I didn't really keep tabs on you and your family. I pretty much hated all of you. I pretended you were all dead or something."

"Well. No surprise there, I guess," he pauses. "There's a lot of dirt, actually."

"I guess I did hear you moved away; you sort of cut yourself off from your family or something, right?"

"Basically. Yeah. I finished college, spending summers at the lake with my parents, but it wasn't pretty. I was partying a lot back then. I had a LOT of anger at my parents, especially my mom."

"Ah-huh."

"They could never tolerate my behavior. Not like they tolerated Blake's. I mean, he partied as hard as I did, but he always got away with stuff."

"Yeah. Like murder."

"Exactly. My parents knew what happened. I mean, I don't know if Blake ever told them the truth, I highly doubt it, but they *had to* have known. I finally accused them one day of being complicit in the cover-up, but they bristled so hard at me they basically kicked me out. They told me they never wanted to see me again. I was in law school at the time."

"Wow. So, you left Minnesota then?"

"No, I finished law school first. Then I moved down here with my girlfriend at the time. Her family lives here. But we broke up a couple years ago. She was a partier, and I was trying to get my life straightened up once and for all."

"How's that going?"

"Good. I'm off alcohol and drugs. I'm into meditation and yoga. We've got a lot in common." Big smiles again.

"Well, that's good you're not partying anymore."

"Very good. But I was miserable for a long time. I had a lot of guilt. I wanted the truth to come out about Blake, but I was stuck in the middle. I kept thinking I was making a bigger deal out of it than it was, or something, but there was this part of me . . . it just . . . nagged at me. It still does."

"How do you know he was driving?" Eleanor wonders. "I mean, I know this. But how do you? Why would you think that about your brother?"

"Let me tell you what I know. What I consider facts. I am a primary witness; I saw things with my own eyes, okay? I mean . . . I was young, but I totally got what was going on."

"Okay. Tell me. I'll shut up." They both ordered more coffee.

"The morning it happened. Believe me, I've replayed it in my mind many times; I remember it well. Blake pulls into our driveway with Candice and his friend Zack in Candice's car. They park right in front of my bedroom window. Blake and Candice get out of the car, and they start fighting. They're so loud, they wake me up. I go to the window and look out to see them having a doozie shouting match. I mean, she's practically hysterical. Zack got in his car and drove off, like a smart man but also probably a drunk man.

"But Blake's left trying to calm her down, and she's wacko. She's pissed that she's had to drive him home at the crack of dawn, she's pissed they had Zack tagging along, and she's tried to maintain her cool the whole drive. But now they're out of the car, and he's about to leave, and she just lets him have it. She's pissed he left the party for so long. She thought they were gonna have a cozy night of reconciliation after their summer apart. She's pissed he's so buzzed, but mostly I think she's pissed because she's found out he had this other girlfriend all summer."

"Well, she had some guy on the line while she was in Europe!"

"Whatever. Doesn't matter to her. She's a super-controlling bitch," his voice snarls on that last word. "You know they're married, right?"

"Yeah. Oh, yeah."

"Well, she peeled off after I think she even slapped him, and I filed that scene away in my head. I didn't think much of it until later. We were all at some charity luncheon, the whole family, but I'd been allowed to go into the lobby and hang out by myself. I was just sitting on one of the couches reading a comic book, and I see Blake sort of sneaking his way over to the payphone, right near where I was sitting. He doesn't see me. I'm behind my comic book, and he's freaked out of his head. He goes to use the phone, and he calls *Zack*. He basically tells Zack the cops are gonna come and question him, and he'd better keep his mouth shut. He says someone was killed on the lake that morning, and he's pretty sure they're in big trouble. He said he was pretty sure they didn't hit a buoy. I heard the whole conversation, and toward the end of it, Blake finally turns around and sees me sitting there. I was trying to keep reading, pretending I didn't hear anything, but he ended his conversation quickly, then he came over and grabbed me by the shirt and dragged me into the men's room. Luckily, it was close," he pauses to take a gulp of coffee.

"He roughed me up, shoved me around, and told me he'd kill me if I said anything. He said I didn't know the whole story, and I would just make matters worse if I said anything. I tried to tell him the best thing to do was to tell the truth. Say it was an accident. He said I was too young and too stupid to understand but that if I told on him, he'd make sure I'd suffer the consequences.

"I was scared of him. He was a wreck. His adrenaline was pumped way up, and he was pretty frantic. He slapped me up, then shoved me out the door and told me I'd better act like I knew nothing and that nothing happened. So, I did. I just played dumb. No one bothered to ask me questions anyway. I never had to lie about anything. I wasn't even a factor in the investigation."

"Wow," Eleanor manages to say, glancing up at the ceiling, trying to sort out all the questions and which one to ask first. "Then what happened?"

"We went home soon after that. My family was pretty tight-lipped. Blake's hated me ever since. We have barely ever spoken for years. Just recently, he's called me for legal advice. But I have a hard time speaking to him, to tell you the truth."

"What's his trouble now? Paternity suit?"

"You know about that?"

"Sort of. His friend, Zack, strangely enough, came to see me at the yoga studio. It's weird how all this shit's coming out now, after all these years. Do you know how long I've been in pain over this?"

"Ellie, I'm sorry." He looks up at the light over the table and takes a long, deep breath. "I meant to start out by saying that. How sorry I am. I really am sorry. I should have said that right from the start. Somehow, when I saw you, it flew out of my mind. I used to have sort of a crush on you, ya know."

Eleanor looks skeptical, but she doesn't say anything. The waitress arrives with the tab. He waits for her to leave before he continues.

"I didn't know right away who got killed. I found out by reading the papers, seeing his picture, and . . . I was so crushed. My heart was broken. I was sort of happy you were single again, and I dreamed maybe one day you'd maybe like me, but then I saw you a couple times, and you were so sad. It just about killed me. Then you guys moved away. I never saw you again."

"Yeah. Well—"

"*I've* never recovered either, Ellie. I've never got over it," he said slowly. "I know it's nothing compared to what you went through, but I suffered. I dove head-first into alcohol and drugs. Go figure. I drove drunk with my girlfriend . . . way too many times . . . home from the bar one night, and . . . we crashed into our garage. That was my final wake-up call. I'd had plenty of others I ignored. I had bad dreams and bad energy hanging on me for a long time," he pauses and takes a deep breath. "I finally got the courage to face the shamble of my life. But . . . I don't think Blake ever has."

"Have you ever confronted him about it?" Eleanor asks gently, "I mean, you said you started talking to him again."

She doesn't feel rage against Brandon like she felt toward Zack when he spilled it all out at the studio. She can see the pain in the corners of Brandon's mouth. The way his mouth trembles ever so slightly as he speaks about this huge thing that happened to him when he was too young, the way he mishandled the situation as he grew up, and his guilt over the whole thing. She can see the young boy he was, the young boy she remembered, always alone on the beach. She feels really bad that he, too, in a lot of ways, was a victim of the tragedy.

"No. God, no. I'm embarrassed to admit I was happy he called me out of the blue. I've been so separated from all of them. They never call me, hardly ever. My sister phones every now and then." He looks down at his empty coffee cup, "You wanna walk over to the old fort?"

"Sure. Yeah. Let's go."

Brandon pulls out two twenties and sets them on the table, and they leave together. Eleanor still clutches the manila envelope. They walk and talk some more. Eleanor's feet are sore from all the walking she'd been doing, but it proves easier to walk and talk, so they don't have to look at each other face to face while they trudge and drudge through the bitter past. She's bursting to talk, but she lets Brandon continue.

"I didn't want to blow what tiny thread of a relationship we managed to hold together after so many rough years. I thought maybe we could put it all behind us, ya know? But then as I listened to him talk, I just kept hearing more of the same antics . . . the same irresponsibility and immunity to consequences. I realized the only reason he called me was because he didn't want his other lawyers, his business lawyers, to know about his personal stuff. Nice, huh. It brings up a lot of these past resentments, I tell ya."

"I get it. Really. I get it, Brandon," Eleanor says. She adds suddenly, "and you know, you don't have to be sorry. You didn't really do anything wrong. I mean, I guess you could have told me. Sometime over the course of these past twenty years, you could have 'fessed up . . . but, I don't know . . . we're all human."

"I did want to tell you. I thought about it so many times. So many times, you just—well, you can't imagine. But I thought you wouldn't want to hear it. Maybe you were leading a happy life, and you overcame it, somehow. I mean, you seem pretty happy. You look happy."

"I am . . . pretty much . . . for the most part."

"You said you have children? Are you married?"

She thinks about bringing up the issue of the girls and the paternity, but it would come too closely on the heels of their discussion of Blake's paternity suit, especially if Brandon might be in the middle of one, too, shortly. Plus, she's not sure they're through with the whole Blake story, and she doesn't want to cut it short, so she says, "No, I'm not married. I adopted my girls. They're twins. I never married. I guess I never got over Neal's death. I . . . really loved him." Though her words come out choppy, she doesn't cry as she says this, and it sort of catches her off-guard. "Neal was a truly amazing person. He had so much going for him. He had so much to give the world. Ya know . . . it just decimated my heart."

"I don't know what to say. Except . . . sorry. I—"

"I think if I would have known the whole story, if Blake would have accepted responsibility, it may have been easier. I don't know . . . probably not, actually. Maybe. Who knows. It wouldn't have brought Neal back. I would probably still have this enormous anger and rage."

"You don't seem bitter."

"Oh, I don't know. I think I pretty much am. I try to leave it alone and not go there, but all this stuff going on in the past few months. My house getting destroyed, Zack coming to unburden himself, Jessie moving back home."

"Jessie?"

"Neal's sister. He has a younger sister. She's another helpless victim in this tragedy. She was left totally alone. Their parents had died a few years before Neal died. She lost her grandparents soon after he died. She literally has no family left. A few cousins, I guess, but no real ties."

"Man . . ." Brandon rubs his eyes. "I can't imagine."

"Well, actually, in a strange sort of way, you two have been in kind of a similar situation. I mean, you're without your family too, basically."

"Yeah. But by choice, I guess. There's a big difference."

"Maybe you can meet her sometime," Eleanor pauses. "She's single. And very cute."

"Really?"

"No kidding. She's here with me, in Florida. You might really like her. And you guys are close in age. But we'll get back to that. Tell me more about his paternity suit. Are you representing him?"

"Well, I considered it. Then I decided I couldn't. And talking to you, thinking about his recklessness, I just can't support the guy. He's a loose cannon, as they say."

"He and Candice, do they have children?"

"No. God, no. Thank God, no. She'd be a nightmare of a mother. She's too worried about her perfect body to ever be pregnant or get stretch marks, whatever. She's had a long-term affair going for years. Blake knows about it. They're so sick. Their marriage is a sham. It always has been."

"How's she doing with the whole paternity thing?"

"I don't know. They're not talking about divorce yet, at least. I don't think she could stand the scandal. Her number-one priority, according to Blake, is to keep the whole thing hushed up."

"Not surprising."

"Zack's wife is trying to get a bunch of money out of Blake. She and Zack are divorcing, you know that, right?"

"Zack told me."

"Candice is furious about Lydia. She's trying to say Lydia's pinning the paternity on Blake so she can get his money. She's pretty much broke at this point."

"Well, did they find out the truth yet?"

"I don't know. I told him I wasn't going to represent him, but he's trying to get me to help in another legal matter. He's got some big project set up for the state forest land on the west side of the lake. Do you know about that?"

"What?" Eleanor's heart flutters.

"Yeah. It's being sold off. Blake's company's going to buy it. He's gonna build another resort, this one with a giant water park. Right next to the lake."

"There's already two water parks in Horton!"

"Yeah. But this one'll be right on the lake, so the little kiddies can see the lake when they're zipping down the slides," Brandon smirks.

"Oh, God, no," She clears her throat. She waits for Brandon to say something. He stops and looks out over the water, and they stand there a minute without talking.

"Elle. We can stop him."

"Right."

"No, I mean it. I'm a lawyer. I'm an *environmental policy* lawyer. And we have all this dirt on him. You and I."

"I've seen so much shit happen on that lake. None of it's stoppable anymore, Brandon. Can I get my house back?"

"They're probably bulldozing it right now, so, no. It's too late for that. They've probably already begun blasting the trees." He turns to her and grabs her arm. "Come on. Let's talk about this. Maybe it could be our way to finally make something good happen from all the bad!"

"Brandon. Wait." She steps away from him. The sun hits his eyes just right, and she sees the hope in his eyes. "Before we go any further in this conversation. I have something to tell you that may change everything you feel about all of this."

"What?" He looks startled.

"It's all right here," she swallows hard and holds up the folder. "See, in this folder."

"Tell me."

She briefly looks out at the water, trying to figure out how to begin. She watches a seagull coming in for a landing on the cement wall near them. The bird looks at her, scrutinizing her for crumbs.

"Just tell me. Say it," Brandon says.

"A paternity suit."

"Another one?"

"It seems to run in your family," Eleanor says, thinking about his brother Blake and Zach and Candice.

"You don't even *know* how true that is."

"What?"

"Nothing." He rasps. "Just tell me what you were going to say."

"No. Tell me what you mean. Who else in your family?" His face looks pained. "You?" She wonders if Joy and Hope have a sibling or two. "Is it you?"

"No. No, not *me*. Forget it, really. It's nothing. Never mind. Tell me: what paternity suit?"

"Well . . . it involves . . . you."

"What are you talking about?"

"You. I adopted two girls, twins actually," Eleanor takes a deep breath. "I think they're yours."

"You've GOT to be kidding!" He looks at her hard. "You're joking, right?"

"No. I'm *not*. And that's why I want you to explain. Do you have other kids?"

"No! Not at all." He looks around, down the sidewalk where they stand next to the old crumbling fort, and is surprised to see no one around them. The shopping street is packed, but where they are is quiet. He's not talking. Eleanor thinks he looks sick to his stomach, but she pushes forward.

"Well, then what did *you* mean regarding paternity suits in your family?"

"Oh, man. I don't know," he shakes his head and shrugs. "I don't mean paternity suits exactly. I guess I mean . . . illegitimate children."

"You have illegitimate children in your family?"

"God, Ellie! You're so nosy!" He says, joking but with a slight edginess. "Let's keep walking. I can't just stand here. Do you mind?"

"No, not at all." They start walking again around the fort. Brandon isn't speaking, and Eleanor glances at him looking down; he's thinking hard.

"Well, come on. Just tell me what you mean." She tries again to get him to cough up whatever he's choking on.

"Alright. I have brown eyes. See, look." He sort of flashes his eyes at her.

"O . . . kay. Explain what that has to do with anything."

"My entire family has blue eyes. Mom, Dad. Everybody. Both sets of grandparents." Silence.

"You?" She asks in disbelief. He turns slightly away as she grabs his arm.

"Yeah. I think I'm a fucking bastard child."

"No way." She almost laughs at the way he says it.

"Well, really, look at the situation. I'm like eight years younger than Donovan. Everyone in the family has blue eyes except me."

"Well, maybe you're recessive or something."

"Blue eyes have only blue-blue genes. They can only contribute a blue gene to the scenario." He shakes his head, "my genetic father has brown eyes."

"Holy shit. This is too much."

"Do you see why my dad hates me?"

"I see why you were alone a lot with your mom."

"Yeah. I was. Right! You noticed? I loved when you guys would invite me over to your bonfires. I used to hang out on our beach waiting for you to come out and make your fires, hoping like hell you'd invite me."

Eleanor doesn't remember Brandon ever being there for a bonfire, but her memories are faded and jaded.

"You guys felt more like family than my own did, until you moved away." She hears the sadness under the words. "I had a crush on your sister Nancy, too. God, my mom hated when I'd go to your house."

"I bet."

"Okay, enough about me," Brandon says. "Are you satisfied?"

"Wow," again Eleanor is tongue-tied. Neither of them talks, but they notice the seagull again because it seems to be trailing them. The bird blinks at them as if waiting to hear this next part of the conversation. Brandon finally looks over at Eleanor, and he swallows before he talks.

He reaches over and takes the folder out of her hands, staring at it for a second. He looks up at her with an open expression. "Okay . . . so tell me about the twins."

CHAPTER 27

Water's Ways

From space, astronauts say they are most startled,
more than by any other vision in the Solar System, by

Earth.

Among the stellar sights, Earth's shimmering blue hues take the breath away
in its uniqueness, with its all-encompassing, sweeping expanses of water.

Gaia dangles, an ornament on the face of the galaxy, alone, illuminated,
swirling, gyrating, and whirling. A blue and white psychedelic orb adorning
the ear of eternity. A surface so dynamically stunning it dilates the pupil—the
cervix—of the universe, like a lens, ready to capture and deliver destiny. The
site of all, seen and unseen.

Does Venus see Earth?

Does Pluto?

Do Orion the Hunter and Cassiopeia and Vega
know of Earth's extraordinary
effervescence?

Does our moon know
viewing us through her panther eye,
just how stealth and earthy Earth has been?
Is now and ever shall be

will be

will be

world without end

amen.

Before humans
had seen Earth from space, great thinkers like Emerson, for one,
believed Earth to be green in the solar system.

How blown
were the minds of men and women to discover Earth is truly
blue.

Earth: one spectacular spectacle in the kaleidoscope of time

How rare are we   to see it,   to view it, to live on it,   to be of it ?

Within Earth's skin, vegetation grows thick and green, and creatures crawl, large and small. The planet is alive with sounds, colors, and endeavors. This living orb, the only one we humans are conscious of in our solar system, exists in great part because of that blue mantle, its intricate quantum web, and delicate cycle of redemptive rejuvenation.

Almighty Aqua glaciates in frozen masses, floats as clouds, and dances as downy snowflakes and cool rain. *Nibi* fills vast oceans, saturates swamps, and splashes around in lakes. *Mni* trickles in brooks and streams and rushes down rivers and waterfalls. *Eau* hides in places never seen, buried in the soil and rocks beneath our feet.

Water's balance on the globe stays the same, but it constantly changes, day after day, second by second, century after century; it transforms itself, from liquid to solid, to vapor in patterns and rhythms untamed. The oldest water molecules, born when Earth was born, still exist somehow in that cool drink, quenching human thirst. Water holds the evidence of Earth's life, her evolution. Agua fuels Earth's journey and transformation. Water's complexities are infinite and unresolved.

When glaciers retreated in North America's last ice age, they left lovely little legacies in lakes. Undeniably drawn to lakes are humans, whose very composition, like Earth, is mostly water. They flock to shores for survival, sustenance, entertainment, inspiration, and comfort.

Vital to life's history and function, presence and destiny, lakes are also playgrounds
        laboratories, homes,
                        and graveyards;
            they are backdrops of
                battles, romances, creations, and yarns;
                they are the focus of eyes witnessing, searching, scanning,
                    delving,
                        reflecting,
                            projecting,
                                perplexing,
                            and through the periscope,
                    the paradox,
                            and before long,
                                        the dawn dances
                        and one particular lake
            laboriously looms into view

in northern Minnesota, one mild morning.

As the light wind shifts, it weaves iridescent sheets of long feathered ruffles of water, like fish scales, glinting the surface.

The lake receives heat and radiance and further cues from our breaking sun.

Gazing in even closer, an old aluminum rowboat bobs into focus, where two old-timers, habitual early-risers, hunker over their fishing poles. The smooth, fluid images of the lake's snakelike skin illuminate their age-worn eyes. Their little boat rocks and sways and an occasional tug of the anchor line gives a subtle nudge. The two talk quietly.

"Let's hope our last day out for the season brings us a bounty we can eat all winter long," says the bigger fella. He holds up his coffee, and they clink their thermoses for good luck.

"Look at that, Red," the smaller fella, Barney, gestures with his pole.

"Wouldn't you think it's a bit early for that?"

Red turns his head, and they both gaze across the curving, shallow bay as another boat approaches. Four sportsmen and their women hold up cocktails, giving their own toast to the fine morning. Music and laughter echo in their wake as they zoom past. They continue some short distance away, then cut their engine and begin preparing their fishing gear. As the sound of their engine dies, the old men hear the music, along with bits of their conversation, wafting across the water. They look at each other; one scowls; the other smirks.

"Even if it's not too early in the day for drinkin'. . . "

"You'd think we'd be past tourist season."

". . . seein' as it is October."

"Should we press on?"

"What do you think?"

"I don't think I can take that woman's squeal much longer. You might have to yank me out of the cold water before long."

'Let's go by the channels," Barney decides. "We haven't fished there in a while."

"Good idea," Red agrees. They reel in their lines and make haste to relocate. Their motor only pushes about six miles an hour, but they enjoy the pace. Barney scans the water, the shoreline, and the skies. On their way, they encounter a couple of other boaters, but they find a calm and secluded spot. Boaters are on the lake at all hours, it seems.

Red cuts the engine. "This is right about the spot where that young man was killed, so many years ago, remember that?" Red says. Barney reaches up and tosses the anchor off the front of the boat.

"Yup. I still think of it, all the time, when I cross here, don't you?" He answers.

"Sure."

"That family, the Havenmillers . . . they owned our house before we bought it. Such a sad story. He had a sister. I heard she inherited a big wad a' money. Wonder what happened to her."

"Probably couldn't take livin' round here after that. It's still hard for me to think about, even after all these years. No one ever figured out who killed him."

"I never heard."

Red yawns. "You know we're probably only going to haul in crappies here."

"I like crappies," Barney says. "Good eats!" He chuckles.

'Yeah. I agree," Red takes a deep breath and lets it out slowly. He tips his head toward shore. "Look at that place. How could someone put something that hideous on the shore of a lake? Such an eyesore."

"No one thinks about it that hard; people want what they want," Barney muses. "Or maybe we're a couple a' old geezers who don't see things the way young folks do."

"It's utter craziness, I tell ya," Red re-baits his hook and casts his line.

"I think I can't take anymore, then I hear about somethin' else. The state forest? It's tagged at four million. I wonder who got that ball rolling."

"I know it, Barney. I know it. I hoped I'd never see the day," he looks over the water. Across the big bay, the bluffs stand out from a distance; the fall foliage is taking hold, and the trees vibrate yellow, orange, and red, translucent in the ascending light.

"Just goes to show, everything has a price," Barney adds. He loosens the lid on his coffee and takes a little sip.

"Aren't people tired of watching the lake go the way of the damn resorts?"

"Have to wait and see, I guess. If it's for sale, there's probably already a buyer lined up," Barney concludes. They're silent for a few minutes on that note. Then Red remembers something in his bag, and he digs in to pull it out. It's wrapped in a couple of hankies, and he gently unwraps it as Barney looks on curiously.

"What ya got in there, a fish zapper or something?" He grins.

"No. Look. I found this the other day. For years I thought it'd been stolen. But when the workers were redoing the kitchen at my cabin, they found it under the sink!"

"What the hell is it?"

Red holds it up. It's a wooden pipe. It's mostly gray now, from aging and use, the sides are worn smooth from many finger grips. The fish image carved along the mouthpiece is still clearly outlined, though the scales of the fish have been mostly worn off. "Here, take a look. This was my father's pipe. He got it from his grandfather, who, if I remember right, got it from his father, the guy who made it. He was a big chief in the Dakota tribes along the Minnesota River Valley. He was part of Little Crow's tribe. Ever heard of Little Crow?"

"No, can't say as I have. I always wondered what kind of Indian you were. Dakota, huh?" He admires the pipe for a minute, feeling its smooth surfaces, then he hands it back to Red.

"Well, I'm Dakota and Ojibwa. Dakota from my father's side, Ojibwa from my mother's. What kind of White are you?" He asks teasingly.

"Oh, Irish, mostly. Some German." They nod at each other as if this information changes something about their friendship.

"Didn't your two tribes fight against each other?"

"Yeah, but when I was born, in the early '30s, the wars were mostly over. At that point, Indians were just Indians, trying to survive, I guess."

"Are you gonna smoke that thing? What is it—like a peace pipe?"

"I think—I will smoke it today. Do you mind?"

"I hate cigarette smoke, but a pipe's alright, I guess."

"Maybe it'll bring us good luck." Red pulls some tobacco out of an old leather pouch. It looked about as old as the pipe, and the two were probably kept together.

"So, what's the story with the pipe?"

"I think it was a council pipe. I think my great, great grandfather used it during meetings. He was a chief. They probably used it at the start of meetings. We Indians are into rituals, you know. It seems like a way to bring everybody together, to unify the group's focus and vision."

"That's neat." Then Barney remembers to ask, "Why're ya *redoing* your kitchen? You sound like my wife."

"Oh, that kitchen was ancient. I've got the place rented out now. I wanted to make the place nice for my new tenant."

"I thought you were going to sell that old cabin to your nephew."

"Nah. He decided to use his money to go to grad school."

"So, you're renting it out?"

"Well, a situation came to light in which someone I know needed a place to live. I never go out there anymore. The place is just sitting there, going to decay. I put some money into it, had it fixed up a little, and now it'll make me some money, and it'll be a nice place for someone to live."

"So, who's your renter?"

"Oh, that crazy gal who runs that yoga studio across the street from the shop. 'member her?"

"Oh, yeah. Nice lookin' gal. She's got a couple kids."

"Yeah. Her story's a bummer. She used to live in Towering Timbers. Ya gone by there lately?"

"Drove by it yesterday. A cryin' shame."

"Seen the shore?"

"Don't think I want to."

"Yeah. But you will. It's inevitable. You can't miss it. In fact, look over there; you can see the bald spot from here." He points. They gaze without talking.

"How's the pipe?"

"Tastes pretty good." He holds the pipe out, offering it to Barney. Barney, who doesn't smoke, feels compelled to take it and have a puff. The tobacco flavor is exquisite, and Barney is surprised to find it quite enjoyable.

They fish all morning, and by lunchtime, they have a satisfactory bounty for several fish dinners to relish over the cold months ahead. Red steers the little motorboat through the narrow channel that connects the lake to a chain of smaller lakes, one in particular, where Barney's dock still extends from the shore. Most of the other docks have been pulled out in preparation for the change of seasons. They slowly putter up alongside Barney's dock. Barney clutches a dock post and eases his way unhurriedly up onto the stability of the dock, and the boat sways as he steps out. Red hands Barney first his loot, then his fishing gear. Barney drops the fish cache into the built-in storage bin on the end of the dock, setting his gear next to it for the time being. He'll be back to clean the fish on the dock after lunch.

"When ya takin' yer dock out, Barn?" Red asks.

"Kids are comin' up tomorrow. We'll be packin' all weekend. All moved out a week from today," Barney sighs. "It sure will be funny not having our place on the lake anymore."

"Ah, you always have the lake. I won't come fishing here without ya. Even if I hafta drag your ol' heiny from the old folk's home."

"I know. But you know how it is. Bonnie and I've lived here over twenty years."

"Well, think of it this way. A lot less to worry about as far as maintenance is concerned, right?" Red smiles.

"Yep. That's right," Barney agrees. "That's right," he repeats, more for himself than for Red.

"Call me up when you're settled in your new place," Red says. "We'll get together for a fish fry."

"Well, Bonnie'll have me callin' ya before that. We're invitin' ya over for a farewell dinner in the next few days," Barney points at him. "Take 'er easy, Red. Thanks for the ride."

He turns slowly, hobbling carefully down the dock toward home. Red pulls the starter cord on the little motor and shifts the engine into reverse.

He guides the boat away and heads back the way he came. He doesn't look back at Barney, but he holds his hand up over his head and gives a wave, just in case Barney's watching him. And Barney is. He stops midway on the dock, turns back to the lake, and briefly hitches up his pants. He looks at the water for a long moment. Behind him, in a tall pine tree, high at the top, a bald eagle perches, gazing. They watch Red's boat fade into the shining sunlight on the water and disappear.

CHAPTER 28

Interlocken

The minivan rolls down the highway, closing in on downtown Horton, and Jessica asks quietly if Eleanor wants to stop at the coffee shop for a pick-me-up. But they're both sick of coffee, so they skip it. Jessica drives, listening to a barely audible news program. The girls are zonked out in the back, and Eleanor, riding co-pilot, has been drifting in and out of sleep since they switched spots at the Minnesota border in the wee hours of the morning. The previous night, they stayed somewhere in Tennessee, but they hit Chicago by dinnertime yesterday, and everybody had a longing to return home, so they decided to push through the night and take turns drinking coffee and driving. The girls fought sleep watching their latest favorite cartoon movie, *Finding Nemo,* until they succumbed to sleep around midnight.

As Eleanor floats back and forth between wakefulness and memory, she thinks back to the last few days before they took off on their trip. She and Red had gone to his old cabin together in Red's ancient pick-up truck. The back was so heavy with tools it amazed Eleanor the vehicle could still move. Red wanted to show Eleanor how to use the new heating system and a few other unique features of the house and property. She smiles, thinking of Red and how pleased he was to show off the place with its renovations. His desire to see her happy overwhelmed her. He had really overdone it. He'd had the log exterior cleaned and resealed, the inside floors buffed, waxed, and polished. The kitchen was redone, the screen porch had been rescreened. The entire second floor had been painted. The bathroom fixtures and toilet had been replaced. He said he was so impressed with the remodel he'd been tempted to move back in himself.

Eleanor set a date to have him over for dinner when they returned from their trip, and she was happy to see the changes. The place had sort of given her the willies when she first drove up. She had been alone. She had gotten directions from Red on a napkin, and she wasn't sure she'd found the right spot. It felt deserted. But the second time she went, with Red, she was completely won over. The place was charming and perfect, especially considering the alternatives she'd seen.

She allows herself to get a little excited for her new place and having Jessica in town, but then her mind wanders back to that pivotal last night at

Pine Hollow, during the packing and moving phase. She remembers how
she struggled to fall asleep. And the dead turtle. Then running home with
a clear sense of what to do. Recalling it, she realizes she still hasn't done it.
The intention temporarily slipped away. So much had happened since the
morning she drove away from Pine Hollow for the last time.

She had shoved the last box into the moving truck and hesitantly looked
back at Pine Hollow. Everything inside the house was gone, and it stood empty
and eerie. It seemed to look askant at Eleanor. It was just a house, a bunch of
boards and nails and insulation, it certainly couldn't know what was coming,
but it seemed to, somehow, which was why Eleanor couldn't look anymore.
She had kept her eyes looking forward as she steered the moving truck off the
driveway onto the dirt road. The girls waved and blew kisses at it, but Eleanor
was stoic.

As she took another turn onto the paved road going out to the highway,
three gigantic tree-felling trucks passed her, coming in with a ferocious roar.
She remembers wondering if the trees felt anything, the ones left standing
after the others had been chopped down. It's up for debate if trees are
conscious or not, but she has no doubt trees are. They must grieve. It must
be weird for a tree, standing in one place its whole life, taking in everything
around it as it grows, then to be confronted with such radical changes. It's
gotta be traumatizing. Eleanor can and does weep at the thought of it.

The development, Interlocken, boasting executive condominiums,
conveys the lofty tone developers know to entice the new breed of buyers.
Eleanor read the massive sign, every blazing word of it, at the turn-in.

Coming Soon:
Deluxe, Private-Entry Row-House Condominiums
Floor Plans Flexible for Individualized Tastes
Some Lakeside, Some with Lakeside Views.
Quartz Lake Water Access with every unit!
Hurry, They're Going Fast!

A sketch of the final product was drawn along the bottom.

As they come upon the first stoplight on the outskirts of town, Eleanor
feels around for that contempt in her heart and in the weight of her body,
but it doesn't seem to be there. Maybe she doesn't have room for it anymore.
Maybe it's hidden underneath the exhaustion of the long drive. She doesn't
know, but the idea of it being gone feels good.

Jessica flips on her turn signal and watches for a chance to break through
the traffic. It's the first day of MEA, Minnesota Educational Association
weekend, a four-day holiday to coincide with peak fall foliage and the chance
for an Indian summer getaway. Early risers who left home to get to their cabin
before the rush are substantial, so traffic in town is thick. The stoplight-filled
trip will be slow across town to the river road where her new place is.

She gazes out the window on all the development, the new strip mall, fast-food restaurants, and classy boutiques filling in the gaps. She sees a black crow, imagining it could be a raven; she's not sure which is which, after all, sitting on a light post arched over the roadway. She wonders if it's forced into scanning the pavement for roadkill, if it's getting lazy, or if it's up there just trying to figure out what a highway is. Whatever its reason for being there, the bird, despite its elegance, disturbs her.

How pavement and wild birds should ever be in the same picture is at the heart of it. Why this price for mobility? Is anyone else concerned? She peers into the other cars around her, idling at yet another stoplight. Everyone looks lulled—half asleep. She holds her eyes shut for a long moment. They sting with tiredness. How can everyone drive so aggressively yet appear so passive?

As they turn down the narrow, dirt, more-like-a-path road to her new home, they drive past the split where the road diverges, and one side goes down to another property. According to Red, an acupuncturist, an older man who opened his own clinic in town, the first one in the area, recently purchased it. She stares down the road and realizes she needs to meet this neighbor because her new place is isolated. The new neighbor might be forward-thinking in his views, seeing as he practices acupuncture. Eleanor brings her mind back into the present when she sees the moving van parked next to the garage.

Her car sits in the driveway behind the moving van. As a perk for helping her move, Eleanor had lent the car to her teenage niece, Carol, to use while she was gone. Carol agreed to meet here to watch the girls and help unpack.

The day looks to be glorious, with a deep, cloudlessly blue sky, incredibly azure beyond the golden hues of the trees. The temperature is predicted to hit record highs all weekend, according to the radio weather announcer they heard this morning. They run down to the river first thing out of the car. The river is low, but Eleanor thinks she might be able to hear the water rushing as in springtime. After a brief sit on a washed-up tree trunk, she calls the girls, and they make their way to the house.

She admires the sturdy logged cabin with its two long rectangular windows in the front, where the living room, den, and kitchen face the river. She meets Carol in the kitchen; she's unpacking a couple bags of groceries her mom had sent with her from the Cities.

"Your mom is awesome. I thought we'd be ordering pizza delivery for the next few days. And I'm not even sure they deliver out here." Eleanor says upon greeting Carol. They divvy up tasks. Eleanor takes the kitchen boxes. Carol handles the linens and upstairs-type boxes. The girls unload their mountainous supply of toys.

Jessica heads back into town to tackle her own moving details, like banking, mail, and a trip to the store for cleaning supplies. She's going to return the rental car and have someone at the rental office drive her to the dealership so she can buy herself a car.

"Eleanor, by the way, I plugged in your phone when I got here because I had to call my mom, and within like a minute, the phone rang. How weird is that? It was some guy from Florida calling. I wrote it down in that notebook next to the phone."

"Okay, thanks. Let's help Jessie tackle the car. I'll call him later."

They empty the car from their trip so Jessica can take it to town. It needs a serious cleaning, but Jessie will tackle it. Eleanor has the huge moving van to deal with. Luckily, the owner of the trucking company is a yoga student, and she told Eleanor, with a wave of her hand, to return the truck whenever she was finished with it. It holds mostly big furniture, so Eleanor has to wait for her two nephews to show up after football practice and MEA traffic.

They had spent the first night in the new house before the trip, sleeping on the floor in their sleeping bags. Now, the girls are eager to get out their bedding. Laughter sounds overhead, and the CD player and Bob Marley muffle through the rafters as Eleanor fills in the kitchen shelves with dishes.

Around noon, she hears a car drive up, and she glances out the window, thinking she'd see Jessica blasting up in her new car. Instead, she sees a truck with a windsurfing board tied to the roof. A man gets out and goes around to his side door, opens it, and pulls out a box. She watches him; his muscular legs are tan, and he's wearing cut-off jeans. His hair is shoulder length and curly, and he has a nice jaw. But her observation of him lasts only until she looks at the box he's carrying. It is an old box from the Harbor View. A box with the logo from the days she worked there, long ago. Her heart skips.

"Are you Ellie Marlow, by any chance?" the man says, holding the box in front of him. He looks at her intently with his green eyes.

"Yes. Me. Just moving in, as you can see," she gestures with her eyes to the boxes behind her.

"Yeah. I heard I was getting a new neighbor. I live in the house up the road, where the fork is." He tilts his head in that direction.

"Uh-huh."

"Well, a week or so ago, this box arrived at my doorstep. The mailman must've got the address screwed up. Or maybe he thought it belonged at my house because this place was vacant. I don't know, but here it is. It's addressed to you."

Eleanor stares at the writing on the box. It sucks her breath out. She feels a twist in her gut, a pang, as if from hunger, but not.

"Oh, my God," she sucks in a breath and puts her hand to her chest. "I have to sit down. Can you come inside for a minute?" She feels faint.

"Sure. Where should I put the box?" He follows her to the kitchen. She gestures to the kitchen counter, the only place to set anything. She stares at it.

"I'm Jamie Morgan." He holds out his hand.

"Huh? Oh. Hi. I'm Eleanor. Eleanor Marlow." They shake hands.

"You don't go by Ellie?"

"I used to, years ago," she says, distracted.

"You moving these boxes by yourself?" He looks around. "You need some help. Can I help? I've got a little time."

"Well, I actually—I have my nephews coming later. They're football players. They love this kind of exercise." She looks over at him. She's been staring at the box. The line where her name was written and the return address in the top corner were written in one person's handwriting, but the mailing address was written in another. Where the hell did this box come from? She glances at Jamie Morgan, surveying the place. She continues, "Ah . . . thanks for offering to help. You look like you're going windsurfing."

"Yeah, I'm not sure," he says, looking out the windows. "It may rain later."

"Really? I can't imagine. Not a cloud in the sky."

"Yeah. Maybe just a passing storm."

"I hate to tell you, but traffic is hellacious," Eleanor says, still distracted.

"What's the matter?" He looks at her. "You freaked out by the box? What's in there, a bomb?"

A gust of laughter escapes her. "God, might as well be." She approaches it and touches it. "I have no idea what's in there. But I can tell you this, this handwriting here, see." she points to her name *Ellie Marlow*. "It's written by a dear friend of mine. Someone I knew years ago, who died."

"What?" His eyes get greener.

"No, really. See how this writing is different from that writing?"

"Uh-huh. Yeah. That's weird." He looks at the side of the box. "Look, here, though. There's an envelope taped to the side of the box."

"Oh, my God." She turns the box.

"Well, hey, I better go." He starts backing up. "You can open this yourself. I'm sure you don't want some strange neighbor guy standing around."

"Oh. Thanks. Sorry. Ah . . . I forgot your name already. I'm not usually like this. Tell me again how you got this?"

"Jamie Morgan." He looks at her curiously, and she focuses on him through her fog. He has friendly, wrinkled eyes. "It was sitting at my doorstep. I'm sure it came by the mailman. It's dated October second. I came over a couple other times to deliver it, but you were never here. I didn't want to just set it outside. I heard cars on the road this morning, so I figured you were here."

She leans in close to see the postage.

"This is certainly interesting," Eleanor says. "I don't know if I should open it."

"If you don't, you won't know what's inside."

"Good point." They turn and look as a car pulls into the driveway. Jessica in her new car. "Come on, I'll walk out with you. You have to move, or you'll be stuck."

They go out. "Well, Ellie, Eleanor, whatever your name is, it's been good to meet you. Do you have your phone hooked up? We should probably trade numbers in case of emergency, don't you think?"

"Yeah. My phone's working, but I have to dig for the number. I'll wander your way in the next few days. I want to see your house anyway. Red Tatéweh told me it was built at the same time as this one. I hear they look alike."

"Yeah. They do. Sure. Please come by sometime. I'm usually home at dinnertime. I have a dog, Emerson. He's friendly, especially if you call him by name."

"Okay. Emerson. Great. Thanks for the box."

"No problem. I've been wondering when someone was gonna finally move in. That van's been here a while." He gets in his truck and looks behind him at the shiny blue Honda Accord. Jessie begins backing up to get out of the way. Then Jamie maneuvers his truck around and sticks his hand out the window in a wave as he drives off. Eleanor stares at the dust floating up on the road and waves back.

Jessie pulls in and hops out of her car. "Who was *that?*"

"Oh, the neighbor guy. Nice wheels, baby," Eleanor gestures to Jessie's car.

"Yeah!" She claps her hands giddily. "Drives like a dream. Do you know that, with all my money, I've never bought a new car right off the lot? That felt goood!"

"Well, you deserve it," Eleanor looks inside. "Nice choice."

"Let's take it for a drive when the girls go to sleep. I want to do a little late-night investigating!"

"What are you talking about?"

"Oh, you know. Brandon says we should go scope it out."

"You're crazy," Eleanor smiles and then winks. "Count me in."

"Help me empty the trunk. And tell me about that *guy!* He's adorable. I thought Red said he was old."

"I'm not sure he's the acupuncturist. I didn't ask. But he says he lives in that house down the road. It's gotta be him."

"He looks your age," Jessie raises her eyebrows at her.

"Stop it now. No match-making," Eleanor thinks about the box. "Wait till you see what he brought!"

"Flowers?"

"No!"

"Speaking of flowers, I stopped by the flower shop," she holds up two bags of tulip bulbs, shaking them slightly as she sing-songs, "He was checking you out."

"You barely saw him!"

"I know these things, my friend. I want to meet him. How can we meet him again?"

"Let's stop by his place tonight on our way to the woods. He said he wanted to get my number."

"See—I told you."

"Shut up, lovebird," She slaps her arm. "You're ga-ga over Brandon, but I'm still somewhat sane. Get your mind off love and into the mess I've started in the house."

When Brandon saw Jessica the first time, his jaw dropped. He couldn't help himself. He had already agreed to the paternity test, but after he laid eyes on her, he fell helplessly into Eleanor's and Jessica's hands. Weird, or not. Hard to tell. Eleanor had seen that the two of them had a profound commonality: loss of family ties. They loved the same food, music, and art. They had similarities in practically everything. Within minutes of discovering they were over the moon for each other, they planned to rendezvous to New York City, but it had to wait two weeks. They didn't know if they could go that long without being together, but by then, he would know if he could claim official father status. Regardless, Eleanor knew he'd be moving back to Minnesota. He had practically started packing before she and Jessie drove away in the minivan. He wanted to be involved, whether he was genetically implicated or not. It would be one weird but cozy family, that's for sure. But it didn't matter how the dynamic played out; Eleanor had never seen Jessica so happy in her entire life. Jessie had struggled with loneliness and depression for years since the collapse of her family; newfound happiness was so deserved and good to see. No doubt love at first sight was real; they had all three witnessed it.

The shift Eleanor felt that day on the dock, the day she saw the dead turtle—she is beginning to see where it was leading. She feels a lightness she hadn't felt in years, not since she found yoga or when she adopted the babies. She might be emerging into brightness, a light at the end of a long, dark tunnel. It's cliché, but it doesn't feel like it. She knows it's time to bring up Neal and his ashes; she's just not sure how.

They work late until all the boxes are unloaded, and all the big furniture has been placed in the house. Exhausted, Jessie and Eleanor put off their late-night escapade. Her nephews return the moving van on their way to their buddy's cabin, where they are staying for the weekend.

It'll be days before everyone feels settled, and she hasn't touched the mysterious box delivered by her neighbor. It sits on the kitchen counter with an empty pizza container on top of it. Jessie had forbidden her to open it in front of her. She said the box was addressed to her only, and the experience of whatever was inside should be Eleanor's alone. Eleanor knew it was true.

So, she waits until the girls and Jessie finally fall asleep and the house is quiet. She's not sure she likes the remoteness. There was a nice balance at her old place. She tries to muster up the courage to open the box. It keeps beckoning as she piddles around the kitchen. She decides she can at least open the white envelope taped to the outside.

Inside, she finds a penned note, somewhat feeble in handwriting but clean and legible. As she reads, her heart flutters. She has to stop a few times just to breathe.

> *Dear Eleanor:*
>
> *I am Barney Gaines, a friend of Red Tatéweh, and coincidentally the current owner of the old Havenmiller place. My wife and I are moving, and we found this box in our basement. We never noticed it years ago when we moved in, but as we prepare now to move out, we cleared out the basement shelves, and there it was. It was neatly and carefully sealed, and though we were very curious, we didn't open it. We had it sitting on the kitchen table, trying to decide what to do with it when Red arrived for dinner. We got to talking about the box, and Red told us he thought he knew this Ellie Marlow and that you are probably the same Ellie Marlow to whom this package is addressed. We met once at Red's shop.*
>
> *We theorized and marveled, really, about how this package, addressed to you, wound up in our possession. We remembered the Havenmillers had a grandson killed in a boating accident years ago. Red's theory is that you and this young fella must have been friends. He gave us your address, and we find it very intriguing you just so happen to be Red's new tenant. If you are not this same Ellie Marlow, please do what you will with the box and its contents. We have no other leads. But we feel confident you are the one. Best wishes,*
>
> *Barney and Bonnie Gaines*

Eleanor's head falls back on the couch. Tears begin to stream out the edges of her eyes. She can't stop them. *Not this again,* she thinks. She pulls herself together for a moment, taking a deep breath and wiping the tears off her cheeks, but then she's back to crying, then sobbing and shaking, and soon hugging herself and rocking quietly, to not wake anyone. She feels like she might vomit, but she takes in a shuddering breath and stops suddenly because she hears a noise.

It's the rooftop. Small raindrops pelt it above her head, and the leaves of the trees are making a tinkling, musical raining noise. *Finally, the rain,* she thinks. She sits quietly listening as it whispers around in the air, and she feels a chill and shudders again. She goes to the kitchen to boil some water. Her reaction to a fall rain is to want to drink hot tea. She stands in the kitchen. The rain is calming but also haunting. She turns on the outside light and peers into the night. It is the atmosphere for Halloween enthusiasts. It's ghostly and gives Eleanor the creeps. New homes take time to feel safe.

She shuts off the light and closes the kitchen curtains. By the time the kettle is whistling on the stove, the rain has gathered strength, coming down heavy and steady. In her new home, the rain seems especially loud. Lightning blinks around, and thunder shakes the rafters ever so slightly. Normally she loves storms. She's never been hurt in one or known anyone to have gotten hurt, so she doesn't associate storms with destruction. To her, rain is food for the flowers and green paint for the grass, yet she also thinks about how waterways have been used as pathways in war, and water kills randomly and unconscionably in many ways. She doesn't want to follow the idea of water destroying. She is tired of this old trope. And if she really thinks it through, usually water destroys when directed by some other force. It mostly performs as a conduit, not an instigator. Curious thing, water.

Tonight, in her solitude, with the package blatantly sitting there, she's unglued,   a little

                                        spooked.

She stares across into the living room, where she moved the box to the coffee table. It's the only thing she sees in the whole room. There are several other boxes, but this one seems to beckon as if neon brown. It occupies space as if it were a person.

"Okay. I'll open it," she mutters aloud. She shakes her head for being a coward. She pours the hot water and flips the teabag around, watching the red color swirl. The steam floats up into her face gently, like breath.

"Okay. Okay." She sits down with a steak knife and begins cutting the clear tape carefully pressed against every seam. The top comes apart easily, and the flaps seem to flop open by themselves. She doesn't look inside right away but takes a breath and tips her head back and forth to get at the tension in her neck. She takes a sip of tea. Then she sits up and peers inside the box. The first thing she sees is a white envelope with a card inside. She opens it and pulls the card out slightly to see it has a Maxfield Parrish painting on the cover.

She's familiar with the painting. Neal knew it was one of her favorite paintings, a girl standing on a cliff, her garments flowing out breezily behind her. She is staring up at the sky, which is lavishly enlivened by puffy white clouds. She slips the card back into the envelope without reading it and goes back to the box.

Inside she finds something square and heavy wrapped in cardboard and plastic and a quart-size jar wound in bubble wrap. She takes off the wrap to see the jar contains water. Along the bottom of the jar, the sediment dances a little with the motion of her lifting the jar out of the box. She removes the cardboard, unwraps the plastic, and discovers a water fountain. It has rocks and small pieces of driftwood. It has three levels, and wrapped neatly underneath is a cord, held together by a twist-tie. Tears well up again.

She takes it over to the dining room table where there's an outlet, and her whole body is quivering uncontrollably as she sets it down, unwinding the cord, letting the plug fall with a plunk to the wood floor. She goes to get the water jar, and she examines it closely. There's been no evaporation after all these years. The jar is sealed tight as if the water's been pickled and canned. The lid pops after several attempts to muscle it open, and though the aroma is not revolting, it's not pleasant.

She pours the water into the fountain, and, in amazement, she discovers it holds exactly one quart of water. There are three black iron plates, three different sizes; the bottom one is almost a bowl, and it holds the most water. The whole structure is cradled in an iron hanger-like tripod that sits close to the ground and hides the pump. Three hooks of the tripod wrap around the lowest plate. The fountain is only as big as maybe a small desk lamp, and it has a handle, surprisingly, so it's easily portable.

She plugs it in and flicks the cord switch. The water begins to trickle as she falls trance-like into examining it. The rocks are mostly quartz. They are glued in place, and the whole apparatus is intact with no loose parts. It feels solid and sturdy. When the rocks are wet, their colors illuminate; a few are dazzling agates. Each one is a study. Three pieces of treated and waterproofed driftwood make a multi-level, layering frame, and the water flows down over one piece, the biggest one, which cuts across the bottom plate, making two halves. It's like a little segment of a trickling brook. On the driftwood are little figures sticking up on copper pins. She counts six, two on each driftwood: a figure dancing with her arms out, a sun, a moon with a star, a turtle, a bird in flight, and a sailboat. The water swishes around the sticks. The figures sit above the swirling water and stay dry.

Every artistic detail delights. It sings and gurgles and sparkles and bubbles and twinkles. She quickly gets her tea and drinks it down; she moves around the house, turning off lights and gadgets. In the dark, the rain seems to be on top of her, but the trickling fountain calls out as if from far off. She intrinsically moves her way to it. She drags the recliner chair over, sits back, kicking up the footstool, and listens. The rain harmonizes with the trickling fountain, the thunder, the occasional jolt of lightning, working in duo vibration with her ears, and within minutes, Eleanor's eyes droop. Tears still wet on her face and her shirt sleeve soggy with snot, she rests in the watery concert, drifting sleep-ward, cradled as

the dream

begins

with flying out of the gray tube, suddenly coming over Quartz Lake, as if carried by a bird. The day blazes hot, the peak of summer. She drops down segmentally to land on the diving dock where a party is going on. Friends, siblings, and cousins are there, diving, giggling, swimming around. A game of ragtag is in progress. Someone has knotted up an old towel, and it's flying around, back and forth over the dock, slapping the back of the next target, who then picks it up to flail it at another. Joy and laughter bubble in her blood.

She notices a handsome young man standing on the tip of the diving board about to jump off. She has to stare at him, focus in, as he looks somewhat familiar. She sees it's Neal. He's doing a little waggle and making a goofy diving pose with his elbows bent and tucked in and his palms together. He's grinning so huge; his eyes are wide and so alive. He lets himself tip over sideways, laughing until he disappears, plunging under the water. She runs over to the edge to catch another glimpse of him. It's really him. She hasn't seen his face in forever. She watches as he surfaces, his curly sunlit hair flowing smoothly back with the water, making his face stick out, his cheekbones, his skin, and grin.

His beautiful face, looking up at her . . . that *beautiful* face. He swims to the ladder and climbs up beside her as she stands paralyzed, staring. He seizes her and hugs her breath away, pelting her face and neck with kisses and laughter. She almost squirms with the sensation; it's so real. She can feel his wet body, and she is dry. She's confused, trying to figure out how he got here. How is this real?

But there's no time for her to contemplate it, because all at once they are laughing, spinning, and twirling; and he's lifting his leg, kicking out in a dance move, allowing himself to twist outward and fall out into the water, holding her in his arms the whole way as they hit the water together. She comes up laughing. He is beside her. The water is so warm, so smooth and thick it feels like warm cream but looks like dazzling sky. The diamonds of light are everywhere. Everyone is there. She looks at the beach; there are all the adults, her mom and dad, smiling, waving, her aunts and uncles. She can't wait to go in and talk to them. Her mom is there. They are sitting, some on towels, some on beach chairs. There's lemonade. There're picnic baskets and toddlers and minnow nets, life jackets, inner tubes, goggles, and beach balls. Everyone is busy; laughter and squeals of exuberance fill in where visuals leave off. She swims and swims. She throws the rag, dives off the board, and glides through the shimmering water to touch the sandy bottom. Neal is there, everywhere she turns; he pops up to smile at her, splash her, push her into the water, kiss her, hold her hand as she gets dizzy.

Then time seems to zoom to a halt, and Eleanor feels like she's in some sort of weird Zen state. It's a dream, but it feels so real. She and Neal are standing together, face to face on the dock, holding each other's hands while everything around them freezes. He leans his face toward hers, and he says quietly, "Happy birthday, my love." And he kisses her. Then he turns and runs off the diving board, gracefully lifting his body into a swan dive and spearing the water poetically with his arrowed spine. She looks to see him underwater, but he has disappeared into the light of the water.

Her heart drops her to her knees, pleading with the depths to send him back up, just one more time, to see his face again.

She startles back into her body, jerking, when a monstrous clap of thunder rattles the house.

The rain has stopped for the moment, and only the sound of the fountain trickling echoes in the still night air. Ghostly empty. She is smoothed out with sudden clarity.

If only she could fall back into the dream, but thoughts and sensations flood her mind. *Water remembers and emotes. Glaciers and ice caps, and melting snow contain stories. Raindrops whisper clues. Streams carve paths to memory, to grid points in time and space. Tears release energy, tiny drops of emotion. The entire globe, vivid and fathomlessly blue, is a living, breathing body pulsing in water. Duh, you say, duh. I know this. . . .* And the sensation of blood pumps through her veins like a rhythmic river. And the river winds and swirls throughout her entire physical entity, flowing out as energy through her fingertips. Her hands are sweating; her fingertips tingle. It's not just the water. It is the force within the water. *We are rivers. Rivers of memory, emotion, history, information, energy. We must flow, or we stagnate. We are all one river.*

Tears flow. She wants more, more, more. She remembers the card. She wants to read it, but reading it means the end of anything more she might ever get of him. How decadent to drag it out! Especially considering she didn't even know before today that there was something unknown left to discover of him. Once she reads it, he will never be new again. Though dead for what seemed like forever, he and the vivid sensation of his presence ripples through her. She stares at the little fountain. It looks tiny and so insignificant. But it is so captivating, inviting you to look and pause.

She grasps the card he wrote to her; it looks surreal, some fragment set apart from time. She wants to put it off, wait as long as she can. Enjoy the fountain, live for a while in the sensation, the anticipation, that there is another little piece of him yet to be revealed in his written words, that he could exist in the present for even just a tremor in time. *Oh, what we would give to get it back!*

She realizes his own fingers were the last thing to touch this before her own hand now does. The thought makes her hug the card to her chest, rocking a little bit. She knows she's nutty, but she doesn't even care anymore. Then she pulls the card out and opens it, and a letter falls out. She ignores it to read the card. The card has the printed message inside *Dream Big*. Underneath, it says simply: *Birthdays are the days to remember our dreams. I love you. Forever yours, Neal.* She studies his handwriting for every little curve and sway. Finally, she unfolds the letter. It is dated the day before the day he died. *My God!* Two weeks before her actual birthday. How?

August 20, Happy Birthday, my dear Ellie!

I wish I could be with you on your birthday,
    but I know it won't be long before I see you again.
My heart aches to be with you,
   I miss you so much.
     I know you are busy starting school, but I wanted to make sure you got this
amid all that excitement, because I know, it will make you slow down, just a minute, to
enjoy it!
          I made it myself, thinking of you with every step.
It's taken me much of the summer. But I've got it all finished now, ahead of
    time. I'm even writing the card early (see the date?) because I know
     I'll be busy teaching when your birthday comes.
      And I don't want to miss it!
     If any of this is dated, that's why.
      I was thinking about how
       you told me your parents have to sell your cabin.
   I know how much you love the lake, maybe as much as you love me!
So, pour the water from the jar into the fountain,
     turn it on, and you have your very own
       Quartz Lake, only I guess
        it's more like a Quartz trickle!
      I took the water this morning,
     right off the end
     of your dock
    while you were sleeping.
     Your neighbor stared at me
   as he geared up to go fishing.
  I'm sure he thinks I'm a freak,
    but who cares?
     When you miss the lake,
      and you miss me,
   just plug it in, and we'll be together—
  me and you and the lake.
I thought you might want to add a few rocks from your own collection
    so put them where you can see I left a few empty spots.
        Always remember the past.
     Yet
      happiness is for now.
   Though we are not together right now,
  as you read this card, we are together in the enduring now of the water.

It will always contain us.
And we will always contain it.
I give it to you.
I love you forever,
my dearest one.
Neal

Over and over, she reads the letter, studying it and memorizing it, astounded by the weight and wisdom of his words. How could he have been that wise, that visionary, at such a young age? She lets herself remember him like she has never let herself before. To really crawl around in the terrain of those bumpy memories. To fully remember just how much he loved her, so deep and so long, for how short of a time they were together. All the stupid little conversations. Small details she didn't see as important then came to her, seemed to zoom into her mind's eye. She saw full facial expressions he had, subtle ones that didn't always make the headlines of memories.

She reads his words and hears his voice in her head as if he were older, as if, somehow, he has aged with her all along. She also reads it distinctly for how he was then, too, so serious and deep, yet frivolous and gregarious. Having lost so much himself, at such a young age, he learned to live cheerfully in the moment; that is a part of what made him so loveable and charismatic. The short time she knew him expands over the decades, and she sees he cannot be extracted from her life. He is there, intertwined, forever. And this feels a little like glue for her insides. She feels held together a tiny bit, somehow, knowing this on a sensory level. The glue of him meshes with her, makes her want to live cheerfully in the now, too, as he would be doing if he were alive. The tragic part of his story doesn't get to overrule his seed of light.

When the whispering wind flutters the leaves,
opening the gates of the morning,
she looks up, and her eyes are drawn out the window to the faint light coming through the trees at the horizon of the riverbed. Something amazing clicks in her heart, another shift of that weird sort of knob within. In the trees by the river bed, a flock of black crows suddenly take flight as if carrying something away.

She gets up.

Talking to Jessica about his ashes will be easy now, and showing her Neal's birthday gift will be as heavenly for Jessie as it is for her.

She walks to the kitchen, where the notebook, holding scribbled messages, sits next to the phone. She grabs a pen and starts writing.

Whatever cracks must needs be chiseled into the rock-hard status quo, she's got her tools ready.

No more playing dead.

CHAPTER 29

Counting Coup

Eleanor scribbles off a note for Jessica before she sneaks out the door to jump in the car and drive to Red's. She's got to talk to him before she goes to the Crandahl's lake house. He'll deliver just the right pep talk, not cheerleadery, more like a shove from Hunter S. Thompson.

She drifted off in the early morning hours and had woken up in a weird state of focused determination. Her cell phone beeped, telling her she had a message. Brandon called to tell her they were going to be at their lake house this weekend. *And, oh, one more thing: time is of the essence! Call me right away when you get this message!* He didn't sound panicked; he sounded excited. Eleanor dials his number as she bumbles down the dirt driveway out to River Road. He answers on the first ring.

"Hi!" He sounds wide-awake. "I've been waiting for you to call!"

"What the heck! Did you sleep last night?" She's smiling as she turns her car onto the pavement.

"Hardly." She feels him grinning through the phone. "But forget about that. Listen. You gotta go over there *today.* I found out Blake is planning on signing a purchase agreement with the DNR on November first, and it'll go into legislation."

"But the land isn't even for sale yet!"

"Well, that's the thing, if the sale can be made privately, with no opposition, then everybody's happy. It's cheaper, faster, and more profitable for both parties."

"Well, how can anyone oppose it when it's not advertised anywhere?"

"Now you're catching on!"

They talk the whole time Eleanor drives to the coffee shop. Brandon coaches her on her argument and strategy. She pulls into a parking spot in front of Harvest Moon and glances across the street at her studio. She'll soon be taking the sign down on the door that reads "Closed for 10 days. See you Monday, October 27."

She walks in, and Red is standing at the cash register, staring at her as if he knew she was coming. "Bout time you showed up."

"Huh?" She says, "It's barely seven a.m.!"

"Here. Sit," he gestures to the counter. "What'll ya have? The usual, or are you back to tea again?"

"Hit me with the usual," they look at each other, grinning. She sits down and sets her keys on the counter. The place is empty except for two other patrons. Red has his back to Eleanor while she bites a fingernail, trying to figure out how to spill it all to Red and do it quickly. Brandon said she should get to Blake's by nine if she's to catch him before he heads out to play golf, what he's usually doing when not working.

"When'd ya get home from your trip?" He says loudly over the coffee grinder.

"Yesterday. The place looks great. We're finally getting moved in. The girls are so happy."

"Well, I'm glad you're back. Place gets a little dull when you and your little people aren't around. Did you have fun?"

"We did. The girls were in heaven."

"Well, I'll have them fill me in on all their adventures." The espresso machine starts gurgling.

"Oh, they will. I have a few amazing adventures to recap for you too."

"Oh, yeah?" He's frothing the soy now.

"I got an interesting package in the mail yesterday from my new neighbor," she throws out finally. "From your friend, Barney Gaines."

"Oh?"

"How'd you know the package belonged to me?"

"Wasn't sure."

"Did you know I knew Neal Havenmiller?"

"I didn't. He's the guy who was killed in his kayak long time ago? Was the box from him, then?"

"Yeah. He was my boyfriend."

"So, no wonder you never got married, huh?"

How does he make everything so simple yet so honest? He seems to get it without having to interrogate her. For the first time since she met him, she wonders about his love life.

"Did you ever get married?" She blurts out.

"I did. I was married for twelve years."

"Kids?"

"Nope. We never had any. My wife couldn't. But we were happy. My sister has four kids. Our house was their second home."

She doesn't want to ask about what happened to his wife. But he tells it anyway. "Elaine Marie," he proclaims into the room. "Met her the day I returned from Vietnam. If not for her, I'm sure I'd be in the loony bin . . . or dead." He stands up straight. "She was a true beauty. Died of an aneurism . . . 'bout twenty years ago now."

"Oh. Sorry to hear that, Red."

"I never remarried. Sometimes the heart just never quite recovers, does it?" He smiles at her.

"I hear ya," she nods. Tears wait behind her eyes.

"So, did you open the box?" He sets the mocha down in front of her.

"Oh, yeah. Totally blew my mind. How weird is it to get something from a long-lost love years after the fact?" How nonchalant she seems to herself.

"I really can't imagine," he says, leaning lightly on the counter.

"It's this cool trickling water fountain. He made it. I can't believe it. It was supposed to be for my birthday. But, then . . . you know. He died. He didn't get to give it to me."

"You know . . . in my culture, there's no such thing as coincidences." He pours himself a fresh brew, then comes back to his lean. "There's got to be something significant about that."

"Oh, there is." I nod. "There was a jar of old water from Quartz Lake in there."

"Interesting." He sips his coffee.

"And I had some crazy dreams. Some weird shit is all coming together."

"About his death?" *How could he know?*

"Funny you say that."

"Oh, not really. Things work themselves out in the most amazing ways," he gives her a long, piercing look.

"Well . . ." she pauses, sipping her mocha, formulating thoughts.

"Want whip cream? I forgot to ask, here," she holds out her mug, and he gives her a whip cream blast. He's still looking at her intently.

"You know my friend Jessica, right?"

"Gorgeous one you're always hanging around with?"

"Yeah." She sips at the froth. "She's Neal's sister."

He shows no reaction except to stand up suddenly and start grinding coffee. A customer comes in, and he gets a couple of coffees to go and a bag of muffins. Then he returns.

"That's very cool."

"She and I want to purchase the state forest on the west shore of Quartz."

"I hear it's in the millions."

"Yeah. Exactly." She pokes at the napkin on the counter in front of her with a stir stick. "Think we're crazy?"

"You got that kind of money?"

"You could say it's been recently acquired."

He's filling his cream and skim milk containers. He looks over at her. "There's usually some high stakes involved when that kind of money moves hands."

"Yeah. It could get ugly."

"Think you got a real shot?"

"I . . . think so."

"Then . . . kick some of that nasty corporate ass."

"But I don't know if I can do it."

He stands in front of her, pausing, holding his big jug of skim milk. "Well. I know you can." He leans down with his elbow on the counter. "Tell me exactly what you have to do."

"Basically . . ." she blinks hard, taking a deep breath. "The guy who has first shot at that state forest is also the guy who . . . killed Neal." She stops to swallow hard. Red continues looking at her steadily. She goes on, "I have to confront him, and . . . possibly . . . blackmail him if he doesn't back down."

"No problem." He's still looking at her steadily. "How long have we been talking about trying to defeat these evil, land-grabbing mutha-fucks? Now's our chance!" His enthusiasm erupts. Eleanor looks at him with astonishment. She sees a flash of his warrior-slash-veteran self. He yanks her back into the present, saying, "What've ya been doin' all that yoga for—if not to hone your prowess? Isn't there some *warrior* pose?"

"God. You are funny," she laughs.

"Well? Get your warrior on, baby! Don't go to battle unless you plan on winning. Okay? Oh, wait! Stay right here. I got something for you." He trots off like he's eighteen years old, slipping into his backroom. He comes out with something in his hand, wrapped in a white hanky. He sets it on the counter next to her mug. She frowns at it.

"It's a pipe. Go ahead. Look at it." He nods his head, eyebrows raised.

"What the hell, you crazy old man!" She picks it up, pulling off the fabric. "What? You think I'm gonna smoke some fancy juju tobacco?"

"No, you crazy-new-age-yoga-freak," he bobs his head and grins. She's feeling its smooth surfaces with her fingers. "My great, great grandfather made it. It's a council pipe. It's good for negotiating."

"You think I should ask the evil creep to sit down and smoke a pipe with me?" She's supercharged with a giggle now, briefly imagining such a scene, her sitting cross-legged, intently packing the pipe, him standing over her with a club.

"No. No, not at all. Just bring it with you. Keep it in your pocket. It has magical properties." Then he holds up a finger, "but maybe you *should* take some tobacco just in case."

She doesn't protest. She holds it up to her nose, smelling it. "Maybe I should smoke *something* out of it before I go?"

"I got good tobacco. Wanna go out back?"

"Naw. I was kidding. I don't do tobacco."

"Hey, it could help. You sure?"

"Yeah. Tobacco makes me dizzy."

"Whatever dings your donger. Or in this case, *doesn't*."

"Hey, I gotta go," she says, glancing at the clock behind the counter. "Wish me luck."

"You don't need luck. Take the pipe."

"Well, wish it to me anyway."

"Good luck then." He adds, "And be careful with that pipe. You're holding generations of Native power in your little hand."

"Okay." She wishes she had the time to tell him about Brandon and the paternity test and everything it could mean, but she'll have to do it later. "I'll be back later with all the details. And a lot more to tell you about lots of stuff."

"In that case, you *better* come back. I'll be sittin' here all day waiting for a sign." He watches her walk to the door. As she opens the door, he says, "You and your friend Jessica bring the girls in later, okay? Really. I'm going through withdrawal over here."

She smiles, "You got it. See ya."

The drive across town and to the north end of the Quartz takes about thirty minutes. Eleanor keeps thinking of things to say, driving in total silence, wading through the stream of weekend traffic.

She switches off her phone as she pulls into the Crandahl's circular driveway. She notes the life-size bronze statue of a Bengal tiger in the middle of the loop. There's a Jaguar parked next to the garage, with the license plate CANDEED and a black Hummer right behind it. Eleanor parks before she even gets to the circle, and she looks around for a minute before she gets out of her car. She can't see the lake anymore. It's blocked by the huge houses and a row of tall shrubs growing along the edge of where the lawn meets the sand. The grounds are completely unfamiliar, even though Blake's house is almost directly in the spot where the Marlow cabins used to be. None of the trees are familiar. No old oak tree. The tennis courts are still in the same place, but there are now four mansions and one guesthouse, or servants' quarters, across the second driveway, further back from the tennis courts. The neighbor who used to live on the other side of Marlow's, Mrs. Wylund, has disappeared too. Her log cabin has been replaced by one of the mansions.

Eleanor estimates the Crandahl compound comprises at least six hundred feet of lakefront, but probably more like eight hundred. It's overwhelming. Eleanor looks down to see her hands gripping the steering wheel and notices her armpits are soggy. She suddenly lets go of the wheel and opens her door, getting out before she has a chance to talk herself out of it. Her head pounds from all the caffeine so early in the day.

She steps up to the front entry; beautiful stones form the base of the house and go up and over the double wooden doors in an arch. Two fall wreaths hang, one on each door. Everything is swept clean. Eleanor examines every corner and joint of the woodwork for cobwebs but finds none. Hearing laughter, she glances across the wide yard to the tennis courts to see three women in their crisp whites stepping through the gate with rackets in hand. She squints at them, thinking one of them has to be Camilla Crandahl, but she can't be positive. She looks back at the door, sighs, and pokes the doorbell button. She waits, and suddenly, the door opens, and Candice is standing there.

Though Eleanor hasn't seen her for more than twenty years, Candice has the same perfect petite body. She's wearing a navy-blue velour outfit with a ruffled collar. Her hair is up in a perky ponytail, but it's lighter in color, highlighted almost platinum blonde. Her face has been made-up carefully and is perfectly framed with a matching navy-blue sweatband.

"Yes?"

"Ah. Hi. Are you Mrs. Crandahl?" Eleanor feels like a frumpy giant standing before her.

"Yes." She leans lightly against the edge of the door.

"I'm looking for your husband. Is he home?"

"No. He's out." *Shit!*

"Hmmm. When will he be back? It's really important I talk to him."

"I'm not sure."

"Well," Eleanor scrambles. She wants to do this now, get it over with. "Can I leave him a note then? Maybe?"

Candice's face tries to suppress a frown. "Oh. Sure."

But she just stands there, as if waiting for Eleanor to pull paper and pen out of nowhere. She's not even carrying her purse. Suddenly she realizes she left the pipe on the passenger seat. She meant to have it on her.

"I don't have any paper," Eleanor holds up her hands and a faint smile.

"What's this about, exactly?" She gives Eleanor a hard look.

"Well, it's kind of complicated. I'm not sure you want me to go into it out here. Can I come in for a minute?"

"Not exactly. I'm . . . in the middle of something."

"Well," Eleanor sits back on one of her heels. "You might want to hear what I have to say. It's pretty interesting."

"I'm not into sales calls."

"This is hardly a sales call."

"Look, just tell me what you want. I don't need to sit here and play games."

"Okay," Eleanor tilts her head. "I am here to talk to your husband about the state forest land on the west side of the lake that he's planning on buying."

"I know absolutely nothing about that. I don't get involved in his business affairs."

"You might want to in this case. I'm also interested in purchasing that land. I don't want to have to go to court over it, but I will if I have to."

"You have *no idea* what you'd be up against, or you'd never say such a thing."

"Actually, I know *exactly* what I'm up against," Eleanor clasps her hands together. "I'm here to tell you what exactly *you're* up against."

"You can't scare me. I have no idea who you are," a little laugh escapes her, "and I really don't care."

"Oh, yes, okay, let me introduce myself. I'm Eleanor Marlow. I was a neighbor of the Crandahls many years ago. I think, actually, that our old cabin—" she looks around a little, "—used to be exactly where we're standing right now." She can't hide her snideness.

"O . . . kay?" She glances back inside the house quickly.

Eleanor sighs. "I was friends with a guy named *Neal Havenmiller*. You may know of him? He was killed in a boating accident about twenty-five years ago?"

Candice stands up straight and opens the door a little bit, squinting her eyes ever so slightly. The women on the court are standing along the back fence, probably waiting for the last of the foursome to arrive. Eleanor has had her back to them, but she's watched Candice's face, her gaze occasionally focusing over at them. Eleanor looks over at them and turns back to Candice, saying, "Ready to let me in?"

"Oh. Of course, yes. You should come in," she steps aside to let her in. Eleanor senses her icy shield as she enters.

"Actually, hold on a sec. I have to get something out of my car."

"Sure." She's attempting niceness.

Eleanor walks back to her car, deliberately going slow, enjoying Candice's impatience. She picks up the pipe and shoves it in her jacket pocket. As she walks back up to the house with her hands in her pockets, she feels something inside the other pocket. She had shoved Neal's letter in there when she put on the coat this morning. She can't remember why she did it, but she's damn happy she did.

She steps through the doorway into the foyer. She can hear someone inside, so she ventures forth. She comes into a wide-open space, a giant living room with an enormous stone fireplace, a bar, an enormous flat-screen television. The whole side of the house facing the lake is windows, and the lake is blinding with the morning sun. Two enormous cream-colored leather couches dominate the room, but everything is creams and whites. The walls display enormous oil paintings, and special lighting highlights stone sculptures of animals in weird dancing poses on pedestals. The kitchen area is off to the left, and Candice is standing in the kitchen drinking some kind of blended drink. Eleanor goes over to the long marble countertop and leans on it with her elbow. The whole place is squeaky clean. Her words sound odd, echo-y when she begins talking.

"You need to talk to Blake. He has to give up the idea of buying that land. He can go find some other place to build his water park."

"I can't imagine why you think anything you say or anything you think you're going to get *me* to say makes any difference to him. He does whatever he wants. He really can't be pushed around."

"Well, maybe I can explain to you just how messy this situation could get if he refuses to back down. I know you're someone who cares what the neighbors think."

"You're hardly a neighbor."

"Oh, I'm not the neighbor you'd have to worry about. That is, if I were your neighbor, which, you're right; clearly, I'm not." She clasps her hands together patiently.

"Look," she leans back against the countertop, "Miss Marlow." She looks up at the skylight for a second. "How do I explain this to you. Blake Crandahl cannot be intimidated. He is one of the most powerful, well-connected men around. His company creates more jobs and revenue than any other company in all of northern Minnesota. We don't even live here, and we're treated like royalty. Anything you think you can do to him is pointless."

"I'm not trying to push him around. I'm trying to get him to listen to reason. A water park on that land would be a disaster for the environment. The whole atmosphere of the lake would change. People who own homes and cabins here don't want that!"

"People need to accept the wave of the future. It's called progress. This lake is meant for entertainment and enjoyment. If you want peace and quiet, *bla, bla, bla* . . . visit the Boundary Waters."

"It's not just what the people want. What about the wildlife and the air quality? What about the water? Chlorinated water parks are toxic and wasteful."

"If he doesn't build it, someone else will. And when he builds it, they will come. People want their fun. Nothing you say can stop the wave of the future."

A masculine voice calls out from another part of the house, echoing through the silent lofty ceiling of the living room, "Candice, come on, let's get back to work."

"That's my trainer. I was in the middle of my circuit when you dropped in without calling. I have to get back to my routine if you don't mind."

"I don't want to hold you up, but I guess I have to take this to the extreme then. It seems that's the way you do things."

"I'm really out of time." She sets her glass in the sink and starts to move past Eleanor. Eleanor moves over slightly to stand in Candice's way. Candice steps back and gives her a nasty look. "I think you should leave now."

"I think you should know this," she lowers her chin slightly. "I'm prepared to visit the county attorney to bring criminal charges against Blake Crandahl for the murder of Neal Havenmiller."

"*What?*" Her face flashes a mix of horror and hatred.

"I think you heard me."

"You *really* have no idea what you're getting into, do you?"

"I *really* think I do. I'm wondering if you know what *you're* getting into."

"You have *no evidence!* The police ran a full investigation. *TWENTY-FIVE YEARS AGO!* Ever heard of the statute of limitations? It's too late for your petty vengeance."

"This isn't vengeance. This is justice. I *have* evidence. I have *solid* evidence. I have four eyewitnesses willing to testify in court that Blake Crandahl *committed* the crime and then *covered up* the crime."

"You are full of shit! You're just a poor, pathetic *loser* who never got over the death of the one boyfriend you ever managed to have," she draws out the part with cynicism. "Any lawyer *anywhere* could see right through you."

Eleanor wants to hit her, but she ignores the urge, staring hard at her as she says, "It's not too late for a criminal trial. New evidence has come to the surface."

"Your evidence is shit."

"Zack Slavin was in the boat with Blake when he recklessly ran over Neal in his coked-up state. Brandon Crandahl overheard Blake telling Zack to keep his mouth shut and was physically threatened by Blake to keep *his* mouth shut. Margaret Hensley, Blake's *girlfriend* at the time, and I, *myself*, witnessed Blake leave your party in the middle of the night in his speedboat. In a real way, you, too, are also responsible." Eleanor is standing up straight now, ticking off the people she refers to with her fingers.

"Candice?" The trainer calls again.

"Hang on, Michael!" She yells. Eleanor hears carefully controlled tension in her voice, and it makes her antsy. Any second now, Candice could go postal. She has to finish fast.

"And if that doesn't cause you to think this through, because I am sure the courtroom would be filled with people—*neighbors*—curious about the royal businessman turned murderer, then a media deluge might be just the thing you need."

"You are a *bitch!* What's your *problem?*" Candice looks Eleanor up and down. "You can't get a new man, so you have to break up happy families with your problems?"

"My God. You so miss the point. Let's get back to what I said I wanted. I want Blake to give up buying that land. I'd never want to break up your *happy* family."

"Blake will not give it up. You just don't get it."

"He won't be building any water park from prison."

"He knows the county attorney, like best buds," Candice sighs tiredly.

"Well. I don't have anything else to say—except—even if the case never goes to trial, the media will be informed, and people will talk. If I don't hear back from either you or Blake by November 1st, I'm going to make two calls. If you prefer to work this out through our attorneys, here's my attorney's card. My number is on the back." She pulls Brandon's card out of her back pocket and hands it to Candice. Then she turns and starts walking toward the door.

Candice stares at the card for a moment then sets it on the counter. Before either of them knows it, Candice is letting out a growl, and she throws her arms up, pushing Eleanor hard against the shoulders from behind, sending her flying forward, landing on her side in the foyer. *"Get out, you fucking bitch! GET OUT!"*

Eleanor is shocked. She tastes blood and realizes she bit her tongue. She gets up slowly as a calm comes over her. She stands facing Candice and thinks how badly she wants to take her down. She's a scrawny little thing, but she does work out. Still, even enraged and fit, she has no physical chance. Eleanor is so close to letting loose a punch but suddenly

words come out instead,

"You know . . . I'd hate to bring criminal charges on you, too."

Candice is calm now, "I said; get out."

"Please try. For once in your life. Be a good person. Do the right thing."

"Michael!" She yells.

"Camilla Crandahl would hate this scandal. She's kept it quiet for so long."

"Michael! Get in here!"

"I'll be going now." Eleanor opens the door and steps out, leaving it open behind her. She doesn't have to wait for the door to shut explosively behind her. The gals are playing tennis now. The late morning sun has dried up all the dew on the wide expanse of abnormally green grass, unhindered with even one fallen leaf. Curious about the door slam, they subtly watch as she gets into her car. Eleanor starts the car quickly. She feels the little bump on her tongue with her finger as she drives away.

She sees an old white pine tree, dappling sunlight lingering around it in a fluffy, green haze. It stands next to the road, huge and spectacular against the yellow birch trees behind it. *That old tree is familiar,* she realizes; *this is the road we used to ride our bikes down and sneak down, in the pitch dark, using the starlight above for bearings. This is the road where I learned to drive, where I used to be so carefree when I was so young.*

It's strangely familiar and yet unfamiliar at the same time. She catches a glimpse of herself in the rearview mirror. Her eyes are clear. She squints at herself, and a mischievous grin, a flash of an expression her face used to make ages ago, appears. A laugh bubbles out. She barely has time to relish it before something else catches her attention.

Down the road, she sees a silver Mercedes coming. It has to be Blake. Who else would be driving such a car down this dead-end road at this time of year? It could be Mr. Crandahl. But she takes a chance and turns her car to the left, blocking the road to stop the on-coming car. She stares as it approaches, peering into the driver's seat to see who's there. As the car draws up and slows to a stop, she sees it is Blake, though he's barely familiar. He's talking on his cell phone.

She turns off her engine and gets out, putting her hands on the roof of her car, facing him. He stares at her a minute, then ends his phone conversation. He opens his car door and leans out. "What the hell, lady?"

"I need to talk to you."

He gets out. As he stands up, she can't believe how thin he is, how short and white his hair is. He looks small. His nice thick brown hair is gone. His face looks drawn, with deep lines in his cheeks. His blue eyes are not twinkly, though they are piercing.

"What the fuck?" He smirks at her. "Who the hell do you think you are? Get the fuck out of the way, bitch, or I'll run you over."

"Can you just stop a second, Blake? It's me, Eleanor Marlow. Remember me?"

"Holy shit. Yeah. I remember you. Barely." He tosses his cell phone down on the seat. "Whatever you want, I have nothing to say to you."

"Isn't there a way we could have a conversation?" They look each other in the eyes for a split second, then Blake looks away.

"What the fuck," he repeats. His head shakes with disgust. "Don't you get what I'm saying? Get out of the way." He makes a flippant sweeping-away gesture with his hand.

"I know you killed Neal."

"You don't know shit." Annoyance mixed with pain flashes across his face.

"You better stop telling yourself that, Blake. You'll be sorry."

"Actually, you'll be the sorry one." He glares at her menacingly.

"What. You're gonna run me down like you did Neal? How many other people have you run down in your stupid life?" She thinks about approaching him, but she realizes he might hit her. "Don't you want to clear your conscience—be free of all this? You have a chance! You don't have to be a dominating jerk!"

"Lady, you are messed up!" He shrieks, dissipating his desperate frustration by holding out his hands, fingers wide like he's squishing an imaginary beach ball. He drops back into his car and shuts his door. He puts his car into reverse and hits the gas. He backs up, then puts it into forward and drives across the grass around her car, narrowly missing a few trees as tufts of grass and cloudy, blue exhaust fly up behind him. She watches as he pulls back up on the road. The red brake lights pop out amid the wake of dust billowing up from the back of the car, and suddenly his car stops, and his car door opens. He leans out and snarls, "If you think you can fuck with me, you're dead wrong, you stupid bitch."

She yells back, "Just you wait and see!" but he slams his door again before she gets the last word out, "Bastard."

She looks around to see if anyone might be listening. The trees seem to be with her on that one. He accelerates away, and the wake of exhaust blasts her face. She ducks back into her car and shuts the door. Her hands are shaking, and her eyes involuntarily tear up. She robotically starts the car and turns it, slowly driving forward. She takes long, deep breaths, dropping her head back slightly, turning her neck this way and that. She clings to how diminished and old he looked.

Pulling up in the driveway at home, she sees the girls on the grass running around with butterfly nets. A huge pile of leaves sits in the middle of the lawn. Jessie is bent over in the flowerbed next to the house, digging bulbs into the ground. When they hear the car, the girls come running. Eleanor gets out, and they leap on her. Jess, her hair spilling out of her orange bandana, comes over, wearing dirty gloves and holding a trowel in her hand. Her face is brooding.

They look at each other, and Eleanor's grin slowly broadens until it's beaming all over her face. Jess finally smiles back.

CHAPTER 30

Miniscus

I stood up to my ankles in the cold water, holding the canoe steady while Jessie arranged herself in the front seat.

"What the heck are you doing?"

"Don't rush me! I'm trying to get everything situated." She digs in her large canvas bag for something.

"Don't tell me you have to go back up the hill—*through the woods*—to get something out of the car, *again*."

"No. No. Just give me a second here. What's the hurry? I can't see anything. It's frickin' pitch dark, for God's sake!"

"You want the flashlight?"

"Yeah. Hand it over."

"What are you looking for?"

"The horseshoe, okay?" She turns back and reaches her hand out. "Here, give it to me."

I hand it to her, "It's in there. I checked. Now I'm shoving off, alright?" I hook the straps of my life preserver and start moving the canoe away from the shore, one hand gripping each side. I put one foot on the tip of the canoe and hop along with the other until the water is past my knee getting my cut-offs wet, then I drop into the bottom of the canoe. The temperature is unbelievably warm for late October. Yet in the wee hours of the morning, the water is chilly, and my leg is tingly cold. I slip my feet into my Birkenstocks and reach for a paddle. Jessica is still fussing ahead, but I begin paddling. I decide to hug the shore for a bit before we begin crossing the bay toward Raven's Point. Jessie finds the horseshoe, and satisfied, she turns behind her to grab a paddle.

"Wait. Before you start paddling, turn on that big lantern thing. God knows we want to be visible."

"That's not funny."

"I'm not trying to be funny." She reaches to turn on the battery-operated light and sets it next to the urn in the middle of the canoe. The light makes it harder to see right around us, but against the shore, the giant rows of white pines are slightly illuminated, and they look magnificent. Humble sentinels of time.

"It's so quiet," Jessie says quietly. "Hear that owl?"

"Yeah. Cool."

"When should we cross?"

"In a few minutes. Let's just get our groove. Luckily, the water is flat, huh?"

"Perfect. Just perfect."

"And it's so warm! I can't believe how warm the air is."

"Me either. It's like this was meant to happen. Right now. Right this very day and right this very minute."

We paddle quietly for a minute. The sound of the water swirling behind the paddles and the whizzing noise of the drops flying off the paddles as we lift them out of the water for the next stroke is synchronized, musical, and entrancing. I hear the owl not far ahead of us. "Sunday. Nice day for church."

"A-huh."

"Look at the light coming up over there."

We stare across the lake to the east. A dimmer switch appears to control the horizon, infinitesimally increasing its brightness. My eyes return to the black water while Jessica looks toward the shore.

"These pine trees are amazing," she gushes.

I glance up at them. She adds, "I hope they stay."

"Oh, I think they will."

I turn the boat just slightly with the paddle, and we start heading out into the open water. No mist on the lake. It's too warm. It might well be the last warm day of the year. We cross, facing east, and we get to watch the light infiltrate the dark stretching through us as we go. Half-way across, the lake becomes fully illuminated, shimmering, and glassy. The canoe leaves a trail, unzipping the surface of the giant liquid garment. The mercury-like façade shimmered like an orgasmic mirror. As if someone lit a fire underwater. I lean forward and snap the lantern off. Looking across the lake in both directions, there isn't another boat in sight. I feel my heart beating steady and strong, and I take long, deep, purposeful breaths. Overhead, the sky clears, blushing to a pale-blue hue. Behind us, above the dark forest, billowy clouds take shape in the new light, swelling with pastel rebirth. The coming sunrise delivers the sun's kiss of hope to the Earth.

As we begin to approach the opposite shore where Raven's Point juts out like a pinky finger, the light intensifies at the tips of the trees as the fiery orb approaches the horizon from below. Suddenly, it breaks up and out, and blaring rays of light hit my eyes. With the glare, we want to get to shore quickly, so we paddle faster.

We arrive with a thud as the sharp tip of the canoe breaks through the rocks and pushes up onto the sand. Jess steps out and pulls the canoe up a little, and I jump out. She grabs the big canvas bag. She's got this all planned out. I finish securing the canoe while she pulls out the purple blanket and spreads it out on the cold sand. I come over and sit down on it while she takes some other stuff out. Jessie lights five candles and sets them in the sand behind us, and she sits down next to me. She pulls out the horseshoe, among other things, and she hands me the glass jar filled with my old Quartz Lake water. Then we just sit a little in silence and watch the world be born. I can't help it; I have to say out loud, "the Boundary Waters is not the only place to find peace and quiet."

"Shhh . . . you're wrecking my "Morning Has Broken" moment!" She looks at me, grinning.

"Funny. Did you bring snacks in that bag of yours?"

"Here." She drags it over and hands it to me. I open it and find a bag of red licorice.

"This is it?" I smirk.

"There's M&Ms too," she doesn't look at me; she's staring at the lake. As I had figured: sunrise extraordinaire. I watch too, without moving for a minute or two, then I give in and open the bag of licorice, taking out a couple of ropes. I hand one to Jessica. She takes a bite, still looking forward.

"Wow," I say, chewing.

"Amazing."

"Yeah," I pause. "I wish he was here with us."

"He is."

"He loved licorice, didn't he?"

"Yeah, he did." She sticks another bite in her mouth. "I like M&Ms better. Hand me the bag, will ya?"

We watch, and I try to catch where a certain color develops, but it can't be pinpointed. Your eyes just have too much to look at. The sun continues toward its zenith, while clouds to the west and north billow and spread. The whole scene is constant yet changing, dazzling, and dynamic. Most captivating to me, of course, is the water. Its luminescence is too bright to stare at. Like the sun, it begins to sear into you, into your mind, causing your ears to ring a little. I listen and hear the magic timelessness and hum of nature. I feel almost like I could self-combust . . . not violently, but rather, seamlessly and instantaneously floating into the wide expanse of it all around me, all within me, all at the same time. Maybe I've been doing too much yoga.

"So, this is how he was going to propose, huh?" Jessica says with a sad grin.

"Yeah," I sigh. "Can you imagine?"

"He never did anything ordinary," she's smiling bigger now.

"I know."

"I sure wish you could've had that experience. Even if he had to die. At least you could've had that memory."

"I guess I'm having it now, in a different way. But we had plenty of great experiences. I'll *never* forget."

"I know. Me too."

"But it woulda been nice."

"Yeah."

We watch a while longer, then I stand up. The candles flicker in the sand; there's hardly a wisp of air moving. I take my jar of water and open the lid. I go over to the lake, step into the sand at the water's edge, and pour about half of the old water into the lake, watching it bubble as it falls in and rejoins itself anew. I hold the jar up to examine the level, making sure I make it as close to half as I can. I don't know why; it just seemed like the thing to do. Then I take the lid of the jar, and I'm about to scoop new water into it. Jessie sits in the sand behind me and watches, but then she says suddenly, "Wait! Let's do the ashes first!"

I stop. I almost forgot. "Yeah. Okay, let's."

"Red gave us the pipe, remember? And some smoke."

"Hmmm." I don't really want to, but I think about Red and how happy he was to give us the pipe for our occasion, so I say, "Alright. Get it out."

So, she gets the pipe ready, and I sit back down next to her. She takes a puff and blows it out, coughing. She hands it to me. I look at the new chip in its shape, from where it broke a little when I fell on Candice Crandahl's marble floor. I take a puff and blow it out over the water.

"Here's to peace . . ." I say, with the smoke.

"You're *such* a cheese ball."

I glance at her, my eyebrows raised, "No. I'm not being cheesy. This is a ceremony. I'm being serious for a minute."

"Okay. Yeah. You're right," she pauses. "Go ahead."

"Here's to peace. Peace on Earth, peace within me. Peace with all of time and the past and what is to come in the future. I embrace and love it all," I say, and take another puff of the pipe.

I hand her the pipe, and she takes a shallow inhale too, blowing out the smoke in little puffs like she's a cloud-maker. Then she says, "I honor the beauty of the world and everything seen and unseen within it. I am grateful for the role I play within this beautiful world. I ask for wisdom and vision as I walk today and in the days ahead. May the universe and the love within my heart guide me."

"Beautiful." We're silent again for a minute, and we finish the pipe.

"Thank you, God, or whoever's out there listening, for this moment," I say, looking up into the sky.

"Thank you, God, for giving me my brother Neal. Neal. I love you. Forever," she grabs the urn and sort of hugs it. Then she stands up, holding out the urn with her hands, sort of timidly, tears welling in her eyes.

"Want me to help you?"

"Yeah. Here. You hold one side, I'll hold the other, and let's drop it into the water and take the lid off. I don't want his ashes flying all over the place."

"Me either."

So, we do it. We stand in the water up to our knees. We take the lid off under the water and sort of swish the urn around, so the ashes come out and swirl around with the water. I'm glad there is no one around to witness what we're doing. I am pretty sure, these days, doing something like this is illegal. I'm sure the government wants anyone releasing ashes to purchase a permit. Somewhere out there, I hope Neal is relishing the illegal release of himself, returning to the place he loved, his burned physical remnants now particles forever mingled into the lake, his essence invited to transubstantiate.

We watch as the black flecks float out and away. I stare at the individual specks for a long time, floating and drifting, until I can't feel my feet anymore in the cold water. Some little gray flecks stick to my legs. Then I say, suddenly, barely audibly, "I love you, Neal. I'll miss you as long as I live. I hope I see you again, somehow."

I step out of the water and get the jar. I refill it, using the lid as a scoop until it is full. Then I screw the cap on tight and tuck it back in Jess's bag. All this time, the clouds from the west have been moving their way over the lake, and I can't believe it, but it looks like it could rain soon.

"We better go pretty soon."

"Yeah. Boaters are comin' out."

"Wanna say anything else?"

"I'm not sure. Let's just sit a few more minutes, and I'll think about it."

Suddenly she says, "Neal. You affect my life every day, and you live in my heart forever. Mom and Dad, I hope you are taking care of Neal. I miss you all so much. I can't wait to see you again. I know one day I will."

"Me too," I whisper. She holds up her open palms, and I take one in mine for a big squeeze. She pulls my hand up to her cheek for a brief moment; we look at each other, but not too long, then she lets go. And we sit on the blanket for a few more minutes. I eat another strand of licorice; Jessie has a few more handfuls of M&Ms. I feel a subtle drop in temperature as we watch the sky. It may take a while for the clouds to spread across the lake, but the western rim is dark already.

Finally, Jessie turns and blows out the candles, one by one. She gets up and starts putting all her little trinkets back in the bag, kissing each one as she does. She has teary eyes, but she's not crying. I find myself amazingly not-so-sad. I help, and we load up the canoe and get in it to start paddling again.

"I feel like I want to be here on the lake all the time, Elle," Jessie says finally, after a little while of paddling.

"Me, too. I know what you mean. You don't have to explain."

"I hope it works out."

"If one way doesn't work, we'll create another."

"Yeah. That's . . . right," she sighs, straightening her posture slightly. It seems like such a small act, the releasing of Neal's ashes into the lake. But it does something huge to our insides. We feel that important thing that so many counselors and therapists talk about in the process of recovering and persisting: letting go. This amazing sensation cannot be pinpointed anywhere inside a person who is working toward redemption. It is an all-over lifting, like a leaf being caught in an updraft, or downy snowflakes flitting directionless in a skittish wind, or a waterway that rips over a cliff and spills into a mist. The sensation knows not where it is going next. It need not care. It allows for the body to float, to gravitate in a new direction, to ground onto something new as it inevitably moves downward. It may seem like a silly moment, but we both know it will never leave our memories. It traces into our life's fabric, now a part of the design and wake of everything that follows. Seeming small, rituals mix mighty manifestations. Rituals redeem. Redemption heals.

By the time we get midway across, I see we might feel rain after all. The air has noticeably dropped in temperature now. Luckily, it seems like the rain will be on and off, no breeze shows up, and the air and water are still flat, so we paddle easily, making good progress. As we approach the state forest, where earlier we had parked at the top of the hill and had hiked down the trail to the water's edge in the dark, a light misting rain begins. The steady, light drops of water hitting the flat lake create a hissing sound. Wispy drops plink over and over each other, steadily replacing more and more rings and ripples. It's a fluffy rain, and it feels warmer than the air, so it almost tickles. The sensation, mingling with the sights and sounds, is so ethereal; it flows through me in waves of wonder and euphoria. The water's color hypnotizes grays, blues, translucent white, black, all in motion, all in sync. Drops falling . . . circling . . . circling . . . round and round.

We hit the shore just as the rain started to pick up. The steady hissing noise is highlighted with the tinkling noise of bigger droplets mixing with the smaller ones. We both hop out, quickly reorganizing and gathering all the stuff out of the canoe, loading it onto our bodies. Carrying the canoe down the steps was a lot easier than it's going to be going up, especially in the slick rain. But we hoist it up over our heads anyway. Jessie has the bag with all the stuff strapped across her back, and I'm carrying the two life preserver cushions through one arm. We pause a minute to look at the water before we head back. The canoe above us is keeping our heads mostly dry.

Now, in the pouring rain, the water's beauty is sad but rousing, and it suspends us just a little longer. I can't see across to the other side of the lake anymore through the water's veil; it's a curtain. The show is over.

It's as if the point, the point of the land itself and the point of the ritual, the truth gleamed from the moment, fades into the wet shroud. The witnessed astonishment of sunrise, our ritual, Neal himself . . . it all retreats . . . is sealed up and closed away, and is now simply a memory like so many others, slipped into the folds of time, into the folds of the mind.

I close my eyes for a moment, and I can't help myself; a slow swell of tears rises in the corner of my eye. But I don't want to cry. I sniff the wet air sharply, and I think suddenly, *we gotta get back to the house and see what the girls are up to. Big Red's probably wearing that crazy headdress of his, and they're probably dancing in the yard in the rain!* The image of them in my mind makes my heart lift. I smile to myself.

"Ready?" Jessie asks.

"Ready."

We start

down

the shore

before turning to cross the sandy beach

where the trail leads up the steep hill.

As we shuffle along,

dry under the rain-pelted shelter of the canoe overhead,

I let go with one hand for a few seconds.

With a quick wipe,

I brush the tears off each eye

and flick my hand over the water.

The tears fly off and drop their way into the lake,

to one day

rejoin

the mighty

sea.

EPILOGUE

. . . that very same morning the drop in temperature seems to instigate a cosmic shift,
some little tiny thing slightly off-kilter in the universe
nudges ever so subtly
into balance.
Blake Crandahl has woken suddenly and unintentionally, in the cracking dawn, to
another sweaty nightmare, chased by some unseen stalker.
The fear of pursuit is so
intense he cannot shake it, and it drives him out of his cozy Egyptian cotton sheets.
He walks absently into the empty living room,
through the kitchen,
onto the porch,
the terrace, even into the laundry room, looking for a spot where
he can comfortably sit,
but he realizes there is nowhere at this moment he can sit and feel at ease.
He wants out of his skin.
He and Candice shouted and argued through most of the night.
The peace of sound sleep fled them both, frightened by the reality of their situation.
Misery took its place. With it came grim thoughts that they really might be irreparably
broken now, and it really could come to divorce for them after all. But things like this just
don't happen to Candice.
Candice has spent her life sheltered and protected
by her influential family. She believes they are immune to exposure and she sees no
reason why anything should or would change now.
Blake wanders down to the lake barefoot;
the grass soaks the hems of his pajama pants, but the cold dew awakens his feet.
He looks to the east, to the rising light, and realizes he hasn't been on an
excursion or dinner cruise, all summer. He walks
into the water's edge.
Tiny waves make rhythmic laps against the cold sand.
He stands for a long time, looking, but seeing nothing.
He drops to a squat on the sand. Then he gives in and sits, sticking his legs out into
the shallow rippling water. . . .

ADDENDUM

November 11

Dear Babies:

I don't know if you are two, but you feel like two. If you are reading this, then it is because the dreams foretold the truth. While pregnant, I dream of being out on a little boat, just me and two little friends floating on the water on a beautiful day, or walking in a garden escorted by two fluttering butterflies. But, also of being plastered between two huge boulders, feeling frozen solid, stuffed, unable to breathe, waking up feeling like I was going to die.

You may grow up angry that I never went to the doctor. But I did go once to the free clinic. I took the bus because my car broke down. The doctor confirmed I was pregnant. He told me everything looked fine and things should progress fine. I took his word for it. I didn't see why I should go back since everything looked okay. Don't hate me; forgive me for dying, if I do. My consolation to this bad dream is that you have lived, survived to read this letter.

I will have it be known, if I die, that I want my sister, Roxanne, to be your legal guardian and adopted mother. She is the next closest person in my family. She has the money to teach you how to make something of yourself. My strongest wish is that you know true love and happiness.

Don't feel bad about my life, that it ended too soon—I had a good life. I was a rebel in my day, and maybe I still am. Being pregnant and having you with me when I've been most lonely has been joyful. You give me hope for the future.

You should know the circumstances of your conception. Some short background is in order. I met the love of my life at a soccer game. His name was Andrew Peters, and he was watching his nephew on the opposite team. It was love at first sight. We married within six months and lived happily married for almost a year. He was tragically taken away from me in a plane crash. My life dramatically altered on that horrible day. I have not known happiness again until you came. I wish I could say Andrew was your father. In all the right ways, he was meant to be your father, but he died before we could make you happen. Still, I think Andrew is responsible for your coming into existence.

I decided to spend a weekend up north with my friend at Lake Island Casino near Horton, Minnesota. Shortly after getting there, my friend's Mr. Right showed up to surprise her. He brought along a friend in hopes we would hit it off, but Mr. Right's friend was a Mr. Wrong. I ended up at the bar where I met a different man. He was younger but adorable and funny. He cheered me up. It was the first time I really laughed since Andrew died.

This man is your biological father. All I can tell you about him is he was kind and loving. He seemed to see me and understand my misery. He seemed like he could be another great love. But it seems not meant to be, somehow. He told me his name was Brandy Crandy, but I don't know if this is his real name. Maybe, someday, you can do your own research and find him.

Knowing I am creating you makes me feel so lucky. I feel certain there are two of you in there. I feel two sets of feet kicking! If I die in childbirth, I am glad I wrote you this letter in case you want to know more about me. It's been sort of fun to tell you. I can't wait to meet you!

No matter what, know I have loved you. You have brought hope and joy back into my life; this is why I want to call you Hope Joy. Or if you are twins, Hope and Joy. Or if you are a boy, Andrew Peter. Or if you are two boys, Andrew and Peter. Or if you are a boy and a girl, Hope Joy and Andrew Peter. But to be sure, I'll have to wait until I see your face or faces.

Grow up knowing you are loved and wanted. Very, very, very much! I love you. I can't wait to hold you tight in my arms and gaze into your beautiful face.

Always your mother,
Heather

ZOOM IN

Reeds and birds talking
    simple,
only essential words are heard;
        words float in with the twittering:
           they float out with the waves

they may ask, we may imagine they ask

    So, how do we redeem ourselves to the Earth? To the stars who witness us
as much as we witness them and more, before the meadows, the mountains,
the prairies, the seas, the lakes?
    The greatness, the minuteness, the moment, the forever, the yin and the
yang
        ask us this question:
          How do you redeem yourselves to your actions,
           your words,
             deeds,
               for what you have done,
               and what you have failed to do
         Red, Raven, Neal . . . me, and you.
           We all finally awaken to our universe
             when we meet death.
            Redemption
        may be ours in that new nonexistence,
    and maybe it doesn't and it won't matter anyway,
        but maybe it will;
and maybe dying into eternity isn't enough
to feel better about what I know,
what I've said and done.
I have damaged and not paid
for the future,
for my ancestral progeny;
      if we are born to procreate,

then what does it mean that I create a sick planet
to give birth in?
Some of this started before us,
a lot of it did,
and has nothing to do with me, really;
and, oh, how long have I been sitting on this cushion?
Earth,
Sky,
Water,
are sick;
they are our people,
I sing for them,
do you?

We all mourn the lost morn.
Now we must come to understand that we all must listen and see and live
differently,
more carefully;
aware, yes,
but more tuned in as well.
It isn't that we must hear them speak to us,
they always are anyway,
but that we
acknowledge ourselves
and what we have done,
how they see us,
we humans   in their eyes,
and offer our presence as a guarantee of our payment.
Nature must become
what it has always been for every living being who dwells here,

the cathedral,
the sangha,
the shrine,
the holy,
the origin of all;
we must be newly reborn
in our collective conscience
and be reborn into it.

We must help ourselves
and each other
                wake up,
just as the chickadee
    and the cattails,
        the turtles,
            rivers,
                winds, trees, lakes, the mighty sea
    help each other.

The chickadee sings while the reed hears;
                                listen you, listen to
                the stories,
    the songs

we   tell   we   tell
         we   sing   we   sing

              And the reed sings while the chickadee hears,
harmonizing as they go, they know,
      we're one,
        we're won;
beauty,
    light,
     love,
redeem me,
redeem thee;
you   me   us

     one

hee hee
        whooo ishhh shishhhh shishhhh
   hee hee

Acknowledgments

Always behind everything is nature. My gratitude goes to the Earth, the great muse. The natural world has provided me with the sustenance and substance needed to write this book. The lakes, mountains, trees, birds, and animals— the rivers and oceans, the crisp air, the forests—hold me captive, provide solace, and are examples of how to persevere and endure. I bow to the animals, plants, sea creatures, and even the annoying and scary insects and spiders; they are my inspiration. I am humbled before every creature, large and small.

In particular, I acknowledge the many places I hold dear in my midwestern homeland, the landscapes of my dream and real-life adventures, my lake friends: Gull Lake, Lake Superior, Mille Lacs, Pelican Lake in South Dakota; my river friends: the Mississippi, Minnesota, St. Croix, and St. Louis; the Boundary Waters Canoe Area and Voyageurs National Park, as well as Big Bog and Jay Cooke state parks. Water is the limbic system of this holy world, and I acknowledge its infinite power and enchantment. It resides with me. It has saved me many times. I was in the borderlands of southwestern Texas, and northern Mexico in June of 2022, where the border wall is an ugly scar and the Rio Grande River is a ghost; when I got home, I was filled with an appreciation for the green trees and grasses, the warm winds, and the gushing riverbeds in my home state. Here, Heaven on Earth is at my feet.

In addition to acknowledging nature, I need to acknowledge the people (who are, of course, a part of nature, too) who have inspired and sustained me through the writing and publishing of this novel.

My gratitude first goes to Wendy Johnson, who patiently and gently directed me through this book's final editing and publishing process. It is one thing to have a book written. It's a whole gigantic other thing to get it into print. I could not have done this without her help. I also thank my friend and colleague Greg Poferl for being our connection and for letting me help him with his book, which brought me closer to finishing mine. Wendy came along at the right time and helped make my dream come true. She's a little bit magical because of that and for so much more. Wendy inspires me with the perfect advice at the right time and because she makes a point to continue to do new things and see life every day as new.

Next, my family: Mark, Hailey, and Henry, who were present with the story, who helped write the story and envision it, and who allowed me the time and space to work on it and retreat to a quiet corner of the world to pore over the pages again and again. I could not have done it without their unwavering belief in me and their encouragement and patience. Mark and I first saw each other at the St. John's University pool. I became very good at the back stroke as I could then watch Mark do crazy jumps off the high dive without being detected. He wondered who the "mermaid-like" swimmer was who could do several laps of the backstroke. Since then, our lives continued to swirl around pools, ponds, lakes, rivers, and oceans, even when the kids came. Every memory of water has all of our surf trips, canoe trips, boat trips, and jet ski rides wrapped into it. It contains every swim adventure, including the excitement of learning to swim underwater and seeing with goggles for the first time. We are forever catching waves and getting humbled by waves. Always the water is new and nuanced because of you, my family, who loves the beach as much as I do. We'll always have that. It is the deepest substance of my life. It will carry me through my life and beyond.

I have overflowing gratitude for my parents, John Francis Markert and Carol Zachman Markert. I must go back even farther to my grandparents, Frances and Aloysius Markert and Arnold and Genevieve Zachman, and extend acknowledgment and gratitude. My Markert birth family, with my siblings Susan, John, Karen, Jeff, James (Jimmy), Jane, and Joanne, provided so much inspiration for the book. My sister, Joanne, often provided me with a place to work, and she never stopped backing my efforts, always providing me with great advice and emotional support. My siblings are deeply embedded in my memories and my limbic system; they are woven into my physical body and soul for eternity. Mom was the patient listener who often had to take deep breaths when attempting to parent me but showed me unfailing humility and courage. Dad was my champion and hero. Among so many other remarkable gifts he had, he also told the best stories and made me want to be a storyteller. The younger four siblings (of which I was one) had to put up with much of my nonsense, theatrics, play school, fairytale-telling, and boyfriend and friend drama. I owe them for helping me grow up safe and sound and loved. Jimmy, for being the protector of his three little sisters and a highly skilled boat driver and turtle whisperer. Jane, for teaching me to never give up and that you can still laugh even when you are sad. Joanne, for all the times you have been there for me. I owe the older four siblings for lots of babysitting (and letting me babysit their kids), lending of money, doling out advice (sought and unsought), teaching me how to swim, sail, and waterski, and for getting me out of plenty of jams in our fervent days at the lake and in St. Paul when it really was "St. Small." Susan watches me from the heavenly realm now and helps me feel safe, just like she did when she was here. Karen, who carried me around a lot when I was a baby, always had my back as a kid and still does, even now. My brother, Jeff, kept the boats running and rescued my upside-down sailboat more than once. My brother, John, gave me the original seed for the story when he intuitively told me I should be a waitress at the lake for the summer. Who would have thought that would lead to a novel? My siblings are living examples of fortitude, and I am proud to have them. I know our parents and grandparents are proud too.

Like a great family, great friends carry you along in life, and I have been blessed to have some epic friends. I thank Julianne O'Connell, one of the oldest and the dearest, for driving around the lake with me that day and fleshing out the story. Her advice to have the accident occur on the water proved essential. Sharing her camaraderie in the writing process, her sense of humor and artistry, the ups and downs, the second-guessing and the fears, and the sometimes-needed ass-chewing of "Get to work!" helped me get out of the stuck places along the journey of writing this book. Where I would be without her is not a happy or successful place.

I thank my college dream-come-true friend, Nancy Delanghe Poole, for inspiring the characters and her unwavering championing of me and my cockamamie plans. As weird as my ideas sometimes get, she never doubts me. What can a person do when they have someone who believes in them, no matter what? I wanted to write a book, and Nancy believed I would. And look what happened. How can you encapsulate a friend like that? She is my Rock of Gibraltar. Even when it took so many years to complete, she knew this day would come.

My friend, Kristine Seymour Thielen, also believed in me and went along on many a weird and wild adventure with me as I plotted and schemed my story and wrote relentlessly in my journal. I was so fortunate to meet her at Sacred Heart School, where we taught middle school together. Our friendship and her being with me on many adventures, one of which involved swimming across a lake with our camping and camera equipment barely balanced and floating on a blow-up raft, has helped me test myself and figure out what to do in tricky situations. She and I have endured a few.

I also owe my friend, Jillian Quinn, so much gratitude for her unrelenting support and belief in me. We met at the first NEH Summer Institute that we both attended in Corvallis, Oregon, with Dr. David Robinson. She introduced me to yoga, and that, along with our shared admiration for the transcendentalists, proved a great foundation for our friendship. We have trapsed around New York and a few other cities on many girls' trips in which we have epic all-night talks. We never run out of things to discuss. Me, writing this book, and Jillian, writing her own book, and transcendentalism and yoga have been threads throughout our friendship. She is there with me in the meanings and depths of this book.

From my days teaching at Hill-Murray School, I thank my counselor friend, Lisa Valentine, for walking some of our life journeys together and collaborating with me on writing. She helped me with self-reflecting. She showed me patience, courage, faith, and perseverance. I am so grateful for my friends who have come into my life at meaningful times and have made such life-altering impacts.

I thank my favorite teacher at the College of St. Benedict for her creative writing class. Sister Mara Faulkner (OSB), a poet and writer, encouraged me to take on the big ones; she told me I could write a novel. I think I had to hear it. It is her appreciation of me and my writing aspirations that I must acknowledge. She often shows up in my head, telling me to outline, organize, and look closely at the details to make sure they are authentic.

Another person I am so grateful for is my friend Christina DeVos, a kindred spirit. We met as teachers at Cretin-Derham Hall and worked together for seven raucous years teaching Values, a humanities class where she taught social studies, and I taught English. She has fueled my passion for environmental studies, taught me so much about racism and sexism, and continues to encourage me to keep offering more actual nature learning for our students. She unfailingly pumps me up and pushes me back to *Waterlines*, reminding me why I care. She is an amazing person who cares about community and making connections more than anything else. Watching her, I get lifted up.

I have experienced some life- and writing-improving workshops and institutes I must acknowledge. They are the backbone of my evolution as a thinker, writer, and person. I am indebted to have been able to attend Orion magazine's 2019 Environmental Writers' Workshop in Rhinebeck, New York, and to have met the enthusiastic writers with whom we created a Sangha. These writers encouraged me to go up to the microphone and speak up. They told me what I had to say mattered. My teacher was Amy Irving. I am encouraged by her courage and skills as a writer and writing teacher. She is an amazing woman; I hope to be as unrelenting as she is one day. She showed me a way into the feelings of the words and how to endure. She made me laugh at myself, but she also said that what I do and say matters a great deal. She said that to help the world, every single person must do something. *Waterlines* is one of my somethings.

I was fortunate to be a part of two National Endowment for the Humanities Summer Institutes for teachers. The first was in the summer of 1996 in Corvallis, Oregon, through Oregon State University. I participated in Dr. David M. Robinson's "Transcendentalism and American Cultural Transformation: Emerson, Fuller, and Thoreau." It was beyond a life-changing experience due to Professor Robinson's passion and brilliance, and because of the teachers I was privileged to meet. One was Jillian Quinn, mentioned above. Being in Oregon that summer was liberating and helped me to see the world in bigger terms; I mean, through all those big trees, Crater Lake, and the ferocious surf. The second NEH institute was equally as impactful. I attended Director Jayne Gordon's "Living and Writing Deliberately: The

Concord Landscapes and Legacy of Henry Thoreau" through the Concord Museum during the summer of 2017, celebrating the 200th birthday anniversary of Thoreau in his proud hometown of Concord, Massachusetts. It was an unforgettable celebration—and to get to see the homes of Louisa May Alcott, Nathaniel Hawthorne, and Ralph Waldo Emerson—such a bonus! Nothing made me want to keep these writers' visions alive more than this group of teachers and Jayne Gordon, the Director of the Concord Museum at that time. These NEH summer institutes fueled my intellectual curiosity and motivation and helped me formulate the guts of *Waterlines*.

Sometime over the many years of writing this book, I met with a woman over coffee for a good chunk of time. She was a Hill-Murray former student's mother; I do not remember her name or the student's name. In my early days and notes about the book, I did not keep good track of important details, like names. I never thought I would forget her name, how could I? I have since learned to write these important things down. All I have are the notes from our conversation. She talked to me about counting coup and helped me understand it. She also talked to me about the Ojibwe language. I owe her big time, and though I cannot acknowledge her name, I won't forget her and her contribution.

There were two books I used throughout writing *Waterlines*. They helped me visualize times and places. The first is *Through Dakota Eyes: Narrative Accounts of the Minnesota Indian War of 1862*. This book came to me in a strange way. It practically fell off the shelf in my friend Julianne's house one time when I was visiting overnight. I bumped the bookshelf with my overnight bag, and this book slipped off the ledge. It seemed to want to catch my eye, and it did. I needed authentic historical accounts of the Dakota War, and it literally fell into my hands. When I asked to borrow the book, Julianne and her family told me I could keep it. None of them recognized the book or even remembered seeing it before. Coincidence? I am not sure. My friend Julianne's childhood home is believed to be haunted; I have no problem taking it as a message from the spirits.

The other book I used throughout the course of writing *Waterlines* is called *Indian Days in Minnesota's Lake Region: The Great Sioux-Ojibwe Revolution, Volume 1: From Invasion to the Intertribal Boundary of 1825*. I got this book from my cousin David, and I want to acknowledge him and his parents, my Aunt Mary (my godmother), and my Uncle Doug (he probably purchased this big giant book!). These three encouraged me to use Indian Days to research and flesh out my story. They have been unrelenting supporters in my pursuit of writing *Waterlines*. It is my Markert family that brought me my love for lakes. I must acknowledge my Markert cousins, especially Jeanne, who has been like a sister to me through the years growing up and beyond. She helped me conceptualize the book and provided much laughter and inspiration along the writing journey. My dad's siblings Eleanor (and Uncle Bernie), Ann (and Uncle Ed), Lois (and Uncle Le), Allan (and Aunt Flo), David (and Aunt Judy), P.J., and Mary (and Uncle Doug) were great role models to me, and I cherish them. They and all my cousins: Andrew, Sara, Matt, Amy, Tom, and Therese; Julie, Lynn, Tim, Babe, Paul, and Mike; Gretchen, Ellen, Rose Ann, and Steve; the seven C's: Chad, Cole, Camille, Cindy, Chris, Cressie, and Clay; Claire, Ann, Mark, and Joan; and Jessica, Elizabeth, and Peter—are a part of *Waterlines*. Though people don't have big families so much anymore, I wouldn't trade mine for anything.

My Zachman family is also intricately tied to *Waterlines* and needs acknowledgment. They have given me many adventures and memories. My mom's siblings, James (and Aunt Mary Ellen), Eleanor (and Uncle Larry), Suzanne (and Uncle Jim), Albert, and Jeff, have inspired me, and I cherish their influence. My Uncle Albert died tragically in a Mississippi River boating accident just two months before I was born (yes, a long time ago). My mom passed away over twenty years ago, but I have never stopped wondering how she must have felt when Albert died, she being pregnant with me. I wish I could have asked her before I lost my chance. I have always been curious about Uncle Albert, and, in a wild and wonderful way, he has provided inspiration for *Waterlines*. My Zachman cousins are also a part of *Waterlines*, especially those closest in age to me: Peggy, Diane, Laurie, and Teresa. We have done much lake frolicking, including skinny-dipping and all-night star-gazing on the dock, to name a few. The ones older than me matter too: Cindy, Polly, Tom, Arnie, Mike, and Cal; Vicki, Andy, Chris, John, Bruce, and David; and Patsy, Tim, Jim, Bill, and Richard. I know I am privileged to have such a family. I am grateful.

The last branch of my family to acknowledge is my yoga sangha, the Yoga Lovelies: Lonna Bartsh, Chris Anderson, Michelle Kagarmanov, Gloria Desjardine, Ranette Ruzek, and Kim Maiello. These sisters show me how to trust the process, even when it's big and shifty, and they are forever with me in every yoga pose I do.

I can't finish this list of acknowledgments without including my nieces and nephews: especially Elly, Nick, Gavin, Rob, and Tessa, but also Julie, Jay, Jana, Luke, Sam, Dan, James, Maxine, Joe, Cora, and Ezekiel. They, too, are a part of *Waterlines* and have helped fuel me to "destination completion." They are a part of the context of my life, and they continue to shape me and what I hope for in the future.

These are my people. They inspire me to keep seeing the world, to keep telling stories, to keep having adventures, and to make memories worthy of stories.

They tell me their stories, too, and I stand amazed.

REFERENCES

Anderson, Gary Clayton, and Alan R. Woolworth, editors. *Through Dakota Eyes: Narrative Accounts of the Minnesota Indian War of 1862.* Published 1988, Minnesota Historical Society Press, St. Paul, Minnesota.

Zapffe, Dr. Carl A. *Indian Days in Minnesota's Lake Region: The Great Sioux-Ojibwe Revolution, Volume 1: From Invasion to the Intertribal Boundary of 1825.* Published 1991, Historic Heartland Association, Brainerd, Minnesota.

About the Author, Jenny Markert

I grew up in a house with seven siblings and my beloved parents, about half a mile uphill from the Mississippi River Gorge in St. Paul, Minnesota. I spent, and still spend, many a day in the company of the Mississippi and the Minnesota rivers, riding my bike and hiking along their banks, listening to their wild songs. I spent childhood summers with my large extended family of cousins and elders, swimming in several lakes in the northern Minnesota lakes region and roaming the forests near the cities of Nisswa, Brainerd, and Pequot Lakes. As I grew up, I expanded my exploration of the world to include hiking the craggy trails along the rugged North Shore of Lake Superior and paddling the waterways of Voyagers National Park and the Boundary Waters Canoe Area. I lived in Los Angeles, California, for a short time and learned to love the ocean, but I missed the wildness of Minnesota. The forests, fresh air, and lakes are second to none.

I made amazing friends and had many influential teachers in my formative years at St. Mark's grade school and Derham Hall High School (when it was an all-girls school) in St. Paul, and the College of St. Benedict in St. Joseph, Minnesota. I married my best friend, and we had a daughter and a son, my favorite people in the world. I teach English at Cretin-Derham Hall (now co-ed) in St. Paul, where my latest passion, in addition to teaching the great authors of United States literature, is writing and teaching curriculums that center around climate and culture, nature writers and writing, and the complex and ever-evolving relationship between nature, animals, and humans. I have written over 30 children's books on wildlife, national park adventures, and nature, published by The Child's World. Waterlines is my first published book of fiction. I hope to write and publish more.

I am, as Ralph Waldo Emerson said, part and parcel of the great cosmos, and so is everyone else, every living creature. Like snowflakes, we are all divinely common and uncommonly divine. When we're all said and done, what remains are our stories: what we tell, what we hear, see, and remember, and where we live. The appeal of nearly every story is its unique characters, times, and places in the world—this natural world— ever-changing and glorious. Influential are the storytellers. Nature endows everything with stories to connect us. Stories inform us, unite us, and keep us going. They are as old as the rivers and lakes. Stories stir love into the world. Listen. Listen to the stories of those around you. You will know love and feel yourself a part of something bigger.

Tell your stories to the world. Tell them, tell them.

Made in the USA
Monee, IL
18 August 2022

11930405R00204